CREDIBLE THREATS

BOOK ONE OF THE SAM ADAMS SERIES

DANIEL MEYER

Credible Threats © 2022 by Daniel Meyer
Published by Daniel Meyer

Cover art by Luke Tarzian

Edited by Sarah Chorn

ISBN: 979-8-98603400-3 (print)
979-8-9860340-1-0 (e-book)

Visit Daniel's website at
www.danielmeyerauthor.com

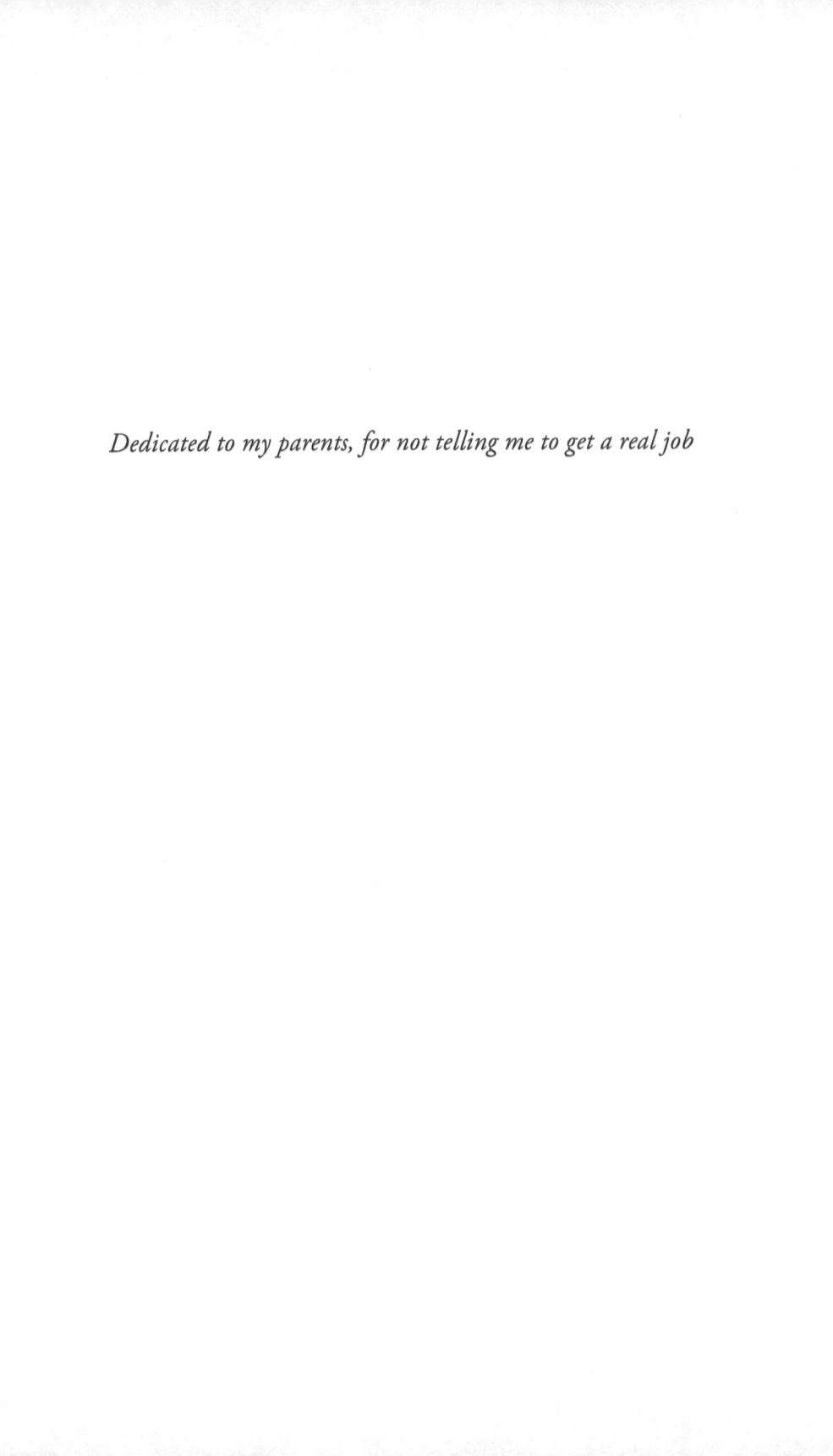

Dedicated to my parents, for not telling me to get a real job

CHAPTER ONE

THE DEEPER I walked into the South Side, the less believable it got when I assured myself I wasn't nervous.

The streetlights were erratic, and their sullen orange glow refused to banish the shadows, letting my imagination fill in the blanks. Wandering around the South Side after dark is never a good decision; it's nearly as dangerous as doing the same thing on the North Side.

Particularly when you're on your way to banish a poltergeist.

My name is Sam Adams, and I'm a wizard.

Yes, I love saying it.

If you think that gives me some desire for heroism, standing between humanity and the darkness and blah blah blah, you're very mistaken. But what can I say? Magic is cool, so I help out where I can.

Afraid of failing your test on the English Civil War? I can talk to my Familiar, who actually fought in it. Guys catcalling you on your way to school? I can whip up a fear spell that'll make them afraid to even look in your direction. Strictly small-time stuff, within the realm of plausible deniability; I avoid attention as much as possible, and never stick my neck out too far.

Until tonight.

Following Mom's advice to "spend some time with your school friends before your summer break is over," I'd wandered down to the beach that morning, encountered a few of my classmates. I'd spotted Brittney Sullivan off by herself, looking forlorn, and like a damn fool, I'd gone over and asked what was wrong. She told me.

In theory, it was completely possible. The catch was, I'd never actually *done* it, hence my growing dread as I made my way to Brittney's house. Unfortunately, magic can be as dangerous to the user as everyone else if they don't know what they're doing. It wasn't out of the realm of possibility that I'd accidentally fry my own face off.

I spotted the house up ahead, quickened my pace, and stuffed that dread down. Everybody's gotta start somewhere, I reminded myself. The fact that I'd never banished a poltergeist was a mere technicality.

Clenching my fists a couple times to stop the quiver, I climbed Brittney's creaky old porch steps and knocked four times. The perfect number of knocks; neither too many nor too few.

There was a moment's pause, then the door opened. Brittney's mom stepped into view, an older version of her daughter, albeit without the neon pink hair or any visible piercings.

She eyed me suspiciously, as people tend to do, but her tone was friendly enough. "You must be Sam. Brit said you were coming."

"Yeah," I said cautiously. "I'm here to help her study before school starts."

She stepped aside, allowing me to enter, faint smile on her face. "Yeah, I know what you're here to study. She told me why you're really here."

I licked my lips. "She… did?" Whatever happened to the good old days of teenagers lying to their parents?

She let out an exasperated parental sigh. "She said you're into all kinds of paranormal stuff. She thinks we have a ghost in the house."

I hadn't planned for this. "Uh, that's not exactly it, I really just came over to—"

She gave me a weary, patient smile. "Sam, it's okay, you don't have to lie." That was good because I didn't have one. "I know something weird is happening. I've seen some of the things Brit's talked about. I don't like it either, but that doesn't mean our house is haunted, for God's sake."

"But you seem open-minded about the whole thing."

She shrugged. "I may not believe in ghosts, but I know my daughter is struggling, and she can't go on like this. If she really thinks this'll help, I'm willing to go along with it."

"That's... level-headed of you."

Her laugh was brittle. "Occasionally, adults can be level-headed, believe it or not."

"I'm not sure I believe it."

"I remember that feeling. I can't say I blame you."

"If you really think something bad is happening," I said, "you should just leave. Get the hell out of here. Not believing in ghosts doesn't mean you're not in danger." I hadn't believed in the supernatural either, once upon a time.

"I said something strange was happening, not something dangerous. It's not the same thing." That had never been my experience. "Besides, it would get expensive, staying in a motel, and I can't really go out of town because of work."

I tried to smile. "Then I guess it's my moment to shine."

She laughed aloud. "Lucky us." I wasn't sure how that was intended. She raised her voice. "Brit, honey? Your playdate is here."

There were footsteps on the stairs, then Brit appeared. Her eyes had a glassy, vacant look that could only be fear, and it did nothing to get rid of my unease. She acknowledged me with a shaky nod. "Hey, Sam."

I managed to keep my voice level. "Hey, Brit."

"Thanks for coming. I'm glad you're here."

I swallowed. "Yeah. Sure. No problem. Hope I can help."

Her face looked drawn, like she hadn't been sleeping, and her eyes were haunted, distracted, the look of someone who'd bumped up against the supernatural, and had their sense of reality shaken because they had no frame of reference for what they'd seen. I'd seen that look in the mirror, maybe once or twice. Luckily, I was so much wiser and more experienced these days.

She turned to her mother. "Mom, it's happening again. It's knocking stuff off the walls. It broke a lamp. I keep seeing it out of the corner of my eye." I could hear how badly she wanted reassurance.

Fear and worry were etched into her mom's expression, and I saw doubt beginning to gnaw at her ever so slightly. I didn't like the sound of this at all. Poltergeists can be aggressive but this one sounded like it was going above and beyond.

Brit's mom stroked her daughter's arm and then looked at me, clearly expecting something. "What did you have in mind?" I could hear the incredulity in her voice.

Calm and professional. "I'm going to perform a banishing spell."

"And how does that work?"

I searched my brain for a more satisfactory answer than the truth but didn't find one. "I'm gonna make it go back where it came from. With magic. Because I can do that."

"That's it?"

"Hopefully." I admit, that wasn't exactly the kind of decisiveness you wanted from your ghostbuster.

"Back to where?" Brit sounded like she dreaded the answer.

"Back to… wherever spirits are supposed to go when they die,"

I said. "I'll let the preachers be the judge of where that is, but this is most likely just some lost soul, in the literal sense, taking out its problems on everybody else." I chose not to mention that a ghost strong enough to do all this was probably a real bastard when it was alive, and death had just magnified that a hundred-fold. Nice people don't become ghosts.

Brit's mom stared at me, probably wondering how her daughter could befriend such a jackass.

"A banishing spell is what you do when you've got an uninvited visitor of the supernatural persuasion," I elaborated, sensing their skepticism. "If they won't leave on their own, that's how you throw them out." Before we could examine that statement too closely, I moved on. "Do you know if anyone ever died in this house?"

"Not that I know of," Brit's mom said. "How exactly was this supposed to work? Were you gonna hide in the closet to cast a spell?"

I snorted. "No." I had been planning to do it while locked in the bathroom, actually. "Do you have any idea where it might be originating? Any area this thing seems to be focused on?"

Brit nodded. "Upstairs, on the second floor. That's where most of it happened. It just *feels* wrong up there."

Something else unsettling. Pro tip: if something just "feels wrong," it is. Run away, lest you be eaten. "I know this is scary," I said. "I've been there. But I'm gonna get this thing out of your house and get you back to normal, okay?" I hoped I could back that up.

"And what do we do if you can't," said Brit.

Run for our lives. "We'll jump off that bridge when we come to it. But I'd feel a lot better if you weren't here. I don't think it'll be dangerous, but I don't want to take any chances. Maybe just wait outside for a while."

Brit's mom shook her head. "This is ridiculous. Brit, honey, if there's something going on with you—"

"Damn it, Mom. This is real. Whatever is happening, it's real, and I'm scared. Please, can you just find a way to trust me?"

I saw Brit's mom waver for a heartbeat, and then I saw her make up her mind. "Okay. Okay, I trust you, sweetheart."

Aww.

She turned to me. "We'll wait outside. Good luck."

"Thanks."

Brit headed for the door, her mom following. I felt my stomach clench, as the time to put up or shut up was thrust upon me. *How the hell did I get into this?*

Brit turned the knob. She turned it again. Then she began shaking it, growling.

"What's the matter?" I asked.

"The door. It won't budge. I can tell it's not locked. It's like something's just—"

Oh shit.

The floor shook, pictures and things rattling on the walls. The lights flickered. Brit cried out in fear, and her mom's eyes bulged out of her head.

My skin crawled as dark, supernatural power filled the air, making me feel as if my hair stood on end. It was here. And it was staring at us. I didn't know how I could feel it, but I could. For a half-second, fear threatened to overwhelm me, and I gave a low growl to steady myself. However out of my depth, however scared I was, they were a hundred times more so. I was the only one in the room who had even a chance at helping them.

Confidence is a must when dealing with supernatural creatures. I swallowed and tried for bravado. "Who are you?" I shouted. "What do you want?"

In the next room, a vague, shadowy, humanish shape appeared, too dark for me to get a good look. The lights around it dimmed unnaturally. Then came its voice, a deep, seething rasp so loud I wasn't sure if it came from the room around me or was being drilled directly into my brain. "I know what you are, Outlaw."

"Then you know what I can do," I bluffed. "What do you want with these people?"

There was a pause I had no doubt was intended to be dramatic. "I want their blood."

There was a choking sound from Brit's mom, where she and Brit were huddled together near the door.

The shape disappeared, then reappeared at the top of the stairs. I had to whirl around to face him, scowling. Robs a man of his dignity, spinning around that way. "Why? They haven't done anything to you."

"They need not *do* anything."

I tried another tack. "What happened to you?"

"Happened?"

"What happened when you died? Why can't you leave?"

"And why would I leave, wizard?"

"If there's something keeping your spirit here, tell me what it is. I can fix it. Nobody has to get hurt."

He chuckled. It was just as disturbing of a sound as you would imagine. "You think me a poor, lost little poltergeist. But I am not."

This was getting us nowhere, and the time for diplomacy was over.

I let magic flood me like a primordial tempest.

Somewhere in the ether, the magic extended and snapped taut, like an invisible chain, linking me to the countless spirit worlds. Raw power flared to life in my soul, leaping and dancing like a flame, waiting for me to spin it into a spell.

The room, the gloomily lit street beyond, the city, the entire *world* became screamingly alive. Every color was sharper, every sound louder, the entire universe humming and pulsing in my veins. In spite of everything, a grin spread on my face and elation surged through me, as it always does when I use magic.

Wizardry is ancient; older than ancient, reaching into the mists of time and beyond, going back to the first wizards, thousands upon thousands of years ago, before even the Mage Wars of the prehistoric era. Those of us that can do it, our souls are like conduits, letting us connect to the power that emanates from all those other realms and use it in all kinds of weird and wonderful ways.

Here in the good old twenty-first century, I stepped up to the plate: "*Get out. I command you to leave this house and never return.*" I felt my words ripple out unseen through the ether, felt the house shake harder under my feet as the ghost struggled against my power. "GET OUT OR I WILL KILL YOU."

There was another rumble, then silence. Everything in the house gradually settled back into its proper place. Panting, the three of us looked at each other.

Brit opened her mouth to speak.

Then every window in the place exploded inward.

There were screams, including my own, as we dived for cover, shards of glass ripping through furniture, shattering against walls, slicing us. I scored a nasty gash on my leg as I threw myself behind the sofa, wishing as I did so I'd picked a hiding place that wasn't so soft and fluffy. Brit and her mom were right behind me.

Oh, right. Shields. Very important in a battle situation. Arms flapping haplessly, I tried to concentrate, finally managed to conjure them. A herky-jerky, uneven sheen of blue-green light flared around us, sparking and flashing faintly as shards of glass buzzed into it to shatter softly and trickle to the carpet. I was glad they worked. I'd never had to put them to the test before.

I saw Brit, apparently completely unaware, had a shard of glass sticking in her back. I tried to warn her but when I opened my mouth the room lurched violently back and forth, and darkness crept in at the edge of my vision.

The bizarrely musical sounds of breaking glass faded. We

exchanged panic-stricken looks, our ragged breath the only sound in the house. I noticed with some consternation they seemed to be looking at *me*.

"Oh my God," Brit murmured. "What are we supposed to do?"

I was spared having to answer that question when Brit's mom screamed and was torn abruptly from my view.

"MOM!"

I cast about the room frantically, my eyes lighting on a bizarre sight: Brit's mom, suspended in the air, face frozen midscream, arms extended outwards, flying upwards, across the room, bouncing against the stairs before disappearing into the shadows at the top.

"MOM!" Brit screamed again.

"Stay here," I shouted. Then I was on my feet, charging after her.

Ignoring the voice of all good sense, I bounded upstairs, around a corner, and into the hall. And froze.

The lights were on, but it was dark anyway, the bulbs dimmer and the shadows deeper than they should be, seeming to move ever so slightly even when there was no reason they should.

Before I made it to the top of the stairs, I had sensed exactly what Brit had been talking about: this place was creepy as hell. And there was a feeling of doom, like bad things had happened here and would happen again. There was no tangible reason to think so, just a niggling sense of dread in the back of my mind.

I felt it, too: not truly in any place here in the physical world, the Curtain was weak, dangerously weak, the barrier between our world and one of the many undoubtedly terrifying spirit worlds whose tentacles connected them to our own. I didn't know what was on the other side, and I didn't want to find out. Little tendrils of fear went slithering up and down my neck, and I didn't know if it was magical, or just my fight or flight instinct telling me it didn't approve of my choices.

Okay Samuel. You got this.

Body surging with tension and magic I stepped deeper into the hall, trying to keep my steps light on the carpet.

Other than a couple broken picture frames on the floor, I didn't see anything out of the ordinary. Brit and her mom's house might not have been big or fancy, but with a hellbeast with bad intentions lurking around, it seemed enormous.

Swiveling my head around, trying to watch every direction at once, I crept down the hall, quickly rejecting the idea of calling out for Brit's mom.

I didn't have to: there was a crash and a scream, causing me to jump out of my skin and nearly collapse.

Disheveled, a trickle of blood down the left side of her face, Brit's mom came lurching out of a door at the far end of the hall and began pounding towards me. "Sam! Sam, run!"

I heard footsteps on the stairs, Brit screaming for her mom.

"Brit, get outta—"

Light fixtures exploded in a spectacular rain of sparks and glass, and I threw a hand over my face instinctively. A shape appeared in the hallway, flying towards me. I caught a brief, murky glimpse of two distended heads on a humanish body, and what bore a distinct resemblance to tentacles.

If that thing was telling the truth when it claimed it wasn't a poltergeist, then we had just entered a whole new level of yikes, but there wasn't time to worry about it. I let out a growl that had a little squeak in it, braced myself, stopped thinking and let my wizardly instincts, such as they were, take over.

If it wanted a fight, it would get one.

The shape was almost on top of me

I let out a scream and attacked.

CHAPTER TWO

IT WAS AN old, flimsy door, for which I was grateful, due to the fact that I was being smashed through it.

The door and I slammed to the floor, the crash half-knocking the wind out of me. I rolled across the room, haphazardly flopping against a chair I suspected the gods had put there just to torment me.

Up, up, dammit.

I staggered to my feet, fumbling to get a grip on my magic.

Before I could, the dark shape flashed into view, filling the space where the door used to be.

I abandoned the banishing spell and tried the direct approach.

Every wizard has one or two things they're really good at, that come easy as breathing. For me, it's levitation. You might picture levitation as simply lifting things off the ground, but it has all kinds of creative uses.

I blasted the chair I'd collided with across the room and through the door, hard enough to brain a rhinoceros.

The creature disappeared, the chair punching a jagged hole in the wall, and reappeared behind me.

I whirled, wanting to attack, but again, it vanished before I could make contact.

It was toying with me.

Then something seized me, something cold and slithery, and my feet flew out from under me. I whirled sharply upward, careening into a ceiling fan. It shattered, glass and wood digging into my back. Force pressed down on me, pinning me to the ceiling and cutting off my windpipe. I gagged for air, the dim room upside down in front of me, my legs hanging awkwardly to the side. Dark spots floated in my eyes.

I tried to focus, call up magic, as my mind began swimming around in my skull and my legs thrashed. One of my shoes bounced off the ceiling.

It was hard to fight the darkness closing in, but I managed to feel a flicker of power, and used it.

Something different this time: fire.

I feared I'd call down a Biblical rain of fire, torching the house and all of us in it, but luckily, I wasn't quite that skilled yet.

A jagged red bloom of flame juddered across the room like an out-of-control Roman candle. The creature let out a shriek that shattered the window in the far wall and then I was plummeting into the floor in a groaning heap.

"Sam? Sam, get up, hurry."

I couldn't tell who said it, but someone pulled me to my feet, causing me to yelp, then they were dragging me along by the sleeve, out the shattered door and back into the hall.

I looked around in dizzy fear. "Where—"

There was a blur in front of us, and I instinctively braced to open fire. It disappeared again, before reappearing behind us.

I was getting a little wiser to him now; he was crafty, materializing physically from the spirit world to attack, then scampering back to the other side when I fought back. And he was too strong for me to simply banish. In the most upsetting turn of events in an evening full of them, I would actually have to fight this thing.

As it reappeared, I pivoted, getting a grip on the wreckage of the chair, along with some of the plaster, and sent the whole mess roaring towards him.

It managed to dodge me again, but it was a little slower this time, and I could tell I'd surprised it. I landed a glancing blow as it disappeared, provoking another cry of pain, cut off as it vanished.

I gasped for air. As it turned out, it was both, Brit and her mom, stamping up and down on the floor, putting out the last remains of some still-smoldering carpet. Oops.

We had exactly no time to hang around.

I grabbed Brit's mom by the shoulder, shoved her forwards. "GO! Get out of here!"

They ran, making it down the stairs and out of sight. I didn't follow far and remained standing in the hall, arms and legs shaking violently.

I had the feeling if this creature had to choose between me and them, it would choose me.

It did.

I heard the front door slam as the shape flickered at the edge of my vision again, and I turned, wrenching off a doorknob with a flick of the wrist, sending it hurtling towards the thing like a cannonball.

It vanished and the doorknob slammed into a wall at an angle, tearing out a jagged furrow through the plaster, sprinkling me with some of its dust.

I grimaced. Hopefully, if I allowed myself to think of something other than not getting butchered, I could avoid demolishing this house, and maybe the neighborhood beyond, both of which were depressingly possible when magic is involved.

If there was a pattern to this thing's attacks, I couldn't find it, but magic made my reflexes a little sharper; I could feel it happening the longer I used it.

I won't say I was ready when it came back, but I was able to react quick enough to keep from dying.

As I spotted it, I hastily threw up my shields, the magical energy squirming into place around me, and batted away a slash from its paws or claws or whatever the hell it was using to slap me around. The impact drove me backwards, nearly sent me off my feet, light sparking and flaring in the darkness where the shield was hit.

I'd managed to keep its blow off me that time, but the shield wouldn't make the impact bounce off harmlessly, just lessen its severity. I really, really wanted to avoid those claws; gods knew what else they were capable of, other than cutting me to ribbons, and my luck would only go so far.

The shape appeared again, still too fast and too dark for me to get a good look, and I threw levitation straight at him, slamming him backwards and was rewarded by a roar that made my ears ring. It was tempting, now that I'd gained something almost resembling the upper hand, to turn and run for my life. The only thing that barely kept my feet in place was the possibility I was saving the lives of the others by giving them time to escape, and the dead certainty that if I turned my back on this thing, I'd get eaten alive.

When you looked at it that way, staying in a darkened hallway to fight a monster in single combat was actually the safest thing I could do.

Huh.

The next half-minute or so lasted a lifetime.

Exhaustion was already clutching at my body, so I figured this was the time to stick to what I knew best, not try anything new and fancy: I lashed out with levitation again, pure force. I doubted that would do much to hurt it, but maybe it could keep it away from me long enough to come up with something better.

Invisible magical ripples surged through the air, forcing the thing back, shaking the walls, as I shoved levitation at it with magical punches. I didn't seem to be hitting much (unless you counted the two or three more chunks of plaster I bashed out of the wall) but I was at least holding him off.

Until I wasn't.

Somehow, he darted in closer, got past my guard.

Claws flashed again and I didn't have time to react, a swarm of tentacles filling my vision. They tore into my shield, the impact rocking me back and forth, sending me crashing into a wall, fearing for a heart-stopping moment the impact would send me off my feet before I barely managed to right myself. I twisted, another shadowy tentacle sailing over my head, another striking a glancing blow against my shields, then I ran out of luck and one of his blows struck home.

It didn't rip my guts out, the way it would have if it hadn't been for those shields, but even the lessened blow hurt, the impact slamming brutally into my abdomen, pain filling my guts.

There was no way I could keep going on like this. I had to change things up, somehow, or I was going to die here. I felt the beginnings of full-blown panic rising within me, like the wind blowing off the ocean in the wintertime. I tried to shove it somewhere far away, where it couldn't distract me at the worst possible time. I threw another lance of levitation; it didn't even come close to hitting the thing, but it made it disappear.

"So," I called to the shadows, "blood. That's what this is all about, huh?" My gaze roamed the hallway, in search of anything I could use, until they lit on the bathroom door. I took a step backward, away from it, back towards the stairs, hoping it would think I meant to head that way.

That chuckle came again. "And why not," it rumbled. "Blood is the life force of the worlds, the nectar of existence, the—"

The creature bought my feint. It materialized on the stairs, behind me, and I was waiting, turning, and sending a surge of levitation so strong it rattled the house. For the first time, I caught the bastard completely by surprise: in a whirl of tentacles, I scooped him up and slammed him into the ceiling hard enough to crack the plaster, sending little rivulets down to puddle on the carpet.

I turned and ran, pounding back down the hallway the way I'd come.

Okay, so "escape the hallway only to fight it in the bathroom instead" wasn't the soundest of plans, but at least it was something.

I had almost made it when it appeared behind me, scaly jaws agape, foregoing the claws and tentacles and going straight to eating me.

I didn't have time to react; pressure slammed into my head, making me see stars and my vision wobble precariously before going dark. My shields rippled against me.

It had tried to bite my fucking head off, and the only thing keeping its fangs off me was my shields. It growled, the sound reverberating through my skull, along with my right arm, which was half-nestled in the fangy darkness of its mouth.

I lashed out in blind terror. Levitation, straight down its gullet. It screamed, and I didn't have to be a demonologist to realize the sound was pure pain. There was a faint cracking sound, then the pressure disappeared, the fangs jerking out of my vision as its head snapped back.

Reeling, I tumbled forward, flung myself through the door, colliding with something hard. A sink.

I tried to focus, waiting for the next attack. My heart thumped brutally against my chest. I was expecting something to come flying through the door or the walls to finish me off, but it didn't happen. It seemed I was making the thing cautious, believe it or not.

How did you kill something that didn't even have to fight you?

All it had to do was wait, and watch, and whichever direction I happened to be looking, it could simply attack from the opposite.

I glanced around the room, once again trying to look in every direction at once.

I saw the mirror on the wall in front of me, over the sink, my haggard face reflected back at me.

Maybe I didn't have to look in every direction.

I stopped and waited. No more frantic attacks. With the mirror, I could see behind me, and with the angles I couldn't see greatly reduced, I could react quicker.

Knuckles white, I clenched my fists and waited. I don't know how long I stood there. It felt like years.

It materialized through the wall, to my right, sliding through the fabric of reality like it was a morning fog.

I used one of its own tricks against it, shattering the shower door into a million pieces with a clench of my fist and sending it flying at the thing in a savagely sharp, twisting cloud. Black, foul-smelling blood spurted onto the linoleum floor.

I let out a shout of bewildered fear and the thing screamed and thrashed, a tentacle thumping against the bathroom ceiling.

I saw more fangs come at me, just before I made my move, casting another levitation spell. Nothing too dramatic: I just picked up the water in the toilet, in a squirming little ball, and rammed it right between those yawning fangs, down the thing's throat. There was a gagging sound and I put all my effort back into a banisher. I wasn't under any illusions I could kick its ass physically; I was lucky I'd done this much damage. And it was too strong for me to banish, either; but if I could do a little of both, hit it while it was weakened...

"BEGONE," I screamed, "SHOO! I BANISH YOU! I BANISH YOU FROM THIS HOUSE!"

As I cast the spell, another scream shook the room, and I

crashed to the floor, as magic came burning out of me, making my skin tingle. Then, abruptly, dead silence. I gulped down a lungful of air that felt much fresher than it had a moment ago.

I looked around nervously, picking myself up off the floor, trying to avoid the dark bloodstains. Nothing. The war was over. I could tell the thing's presence was gone. The creepy as hell vibe disappeared. I hadn't realized how oppressive it had been until it was gone, and I was back in a normal house again.

I sat on the edge of the tub for a few moments, catching my breath and trying without success to stop shaking.

Eventually, I made my slow way out of the bathroom, down the stairs, and out into the yard where Brit and her mom were crouched down behind their car, clutching at one another. They'd waited for me. They stood up stiffly when I appeared, but didn't speak, as if they were afraid to ask the questions swirling in their minds. They looked as if they'd just woken up from a nightmare and still weren't quite sure whether it had been real.

I jerked my head behind me. "It's gone. Whatever that thing was, it won't be bothering you anymore."

They cast uncertain glances back towards their house, both wiping away tears. "Are you sure?" Brit said.

"If anything strange happens, let me know, but yeah, I'm sure. It was pretty final." They stood there, still plainly frightened and overwhelmed, and didn't answer.

"Oh. There's some, uh… damage. I'm… not responsible for all of it." Recalling what Brit's mom had said and feeling a stab of guilt, I dug out my wallet and produced a depressing eleven dollars. "Here. I'd offer to help fix the place up, but this'll do more good than my carpentry skills."

Brit's mom shook her head. "It's okay, Sam. There's nothing broken in there that can't be fixed. If this is what it took to keep us safe, then it was worth it."

"What are we supposed to do now?" Brit murmured, the question encompassing a whole lot of territory.

I knew how hard this was for them to process. The supernatural had been common knowledge to me for a long time now, but for them, it was unfathomable. I tried to think of something properly comforting. "That thing is gone, at least. I know it's not that easy to just forget it happened. Look, I know how you feel. When I first found out about this stuff, I was afraid no one would believe me. Thought I was losing my mind."

"What did you do?" Brit's mom said.

"Well, I met a guy who helped explain things, which is the position you seem to be in." I felt a stab of uncharacteristic reflection, wondering how many other people had seen something like this and been too afraid to say anything. What had happened to them? I put it out of my mind and forced a smile. "I know the world's a little weirder now. But... it was weird already. What's a little more weirdness? It gets easier." It wasn't much, but it was the best I could come up with.

Brit scraped more tears away from her eyes. "It still doesn't seem real. I don't know what's happening. I don't know what to say. Thank you."

"Uh, you're welcome. I'd appreciate it if you didn't tell anybody about this."

"I won't," Brit said.

"Neither will I. I promise," said her mom.

We all stood there a moment, shell-shocked, and I broke the silence. "I should go."

Brit's mom nodded. "Yeah. Sure. Thank you again."

"You're welcome."

"Bye, Sam," she said.

"Bye." They headed back inside, though Brit, crooked smile on her face, turned back and took the eleven dollars still in my hand. *Smart call.*

I gave them a wave as they walked away, then limped for home.

I kept my eyes open, unable to shake my nerves, tense and ready to fire magic the whole way. I swiveled my head once, towards what sounded like flapping wings, but that was the extent of the excitement. It was late by the time I made it back to a friendlier, more familiar part of town.

The streetlights worked better here, although all the houses I passed were dark, including my own. I tromped onto the porch and fumbled with the key. As I felt the lock slide open, a twist of movement I couldn't quite identify caught the corner of my eye, making the hair on the back of my neck stand up.

I spun around and saw, just for a heartbeat, the silhouette of a woman smudged in the shadows across the street, long hair tumbling down past her shoulders. Then I blinked and she was gone.

Because I didn't have enough problems.

Reminding myself of the precautions I had taken to keep otherworldly prowlers out of my house, I relaxed, slightly, heading inside and relocking the door. Who she was, I couldn't even begin to guess. Just when I'd gotten one crisis settled, here was another, come to party. I shut it out of my mind for now.

I let power come coursing through my body on the way home, and the pain of my injuries was receding to a dull roar rather than an insistent howl, the presence of the magic within me acting on its own to relieve my injuries. The cuts and bruises were nasty, but by this time tomorrow, the pain would disappear completely. I was exhausted, though, weariness sucking at my limbs. Magic makes you powerful, but not superpowered, and just like physical exertion, if you push yourself too hard, you're gonna collapse, though in this case, the bone-chilling terror probably had as much to do with it as the spellcasting.

I reached out for magic again and was relieved to feel it still thrumming away, ready to spring to life. Another obnoxious thing about magic: hit it too hard at a time, and you can find it getting less and less reliable, until your connection to the spirit worlds finally goes dead like a blackout after a power surge.

I picked my way through the darkened living room and up the stairs. To my relief, my parents were already in bed, and my sister Ella too. My injuries weren't really visible, but I feared they would see "amateur demon fighter" written all over my face.

I knew I had been damn unwise tonight. I knew how to use magic in a fight, intellectually, but I'd never been in a real one. I could barely manage to chase the possums out of the garbage.

A cold wave hit me, like an invisible current cresting over my shoulders. I could have gotten killed. I almost had. Where would that have left my family? Or, at the risk of stating the obvious, *me?*

What the hell were you thinking?

You weren't, the little voice in my head replied.

That'll be quite enough out of you, I shot back at myself. I was alive, Brit and her mom were safe, and to hell with everything else.

When I reached my room, I didn't even bother to undress, just flopped into bed. I feared I would be too keyed up to sleep, but it took only a moment for the exhaustion to set in and make my mind go fuzzy. Whatever was out there, it would have to wait until morning.

Tomorrow was the first day of school.

CHAPTER THREE

TAP. "SAM?" SOMETHING warm and furry was on top of my head.

Tap. "Sam?" My brain was too scrambled to respond.

Swat. "Sam!" This time there were claws involved.

I yelped and pushed the creature off my head.

I sat up and looked around, the room spinning. I glared at the clock, then fumbled with it until I shut the alarm off.

I swung my gaze over to Catrick Swayze, (who, to be clear, was a cat) perched at the foot of my bed, absentmindedly swishing his tail. "This couldn't have waited another ten minutes until the alarm rang?"

"Good morning to you, too, Sam," he said, the words apparently coming from his mouth, though I'd never quite figured out how he was able to do that. "Welcome to the first day of sophomore year, and, if you want to get philosophical, the rest of your life. And no, it couldn't wait. Tell me about last night."

I flinched, as I remembered last night's fiasco. "It was a little more complicated than I thought."

"I'm shocked. Shocked I tell you. What happened?"

I staggered out of bed, still in last night's clothes, looking and feeling completely bedraggled. "Remember how I said Brittney's house had a poltergeist?"

"You mean the one you assured me would be so simple to banish?"

"Turns out it wasn't a poltergeist. It was a demon. Live and in person."

His whiskers jumped. "A *demon?* Are you sure?"

"Yeah, I'm pretty sure. I figured it out somewhere between the door and the ceiling fan."

"*Shit,*" he merrowed. "This is not good."

"I noticed."

"Demons don't just come wandering into your house. That only happens when magic is getting thrown around, and a lot of it."

I didn't like where this was going. "A lot more than what I use, is what you're saying."

"Yeah, you have many flaws, but you didn't do this. This was dangerous magic, the kind powerful enough to eat away at the Curtain."

"I was afraid you'd say that."

"I don't know what kind of magic it was, but whoever's using it isn't exactly somebody of high moral character. They have to know the risks, and apparently it doesn't bother them at all."

Involuntarily, I cast a suspicious look toward my window, saw nothing but the empty street. "I was afraid you'd say that, too."

"Do you think your friend was involved in some kind of magic? Or somebody else in there?"

I chuckled at that idea. "I don't think so. I didn't sense anything like that."

"Well, that's even worse. That means we don't know where it's coming from. Did you recognize your not-poltergeist?"

"No," I said. "I've never met this guy before. Didn't exactly get much chance to talk. Whoever he was, he wasn't what you'd describe as even keeled and rational. You think it was a fallen angel maybe?"

Catrick shook his furry head, orange and white like the rest of him. "Anything's possible but I doubt it. They don't spend much time on earth these days. Too busy fighting each other. No, he was probably just some small-timer who went looking for trouble and found some."

"Oh yeah, I almost forgot. I saw a mystery woman following me around last night. Pretty sure there was something supernatural about her."

Catrick flopped his head down on his paws. "Why is nothing ever simple with you, Sammy?"

"You think she could be the one using all this magic?"

"Could be. It worries me that she seems to know who you are."

"Imagine how I feel. What do we do now?"

He regarded me incredulously. "*Do?* We do nothing. Lay low for a few weeks. No magic, no sudden movements. Whatever's going on, it's probably something that has nothing to do with us."

I found his optimism somewhat ill-founded. "Okay. Fine. I have to get ready for school. Another crisis."

Swayze strutted downstairs to mooch breakfast scraps, and I showered and dressed, then headed downstairs to do the same thing.

School. Where every corner would hold some half-buried memory, waiting to jump up and bite me. It seemed ridiculous, with what I'd been through last night, but the thought of starting a new year was daunting. I'd managed to put it out of my mind, almost, and when Brit had told me about her poltergeist situation, the distraction had actually been a relief, something magical to throw myself into so I didn't have to concentrate on real life. But I couldn't avoid it any longer.

"Morning, family," I said, getting bleary-voiced greetings in return from Mom and Dad and a half-hearted nod from Ella. I filled Catrick Swayze's water bowl and poured his breakfast kibble, then flopped down at the table.

"You came in kinda late last night," Dad said, after gulping down a chunk of toast.

I shrugged. "I had things to do."

He laughed. "I'm sure you did."

Ella snorted. "He was probably out committing crimes and stuff."

I gave her a hiss Catrick Swayze would have been proud of, hoping my parents wouldn't take her seriously. I didn't think banishing spells were a crime, per se, but it was a legal gray area I wasn't keen to explore. Dad's grin continued. "First day of school, huh?"

"I will never understand why people your age think that's something to be happy about."

"It's exciting. Whole new year ahead of you, all the possibilities, the unknown. A new chapter of your life about to start. You're making memories."

"Well, aren't you a poet?"

"Got any plans in particular?" Mom asked, sipping her coffee.

Dodge a mystery stalker. Hope dark magic isn't headed in my direction. "Not really." A thought struck me: if that mystery stalker was onto the house, that meant she was onto my family. "I did notice something strange last night," I said. "I thought I saw a woman lurking around across the street. Seemed weird to me."

Mom and Dad glanced at each other. "Did she do anything in particular?" Dad asked.

"Nope. Just thought it was a good idea to be on the lookout for prowlers."

"Well, it's not like prowlers are unprecedented in Williamsport," Dad said.

"I think she just exists in Sam's pervy imagination," Ella said.

"I've thrown my breakfast at you before, and I can do it again," I told her.

"What about you, Ella," Mom said, "any plans for your first day of junior high?"

"Not really," Ella said. "I'm kinda nervous, to be honest."

"Don't be nervous," I said. "They hardly ever make the middle-schoolers drink from a toilet anymore."

"Sam, be nice." Mom said. "With everything different for Ella this year, it would be good if you watched out for her a little, until she gets her bearings, since you'll be in the same building and all."

"What am I supposed to do?" I protested. "Don't I have enough problems? Our schedules don't even overlap."

"I don't need him to look out for me," Ella said, jumping in.

"See? She's a strong, independent woman now, she doesn't need me looking out for her."

Mom rolled her eyes, a distinctly familiar expression I may have inherited from her. Then her face grew serious. "Are you sure you're doing okay?"

I flinched, causing the table to rattle a little. "I'm fine."

"Are you sure?" Dad said. "I know going back to school can't be easy." Ella watched us moon-eyed, for once keeping her mouth shut.

"Yes." I muttered into my breakfast. "Really. Everything's fine. Thanks." The temperature in the room seemed to plunge several degrees. Thankfully, they let it drop after that. I had feared I was in for some "talk about your feelings" conversation, but I still hadn't been prepared for it.

I scarfed down the rest of breakfast, then Ella and I grabbed backpacks and jackets, I gave Swayze's head a scratch, and we made our way out the door amidst a flurry of goodbyes and admonitions to have a good day at school. "And watch out for your sister, if you can," Mom said as I managed to get a foot out the door.

The September air was breezy but still warm as we made our daily journey.

Passing through town, past the houses, the old church, the barking dogs, all of which conspire to give this city its veneer of normalcy, is always my favorite part of the school day.

Unfortunately, I always end up in the same place. My pleasant residential neighborhood gives way to Archibald J. Keller High School, blotting out the view and my optimism like the Death Star. It's almost like a living, breathing creature, one that daily plots new and exquisite ways to fuck up my life.

I was too absorbed in my own thoughts to notice Ella wasn't her usual chattering self until we turned onto the street that led to the school, a few other students making the same trip scattered here and there on cracked sidewalks, sprigs of grass thrusting through them. I turned to see her eyeing me. "May I help you?"

"You're limping," she said. "You weren't doing that yesterday."

I hadn't noticed it, but yeah, there was a little hitch in my step. "I fell yesterday, playing soccer at the beach."

By that time, we had crossed another street and made our way into the bustling parking lot, crowded with the various colorful denizens of our school, psyching themselves up for another year of hell. It was all depressingly familiar.

Three or four stories tall, the school towered over the wide, grassy lawns now filled with milling people and a clamor of noise: voices, engines, a car radio playing faintly somewhere.

"I know you're lying to me," Ella piped up as we picked our way through the press. "I can always tell when you're lying to me."

We approached the big double doors and I pulled them open. "When you put it that way, I don't care."

We stepped inside, into the roar of hormones and desperation. I gave her a hard nudge. "Don't get murdered today. There, you can tell Mom I looked out for you."

"Thanks. Your sympathy is overwhelming as always."

We parted company, and I steeled myself, pushing through the surging mob of bodies, dodging back and forth, in search of this year's locker. *Oh yeah, we're making memories.*

I dodged and thumped and got battered along as I made my way down the hallway, looking askance at those around me. Things tend to get lively around here. I saw nothing out of the ordinary, though: just North Siders and South Siders, roving in packs, as they usually did, many of them with the same askance looks I had.

In most ways, we're perfectly normal: we've got our stoners and jocks, our cheerleaders and the nerds that will never date them; all the stereotypical things you'd expect to find in an all-American high school. But this was Williamsport, and in these parts, we're over-achievers: we just have to add a little extra twist of suck all our own.

See, around here, the only "clique" that mattered much was the "haves" (the North Siders) and the "have-nots" (the South Siders). The Williams River splits off from the bay and cuts across town east to west, providing a convenient dividing line.

There were probably complex historical, economic, and social factors that explained why a seemingly arbitrary amount of dollars deposited you on one side of the river or the other, but I didn't know what they were. I just knew our two geographically themed social classes had hated each other since time immemorial. You'd think the North Siders would send their kids to some fancy private school, leaving us South Siders to wallow in public education, but no, for some arcane reason, we were all sandwiched together in this ancient brick building that had been there since pilgrim times.

It wasn't out of the question for a fight to break out, here and now, over a misheard comment or an accidental collision or just for the sheer bloody-minded sport of it. When that happens it's best to hole up in the nearest restroom.

I dodged past two more of my fellow students, then spotted my locker: 373.

I turned the dials on the lock (a must at Archibald J. Keller) and got it open on the first try. I tossed my jacket and backpack into the darkness of the locker, grudgingly dug out the textbooks and deposited them on the shelf. Nice and organized, though I knew it wouldn't be long before I began the year-long process of trashing it. I wondered how Ella was doing in this madhouse, so different from the elementary she'd been in until last year. I had been only half-joking about drinking from the toilet.

I had barely gotten my locker packed when the bell screeched, the signal to start my first round of education. With a groan, I pulled my math textbook off the shelf, shoved it into my bag, and thrust myself back into the mob.

It was a long walk, nearly on the other side of the school and on the next floor up, which meant navigating the always-sketchy stairs. I bobbed and weaved without incident, although once or twice I heard an angry shout, audible over the clamor, suggesting we were already getting started on this year's feuds. I passed by Brit, briefly, who gave me the awkward smile and wave you give someone who exorcises your house.

When I arrived at my classroom, Mr. Wilkins was outside by the door, as he always was, greeting his arriving students.

"Morning, Sam," he said, giving me a smile and a nod.

I gave him a salute. "Yes, sir."

He chuckled. "Nice to see you again. I'm glad your sense of humor is back." Then his face collapsed in dismay.

I froze. If he hadn't had such a reaction, I wouldn't even have noticed what he'd said. Was the entire school fretting about my state of mind? Were the mathletes going to sit me down to talk about my feelings?

I held up a mollifying hand and forced a smile. "No biggie."

I used to have something of a reputation as a class clown. Until Abby died. After that, I'd felt more like one of those creepy clowns you see in the movies. It had been well into summer before I'd started feeling like myself again. Almost. That almost was never going away, was it? The realization turned my blood cold, blotted out the roar of voices and footsteps around me.

I entered the room. Jesus, this day was going to be endless.

I had just ducked out of math class when a booming voice cut through the perpetual noise of the crowd: "SAAA-AHAHAHAAM!"

I whirled, spotted Jason Clay several feet away. "JAAA-SOOON," I responded, and we closed the distance, pulling each other into a thumping hug. Jason was an athletic dude with blue eyes and shaggy dirty-blond hair, and he looked like he escaped from a cologne commercial. His family was loaded, and of course, he got straight As.

But you couldn't hate the guy because he was just too damn decent, more likely to pull a nerd out of a locker than throw him in one. That's why he's one of the only people nominally respected by both North and South. (Whereas I'm respected by neither.)

He's also the best and quite possibly only one hundred percent human friend I have in the world.

We first met in junior high when I was around Ella's age. I was just coming into my magic, and it's fair to say I'd handled it poorly. Thanks to meeting Swayze, I'd managed to get it mostly under control, but still tended to spend my days wandering around with a haunted look on my face. Despite that, or perhaps because of it, Jason had simply walked up to me one day and, without preamble, became my friend. The haunted look didn't last long after that. And yeah, he knew all about my magic. Long story.

"It's been too long, bro," he said, giving me another thump.

"I know," I said. "What was it, like a month?"

"Even longer, I think. Sorry it's been so long. Well, not that sorry. Europe was awesome." He flung an arm over my shoulder, and we began to walk. "How's Williamsport? How's everybody?"

"Well, Williamsport's still here, unfortunately." We did a little fancy footwork, dodging someone carrying a bow who I hoped was on the archery team. "Oh yeah. Ella's in here now, cause she's in junior high."

He shook his head gravely. "They grow up so quickly."

"Our schedules don't overlap, but maybe you could keep an eye out for her, make sure she doesn't get lost or hassled or something."

He nodded. "I'll keep my eyes open."

"Thanks."

"So, what about you," he said. "How was your summer?"

I grimaced as I thought back to last night when my head was in a demon's jaws. "It was magical."

Half an hour later, I tried to come up with an answer to the same question as I stood in front of my second hour class. Twenty-six bored teenagers stared up at me from their desks, plus Mr. McKinley off to the side in his creaky rolling chair. I blinked and repeated his question. "What did I do on my summer vacation? Um, well, let's see here." I tried to cast my mind back over the past few months and dredge up something school appropriate.

I used an old microwave for target practice with a fire spell. "Jason got me into Premier League soccer. Go Liverpool."

I met my first water spirit, an interesting lady. "Visited my aunt and uncle in Minnesota."

And of course, performed my very first banishing spell. Who could have predicted the ensuing property damage? "And I helped with a food drive. I guess that's it." I walked back and sat at my desk.

As the next person went to the front and began droning, my attention wandered. A sense of strange, uneasy déjà vu stole into me.

I found my gaze on a desk in front of me and to the right, currently occupied by Lucas, a dopey, mop-headed linebacker. Before I was even aware of it, memories enveloped me.

It was a year ago. In the same classroom, in the same desk even, staring in the same direction.

At Abby.

Unease stabbed me. I tried not to think of her much. But it was too late for that.

I saw her, as clearly in my mind as if she was in the room. Her dark hair, which she never seemed to style, not that I know about such things, tumbled down her shoulders as she stared at her textbook, pen in her hand, equally dark eyes bright, focused. I felt a ridiculous little smile appear on my face.

"Sam? Sam?"

I flinched, snapping painfully back to the present. Lucas was back at Abby's desk. Sadness punched me in the stomach so hard that for a second, I feared I would actually fall out of my desk. I wanted so badly to be then and not now. Life now was just... wrong. Too wrong for me to deal with. I grabbed the edge of the desk. "Um, sorry. What?"

"The intercom," McKinley said. "It was for you."

I hadn't even heard the damn thing. "It was?"

"Yeah. They said you're supposed to go to the office."

For God's sake, now what? "Okay."

At least it would be a break from class. I hauled myself out of my desk. A few people around me snickered, and I flashed them a smug expression as I walked by.

Mr. McKinley gave me a sympathetic look as I passed. "Good luck."

"Thanks."

I knew I shouldn't, but as I walked by the desk that had been

Abby's, I couldn't fight the urge to look in the direction where she was supposed to be. She still wasn't there.

I walked out the door and into the halls. Luckily, I was in a completely different wing of the building than the office, meaning I could drag out my respite from schoolwork that much longer.

The school was quiet now, all its factions safely locked up in classrooms.

I wondered again what this could be about. Had I done anything questionable lately? That didn't make sense, it was the first day of school. Maybe a family emergency of some kind? They hadn't called for Ella, though. It was probably completely mundane, but anxiety squirmed around in my guts anyway.

Eventually, I found my way to the office, pushed through the glass door, and saw the receptionist, Mrs. Linsky, sitting at her desk. "Hey, Mrs. Linsky. I'm here. Do you happen to know what this is about? I haven't—"

I stopped talking. Mrs. Linsky wasn't moving a muscle. She didn't even seem to notice I was there.

"Mrs. Linsky?" There was no response. Shaking, I waved a hand in front of her face. Nothing. She wasn't slumped, like she was unconscious or dead. There was no blood. She was just frozen.

I caught sight of other figures around the office. A girl, pale and drawn, probably going home sick; a teacher, a flyer for the back-to-school dance in his hand, mouth open like he was about to speak. Through the half-open door of Principal Johnson's office, I saw his bald head hunched in front of a computer screen. I didn't have to go in to know he was in the same state.

Were these people dead? Dying? Was this a precursor to some kind of full-scale, magic-themed attack on our school? Was whoever let the demon loose about to make their move?

I cast about the room, in search of I don't know what, hoping for a lifeline.

"They're fine, if that's what you're worried about."

Trying to push the shock out of my mind, reaching for magic like it was a gun, I spun around.

That's when I got my first look at the thing that had invaded my school. It had long, black, gothy hair, dark bluish skin. Flat, slitted eyes. Talons. Fangs. Vaguely medieval garb, down to a sword at its hip.

It took me several seconds to gain the presence of mind to figure out what I was seeing. It was a Shal'Gasa. They were the inspiration for countless terrifying folk tales, legendarily bloodthirsty and Machiavellian, and they played at a level far, far above my own. The "gods and archangels and eldritch empires" kind of level. And one of them was standing in the high school office like it had just dropped by to help itself to some breakroom coffee.

I wish I could tell you I made some heroic wisecrack, but I just made a groaning sound, my knees about to collapse out from under me as I stared at it in shock.

"Good morning," it said.

You've probably never heard of the Shal'Gasa. Some say that's because they choose not to interact with humans much. My theory is that everyone who meets one just ends up dead. Take it from me: the creatures you've never heard of are the ones that should scare you the most.

I cleared my throat. I suppose I should have done a better job hiding my fear, but I doubt the Shal'Gasa would have bought it anyway. "G-good morning." I jerked my head toward the still forms around me. "What did you do to these people?"

He shrugged. "I merely made them be still so we could have some privacy. They'll come around in a little while with no idea anything happened."

My mouth ran away with me: "If you hurt them, you're gonna have a problem you can't handle."

As last words went, those weren't too bad.

The Shal'Gasa laughed, a far more pleasant sound than it had any right to be. "Now *that* is the fighting spirit we need. My name is Eressen, of the House al'Barra, sworn to the Crimson Throne. I'm pleased to finally make your acquaintance."

I nodded several times. What the hell do you say to a Shal'gasa making small talk? I mustered a little courage. "If you wanted me dead, you could have done it already. So, you want something."

"Precisely. I have need of a man with your talents."

Careful, Samuel, careful. "And what could I possibly do for you? I'm just a low-level guy. If you went to the trouble to seek me out like this, you should know that."

"Don't sell yourself short. A 'low-level guy,' as you put it, can rise very high indeed, if they seize the moment."

I tried to stay calm. Here's a little something David Copperfield failed to mention: when you enter the wonderful world of wizardry, gods, demons, spirits, and other shady characters sometimes try to recruit you into their coven; they'll boost your powers, grant your wishes, kill your enemies, in exchange for certain (typically hor-rifying) tasks. They're kind of like organized crime families, albeit without the mob's easygoing nature and generosity of spirit.

That's one way to do magic. Then there's the way I do it; I cut out the middleman, and draw in otherworldly energy myself, directly from the other side. I'm like a human combustion engine; I take that raw power and whip it up into something magicy. Wizards like that are called Outlaws. It gives you a certain swagger, but the only way to stay alive is to be powerful enough to survive on your own, or not to draw any attention to yourself. I'd gone for number two, and apparently it hadn't worked.

I swallowed. *Stall.* "How did you find me?"

His voice was deep and rich, and he spoke with a fancy British accent, because of course he did. "I looked. It really was that simple.

My young friend, you have no idea how spectacularly you've found yourself in the right place at the right time."

"That's great and all, but you still haven't told me why you're here, disrupting my education."

"Simple: I'm here to ask a favor."

If I thought my alarm couldn't get any worse, I was very mistaken. "A favor."

"Indeed, and perhaps do you one or two as well."

"Well, I'm not sleeping with you." He laughed at that, genuine amusement dancing across his face. "And I'm not selling you my soul, either."

His laughter faded and he sighed theatrically. "Oh, Mr. Adams, what would I do with your soul if I had it? I won't ask you to swear an oath to me. All I ask is that at some date in the future, you assist me in an endeavor."

"Which is?"

He shrugged. "I confess, I'm not entirely sure. Things are quite complicated among the Shal'Gasa at the moment. Many moving parts and such. I'm involved in something that may require your services. Forgive me, I can't say more. I realize how that must sound from your perspective, my asking for a favor I don't even know myself, but I'm afraid that's the best I can do."

"The answer is no."

He held up a taloned hand. "Don't be so hasty. I'm not demanding something for nothing; what I have in mind would be quite reciprocal, I assure you."

"That begs the question of what you could do for me." I dreaded the answer.

"I believe you noticed a demon prowling about last night, slobbering, knocking things over, doing all those nasty things demons do. And sooner or later it occurred to you that its presence must have been caused by the spells of another practitioner who was entirely unconcerned their magic could invite a demon into your realm. It goes without saying such a person would undoubtedly be both powerful and up to no good."

"And you're telling me you'll help me put a stop to this mystery person, in exchange for a favor in the future, is that it?"

"Precisely, my young friend. It'll all be a grand adventure."

My mind raced. One wrong word could turn this into a fight I had no doubt I would lose. Still, I had to roll the dice. I didn't see any other way. "The answer's still no. I know a trap when I hear one."

I tensed, half-expecting him to slaughter me on the spot.

Instead, he held up a conciliatory hand. "Mr. Adams, it would be degrading to both of us for me to start issuing threats. I'll simply be blunt: this is beyond you. As you said yourself, you're merely a low-level guy. I don't deny the situation is murky, but I've still seen enough to know that if you try and dance at this particular ball, you are going to die, and that's all there is to it."

"You're operating on the assumption that I'm going to do anything. Maybe I'll just stay out of it. Whatever 'it' is."

He gave me a casual look. "I can't deny that would be wise. Judging by your reaction when you thought these people were in danger, I somehow don't think that's the choice you'll be making. In any case, I wish you luck."

He made a motion with his hand. A tangle of golden motes swirled through the air, causing a perfectly round slice of reality to distort, then disappear. A portal opened directly in front of Mr. Johnson's office. A cold wind blew through it, chilling me right down to my boxer shorts. Beyond the portal, I could see indefinable shapes moving around in near darkness. Noises I couldn't make out sounded faintly on the other side.

"Mr. Adams, I can tell you're a bright fellow, intelligent enough to know when to ask for help. When you need me, simply cast the most basic of summoning spells and I'll be waiting. I look forward to working with you. Good day."

"Uh… good day."

He stepped through the portal and it closed instantly, the mundane reality that was supposed to be there clicking back into place. For a long time, there was simply silence in the office, as I panted for air.

Then, Mrs. Linsky began to stir back to awareness, so I hurried out the door and back towards class, still shaking.

The bell had rung by then, and the hallways were filling with people, arguing with each other, couples holding hands, laughing or worrying over something or other, little slices of life played out in five-minute bursts.

I weaved my way through, trying to focus enough not to collide with anyone. An offer I couldn't refuse from a Shal'gasa, on the first day of school. My brain couldn't quite wrap around what the implications of that might be.

Apparently, I was more popular than I ever realized.

CHAPTER FOUR

EVEN IF THE cafeteria food had been better, I still wouldn't have had much of an appetite.

In the space of twelve hours, I'd banished a demon that had nearly eaten me, spotted a mystery woman stalking me, and mouthed off to a Shal'Gasa warlord. And I already had homework.

Help.

I had taken my lunch outside, at one of the tables, thinking I could at least enjoy the fresh air, because I was quickly running out of anything else.

I'd started off my lunch break staring blankly at the parking lot, wondering how a person went about writing a will. Whenever I tried to get my brain into gear, it did nothing but stir up questions I didn't want answered. Why a Shal'Gasa should come wandering in from the great beyond to seek me out, I couldn't even begin to imagine. There wasn't a single reason, however tenuous, that the Shal'Gasa should have any business with me, especially one as high-status as Eressen's garb and manner of speech suggested he was. And then there was the small matter of some mysterious, unscrupulous other wizard prowling Williamsport. I'd downplayed it in front of Eressen, but I really, really disliked the sound of that. We wizards have many flaws, and not playing well with others is high among them. One wizard in this town was more than enough.

I was startled back to reality by Jason, sitting down across from me. "You look... bad."

I shook my head. "Uh. Yeah. School year's not off to a great start."

As soon as the words were out of my mouth, I regretted them, because I knew he would think I meant something else entirely.

He did. A look of tremendous sympathy washed over his face. *Here we go again.* That was the thing about Jason. It was all "dude" this and "bro" that, and then *bam.* When you're least expecting it, he hits you with sincerity.

"How are you holding up?" His eyes were deep wells of concern. I couldn't exactly get mad at him for that.

I opened my mouth, closed it, tried to think of something to say. I wanted to keep up the official line that I was fine. What came out was "Why didn't I know?" Damn it, I hadn't meant to say that. I fought the urge to flip the table over.

He leaned forward and gripped my shoulder. "Nobody knew Abby was using, Sam." *Not until the day she OD'd.* "Not you or me or her family or your family or anybody. You can't blame yourself."

"I don't blame myself, I just..." I couldn't finish, because I didn't even know what to say.

"She hid how much she was struggling, from everybody. And she wouldn't want you to go on like this. That much I do know."

"What do you mean, 'like this?' I've moved on. Everything was fine until today."

He gave me a sympathetic look. "Sam, I know how you felt about her."

"I don't know what you're talking about," I lied. I needn't have bothered.

"It wasn't exactly a secret."

I shook my head. "There's nothing I can do about it now. I just want to put it behind me."

He gave me a forced smile. "Right. Happier thoughts. Are you gonna go tonight?"

"Go? Oh, yeah. The bonfire."

"Yup, it's tradition."

"Sorry man. I don't think I'm up for it this year."

"Come on, you gotta go. Might be just what you need to get your mind off everything. You might see a fight or two. I know you love a good North Side/South Side fight."

"True. That is an oddly specific Williamsport pastime I'd hate to miss."

"Exactly. You'd go to school the next day, and everybody would be talking about it but you. Come on." He laughed and nudged my shoulder.

He didn't know the extent of the problems I was dealing with, but then, neither did I. I couldn't hide out forever, I supposed. "Fine," I said. "I'll go."

Sea air mingled with woodsmoke to light up my nostrils as I walked down a quiet side street. If I didn't know where I was going, the pleasant smell would have told me I was moving in the right direction.

I felt a vague sense of unease as I topped a rise and saw the glow of the fires in the fast-darkening night, human figures stirring around them.

I hiked down to the beach, watched the fires grow closer and the figures more distinct. Ostensibly a school-sponsored event, it tends to be grossly unsupervised. Music mingled with voices as I wandered into the press of bodies.

As I prowled, I happened to pass a couple curled together in some shadows, leaning in for a kiss. I looked away, but I couldn't keep it from sending my mind spinning off, to some other bonfire that could have been.

This would have been the perfect time to talk to Abby: the music, the beach, the possibilities of a new school year in the air like Dad had talked about. I could have suggested we go out sometime, for coffee, or something to eat, or anything. Nothing serious. If she had wanted to. If she had been alive.

If, if, if.

Bonfires blazed up and down the beach, little torches against the darkness over the ocean just beyond, and hundreds of my fellow teenagers mingled all around them, voices and laughter a dull, pleasant roar, managing to hide the tension that lurks under the surface of pretty much everything around here.

I studied the milling faces for a moment, then went searching for Jason. Even here, both sides kept their distance, congregating, amusingly enough, on the North and South side of the beach, respectively, although I doubted anyone had put that much thought into it.

Luckily, it didn't take much wandering to catch up to him. He was standing near one of the fires with a couple of his North Side buddies. When he saw me, he bounded over and we bumped fists. "Sam. Glad you made it."

I forced a smile. "Well, I wouldn't want to miss the inaugural fight."

The two guys next to him gave me wary glances. Kyle and Brian, I recognized, best friends themselves. Probably inspired by Jason's presence, they made an effort at friendliness and grunted hellos.

Kyle, a stocky, red-haired guy who had caused a minor scandal last year when he'd quit the football team to "concentrate on his rowing," spoke up. "You're…" He waved a bewildered hand. "Riley?"

"Sam. Sam Adams."

"Oh. I knew it was one of the founding fathers. Sorry."

"No problem."

Brian reached into a nearby cooler and thrust out a beer. "Want one?" He still had his whiskers, I noticed, which he dubiously claimed made him resemble a "young Denzel Washington." The whiskers arranged themselves into a weak smile.

I waved it away. "No thanks." Shrugging, he tossed it back in the cooler. It wasn't moral conviction that made me abstain. There's no telling what a drunk wizard will do, but it'll likely be something dramatic, which I knew from experience.

The day of Abby's funeral, to be more precise, when I'd started drinking my parents' wine straight from the bottle and the next thing I knew, I was sprawled face down in the backyard and the power was out on our street.

But those dark thoughts were easier to ignore than usual, with the noise and the crowds, and they quickly faded and crumbled away, at least for now.

"I'm glad I came," I admitted to Jason.

He thumped me on the arm. "Good. I knew you would be."

There was a crash, shouts rising over the din. We turned our heads to see a couple guys rolling across the ground, sand flying around them, while onlookers cheered them on. They were trying to land punches without much success.

It didn't take long for them to plow into someone else and send them helicoptering down as well. This provoked more shouting and others to jump in. As the mass surged towards us, Jason and I both danced backwards, laughing. I caught a glimpse of Kyle off to the side, screaming encouragement to one of the fighters. The cooler quickly became the evening's first casualty.

In the end, it fizzled out. A few cooler heads waded in and dragged their buddies apart, there were a few more shouts as the two groups slowly disentangled themselves, then things died down and began returning to normal levels of debauchery.

"Just when we were getting somewhere," I said.

"Look on the bright side," Jason said. "We have a whole year to see more. That was just the warm-up."

He was probably right: even by normal standards, this bonfire seemed teetering on the edge of chaos. Voices were a crescendo, tension and jubilation mixed, alcohol flowed and those closest to the speakers were dancing in a fashion adults would call "suggestive."

I remembered the anonymous wizard still lurking out there somewhere, no doubt plotting villainous plots, and my spine tingled. Involuntarily, I glanced around the darkness, saw crashing waves and silhouettes by the fires. No demons, no black-robed sorcerers. But the night suddenly seemed more dangerous anyway. This was a well-lit, public area, but that was no real deterrent: the supernatural, in whatever form, can manifest pretty much anywhere: in a crowd or the middle of nowhere, night or day, big city or small town, pleasant suburb or literal haunted house. The only commonality was that it showed up where you least expected it.

I tried to smile. I was expecting supernatural trouble now; did that mean that would ward it off? That seemed a little too superstitious even for an actual wizard.

Something thumped into me, sending me reeling. "Hey!" the shape shouted. "Hey, hey, hey! Break it up!" If anyone could hear it over the music, they continued with their regularly scheduled partying, already in progress. The shape revealed itself to be Mr. McKinley, who looked around, realizing he'd missed the whole thing. "Oh. Hi, Sam. Sorry to bump into you like that. Enjoying the bonfire?"

"Yeah, it's been great so far."

"Good, good. Everybody seems to be having fun."

I sniffed, noticing his highly impractical shirt and tie were damp, and his normally curly brown hair was plastered to his head. "Is that beer?"

"Uh. Yeah." His voice was sheepish. "I caught some kids drinking earlier and took away their beer. It didn't exactly work out like I planned."

"You mean people were drinking?" Jason asked, face a mask of shock and horror.

"Funny man. Taking some lessons from your friend here I see. They don't pay me enough for this shit." He jerked his head up, stared into our eyes like a hawk. "Don't curse in school."

"We're not in school," I pointed out.

His anxious eyes roamed the revelry. "Well, it's a school function, God help us, so it still counts. Look, I gotta stay on the move. Thanks for not being the worst. Good talking to you."

"Good talking to you, too. Be careful out there."

He gave me a weary look, steeled himself, and plunged back into the crowd. "Good luck, Mr. McKinley," Jason called. McKinley raised a hand in farewell.

"When I grow up, I think I'll be a teacher," I said.

Jason laughed, then his face grew curious. "What *are* you gonna do when you get outta here?"

"I don't know, but I'm getting out of Williamsport, I can tell you that much."

He barked a laugh. "Me too. College is gonna be awesome."

"What, and leave all this?" I gestured around.

He laughed again. "Yeah, I don't want to spend the rest of my life doing the whole North Side/South Side thing. I'm not in any rush to get there yet though. And don't worry, I'm gonna stay in touch with all my high school friends, I promise." He gave me a punch in the gut, which I returned. "Hey," he said, "we should apply to the same colleges. Keep the friendship alive."

"Sounds good." I hesitated, then decided to speak, not wanting to disappoint him sometime down the road. "I don't know, though. I don't know what kind of college I'll be able to afford and I'm not exactly brilliant enough to get a scholarship."

To my relief, he was completely nonplussed. "You should get a magic scholarship." I laughed. "Besides, that's tomorrow's problem. We still have three years of high school left."

"I can hardly wait."

As my eyes roamed the crowd, only half-paying attention, they raked across something familiar but out of place. I turned my gaze back, and this time picked it out almost immediately.

Ella.

I turned to Jason. "Hang on just one second."

I began tromping across the beach, trying to intercept her. She was ahead of me, and I nearly lost her once or twice. Where she thought she was going, I had no idea.

My strides ate up the sand until I closed the distance.

She hadn't noticed me at all, apparently going for the "blend in like I've been here the whole time" strategy, sitting on a log near one of the fires. It would have worked if she'd managed to slip past me.

I hesitated. Did I really want to be some responsible voice of reason? Not really. But, I decided, the look on Ella's face would be funny.

I crept behind her, and leaned in, peering upside down at her face, which registered sudden guilty shock. "Sam?"

"Good evening."

She jumped up and scowled at me. "What are you doing?"

"I could ask you the same question, and I think I will: what the hell are you doing here?"

She gave me an exaggerated look of innocence. "I just wanted to come to the bonfire, okay? Everybody always talks about how wild it was at school the next day; I wanted to see it for myself."

I adopted a tone of stern authority. "I remind you that this is a high school event and middle schoolers aren't invited."

She gave me the biggest eye roll I'd ever seen. Yeah, it definitely ran in the family. "Oh God. Are you actually trying to be responsible and brotherly and shit?"

"Yes, as a matter of fact I am. It amused me."

She groaned. "Just leave me alone, okay? I'll be fine."

"Ella, what I said about getting murdered actually applies here. Look around; you're twelve years old, this isn't safe."

We both sucked in deep breaths, almost simultaneously, preparing to argue further. Before I could start firing, a sound caught my attention, a little away from the party, not a demon, thankfully, just shrill, tense yells. Well, Williamsport had plenty of problems that weren't demonic in origin.

It didn't take long to spot the source: a tall, dark-haired North Sider I recognized as Trevor... something. I'd seen him around but never spoken to him or felt much reason to. There were a couple other North Side goons with him. No, not just them: four or five wide-eyed, nervous freshmen.

The back-to-school bonfire isn't exactly a great place for freshmen; the upperclassmen tend to use the occasion to terrorize them. It's kinda heart-warming: for one magical evening, our class prejudices disappear, and North and South put their differences aside to dump beer on the freshmen and draw penises on their faces. (One suspects the freshmen don't see it that way.)

I found my mind wandering back to last year's bonfire when I had been a freshman. A bunch of us had been herded in front of the water, trying to dodge an endless supply of water balloons some upperclassmen were hurling at us, much to their amusement. Dodging and weaving, I nearly collided with someone, forcing me to sidestep. Abby.

Her dark hair was plastered to the side of her head, droplets of water running down her cheeks and onto her neck. And she was smiling. "So, freshman year, huh?"

"Yeah, it's been a blast so far."

"Look on the bright side: they could have made us do something a lot worse."

"They still can."

"One problem at a time."

"That's what I like about you. You're an optimist." That was one of many things.

"Duck." She grabbed my shoulder and yanked us both downward, as a water balloon sailed over my head.

"Thanks."

"No problem."

We scrambled up out of the sand, avoiding a sudden volley that soaked a couple of others who hadn't moved fast enough. "And you're a pessimist," she said.

"No, I'm a realist." She had a point, though: wizards are destined to be on the cynical side.

"That's exactly what a pessimist would say." Another balloon arced in, splattering against another freshman well wide of me, but the droplets still managed to soak me. Abby giggled.

"Very funny."

"I agree."

"You're part of this too, you know."

"Yeah, but that's the optimism you like so much." A balloon came at her, which she narrowly managed to swat out of the sky, spraying her but avoiding a direct hit.

I saw another flurry coming in, and with unapologetic ruthlessness, gave another freshman a little nudge that let him soak up the worst of it. I hurried back towards Abby in case he was curious who got him soaked.

"That was terrible," she said. "You should be ashamed of yourself."

"But I'm not. Makes things so much easier." A water balloon splatted against my hip.

"See?" she said. "Karma."

"There's no such thing as karma."

A balloon ricocheted off her leg, but she hardly noticed. "You don't fool me," she said. "You act like nothing gets to you, but I know you too well to believe it." She gave me a look that mingled playfulness and sincerity. "I can see right through you."

I hesitated, unsure what to say. I was saved from a response when, almost simultaneously, a pair of water balloons got us both in the face.

I shook my head vigorously, coming back to the present. I really was losing it, getting nostalgic for freshman hazing.

A small crowd, smelling blood, was migrating in Trevor's direction. Trevor held up a wine bottle of uncertain vintage. "How about a toast," he roared, "to our new freshmen class!" He flung the bottle into the hands of one of the freshmen, a redheaded girl who looked like she'd been poleaxed. "Drink up."

Mr. McKinley won't like this. Unfortunately, he was nowhere in sight.

Ella had only got a couple angry words out when I cut her off, jerking my head in their direction. "There's some of the trouble I was talking about. Go find Jason." My eyes picked him out of the crowd, and I pointed him out.

She scowled. "Jason?"

I gave her a push. "*Go.*" To my surprise, she got moving, if slowly and indignantly.

"What am I supposed to do with Jason?" she called over her shoulder.

"I don't know, maybe I'll get lucky, and he'll decide to adopt you."

She gave me one last glare, then disappeared in his direction.

I wasn't exactly sure what made me head towards the gathering crowd; maybe high school drama just seemed like a nice change of pace from the supernatural, or maybe remembering Abby made me sentimental, but I found myself walking across the beach until I was standing among them. "Trevor. Hello there. Happy school year."

He greeted me with a befuddled scowl. There were a few snickers here and there, and the freshmen turned anxious glances toward me. "Do I know you?" So much disdain dripped from his voice I could have slipped in it.

"Not really. Sam. That's my name. Don't worry about my last name because I don't remember yours either."

Another scowl. "What do you want?"

I looked at the bottle, then back to him. "I thought we were toasting. Are there glasses?"

"Glasses?"

"Yeah, for the toast. It looks like nobody has theirs yet." There were more snickers, including from the girl who held the bottle.

He blinked. "It's for the freshmen, genius."

"But they don't have glasses either."

He stepped closer. "What the hell is your problem?"

"Yeah, what's the problem?" Jason picked his way through the crowd to stand beside me and I nearly collapsed with relief.

Trevor's eyes flicked towards him. "No problem. Your friend here is just looking for trouble."

"Yeah, he does that sometimes."

"It's true," I said.

"I can see it's true."

Jason, ever a peacemaker more than a fighter, didn't rise to the bait, shot a glance at the freshmen, crouched like gazelles in a lion's den and watching us. "Found some freshmen huh?"

"Thought I should welcome them to high school."

"What for? There's so much other stuff going on here. Doesn't seem like a very fun way to spend the evening."

Trevor smirked, weighing options in his mind, then gave his head a shake. "Just stay out of my way." He sauntered back and disappeared into the crowd. It takes a special kind of douchebag to be able to saunter. The people around us slowly dispersed, the freshmen scampering away, leaving the bottle in the sand.

"Thanks," I said. "I had him right where I wanted him, but thanks anyway."

Jason rolled his eyes. "You're welcome. You really do need to find some way to keep out of trouble. It's only the first day, you don't want to peak too soon."

We began walking back the way we had come. Kyle and Brian appeared through the crowd, meeting us. Jason glanced back and forth between them. "Where's Ella?"

Kyle jerked his head behind them. "Back over there, by the fire."

"You were supposed to watch her, dude."

"We were coming to help you two," Brian said, voice vaguely indignant. "She thought you might need some help."

I growled, scanning the beach again. Luckily, she hadn't gotten far. I intercepted her and began hauling her back toward the others. "Nice try."

"I was trying to help."

"Thanks."

She scowled up at me furiously. "Are you gonna tell Mom and Dad?"

"I'm no rat. But I'm taking you home."

Jason began backing away. "I'll let you two sort this out. If anybody needs me, I'll be… somewhere else."

"We don't need to leave," Ella said, pulling away. "I'm already here, you can, like, supervise if you want. We just got here."

"Spending the night supervising you at the back-to-school bonfire sounds like my actual hell."

"I think you're being pretty unreasonable," said Brian. "It's not like she got hurt or anything."

"Yeah, this isn't your best look," said Kyle.

I glared at them. "What if somebody puts something in her drink or something?" I shuddered at the voice of reason in my tone.

"Actually, maybe you're right," said Kyle, his gaze wandering away and his tone getting uncharacteristically serious, serving only to make him sound comical. "The Reapers are here."

"The *who?*"

"The Reapers. He lowered his voice. "I swear, I just saw one of them walk by.

"It's just an urban legend," Brian said, in the tone of voice of someone who'd said this many times already and got nowhere.

"It's not; that's why Ella doesn't have to worry about getting something in her drink. The whole town's going dry because of them."

I gave him a skeptical look. "Going dry? When is Williamsport ever going dry?" He glanced at me, at Brian, his face going uncomfortable as he realized he's said too much. "Come on, man, just tell me."

"It's just some rumor going around," Brian said, "You don't know about it?"

"What, just because I'm from the South Side I'm an expert on crime?"

A smile flicked across his face. "Everybody says there's this scary-ass new gang in town called the Reapers," he said.

From his dismissive smirk I could tell he didn't believe it, but I felt unease creeping up my spine. Williamsport was hardly immune to gang activity; it could be a complete coincidence that some new faction showed up in town, but at the same time as dark magic? I didn't like it. "And they're running off all the other dealers, is that it?"

He shrugged. "That's what people say, anyway. Like I said, it's just some rumor."

That didn't make me feel any better. Monsters and wizards qualified as "just some rumor." I turned to look at Ella. "See? If I wasn't here, you might have been carried off and eaten by the Reapers."

"Why did the intercom call you today, anyway?" she said.

"I got the wrong textbook by mistake, and they needed to replace it. And changing the subject won't work."

"It's true," Kyle proclaimed, his gaze returning to us. "And I can prove it."

"How?" Ella said.

"Because I just spotted that guy," he said. He raised a finger to point at something, then slammed it back down to his hip and began pointing more surreptitiously. "That's one of them," he whispered.

"Where?" My head swiveled in the direction he'd pointed, but I couldn't make out many individual faces.

"Dude, come on," Brian said. "Are you serious?"

"Yeah, I'm serious." Kyle said. "I know they're real because I've seen them. I ran that guy off yesterday when he tried to sell to my little brother."

I tried to keep my voice level. "How do you know he's a Reaper?"

"Because of the tattoo on his arm. I didn't get a good look, but they say all the Reapers have them. Super fancy, not the kind a street rat could afford."

That wasn't exactly hard evidence, but then, the world didn't think there was much hard evidence for magic, either.

I looked around, but all I saw were revelers, flowing beer, and smoke blooming from the bonfires. I found it hard to believe any of this crowd was dabbling in the dark arts. I would have been surprised if most of them dabbled with a cookbook. "Where did he go?" I muttered tightly to Kyle.

"I don't know. I lost track of him."

My glances around the bonfire landed on Jason, red solo cup in his hand, moving in our direction. I lighted on a figure, on the periphery of the gathering, walking slowly. Right towards him.

"Is that him?" I muttered to Kyle.

"Yeah, I think so."

With no actual plan, I found myself moving rapidly in Jason's direction. The closer I got, the more certain I became there were traces of magic coming from the guy. Now that I knew where to look, it was unmistakable. My stomach turned cold as any hopes I had that this wasn't magic-related disappeared.

Of all the damn times for Ella to sneak out.

He got to Jason a little before I did, but I was close enough to hear their muffled voices. "Hey, man," the guy said. "You looking to party? I got some stuff."

Jason, nice even to a stereotypical drug dealer, waved a hand. "No thanks. I'm good."

"Come on, it—"

That was when I got there. "Hey," I shouted. I sent a blast of magic into him that provoked a surprised cry. His feet flew in the air, and he landed in a spray of sand and flailing limbs.

He sat up, leaning on his elbows, and looked at me with shock and understanding. He understood what I was and what I had done. I wondered for a split second if he would make a fight of it, here and now, but instead, he scrambled to his feet and ran back up the beach, quickly disappearing into the darkness.

"Are you okay?" I asked Jason.

He looked puzzled. "Uh, yeah. I've seen drug dealers before. Most of them aren't gonna just shoot you for turning them down. You didn't need..." His eyes widened. "Oh. That was..." He dropped his voice. "Magic?"

"Yeah," I said, half-listening, staring at the smudge of night where the dealer had gone.

"Do you know that guy or something?"

"No, never seen him before. You should see if you can break this party up. Maybe it's nothing, and I doubt you can do much with these people anyway, but I'd feel a lot safer if we all got the hell out of here."

"Sam, you're freaking me out. What's going on?"

"I'm gonna follow him."

"You're *what?*"

"I'm gonna follow him. I want to figure out what the hell he's up to."

"Are you kidding me? What do you think he's gonna do? He might have backup around here somewhere."

These arguments would have seemed very sensible, to a more sensible person. "I'm gonna follow him." I doubted I could get a line on him, knew it would likely be smarter to sit tight and do nothing, but I wanted some answers. I didn't know how all these weird-ass dots connected, but whatever it was, I didn't like it. I dared to hope I could find some way to get ahead of it before things really blew up.

We're making memories, everybody.

As it turned out, I didn't end up doing something so dangerous and foolhardy, because a far more dangerous situation came out of nowhere.

I had only taken a handful of steps after the dealer when I stopped, doubled over, crying out in surprise and fear. Something hit me, like icicles burrowing into my mind, like death and decay carried on a cold wind into my guts.

Black magic, like most people think of it, doesn't exist. There's no list of good spells and bad spells. But some magic, the kind you get from the more disreputable spirit worlds, is more dangerous. Flat-out scarier. The kind that eats away at the Curtain, like Swayze said. All spells give off a psychic vibration, but that kind has a sense of cold, and darkness, and intangible fear that worms its way into the back of your mind, making your skin crawl and convincing you every shadow holds some ghost come back to haunt you.

That was the kind of magic that had just went off, somewhere on the beach.

CHAPTER FIVE

"SAM? SAM, ARE you okay?" Jason's hand clasped my shoulder, dragging me back to reality, away from the dark, nauseating feelings that stabbed through me.

I whirled on him, grabbed him brutally by the shoulders, stared into his eyes. "Jason, listen to me. We are in the middle of a magical emergency. You need to find a way to get everybody out of here, especially Ella, or at least as many of them as you can. I know it'll be herding cats but maybe you can do something. And I'm gonna do what I can with my skills. Do you understand?"

He swallowed; fear burned deep into his eyes. He nodded twice and his face took on a look of ferocious determination. "Got it. Let's do this. Good luck, bro."

He turned and dashed away into the night, and a moment later, I heard him yelling, the words indistinct. I always knew there was something I liked about that guy. I feared he wouldn't be able to do much, but it was better than nothing.

Okay, my turn. I needed to figure out who or what was the source of that magic before it murdered anyone. I didn't bother to contemplate the suicidal insanity of that idea.

Nothing had happened yet, no blood, no screams, no apocalyptic destruction, so at least that much was working in my favor. The taint of the magic seemed to fill the air, everywhere all at once, but there wasn't an easily identifiable place to start looking.

Think, think, you bastard of a wizard.

An engine roared, loud even amidst the noise of the party, and I turned to see a car, a dark beast in the shadows, lurch around a corner and come plowing down the beach, tires foaming sand, headed directly for the crowd.

There were shouts, screams, people scrambling to get away. The car took out a grill, sending it rocketing into the air, a rain of sparks around it.

People stampeded, the ones nearest me buffeting me to the ground before I had a chance to react. Through a tangle of legs, which I had to dodge to avoid being stomped, I saw several others going down.

I forced myself to my feet, then extended my hand and sent levitation flowing towards the car. The car jerked hard to the left, bouncing, then crunched against a pylon. It sat there, dead still, engine groaning.

The crowd had scrambled away by now, leaving the detritus of the evening's party in their wake: beach blankets, backpacks, bottles, coolers, a sandal. I eyed the car, still unmoving, unsure what to do next. Was it possible the whole thing had been a coincidence? Either option seemed plausible, given the way this party was going.

Any uncertainty I had on that front was banished about three seconds later. I felt a psychic twist of magic, too fast for me to do anything about it, then there was an ear-splitting roar, a burst of brilliant blue-white light that filled the world and knocked me off my feet.

The ringing in my ears gave way to the sounds of screams and stampeding feet. I hoped Ella and everyone else were okay but couldn't see much. There was a faint smell of smoke in the air, and a few small fires burned nearby, near a massive, jagged rent in the ground. Lightning, I realized. Some fuckhead had just called in a magical lightning strike. I knew the back-to-school bonfire could get out of hand, but this was ridiculous.

I tried to stagger up, but as I was still half on the ground, I felt it again, that dangerous whisper of magic.

I got my shields up, barely, not wrapping them around myself but casting them, as strong and as wide as I could, directly over my head, in a shimmering dome, to cover as many people nearby as possible. Half a second later, another bolt of lightning, retina-searingly bright, slammed home, scything down from a cloudless sky. The electricity never actually touched my body, but I felt the impact anyway, a psychic shovel to the face that, for half a second, briefly convinced me my head had exploded.

Light swallowed my vision again and I was thrown twenty feet through the air as the crash of thunder slammed through my ears and brain. I crashed into the sand and rolled, groaning and flailing, several more feet until I finally came to a stop, right hand in the gently lapping surf. My ears were ringing again.

I sucked in a relieved breath and let it out again. The magic was gone. Whatever and whoever that was, this round was over. I guess you'd call this one a draw.

Cheek in the sand, hand and forearm soaked, I stared at nothing and wondered what quirk of the universe had gotten me into this situation. I stayed like that until something hauled me to my feet. Jason, I realized. "Jashun," I slurred. "Everybody okay? Ella?" I still wasn't up to full sentences.

"She's fine," he said. "She's on top of the hill. She's really scared, even though she won't admit it, but she's okay. I don't think anybody got hurt too bad. A couple twisted ankles and bloody noses but that seems to be the worst of it."

I gave him an exhausted smirk and smacked him on the arm.

"Well. There have been worse injuries than that at a normal, non-magical bonfire."

He nodded. "Yeah. They really should think about getting rid of this tradition."

"They really should."

"Did I see a lightning strike?"

"Yup. Don't ask."

My gaze found the car, engine idling, jackknifed awkwardly and unmoving. I reached for magic again. Jason's gaze followed mine. "What the hell happened there?"

"I don't know."

"Look." Jason pointed and I followed the direction of his finger and saw what he saw: two dark human shapes in the front seat, completely unmoving.

"Are they okay?" he said.

"I don't know." Dread began to fill me again. Were these the people who attacked us? If they were, they didn't seem too dangerous now. I continued to stare, and they continued not to move. We exchanged glances, came to a wordless decision to check it out.

The car loomed closer, the faces taking shape, a girl and a boy. The girl was closer. Nina? I recognized vaguely. "They ain't moving," I told Jason tightly.

"I know." With a bound, he closed the distance, threw the passenger door open, me right behind. Nina's body flopped limply out, bouncing off Jason, causing him to yell out in surprise and jump back. My stomach burned and the air hissed out of me as I looked down.

Her glossy black hair was splayed out around her head, her limbs frozen in awkward positions. Her mouth hung open, along with her eyes, staring up at nothing. An irregular pattern of dark color marred the whites of her eyes, like dirty, congealed ink. Her skin was already blue. *Jesus.*

And under the surface of reality, invisible to everyone there but me, was the faint reek of magic.

Ella and I stood in the shadows, watching the ambulance finally drive off, sirens silent. Jason approached us, face grim. He was shaking his head already. I hadn't been expecting good news. "They're both dead," he said without preamble. There were murmurs from the few still gathered around, those who hadn't had the sense to make tracks before any authority figures showed up. I heard Ella suck in a breath, noticed she took a step closer to me.

"Who was the other guy?" I asked.

"Reggie Thomas. I knew him, a little. Reggie was a North Sider. Nina was a South Sider." He didn't have to elaborate further.

A North Sider and a South Sider, dead in the same car, was gonna go way beyond opening a can of worms. I swallowed. "Do they know... w-what happened?"

He stared directly into my eyes, looked away, looked back, hesitated. "They think it was an overdose," he said. He said something else, but I couldn't hear him, because something in my brain was screaming.

The world spun off its axis.

There are public restrooms on the hill overlooking the beach, and some vague instinct deep in my brain managed to remember this as I made a beeline for them, bashing my way through the door, not even sure if it was the men's room.

I made it to the bathroom sink before I threw up.

Several minutes later, I staggered outside, and as I turned a corner something banged into me. I yelped, convinced I was about to fight for my life again. I was surprised to find myself facing a middle-aged man, hair going grey, but tall and powerfully built, nonetheless. Light blue eyes stared at me good-naturedly. I held up an awkward hand. "Oh. I'm sorry."

"Don't worry about it. Tough night for everybody." I had started to walk on when he spoke again. "You're Sam, right?"

I stopped, eyed him suspiciously. "Yeah."

He gave me an awkward smile. "I'm Jack. Jack Deacon. Trevor's dad?"

Oh right. That was his last name. I couldn't see any positive reason for us to be interacting. "Yeah?" I said, the most noncommittal thing I could think of.

He shifted, still smiling. "Uh, he told me you got into it earlier."

"Oh. That." With everything else going on, I'd forgotten all about it. "It was no big deal."

"Yeah, sure, I know." He seemed to sense my train of thought. "Oh. I'm not mad at you or whatever. Just the opposite. I wanted to say I was sorry."

I hadn't expected that. "You are? Why? You didn't do anything."

"I know, it just... seemed like the right thing to do. Trevor's been going through a tough time lately. I think he feels bad but he's just too stubborn to apologize."

"Oh. It's not a big deal, really."

"That's good. Anyway, I just wanted to let you know everything's okay."

"Great. Thanks."

"No problem. Have a good night."

"You, too."

We parted ways. I wasn't sure how that guy had produced a son like Trevor; maybe he took after his mother, I didn't know, but I doubted Trevor was as remorseful as he seemed to believe. It seemed more realistic that I'd earned his undying enmity. Oh well. It would be downright comforting to have something as normal as a high school bully to worry about when this was all over.

When I eventually made my shaky way back, I saw Mr.

McKinley standing with Jason and Ella. He turned at my arrival and gave me a sympathetic look. "Hey, Sam."

"Hey, Mr. McKinley."

He shot an exhausted glance back towards the beach, where I could distantly see a few cops still roaming around the car. "I'm sorry. This is not the way your night should have turned out."

"It's okay," Jason said. "Nobody could have predicted this."

He shook his head. "I just keep thinking if I'd been more on top of things, if I'd just done a better job—"

"It's not your fault," I cut him off. "There's nothing anyone could have done to prevent this." *Except maybe me.* "Don't blame yourself."

"He's right," Ella said.

He shot her a ragged look, looking a bit more like his old self. "I'm not even gonna ask how you got here. Please, never tell me."

"Okay."

"Do all of you have rides?"

"Yeah," I said. "They should be here in a few minutes."

"Okay," he sighed. "I guess there's nothing else for me to do then. Well, good night. See you at school tomorrow."

We mumbled goodbyes and he disappeared into the darkness, shoulders slumped. "I hope he'll be okay," Jason said.

"Me too."

"What about you?" Ella asked abruptly.

"Huh?"

"You took off like you'd been shot," Jason said. "I was about to go looking for you. We were worried."

I couldn't keep a grimace off my face. Yeah, to the outside observer, I probably looked... strange. "I'm sorry," I said. They were still staring at me. I couldn't really cover this up. "The ODs... it was just a lot, okay? I'm fine now. Sorry I worried you." I glanced at Ella. "Are you okay? I told you this place was a public menace."

She shrugged. "I'm fine. I didn't see those bodies like you two did. Jason basically just grabbed me, and everybody ran." She glanced at him. "Thanks, by the way."

"No problem, Small One."

Ella returned her gaze to me. "And you're changing the subject again."

"Maybe that should be a hint." The words were bitter, but I didn't have the strength to put much heat in my tone. Ella understood; I could see it on her face. She tried to smile, reached out and awkwardly rubbed my arm. I patted her arm in return, hoping she knew I appreciated the gesture.

It wasn't long until Dad came to pick us up.

I felt a lurch of dread at the conversation that was about to follow as his car rolled into the parking lot, headlights streaming outward, coming to a gravel-crunching stop. He seemed to have been moving at a high rate of speed.

"Do you need a ride or anything?" I asked Jason. "Please say yes."

He gave me a rueful look. "Sorry. My mom texted me just a minute ago. She's coming to pick me up."

I sighed. "Okay."

"Sam? Ella?" Dad's voice came across the parking lot as he hustled up to us. "Oh God, are you two okay?" Worry filled his voice.

"I'm fine, Dad. Really."

"So am I," Ella said.

His gaze swung to her, still too worried to look particularly angry. "And how you got here, I have no idea."

Ella shuffled, looking suddenly tiny and much younger than her twelve years. "I'm sorry."

Dad dragged a hand through his hair, seeing the same thing. "We can talk about it later." His gaze returned to me. "Do you need to stick around for some reason?"

"No, I'm fine to go."

"Okay. There's no reason for us to be here anymore then." He tossed a glance at Jason. "You okay, bud?"

Jason nodded, but his eyes betrayed him. "I'm fine, Sam's Dad. My mom will be here in a few minutes."

"We can wait with you, if you want." *Yes. Please.*

Jason nodded. "I'd appreciate it actually. Thanks." *Good man.*

This, I reflected, was never supposed to happen. Jason, Ella, Dad, none of them were ever supposed to be around this kind of magical horror show. For that matter, I'd planned on going my whole life without it myself.

Dad squeezed his shoulder. "If you need anything, don't hesitate to let me know." He glanced at me. "While we wait, I'll shoot a text to your mother. She'll want to know everything's okay."

"She's probably pacing the floor with the cat," I said, struck by the mental image.

He rolled his eyes and began fiddling with his phone. As he did, another car appeared, pulling up close to us, driver's door swinging open with the engine still running.

A blonde woman, well-dressed despite the assorted horrors and tragedies, on the younger side of middle age, flew out. "Jason."

"Hey, Mom." She gave him a hug which he returned.

I stood there, a bit flustered, as I always am in the presence of Jason's hot mom. She glanced at us, back at him. "Oh my God, Rich, what is happening here?"

"There was an overdose," Dad said carefully. "A couple of high schoolers died."

Her hand went to her face. "Oh my God. Are you serious?"

"Yes, unfortunately. The kids are okay, though."

"It's true, Mom," Jason said.

She lifted her hands, seemed to be on the verge of sputtering all kinds of things, then blew out an exasperated growl. "Okay. I'm glad all of you are okay. Let's go."

We muttered goodbyes and they climbed into their car and disappeared.

"Looks like we're the last ones at the party," I said.

"Yeah, and it's time to go," Dad said.

We clambered wordlessly into the car and pulled out onto the street. I was hoping we would keep things nice and quiet all the way home, but no such luck.

"Are you sure you're okay, Sam? It couldn't have been easy seeing those bodies." I was glad he didn't say what was clearly implied, which was "after what happened to Abby."

The bodies, the ODs, it was like they'd shaken something loose in my brain. Half-focused memories of Abby slid around through my mind like shards of broken glass. Abby in her fuzzy winter hat. Her blowing out birthday candles. Singing faintly, headphones covering her ears. I hadn't realized I had so many memories of her, until she was gone. I squeezed the door handle until I was able to speak. "Yeah, I'm fine. Really." Streetlights zigged past us, making cool lights dance around the darkened front seat.

"I wouldn't be fine if I were you. A good buddy of mine died when I was in college, in a car accident. I know it's not the same thing but sometimes it still hurts, all these years later. You can talk about it." He paused. "You need to."

"To be honest, I thought you'd be pissed at me."

"Why would I be pissed at you?"

"I don't know. Accessory to teenage debauchery. Criminal proximity to a corpse. Something like that."

"You did the right thing, Sam. You checked on somebody you thought was in trouble, and you called 911. I can't be mad at you for that." His glare in the rearview mirror swung to Ella. "You, on the other hand."

"I think she should be hanged, or sent to a convent," I suggested.

"Oh, hush."

"I'm sorry, Dad," she protested. "I wasn't gonna drink or do anything like that, I swear, I just wanted to see it. Nobody could have had any idea something like this would happen."

"You weren't supposed to be there at all. It wouldn't have been an issue if you'd been where you were supposed to be. You could have gotten hurt. And you compromised your brother's integrity."

Her mouth worked and it was a few seconds before she could speak. "His...*integrity?*"

"Yeah. You put him in the position of having to decide whether to tell us what you did or not. He was in a bad spot either way."

"That's right," I crowed, the dark clouds momentarily banished, "my integrity. I'm very integritous."

Ella stared sullenly out the window. "Maybe it's not too late for me to be hanged."

Anxiously, I noticed we'd turned onto our street, and it was only a moment longer before we pulled into the driveway, where I knew a disturbingly heartfelt conversation awaited. It probably didn't bode well, I figured, that I'd chase a magical drug dealer off into the night without a second thought but talking about Abby made me want to collapse. "Ella, go in the house, please," Dad said as he shut off the engine and it rumbled into silence.

Unfastening her seat belt, she gave us the kind of wary glare Catrick Swayze gives me when he suspects he's about to get a bath, then stalked inside. I heard the door open and shut.

Dad glanced over at me. "You need to know you can trust me, Sam."

"I do." *I just can't tell you certain things.*

"You need to know you can talk to me, and your mom."

"I can talk, okay? It's just... not easy." I knew he was talking around Abby again.

"I know it's not," he said. "Just remember, you're not the only one who knows what it's like to lose a friend."

"She wasn't just a friend," I found myself muttering. I was too tired to curse myself for admitting it out loud. I supposed it didn't matter anymore, did it?

"I know."

I looked up at him in surprise. "You knew? How?"

He gave me a sad smile. "From the way you found excuses to bring her up in a conversation. From the look on your face every time someone mentioned her, and the way you looked at her whenever she was around." His face grew serious. "The look you get when anyone mentions her now."

I was afraid to voice my next question but the words slipped free anyway. "Do you think she knew?"

"I don't know, pal."

I hated this conversation. "It doesn't matter anymore. The past is the past." I climbed out, slammed the door.

Dad followed. "Yeah, until you turn a corner and there it is."

"You're just on fire with the philosophy today."

"Thanks. It just came out of nowhere, and I thought I'd roll with it."

"Well, it really worked. I'll have to write that one down."

I reached for the doorknob, but Dad pressed his palm on the door before I could swing it open. "Just think about it. When you need to talk, I'll be waiting."

I nodded uncomfortably. "Yeah. Sure. Okay."

I walked inside to face the next hurdle. Mom bounded up from the couch. Ella, it seemed, had already been exiled to her room, where hopefully she'd spend the next few years. I held up a hand. "Yes, I'm fine, like I already told your husband here."

"It's true," Dad said. "He specifically told me he was fine."

She pulled me into a hug, released me a moment later. "You never should have been in that situation."

"To be fair, I don't think anyone really could have predicted this."

"They should have. That damn party gets out of control every year and the whole town knows it. Everybody knew something like this would happen eventually."

"Your mom's right," Dad said. "I lived in this town most of my life, except when I went to college. It's always been a mess. North Side, South Side, whatever. It has a seedy underbelly."

"I don't think it's even the underbelly anymore," I said.

"No. It's not."

"Sam, I don't want you involved in this," Mom said. "You've seen too much already."

"I'm not involved."

She pursed her lips. "You know what I mean. I don't want you charging in trying to save the day. I don't want you using your magic."

So, here's the thing.

I would have liked nothing better than to keep my wizardry as some kind of secret identity. But when magic is flooding one's veins without them knowing what it is, when one is wandering around muttering to themselves and accidentally levitates an easy chair through a window, well, one can't really hide it from one's loved ones. In the years since then, since meeting Swayze and learning how to use it, my parents had gotten as used to the idea of having a wizard for a son as it was possible to get. That didn't prevent the occasional uncomfortable conversation about the topic. Like now.

I grimaced, trying to come up with an answer that wouldn't horrify her. I wasn't about to mention the scary magic I'd sensed. "Look, this is probably just typical Williamsport gang stuff that's got nothing to do with me. Trust me, whatever's going on, 'involved' is the last thing I want to be. What would I even do about it?"

Mom visibly hesitated before speaking. "After what happened to Abby, I have no idea what you might do."

My blood turned to ice. "Abby OD'd, and now more people have OD'd, so I'm going to go off the rails in a blaze of magical glory, is that it?"

"Sam, nobody thinks that," Dad said.

"We're just worried about you," Mom said. "For a lot of reasons."

"I'm sorry," I sighed. "I don't want to make anyone worry. I'm holding it together, I promise. If anyone charges in to save the day, it won't be me. And for the first time in my life, I want to go to bed early."

For a moment, Mom looked like she wanted to argue, then shook her head and sighed. "Fine. Go. Get some rest."

I hurried upstairs before they could change their mind. The cat was asleep again, this time on the windowsill, which was fine with me. I'd had more than enough explanations for one night. I at least had the presence of mind to change into my pajamas this time, before flopping into bed and turning out the light.

The first day of school, everybody. A mere one hundred and seventy-nine to go.

CHAPTER SIX

"YOU'RE MY FAMILIAR," I told Catrick Swayze as I stood in front of my dresser. "Do your job. Familiarize! How do I handle this?"

He sat curled in a ball on the floor at the foot of the bed. "I guess you could turn yourself into a hamster, or some other small animal."

"Terrific. I can either be a fall guy for the Shal'Gasa or spend back-to-school week jogging on a hamster wheel. Come to think of it, that might be an improvement."

"You could always do nothing, which you may remember me loudly and profanely advocating, not ten minutes ago."

"I think the gods have other plans."

"The gods, huh? You sure it's not about that girl?"

I rounded on him. "Not you, too."

"You know I'm not big on the emotional stuff but come on: this isn't really about this thing with the Reapers. You couldn't save the person that really mattered, so you're gonna save somebody else instead. And you don't care what happens to yourself or your loyal kitty in the process. I've seen this hero complex thing a million times and it never ends well. Which is why you neglected to tell your parents about the Shal'Gasa and the alleged mystery wizard."

"I didn't want to freak them out when we don't even know if there's anything to freak about."

"Yeah, and you didn't want them interfering with your noble suicide mission."

I considered chasing him up a tree. "Well, thank you, Dr. Phil." I changed the subject. "What do you think Eressen's up to?"

"Him, I can't figure out. I know his name, but that's about it. Heard of his family, though. The al'Barras. One of the most powerful houses in all the Shal'Gasa tribes. Your friend Eressen is on the young side, relatively speaking, so he doesn't have the rep his brothers and sister do. Or gods forbid his parents. Be glad we're not dealing with them."

For the sake of my sanity, I decided not to press for details. I began shuffling through the mess of my dresser, pulling out various charms, amulets, talismans, and so on, which supposedly protect the wearer against evil. Rather than buy them from some mystical wizardly curio shop, I'd just bought them from shady online stores, which always gave me some doubts about their reliability. I wear some combination of them every day, and if anyone takes notice, they assume it's some teenage fashion statement. Today, I put on everything I could find.

A pendant that warded off curses? Check. A charm bracelet that claimed to help your ancestors identify your soul if it wandered free of your body? Better safe than sorry. A ring that helped you heal faster? Yeah, definitely.

I continued to rummage through the mess. "Have you seen my anti-madness ring?"

"No."

"Well, it's not here."

"Why would I have it? Cats don't wear rings."

"Forget it." I blew out a breath. "How much trouble am I in? Really?"

He scratched an ear. "If I'm being honest, quite a bit."

"Do you think I'm gonna live through it? Is my family gonna be okay?"

"I don't know. Whenever the Shal'Gasa are involved, things aren't exactly gonna come to a warm and fuzzy conclusion. Throw in these Reapers…"

"Yeah, I get the idea." Deciding I needed something a little more solid than just the talismans, I rooted around in my drawer until I found my knife, concealing it in the lining of my trusty old denim jacket. *Sure, Samuel, a knife will make all the difference.*

They think it was an overdose.

The words kept swirling through my head, banging up against the walls of my skull, bringing a fresh surge of pain every time they did.

One thought in particular came to the surface: if I had taken Eressen up on his offer immediately, would Nina and Reggie still be alive? That seemed unlikely, but I suspected I could come to believe it if I tried. I pushed those thoughts away. I was good at that.

Ella and I made our way to school, a lot more than just beginning of the year jitters jumping around under my skin. "Be careful today," I told her, in a fit of brotherly concern. "It's gonna be tense, might get violent. Keep your eyes open, and be wary of everybody, north, south, and any other direction, including the adults."

"You really think it could get that bad?"

"Yeah, I really do."

"Okay." She didn't argue for once. Things were getting serious indeed.

Recalling that Ella didn't have any magical means to defend herself, I considered slipping her my knife, but, in a rare moment of prudence and maturity, decided that arming a middle-schooler with a Ka-Bar might not be the wisest move. I settled for another admonishment to be careful before we parted company.

When a school is so quiet you can hear your shoes tapping on the tiles, that's a godawful bad sign. You don't need the dark arts to figure that one out.

Normally a seething mass of humanity, today it was completely, terribly silent. The kind of silence you hear in a movie shootout when everyone pauses to reload.

I heard footsteps, lockers banging open and shut, a phone ringing somewhere, but not a single voice. It was beyond eerie. If there was something positive to be observed, it was that everyone was still in too much shock to start killing each other. I doubted it would be long, though: North Siders and South Siders were roaming around looking at each other with undisguised loathing. Here and there people had tears in their eyes.

There was still the awkward question of what I was supposed to *do* about all this. What the hell *could* I do? Even if I'd wanted to get involved, I had no idea where to start.

"Bad day to be a South Sider," remarked Eddie, my locker neighbor, when I stowed my backpack.

"Yeah."

Eddie's face was downcast. "Nina was my friend. I wish she hadn't gotten involved with that Reggie guy."

"I'm sorry." I couldn't muster up anything brilliant to say. It's not like there was much I could have said that would make a difference.

The day was a long, gloomy-ass blur.

In half our classes, our teachers awkwardly ignored the big dead elephant in the room. In the other half, they wanted us to talk about how it made us feel. I thought it was best I didn't share my feelings.

Unfortunately, I was in the minority on that score.

I sat with my head slumped on my desk while Mr. McKinley's class, a nice blend of North and South Siders, sniped at each other, McKinley sitting behind his desk, looking befuddled. No doubt Teacher School hadn't prepared him for this.

"Do you know how many people OD in the South Side?" someone in the back of the room bellowed. "It happens *all the time* and nobody gives a shit until it happens to a rich kid from the North Side."

"Why the hell should we?" a girl shot back, her tone just as venomous.

"Language," groaned McKinley, sounding like he was about to be murdered and begging for his life.

"My brother was hooked for *years* on your people's drugs. I hope all of you OD, it's what you deserve."

"Are those really the only two letters we know anymore," I grumbled, trying to not look towards Abby's old desk again.

I didn't think anybody heard me, due to the general commotion that ensued, but McKinley did; I could tell from the way his eyes locked on me and his mouth twitched. He stood from behind his desk, visibly taking a gulp of air. "SIIIILEEENCE," he roared, thumping a stapler on his desk several times. "SIIIILEEENCE!" The clamor faded almost instantly. McKinley had never been much of a disciplinarian and was well-liked for it. He glanced around the room, still looking more befuddled than angry. His words were slow and careful. "This is a very painful situation for all of us," he said. His gaze flicked towards me again in understanding, and I managed a brief, thin smile to let him know I appreciated it. "And none of this is making things any better. So... be quiet. Do your homework. If you don't have any, just pretend, I don't care. But no more sharing of feelings." And that seemed to work. There were a few occasional grumbles, but for the most part, we spend the rest of class in frigid SIIIILEEENCE.

Between classes, every soul in the building was in a state of riot, the deathly quiet of that morning quickly becoming a distant memory. The teachers had, momentarily, tried to stop the endless rumor mills before giving up and joining in. The overdoses had overshadowed the freak magical lightning strikes, which were alternately chalked up to drug-induced hallucinations or the detonation of fireworks, depending on who you talked to.

I didn't understand what had happened to Nina and Reggie, not really. All I knew was it was magical, and nasty, and apparently made to look, somehow, like an overdose. Every time my thoughts began turning in that direction, my mind seemed to fly to pieces, my brain stubbornly refusing to think about ODs. But whatever people were theorizing, the truth was worse, and the suspect pool far, far more dangerous than even the scariest of the local drug dealers.

I wish I could say witches, demons, gods, werewolves, vampires, and a hundred thousand other things from every urban legend you've ever heard were just metaphors for the perils of adolescence. Well, gosh, that would make my life easier. But no. They're all real. And they all want to cook and eat you for brunch. (Well, except leprechauns. Leprechauns are delightful.)

I was surprised it took until fourth hour for a fight to break out.

I had just walked out of social studies, dreading heading back into that hair-trigger press of bodies, when I heard profanity and a crash.

I turned to see a couple students, who I recognized as a North Sider and a South Sider, respectively, grappled together, growling, and careening into an inconveniently placed trash can. All three of them toppled to the ground.

A couple others joined in to help their buddies, and the whole thing turned into a dogpile. Somebody threw a punch. Screams filled the hallways as everyone cheered on their comrades to more and better acts of violence. Someone, in the midst of a hearty fist pump, landed an elbow in my ribs.

Just as things were getting good and wacky, a few teachers appeared, throwing themselves heroically into the fray, dragging the screaming combatants apart. Mr. Miller, the gym teacher, got a right hook to the face that sent him staggering. After a lot of shouting and thrashing, the perpetrators were hauled off, the crowds died down and started moving again, and things slowly returned to as normal as they can be around here. The teachers staggered away, looking shell-shocked, and I noted that Mr. Miller had a little blood streaking the side of his head.

"Hey, man."

I turned. "Hey, Jas. How's your day been? Anything interesting?"

He snorted and didn't answer, eyes downcast.

I took a stab at cheering him up. "We were on our way to a real hall of fame fight before the teachers stepped in. Would have been tough to beat that fracas in the library last spring, though."

He gave me a weak smile. "I still say the fight at the homecoming dance was better."

"Interesting choice." I could tell his heart wasn't in the humor.

He sighed. "I'm sorry, it's just tough for me to find it funny anymore. Now that people are dead. This North Side/South Side war, it's bullshit."

"How are you doing? I know you were pretty shaken up, even if you didn't say anything." *You're a fine one to talk.*

He shook his head. "I'm fine. Really, I'm not just saying that. I'll be fine, anyway. Just freaks a person out, having a corpse land on them. But that's not what I'm really worried about."

This serious side of him was worrying indeed. I'd never seen him like this, and it bothered me. "What is?"

He gestured around. "This. All of this. What you just saw. It used to be worse than this. I was talking to my parents about it;

they said when they were my age, there were riots, people bringing knives, guns to school sometimes. It was bad. I'm afraid that's what's happening again. Nobody really *wants* to fight. They just think the other side is out to get them, so they have to take them out first."

"To be fair, given everybody's history, there are some pretty good reasons to think the other side is out to get them."

"Yeah, I know. There's too much bad blood for people to forget about it now. This whole thing is gonna really get out of control."

"This isn't the first time North and South have been at each other's throats. They'll figure out what happened, lock some people up, then everything will calm down. It always does."

He could tell I didn't really believe it. "I hope so."

I needed information, and Jason would have his ear to the ground. "Have you heard anything more about what's going on? I haven't; nothing believable, anyway."

"No, nothing more than what we already knew. Nina was a South Sider, Reggie was a North Sider, like it even matters. The fact that they were a couple just makes everything worse."

"Regular Romeo and Juliet, huh?"

"I guess. Ended up the same way too." His face grew even more grim. "Their parents are a wreck, obviously. And Reggie's aunt is super connected thanks to her real estate and stuff and they're saying she's pissed enough to kill somebody. Both sides are blaming each other."

"The North Siders think the South is putting drugs on their streets, and the South Siders are pissed because this is the umpteenth OD of the year and nothing ever gets done, is that about right?"

"Yeah. And I've heard people on both sides saying they're gonna do something about it, not that they know what." He shook his head. "Nobody is too sympathetic to somebody dead on the other side. Jesus, I don't know how it got this far."

"Nothing about who sold them the drugs?"

"No, nothing. I told the cops about that guy we saw, and supposedly they looked for him but didn't turn up anything."

"We don't exactly have a shortage of dealers around here. Ever seen him before?"

He shook his head. "I didn't talk to him but a second. It's the South Siders according to the North Siders, and vice versa. The truth is, either one of them could be right. There are gangs on the South Side, everyone knows that, but there are dealers in the North too. Rich kids who get their hands on prescription pads, stuff like that."

"The urbane, sophisticated drug dealer."

"Exactly."

That didn't narrow down my suspect pool. I had a suspect pool now? I didn't like the sound of that. And this was opening dark avenues I was terrified to explore, for reasons that went far beyond magic. "What about you," Jason said. "I know this must be…" His voice trailed off.

"Bringing up bad memories?"

"Yeah."

I shrugged. "The bad memories were already there. This didn't change anything." I gave him an "I'm perfectly fine" thump on the shoulder and sighed. "This is gonna be the longest back to school week ever."

When the last bell finally had the decency to ring, I practically ran from the school.

It was still an uproar, voices buzzing, and people clearly on the edge of erupting, as I made my way across the parking lot to freedom, dodging and weaving through others trying to do the same thing. Here and there teachers stood watching the crowds with the watchful, nervous eyes of people who knew there wasn't much they could do if trouble popped off.

Recalling Ella, I slowed my pace and glanced around trying to spot her, supposing waiting around for her was the least I could do, since Williamsport was on a war footing.

I hadn't gone far when something assailed my senses, all at once, hard to identify. A foul scent burned through my nostrils, and the voices around me rose in pitch, clattering together, unmistakably fearful, and under it all a sound I couldn't quite place.

It took only a second to find the source: on the other side of the parking lot, I spotted a school bus. On fire. Sullen flames licked out of windows, dirty smoke curling upwards as paint began to scorch. I couldn't sense any magic in the air. No, this was just Williamsport being Williamsport.

I stared at the mess, as the flames began eating through the bus and the smoke got darker, puffing up to smear the blue sky and sting my eyes and nose even further. I recalled Jason's fear of all-out war.

A crowd of onlookers had gathered, babbling anxiously. At least there weren't any more dead bodies. Yet.

I had no idea who'd done this, or what they'd thought to accomplish by molotoving an empty bus, but whatever it was, they'd just fired the opening salvo. All of us watching knew that. The teachers, certainly earning their money today, finally got us herded back a safe distance, as sirens began to hum faintly nearby.

"Is it bad I'm almost happy to be grounded?"

I turned to see Ella picking her way out of the slack-jawed, squawking herd of people. "There you are. I was about to go looking for you."

She glanced towards the metallic bonfire on the other side of the parking lot. "Things are really going to shit around here."

"Yeah, and that's why we need to be somewhere else."

I started walking, separating myself from the people, and Ella followed. Avoiding a very distracted crossing guard, we hit the streets.

I guess you could say my feet got away from me. I had planned to head home, maybe have a strategy session with the cat, but when I reached my house, Ella went inside, but I kept going, on down the street.

Abby hadn't been the girl next door, technically: she'd been the girl across the street and four houses over. Without much in the way of conscious thought, I found myself standing on the sidewalk outside her fence, shuffling awkwardly, impelled by some mysterious force that had nothing to do with magic.

This was a mistake. I told myself, over and over, to move on, get out of here, but my feet never quite got the message. It was a pleasant place, though I couldn't think of it as such anymore: there was a neatly mowed yard, red picket fence, tire swing. It looked so damn empty now.

Something stirred in the back of my mind, and I felt my thoughts about to wander away again. I had the feeling that regular flashbacks probably weren't indicative of stable mental health.

It was nothing new, the memory my brain dredged up; it was one I'd seen countless times already. The last time I'd seen her.

The final bell had just rung, and the halls were swarming as usual. I was making my way out, swept up in the crowd, and passed her locker. I hadn't noticed her standing by it until she spoke.

"We still gonna study tomorrow?" she called, raising her voice over the din, and shouldering her backpack.

I tried to turn around without getting trampled. "No, I'm actually dropping out of school tomorrow." She gave me a sarcastic smile and with a little toss of her hair, turned and disappeared in the opposite direction.

The next morning, I found out she was dead. No, that wasn't right. Those memories threatened to come rushing back as well, something else prickling my mind, as all those thoughts came welling up.

"Sam?"

The voice drug me out of my reverie, saving me from the torrent that would have drowned me. "Huh?"

I looked around and my heart lurched. It was Jenna. Abby's mom. Her long brown hair, so eerily reminiscent of her daughter's, tossed a little in the breeze. "Sam," she said. "You okay?"

Not lately. "Uh, yeah. I'm fine." I realized how weird it must look, lurking around in front of her house. "I was just walking by, stopped to answer a text."

"Oh." It didn't sound very believable, and I doubted she bought it but at least she didn't say anything.

I shuffled, uncertain what to say, trying to think of a way to extricate myself. "I should get going."

"Yeah, sure. It was good seeing you again."

"Yeah, good to see you, too." I had an opening, but something kept me from walking away. "How are you doing?"

She shrugged. "I don't know. I just…" Her voice trailed off and guilt stabbed at me.

"Yeah," I said. "I get it. I'm sorry I said anything."

She wiped an eye. "No, it's okay. I'm glad you did. It's just hard, that's all. I haven't seen you in a long time."

"I'm sorry," I mumbled, wishing I had never come here. There was a reason I hadn't seen Abby's family in months. Why I didn't even walk by her house anymore.

"You don't have to feel bad," she said. "I know why you haven't been around."

I nodded uncomfortably. "Yeah. I should go."

"Bye, Sam."

"Bye."

I turned and began briskly walking away, as fast as a person could walk before it could be called a run.

I risked a subtle glance back at Abby's mom, who was making

her way across the yard to the house, looking desolately alone. Was that how I looked?

If I didn't get myself killed in the near future, I decided, I would stop by more often.

But, right now, people were dying.

If there was anybody else in Williamsport who could do anything about it, I didn't know who they were.

And more people would die, wouldn't they? That, I thought, was a complete certainty.

Son of a bitch.

CHAPTER SEVEN

FOR ONCE, I decided to apply a little logic to the problem.

Nina and Reggie had supposedly died of a drug overdose, and the most likely scenario was that the guy who approached Jason had sold them the drugs. And magic was involved, somehow: the magic I'd sensed on the corpses was unmistakable, to say nothing of the supernatural lightning storm that had tried its best to fry me.

I had no idea how it was connected, but the only real place I could think to start was with the dealer. The problem was, I didn't know who he was, where to start looking, or what he might have waiting for me if I tracked him down.

But if I couldn't get to him, maybe I could get close. As I told Jason, it wasn't as if Williamsport had a shortage of drug dealers. And it wasn't as if their activities were much of a secret, either, at least to those of us at Archibald J. Keller.

I ran through a mental list of the dealers I could remember off the top of my head and settled on the one that seemed the least intimidating: a guy named Nick, who could often be found plying his trade at Washington Park, which was where I headed.

I knew it was thin, especially if what Brian had said was true and the Reapers really were running everybody else out of town, but I was gambling that Nick would be low enough on the criminal totem pole it would be a while before they got to him.

I was about halfway there when my phone vibrated once, then began croaking out "I'm the Only One," by the incomparable Melissa Etheridge. I stopped, pulled it free of my jeans pocket. Mom, the screen said. Against my better judgment, I decided to answer. "Dearest Mumsie, what can I do for you?"

"You can tell me about this explosion."

I had no idea good news would travel so fast. "Well, it was a fire, not an explosion. Words matter, you know."

"Was anybody hurt?"

"Only the parents that'll have to drive their kids to school tomorrow."

"Are you and Ella okay?"

"Of course we are."

"Where are you? Did you go home?"

"Where else would I be?" I started powerwalking.

Washington Park was a nice place, lots of low, grassy rises, big trees, a pond, playground equipment. It wasn't quite the seedy place you'd imagine a drug dealer to hang out, which may have been why he picked it.

I roamed the park, eyes sweeping the place, until I spotted him, trying to look like the picture of innocence, loitering around behind a shelter house.

I made a beeline for him and closed the distance. One more cautious glance told me there weren't any prowling authority figures nearby. He looked up, spotted me. "Hey man."

"Hey, Nick."

"What can I do for you?"

What was the best way to handle this? "I'm looking for something," I said.

He laughed. "Well, you're in the right place."

I glanced around. "Isn't this a little old school? Loitering around in a park?"

"Yeah, but that's the point. Other people use phones and the internet and stuff, but this you can't trace." There was a note of professional pride in his voice. "What are you looking for?"

I studied Nick as we talked and concluded he wasn't the guy I saw last night; a little too short, a little too young, hair a little too dark. Getting it in one would have been too easy, I guess. "That depends. I damn sure don't want any of what Nina and Reggie had."

His face darkened and he shifted uneasily. He held up an unsteady hand. "Um, you don't need to worry about that. I don't have any of that stuff."

Hmm. "What was it? So I can make sure to never take it."

He shook his head uncomfortably. "I don't know, just some nasty stuff going around. Like I said, I don't have any."

"Who does?"

He shrank back a little, beginning to realize he was in over his head. "I don't know. I thought you said you didn't want any." His eyes began to widen in alarm. "What do you want? I know you're not a cop." He shook his head. "Never mind. I'm outta here."

He turned to go. I gave my hand and wrist a twist, then magic concentrated around his ankles, spewing a few dead leaves around and tripping him up, sending him sprawling into a heap. I'd thought about lifting him into the air but decided that was a bit much.

He whirled back to me, one shoulder on the ground, eyes aghast. He knew something strange had happened, even if he didn't know he'd been scooped up by magic. "Wha... what did you do?"

"What did they take, Nick?" I demanded, going for an intimidating baritone. "I know you know what it was."

He tried to leap to his feet, but another twist of magic sent him careening back down.

He managed to jab a shocked finger at me. "Stop doing whatever the hell you're doing." His voice was getting hoarse.

I really should have found some subtler, more scientifically explainable way to keep him from running off, but that's the trouble with magic: you kinda forget there's any other way to solve a problem. "I will when you tell me what they took."

He swallowed and managed to thrust the words out of his mouth. "It was Hex, okay? It was Hex. I swear to God, I don't have any. I don't mess around with that stuff."

He staggered to his feet, eyes wary, but didn't try and take off this time. I stared at him. "Hex?"

His eyes bugged and his face was slack with fear. "Y-yeah."

"What the hell is Hex?"

He shook his head. "It's…" Something crossed his face, pure, uncomprehending shock that washed away everything else, and unsettled me to look at. "Oh my God. Oh my God. You gotta be kidding me. Oh shit."

I held up a hand, cutting him off before he went completely off the deep end. "It's what? What are you talking about?"

He waved at me frantically. "Oh Jesus, that's what you just did. It can do that."

"Do what?" Creeping realization sunk into my brain. Goosebumps chilled me. *No way. No fucking way.* "Are you saying Hex is magic?"

He flinched like I'd slapped him. "Yeah. I mean, that's what they say. I never believed it. Thought it was just hype, you know? But… but now…"

Suddenly, I felt a wave of shame for terrorizing someone with magic, even if the worst he'd gotten out of it was dirty jeans. I recalled how I'd felt when I'd first learned about it. Believe it or not, Nick was taking it better than I did. "Relax," I said. "I'm not gonna hurt you. I just want to know what's going on."

He shook his head back and forth. "I don't know anything, I swear."

"I know you know more than nothing."

"They'll kill me."

"They'll never know you talked to me. Magic doesn't make you all-knowing and all-seeing. I can appreciate not being a snitch, but this goes way, way, way beyond the normal stuff, and you know it." I tried to soften my voice. "Come on. Just tell me what you heard, please. Before anybody else gets killed."

He drew an uneasy breath. "Not much. Just rumors. Like I said, I thought it was all just a marketing thing."

"Do you have a name?"

He licked his lips and visibly had to force the words out, voice low. "They call him King Death." From the way he cast nervous glances back and forth, he seemed to expect thunder to rumble and wolves to start howling.

I glared. *"King Death?"* We wizards can be grandiose but come on.

"Yeah. That's his street name."

"You don't say. What do you know about him?"

He shook his head vigorously. "Nothing, I swear. I've never met anybody that actually knows him."

"Then how does he get his product on the streets? The Reapers?"

"Yeah, I think so. I stay away from those guys." He shuddered. "They're not normal. They give off bad vibes. It's creepy. If one of them shows up on my turf, I get the hell out of there and don't come back for days. One of them cornered me the other day. Wanted me to start selling Hex. I told him I'd think about it to get him to back off, but I don't think they'll take no for an answer. I wouldn't even be out here if I didn't need the money."

"Where do I find these people?"

"You don't want to find them, for Christ's sake."

"If I did, how could I?"

"I don't know. You don't find them so much as they find you. They started out in a neighborhood on the South Side a couple months back. I don't know which one. But they're spreading out. Into the North Side now. Wherever there are people, they show up. They don't have turf, really. One day they're here, the next day they're not and they pop up somewhere else."

"You have to have some idea. If they're 'wherever there are people,' where might that be?" He looked towards the sky. "Come on, I know you thought of something just now. Tell me."

"Well, there's this rave. Tonight."

"Sounds like a good place to look. Where is it?"

"In one of those abandoned buildings on Gregson Street. I don't know where, exactly."

"Well, it can't be too hard to find."

He gaped at me. "You're saying it's all real? This magic stuff?"

There didn't seem to be any point in lying. "Yeah, Nick. It's all real. This magic stuff." So much for plausible deniability, but maybe the knowledge would keep him from getting himself killed.

He rubbed his face. "Oh my God. People say he can walk through walls, fly, move things with his mind. I never believed it. But you…" He gestured at me.

The stuff he described was all in the realm of depressing possibility. "Yeah, me," I said. "Relax. I'm not with him, I'm trying to stop him, before he hurts anybody else." I jabbed a finger at him. "But you should lay low for a while. You won't need money if you're dead. It's gonna get dangerous around here and I might not be able to look out for you if you're caught in the crossfire."

He held up a hand, eased a step back. "Yeah, sure. I'll lay low, I swear."

"This is Top Secret Magical Business, and you need to stay out of it."

"I will."

"Good. Thanks for the help. Sorry about, uh, scaring you."

He started to ease away, and I was ready to leave myself, when I was surprised by the sound of my own voice coming out of my mouth. "Abby Scott. Did you ever sell to her?"

He froze, seeming to sense a dangerous edge in my tone, though it had sounded perfectly normal to me. "No, I didn't. Never." He must have seen suspicion in my face because he kept talking. "I remember when she OD'd. I just sell molly, bro. She took prescription pills. I have no idea where she got them, I swear."

I knew he was telling the truth. She'd probably gotten the pills out of somebody's medicine cabinet. This guy had nothing to do with it. I really was losing it. "I'm sorry. Forget about it."

He hesitated, as if, strangely, he wasn't quite ready to leave now that he finally had the chance. "I'm sorry too."

"For what?"

He fidgeted. "Well, I just… I can tell she meant something to you. Seemed like the thing to say."

"She did," I mumbled, swallowing hard. "I have to go. Just stay undercover for a while."

"I will."

We hoofed it in opposite directions.

"What exactly is the plan?" Swayze yowled in exasperation. "You're going to fight evil by… going to a party?"

"No," I said firmly. "I'm going to fight evil by going to a party and *keeping an eye on things*. Make sure whoever is behind this doesn't try anything else. And I'll keep my ear to the ground, see if I can learn anything. It's the perfect place to sell Hex, and I'm sure they'll be there."

"Yeah, them being there is kind of the issue."

"Do you have any idea what could have killed Nina and Reggie?"

He screwed up his face in whiskery concentration. "My guess would be you and the authorities are both right: it was an OD and magic."

"What do you mean?"

"I'd say their drugs were spiked, but not with the kind of stuff drugs usually get cut with. With magic. Nasty magic. I'd say you have a dealer who dabbles."

"And he's using magic to juice up his product. Which goes predictably badly."

"Exactly."

"How is that even possible?"

His feline face took on a thoughtful cast. "Well... huh."

"'Well, huh'? That's the best you got?"

He glared. "It has to be some kind of enchantment: they slather it up with magic, then, when the sucker takes it, the spells go off."

I followed his line of thinking, and it clicked into place. "Their souls."

"Exactly. Human souls aren't built for magic, like ours. When they try to use it... yeesh. The magic eats away at them. Tears them apart until there's nothing left."

Writhing snakes of dread wrapped around my ankles and worked their way to the top of my head. I tried to focus. "It doesn't make sense: his customers are dropping dead, so they can't pay him anymore, and soon word will get out and then everybody looking to get high will go somewhere else and put him out of business. And besides, a wizard smart enough to cook up a spell like that would be smart enough to know what it would do. So why do it?"

"Why, that's an uncharacteristically reasonable and level-headed assessment of the situation, Sam. Of course, we all know how reasonable and level-headed your average drug dealer is."

Was there really an entire gang of these people out there? I couldn't imagine what a street gang of wizards could accomplish but it would be premium cable levels of violent. "I don't care for the idea of fighting my way through Williamsport's drug scene until I get to a dark lord."

"Well, you're the one who wanted to do hero stuff. What are you gonna do if something does go down at the rave?"

"Uh, fight it off?"

"You weren't really supposed to answer that with a question."

I couldn't think of a good response to that, so I scratched him behind the ears and headed downstairs.

My parents were in the kitchen. "I'm heading out," I said.

"I still think you shouldn't go," Dad said.

"It'll be fine, really," I said, hoping it was true. "People are blowing this up to be worse than it actually was."

"Kind of a poor choice of words," he said.

"Again, it was a fire, not an explosion."

"Your dad's right," said Mom, appearing from the kitchen. "It's better if you stay home. That's what we're gonna do for a while."

"Come on," I said. "It's not like the school's far off, and it can't get too out of control at a pep rally." The pep rally was the next in Williamsport's back-to-school traditions, and it made for a plausible excuse. I felt bad about the lie, but you can't tell your parents you're going to hunt down drug-dealing death wizards at an underground rave. That's just out of the question. "I'll be careful, I promise. If anything looks weird, I'll get out of there. I might not even stay that long."

Ella stuck her head in. "If it's so dangerous, why can he go out when I can't?"

"Because you're grounded," Mom said, "which I thought you were aware of."

"But mostly because they love me more," I interjected.

"Sam, be nice," Mom said.

Ella came all the way into the room. "Hold on. You already said I could go."

"Where did I say you could go, and when did I say this?"

"Four days ago," she said, with the confident tone of someone who'd done the math. "Ava wanted me to come over, to help her study, and you said I could."

"That was before you were grounded," Dad said.

"But she's expecting me. *I gave my word*."

I started angling away. "I'll let you fine people sort this out. Bye."

"Be careful," Dad called, as I opened the door.

"Father, when am I not careful?"

The walk through town looked a lot different in the dark.

Nothing happened, nothing was amiss. The night air was pleasantly cool. There was no dark magic swirling through the ether, making my hair stand on end. There were no fires, no riots, no shootouts.

I was just nervous. I couldn't shake the feeling that something was about to go down, something even worse than last night, and I was about to blunder right into it.

What would Abby think about this, I wondered, then wished I hadn't. She would say something very nice and kind and considerate, and everyone who heard it would think what a wonderful soul she had, and then they'd kick the shit out of each other anyway.

It was hard to remember her voice, I realized. The realization made me freeze in my tracks, there on the empty sidewalk. Why was it so hard to remember? I'd heard it every day, had heard it fill my head countless times. I concentrated, and forced the sweet, soft sound into my mind. It was simple, boring, just a conversation we'd had walking down the hall one day, talking about the eccentricities of Mrs. Harris, social studies teacher.

Satisfied, I kept going. I had been trying so hard to bury everything. Apparently, I'd been succeeding.

I was supposed to be over this. I had gotten myself together by now.

Hadn't I?

I had convinced myself I was fine, until yesterday morning when I realized it was all apparently just a scab over a still-raw wound.

The path to Gregson Street was convoluted but easy enough to find. This was the second time this week I'd ventured into the South Side after dark. It didn't seem like a very wise habit.

I made my way out of my neighborhood, hung a right, went another four blocks, hung a left. It wouldn't have been too bad in a car, but on foot, it was far enough to be obnoxious.

I shot a glance back and forth, did a quick jaywalk, then found myself on Gregson. Say one thing for living in Williamsport, it makes a person good at geography.

The streets had been almost deserted when I'd made my way there; apparently, most people had been smarter than I was and stayed home. Only the occasional car whizzing by had reminded me Williamsport was still inhabited. That changed on Gregson.

Slowly but steadily, I began to see more dark shapes shuffling in and out of the streetlights. South Siders, North Siders, I had no idea, but they'd all made their way to this dump for a little illicit fun.

I knew why Nick hadn't known exactly where the place was: there were at least three or four abandoned buildings on Gregson, clustered together, all of them looking disreputable in the sober light of day. At night, they were downright sinister, scrawled with graffiti and the windows long busted out, darkness yawning beyond.

It wasn't hard to spot the one I needed. Small clumps of people made their way through the front door of the largest one, trying to look surreptitious. It wasn't long until I could hear music softly thumping through the walls and see light leaking out here and there.

I doubted you had to go through a metal detector or produce an invitation, so, rather than appearing as easy meat to any human and/or magical troublemakers who might be lurking around, I quickened my pace, squared my shoulders, and marched the rest of the way down the sidewalk and through the door, ready to draw magic.

Music and unidentifiable smells hit me instantly. The place was packed; apparently, the fear of ODs and bloodshed hadn't kept any of these party animals at home. I couldn't say I was too surprised the people of Williamsport hadn't chosen to exercise prudence and good sense.

I couldn't tell what this place had been in its heyday, if it'd had one, but whatever it was, it was the perfect venue: wide open floor space had been converted into a dance floor, with stairs leading to another half-floor overlooking the one below. More graffiti decorated the walls in a cheerfully colored riot, and unidentifiable bits of trash dotted the floor here and there. The people around me danced and collided, the music swallowing me as I picked my way through the press. This place made the back-to-school bonfire look like a children's movie.

My eyes roamed over the people. Even here, the local class war was present. The lighting was predictably lousy, but I still spotted North and South Siders passing each other with pure hatred in their eyes. It wouldn't take much to turn this place into a battle scene from *Braveheart*. Magic or not, the likelihood of violence was damn near a certainty. Hopefully, I could get something to work with and get out of here before that happened.

Well, you're here. Now what?

That question didn't have much of an answer. I looked around for a good vantage point; the second floor might be good, but with so many of these people crowding around, I doubted I could see much wherever I was.

I carved an anxious, erratic path through the free-for-all, the music banging away. Alcohol was flowing freely and the faces of the dancers around me were ecstatic. They had a lot less to worry about than I did. I collided with people several times, but no one noticed or cared, until the last time it happened. Some guy I vaguely recognized from gym class spun around, heedless of the crowd around us, to glare at me. "Aren't you a South Sider?" he said, straining to be heard over the walloping beat. He was plainly wasted.

"No," I roared back, "I'm an East Sider. Why does nobody ever talk about us? We make valuable contributions."

He started to babble something angry and nonsensical, but I was already turning away, disappearing into the crowd. I'm not sure how long I milled around, ready to start casting spells at the drop of a hat, but it couldn't have been long. I had just felt my stomach rumble and wondered how safe it would be to eat something when I felt those magic currents again, the ones coming from a spell being worked nearby, twisting and turning somewhere beyond human vision.

I recognized it immediately, coming to a nerve-shredding halt. It was the exact same bad vibe I'd gotten at the beach last night. I got thumped again but hardly noticed. My appetite vanished and cold sweat prickled my forehead.

I let magic fill me, sounds getting louder and colors getting sharper. It was amazing. For a moment, it took my breath away, despite my fear. The music, the colors, the smells, they all became more powerful, more intense. I understood in that moment why people would take Hex.

And it made me angry. The people who took Hex had no idea what they were getting involved with, no idea what was happening to them. But the guy who cooked it did.

I glanced around. Nothing was amiss; people continued to mill and dance and glower at one another, but no one else had realized anything was wrong.

But something was. Very, very much so.

Okay. I had to think. Plan. I knew something was coming this time. That meant I could do something about it. The "what" still eluded me. I scoffed. Such details were for amateurs.

I got a burst of inspiration and forced my way through the crowd as quick as I could without getting trampled until I broke free and made it to the edge of the room. There were people there too, talking, drinking, sitting on the floor, but I picked my way through them. I thought to make my way around the perimeter until… I don't know, until something terrible happened, I guess, then maybe head upstairs, or go outside and check the street.

My "wait for something terrible to happen" strategy worked.

A bizarre noise tickled my ears, hard to identify over the music even with my senses heightened. I concentrated and realized it was a scream, high and shrill and loud.

Well, that would be a place to start.

I pushed my way through the crowd, shouldering people out of the way, heading towards the sound. I didn't know where it was; sound carried strangely in here, especially in so much noise, but I figured when I found the horror and bloodshed, I'd be in the right place. I tried to ignore the knot of fear slithering out of my stomach and into my throat.

What the hell was I thinking? I didn't do stuff like this. This was suicide. I remembered I was supposed to ignore those thoughts and kept moving.

The scream came again, loud enough to be heard over the music, materializing into the word "help."

I was finally close enough. It had come from the restrooms,

several feet away. I closed the distance and kicked the door open, braced to fight.

The first thing I noticed was that the place reeked. Half a second later, I saw something far more disturbing. Standing in dingy fluorescent light, back against the stall, was a man, college-age maybe, stocky, with a buzz cut. Empty blue eyes pierced mine like a spear. Even from the other side of the room, I could see those strange colors in his irises.

He'd extended himself to his full height, head raised, arms down. His muscles were straining, but I knew he didn't notice the pain. He made a few soft grunting sounds as he did, body spasming now and then. And then his face broke into a ridiculous, skull-splitting smile.

On the other side of the room, lying half-under the sinks, a man lay sprawled on the floor, blood pooling around him. The mirrors above him were shattered.

A young woman was next to him, shaking his arm futilely. Without taking her eyes off him she screamed again for help, this time ear-splitting in the confines of the restroom. I could see the raw fear in her eyes that came from her screams going unanswered. I wasn't convinced she'd be relieved when she saw what form "help" had taken.

I closed the distance, pushed past her to crouch over the wounded guy. "He took Hex," she sobbed miserably, gesturing at the guy against the stalls, who started cackling.

"I know."

"Things just started flying around."

Great. A fellow levitator. As I studied the guy on the floor, I realized what had happened: a jagged piece of mirror glass was lodged in his stomach at a strange angle, dirty grey glass mingling with blood spreading all over the tiles.

She shouted something else, but I blocked it out, though I did note that a couple of fearful-looking people had stuck their heads in the door to see what was going on. *Terrific.*

Then I did something you're very much not supposed to do. I grabbed the glass and yanked. He didn't scream, just stirred.

I tossed the bloody slice away, then hovered my hand over the wound. Power flowed from my fingertips. I could imagine the looks I was getting from anyone who happened on the scene. Secrecy is supposed to be standard operating procedures for wizards, but events, yet again, had gotten away from me. Eyes closed, concentrating, power rippling and twisting through my body, I sensed the wounds in his gut beginning to change, mend. Hey, I'm a wizard, not a doctor. Satisfied, I released the magic. The guy groaned and stirred, which I took for a good sign.

Then there was the scream of rending metal and I looked up to see the wall of a stall being torn loose from the floor and come flying at us.

I barely got my shields up before the metal slammed against them, light flaring, the metal bouncing away with a thunk. I sent a wave of magic that picked it up and tossed it back into the shadows of the restrooms, bouncing off the tops of the other stalls, before crashing and clanging to the floor. The girl screamed again.

There was another crunch, then the paper towel dispenser was ripped from the walls. I batted it away with a wave of force, sending it crashing into what was left of the mirrors. Wizards and Shal'Gasa were one thing, but I flat-out *refused* to be murdered by a paper towel dispenser.

I glared toward the guy on the floor, ready to take the fight to him, clenching my fists, but before I could make a move he bounded to his feet and dashed out the door, into the crowd. I jumped up, tried to wipe the blood off my hands but succeeded only in getting it on my pants, and bounded after him.

In the least surprising event of the evening, all hell broke loose.

There were screams, as people stampeded, practically climbing over one another's shoulders, colliding as they ran in opposite directions.

It only took a few heartbeats to realize what had gotten into them. A metallic scream boomed out across the room, loud over the din, drawing my attention upwards. Bits of metal and plaster showered down from the ceiling as a massive metal strut gave a groaning heave, then tore free, plummeting towards the crowds.

I knew instantly what was happening: the guy I'd seen OD was loose in here somewhere, and this was the result.

The metal careened downwards, filling up my vision. I reacted, shouting and throwing up a hand. The thing froze in midfall, creaking, laws of gravity be damned. It thrashed in the air, as if it wanted to fall and crush someone, and was waiting for the first chance to squirm free.

I could tell my grip was tenuous, and I wasn't planning on giving it that chance: I looked around frantically for somewhere safe to plunk it. Nowhere qualified. Unless...

I stopped fighting the magic tugging on the metal and leaned into it, sending a wave of my own that propelled the thing sideways and upwards, forcing still more magic into it, increasing its speed even further.

It didn't take long. The metal slammed into the ceiling, smashing through the surface with a roar that made its previous noises sound like one of those machines that plays ocean waves to help people sleep.

More debris rained down, and I saw some of it land amongst those still fleeing, but that was better than a gigantic hunk of heavy metal in the most literal sense. It tore a massive chunk through the ceiling, then punched out towards the night sky, coming to a grinding halt on the rooftop, the last few feet still hanging over the hole I had left.

Danger abated for the moment, I glanced around for the perpetrator but there was no chance of spotting him in this mess. Some people had made it through the doors, a few of them busting out windows, but there was still plenty inside, the place gone berserk, as shouting people entangled with each other trying to get away. Here and there, someone was huddled on the floor, doubled over, clutching an abdomen or an ankle. At least no one seemed to be dead. Yet.

If this kept up, they wouldn't need any outside help to off each other.

A wave of people surged towards me, and I didn't fight it, kicking up my heels and letting it roll over me, sweeping me outside, into the cool night air, in a rush.

I forced my way free of the press, into more trouble.

A brawl had started. Someone had probably gotten stomped on by someone from the wrong side of town, throwing a punch in revenge, and off to the races they'd gone.

And the cops were here. I hadn't even heard the sirens.

There was a writhing dogpile in front of me, ringed by combatants flailing at each other. Cops waded in, taking people to the ground, trying to stuff some into handcuffs without much success, shouting rather pointless commands to stop. Nightsticks collided with skulls, and I saw a cop go down from a right hook to his jaw.

There was a whump, a gout of light like a firework in front of me. A fist of hot air pummeled my chest and my ears rang. Around me, I heard more debris thumping down.

Smoke smeared the streetlights. There was a metal hulk far off to the side, soaked in flames. It looked like it had once been a cop car. Apparently, we had a pyromaniac to go along with the levitator.

I spotted the levitator, picking him out of the crowd, that same inhuman grin on his face, drawing back his arm to hurl more magic.

I got there first, sending him tumbling ass over teakettle back towards the building.

I headed after him, as he got up, dodging people throwing haphazard punches.

He made it inside, and as he did so, the metal doors came ripping off their hinges, heading straight for me.

I got my shields up, barely, then sent a wave of magic of my own that sent the doors crashing back the way they'd come.

I bounded over them where they'd fallen, threw myself inside.

He was right in front of me, and surprise registered on his face, managing to cut through the haze of drugs and magic.

Before he could react, I picked him up in a whirlwind that tossed him through the air, limbs flying, and thumped him to the ground halfway across the deserted, trashed dancefloor.

Magic burning within me, I bounded across the room, to where the levitator lay face down and motionless. I nudged him onto his back with one foot, but he didn't move. He was plainly dead. I doubted my gust of wind could have done it; no, it was just the Hex doing its thing, again. His face was lifeless and empty, staring at nothing.

The same way Abby's must have looked when they found her body.

STOP IT.

Light burned in the corner of my eye and instinctively I threw my shields up, right before I would have been barbecued alive, as my other quarry sent a baby elephant-size jet of fire directly into me.

Orange light washed over the shields, twisting and writhing, hard enough to make me stagger. It's rather terrifying, being smothered in fire, and I won't say I handled it with stoic courage, screaming and flapping my arms like I did. Heat seared through my shield, not enough to fry me, but enough to be alarming.

It finally dissipated and I spotted its source: the pyromaniac, standing up on the second floor, staring down at me, too distant to make out his features.

Already there were small fires burning here and there. I couldn't let him keep that up; I cast my magic, sweeping up the debris from the dancefloor, beer bottles and chairs, mostly, and sent it towards him in a tornado.

I heard a squawk of pain and fear, combined with a pulverizing crash, and while the debris was still in the air I bounded across the room, to the stairs, taking them two at a time.

It must have looked ridiculous but figuring it just might save my life, when I crested the stairs, I threw myself down and hit the floor in a roll, coming up ready to fight.

I needn't have bothered: before I could do anything, he took off through a door marked 'exit', on the other side of the room. Apparently, my counterattack had thrown a scare into him. The guy I faced was clearly just some ordinary person high on Hex, which was better than dealing with an experienced wizard, but far from good news: I'd long ago realized this attack was more powerful, lasting longer than what happened last night. *Of course it is.*

What was going on in his head, I couldn't imagine, but I had to stop him before he hurt anybody else. I didn't want to kill the guy, whacked out of his mind on things he didn't understand, but I wasn't convinced there would be another way.

There was nothing to do for it but go after him: I scrambled through the debris, out the exit he had used, then went clanging down a rickety flight of metal stairs to the ground. I was in a large, gravel-strewn lot, maybe employee parking back in the day, and it had been taken up by tonight's partygoers, scores of vehicles haphazardly packed together.

I spotted him, running pell-mell towards gods knew where, and threw a blast of force at him. It sent him spinning to the side and off his feet, bouncing off a parked car. What was I supposed to do if I didn't kill him? Ship him off to Magical Rehab?

One problem at a time: I had to find the bastard first. I hunkered behind the nearest car, raking my gaze across the night, having no interest in sticking my head in shadowy crevices until I found him. I saw nothing.

This kind of magic was bound to be raising an ethereal stink. I concentrated, closed my eyes, tried to block out everything else, and feel the faint radiance of magic. It didn't take long: almost straight ahead. I squinted.

Illuminated in the lurid, wavering light, I saw a figure: it was too far away to pick out its features, but once my gaze locked on it, the dark magic was unmistakable, like little knives in my psyche.

I broke from cover and threw another lance of movement at the figure, hoping to trip him up, knock him out. He rabbited, his timing probably the result of pure luck rather than magic, and the magical force slamming into a parked car, crashing it violently into its neighbor.

I crept outward again, staying low but moving forward, ready to fight or flee, as the situation called for—although I think it already called for flee—invisible power dancing and surging at my fingertips, rippling through my body, potential spells practically begging to be cast.

At first, I saw nothing, just thin waves of smoke from the fires wisping under the streetlights. Then there was another jet of fire, bigger, brighter than the one before, blazing towards me from up ahead, between two cars.

I dodged away with a yelp, and it whirred by me, close enough to feel the heat against my shields. It smashed in and out of the glass of one pair of car doors, slammed into the one behind it, and, remembering the exploding cop car, I ran for cover.

I was nearly too slow: as happens in every action movie ever, and apparently in real life, the car blossomed into violent flame, setting off the one next to it for good measure, the explosions arching up and out into the night, a massive gale of heat and force. One of the burning wrecks jerked madly into the air like it had been yanked on a string, fire gouging out beneath it, and came careening towards me.

I scrambled away, bouncing off a car, wondering if my shield could stop thousands of pounds of American horsepower.

I doubted it, but it managed to stop the shrapnel that rained down. With a squawk, I managed to throw myself far enough away, between two other cars, that I was shielded from the flaming metal tornado that roared and bashed through where I'd been standing, breaking apart and flying away past my line of view, what was left of the hulk shredding a chain-link fence and disappearing into the dark street. I winced as I watched it tumble away; this would bring down attention that I didn't need.

Another car went up before I realized it, terrifyingly close, and burning shrapnel bounced off my shield, rattling my bones, throwing me back against a car door, but managing to keep me from being vaporized. When the blast died down, I managed to get a look at Fireball Guy again, standing atop a car, plainly about to strike.

A long beam of fire shot out from his hands, straight for me.

I slammed more magic into my shields, tried to brace myself, and let the heat and force bowl into me, forcing me to scramble backward on the ground. Gravel crunched and I tripped and fell, but the shield held, and the fire flared for a long moment, then winked out.

I blinked away the colored spots in my eyes. If that was the way he wanted it, that was fine with me.

I sent magic outward and yanked the car from under his feet, and the two on either side of it for good measure.

They careened upwards, somersaulting before smashing back down to earth in a thunderous tangle. I was rewarded by seeing Fireball Guy flip upward into the air, limbs flapping in a thousand directions.

He disappeared from view, and I propelled myself forward, away from my pitiful cover, bounding across the parking lot into the wreckage.

I was hoping to find his corpse but came up empty.

I knew it almost instantly, kicking through the wreckage, the shattered glass, unhinged doors, and parts I couldn't identify strewn in all directions, but I kept searching, wanting to be wrong.

I wasn't. I growled in frustration. I glanced back towards the front of the building; I couldn't see much, but I made out silhouettes running pell-mell, illuminated by the Christmassy glow of sirens. Apparently, the fight had caused some consternation. I needed to bolt, but the guy could be anywhere, and I was the only one with the skillset to stop him. How badly had I hurt him? Maybe I'd banged him up too badly to fight, and his only thoughts now were of escape, fearing how easy it would be for me to finish him off.

That seemed wildly optimistic, but at least it was an idea. How much the Hex affected his judgment, whether it made him aggressive or scared, if he even knew what he was doing, I had no idea. *Wait a minute.* I had to have done at least a little damage, even if it was less than I would have preferred. Trying to block out the sounds of pandemonium, glancing anxiously over my shoulder, I knelt in the area where, roughly, he had been. It didn't take long to find what I was looking for: blood.

It was hard to see, but there was a thin, dark trail leading off to the right, back towards the building. I had a direction, at least.

I pounded off that way, keeping an eye on the little traces of blood in the gravel, wishing he'd picked a less dangerous direction to run. I caught a faint bitter scent in my nostrils, felt a trace of moisture there, and goosebumps chilled my skin. Blood. I was pushing my magic too far, and it was catching up with me. I growled. Now was not the time.

I followed the trail, out towards the edge of the parking lot. The streetlights were brighter here, allowing me to make out the models and colors of the vehicles parked around me.

Another sound rose, shimmering out of the tangle of shouts and screams and sirens nearby. Voices. I couldn't make out many individual words, but I could tell their determined tone was masking fear.

Two beams of flashlights cut through the wisps of smoke. Two silhouettes emerged, guns in their hands, aimed into the darkness. My stomach lurched. Cops. Damn it. No doubt the exploding captured their attention. I shoved myself deeper into the shadows by the building's wall, slowed my gait to a stealthy creep. They hadn't seen me, but if they did, things were going to get awkward.

Then Fireball Guy appeared from nowhere and the cops became the least of my problems.

He saw me and bolted. He was limping, I noticed. My theory had been right. I ran after him, gratified to have him on the run instead of the opposite.

He turned as he ran, arm lashing out behind him and another long, orange jet of fire sailed out, way over my head this time, hissing down into an open space well behind me, sending up a bonfire but, for once, managing not to blow anything up.

I stuck with tried-and-true levitation: I lashed out but missed, barely, the force smashing into a car, crumpling the door and shattering the windows like it'd been T-boned by another vehicle.

A radio crackled, and the cops scrambled towards us, raising their guns. "HEY. STOP."

I dodged away on reflex, stomach flip-flopping, nearly losing my footing in the gravel.

I'm not sure what Fireball Guy did, but before I realized what was happening, before I could even think, a pickup truck off to the left erupted in a pummeling, ear-ringing explosion.

My shields were still wrapped tight around me, and it happened too fast for me to react. I was far enough away to avoid the worst of it; a couple of pieces of hard, hot plastic, from a dashboard, maybe, bounced off me, but that was it.

The cops had no such protection.

There were wet thumps, muffled cries, and bodies falling to the ground. One of their guns went off. Blood spurted, shiny red blurs under the streetlights, as hot shrapnel ripped through flesh.

I couldn't even scream, just reached out a hand futilely.

I didn't see Fireball Guy anywhere, but I staggered toward the human wreckage in the gravel.

I risked a look at the bodies. They were bloody, completely still. I could hear fearful cries receding further on, as the people out there fled the chaos. And the people left here were done moving. It was too late to heal them; I could tell almost instantly. There was nothing I could do for these two. *Add them to the list.*

I screamed and threw a spiteful gust of wind in Fireball Guy's direction, accomplishing nothing but kicking up some leaves.

I heard more sirens on the way, ambulances and fire trucks and the riot police, if Williamsport had such a thing.

I had to get out of here.

I bolted, into the dark void beyond the building, leaving destruction and failure behind me, desperation howling at the edges of my mind. How had I ever thought I could win a fight like that?

I wanted nothing now but escape, but this night had one more horror waiting for me: I turned a corner and collided with someone.

A young man. North Siders and South Siders are usually distinguishable by the difference in name brands they wear, in the sense that North Siders wear name brands, but this guy was unidentifiable: his clothes were too covered in blood and dirt to recognize.

With a jolt, I realized it was Fireball Guy. I braced to fight but knew it was pointless: he was done for. The magic had already faded from him, and his soul didn't seem far behind.

He stared at me with bloodshot, unseeing eyes. I grabbed him by the shoulders, unsure what I was supposed to do with him now, but he shook me off, firm but no longer aggressive. He seemed to be trying to say something. It came out as a few babbles before he managed to turn it into words. "Seen it all," he said. "It's coming. Finally. Gonna be a beautiful day. So beautiful the sky. Judgment day. Washing away... everything. Everything will be okay, everything... I... I...."

He pitched forward, face-first onto the gravel, brushing against my shoulder as he fell limply. Lifeless eyes stared into the night sky. *Damn it.* I bent over him, though I knew it was no use, turning him over, checking his pulse, listening for breath. Nothing. It was too late for me to heal him if I even could have. His face was already turning blue, visible even in the dark, and his eyes had taken on that same strange color.

My first thought was to run for my life; as my legs tensed, my second was that I needed information. It wasn't the kind of thing you wanted to be caught doing, but I didn't think I'd get another chance. Fighting off my revulsion, I crouched and began rifling the dead man's pockets, hoping nothing bit me, spilling out a cellphone, keychain, mints, and finally, a baggie. Bingo. I'd look it over later. I was about to take off when something else caught my eye, something that had spilled out of his pocket. A card, a few inches wide and long. On impulse, I picked it up, stuffed both into my pocket.

Demons, explosions, now felony possession and corpse-robbing. Throw it on the pile.

I fled into the darkness, across the parking lot, away from the madness, the sounds fading behind me until I got to an open space. I knew more or less where I was now, and it would be simple enough to get on the street that would take me home and far away from here.

I had just hopped a chain-link fence onto the street when the voice came. "Stop."

I froze, stomach lurching. That was pretty much the last thing I wanted to hear. Body tensed, I slowly turned, and my dread increased. It was a cop, standing on the other side of the fence. His hand was on his gun. But it wasn't drawn.

I hesitated, poised to run, to cast a spell, trying to run through scenarios of what to do next if I did either of those. I didn't want to fight a cop, but I didn't see a ton of other options. Going to jail now wasn't on the menu.

His face was uncertain, troubled. I figured that was a better sign than the alternative. "What seems to be the problem, officer?"

He swallowed. "I saw what you did."

Oh shit. "Are you going to arrest me?"

His name tag, I noted in the streetlights, read Rodriguez. "I should," he said, his voice lacking the authority you'd expect from a cop. It sounded like he was trying to convince himself. "I mean, I would. But I don't know what we'd charge you with. I know you didn't hurt those people. It was that other guy. I could tell. I saw it happen. He threw fire, somehow."

"Yeah."

"But you tried to stop him."

"That was the idea."

"There's a lot…" He ran a hand through his hair. "There's a lot you don't know. A lot I don't know."

I hesitated, then rolled the dice. "Maybe we can help each other figure it out, huh? Whatever's going on here, it's not the usual cops and robbers stuff."

"I know." He shifted uncomfortably, clearly uneasy about getting involved with a crime-committing, spell-casting high schooler, which was, okay, understandable. "Yeah, I think maybe we should," he said slowly.

"Great. We'll touch base again soon, see what we can figure out."

He nodded once, as if to psych himself up as much as agree with me. "We will."

I tossed a glance over my shoulder. "I'm gonna go, unless you're gonna arrest me."

He stared, then shook his head. "No. Go. We'll talk soon."

"Right."

Before he could change his mind, I walked away into the night, head darting back and forth, keeping an eye out for Rodriguez's buddies. Once I was a safe distance away from any onlookers, I broke and ran.

CHAPTER EIGHT

SCHOOL WAS CANCELED the next day.

I had stumbled in last night and managed to keep a straight face while I assured Mom and Dad that nothing interesting whatsoever had happened at the pep rally, before fleeing to bed.

I'd had a moment of panic when I remembered the bloodstains on my jeans but luckily, they didn't notice. It was, I reflected, a gloomy marker of how screwed-up my life had become that "my parents didn't notice the bloodstains" was considered a stroke of luck.

I came downstairs the next morning, still edgy, only for Mom to inform me that school wouldn't be in session due to "credible threats." Considering it a minor miracle, I went back upstairs and slept another two hours, while they went to work. I'd fired off more magic than I ever had last night, though I hadn't stopped to realize it at the time, and I needed time to build it back up, in addition to being flat-out exhausted. I had a feeling I was going to need all the magic I could get soon.

After I woke up, I went looking for Ella, my most immediate problem.

I found her in her room, lying on the bed staring at the ceiling, plainly contemplating the cruel and unfair nature of life. I knocked on the open door. "I'm guessing you're pissed that you're stuck here when school's out, huh?"

She turned and glowered at me. "How did you guess that?"

"Did you end up going to Ava's house?"

"No."

"You should go. She'll be home too."

"No. I might get caught and then they'll ground me for longer."

"You and Ava were gonna study, weren't you? Her grades shouldn't get screwed over just because you're in trouble."

"Yeah, well, tell that to our parents."

"Just go. It's only a couple blocks, and if you don't stay long, you'll be fine. I won't tell them, I promise."

More glowering. "Why do you want to help me sneak out?"

"Sibling solidarity?"

"When have we ever had sibling solidarity? You want me out of the house."

"I always want you out of the house. Are you gonna go or not?"

"Is this a trap?"

I heaved a sigh. "No, it's not a trap."

"I should stay here out of spite."

"Would you rather be cooped up here all day to spite me or go see Ava?"

She bared her teeth. "Fine."

"Fine."

When I heard the door shut, I got to work.

First, I went online and got a fuller picture of last night's events. Four people had died at the scene; cause of death was "pending." At least there hadn't been any more deaths than the ones I already knew about. Eighteen people were in the hospital, two dozen had been arrested. Predictably, only two of them were North Siders, one due to a case of mistaken identity (he planned to sue) and the other because he kept biting a cop. The fire department had arrived in time to keep the fires from getting out of control.

As I knew it would, the two dead cops had escalated things. Mostly it was confined to Williamsportians (Yes, we're really called Williamsportians; it's on the official website) seething online, but there were two different cellphone videos of payback-hungry cops tooling up South Siders.

Once I'd had my fill of bad news, I went searching for Swayze, apparently tucked away somewhere enjoying sleeping in as much as I did. While I did, I concentrated. "Al? Al, are you there?"

A moment later, his voice reverberated in my mind, causing me to sag with relief. "I'm here, Sam. Is everything all right?"

Alganorath'Dantaine, or Big Al, if you prefer, is a gigantic snake demon and a genuinely nice guy. We had cut a deal years ago for him to watch over my house from the other side, in case of any uninvited visitors. "No. No, definitely not."

"Are you expecting trouble?"

"Yeah. You need to keep your eyes open. Things are gonna be a little more dangerous than usual. Or a lot more."

"Very well, Sam. If anyone threatens your home, I'll tear them to bloody shreds. Should I be prepared to go to Plan B?"

"I don't think it'll come to that. But if it does, somehow..."

"I'll be ready."

"Thanks, pal."

I found Catrick Swayze sleeping, for once, in his appointed spot, a round cat bed tucked into a corner.

Creeping up on him, I filled my lungs with air and started barking.

There was a screech, and he flew into the air. Landing on the floor, paws skidding, he turned and growled at me, eyes vicious slits. "That was for the other day," I said.

"Very funny. Did you learn anything?"

"I don't know. We'll see." We trudged back up to my room as I filled him in on last night's events.

"The *cops* are onto you?" he said when I got to Rodriguez.

"I don't think they are," I said as I rifled through my closet. "I think it's just him."

"You can't trust him."

"I don't, but I don't not trust him either."

"Makes sense."

"I told him we'd talk soon but it's not gonna be now. There's other stuff I need to take care of." I didn't tell him what it was; he'd only try and talk me out of it, and in my experience, when you're about to make a bad decision it's best just to stop thinking about it and take the plunge.

I fished what I was looking for from the back of the shelf where I'd stashed it last night. I held the baggie up with two fingers, a few pills nestled in dingy plastic. "What do you make of this?" I asked him, tossing it to the floor in front of his paws.

He hissed at it, fur standing up from his head to the tip of his tail. "Bad, bad vibes, that's what."

"I thought the same thing. Do you know what it is?"

"I don't know. Ecstasy maybe?" He hesitantly reached out a paw and gave it a smack. "Whoever made this took regular old drugs and enchanted them somehow, like we thought. I'm not even sure what kind of spell it was, let alone what hellhole of a realm it was pulled out of. Whatever it was, they reached way into the fringes of the other side to get it. And this gives normies magic powers?"

"Yeah. I wasn't sure if it was possible at first, but there's no mistaking it after last night. I've never heard of anything like it."

"Neither have I, and I'm seven hundred years old. Jesus, if vanilla humans start running around, whacked out on magic that even us brilliant practitioners have never heard of…"

"I know. Williamsport goes up like a Roman candle. Is there any way to counteract it? Help the people who take it?"

He gave his head a rueful shake. "Like I said, I've never even heard of this. I can hit the books, maybe talk to some contacts, but don't expect much. It's like I said last night: if a normal human takes this stuff, they're good and doomed, period, full stop, do not pass go."

"I was afraid of that. Is there anything else you can tell me?"

"Not that I can think of. Just get this out of here as soon as possible."

"With pleasure. There's something else, too." I picked up the other item I'd lifted last night, easier to study now that it was daytime and I wasn't in a stone-cold panic.

"What's that?"

"It's a card." I set it on the floor where he could see it. "A tarot card. The death card, which seems appropriate."

He gave it a suspicious sniff and another tap with his paw. "Nothing magical about this, as far as I can tell."

"Yeah, I didn't think so either. Seems more like it's just a calling card of some kind. Know any wizards that use those?"

"Maybe a couple. None that use this, though."

"Huh."

"Yeah. Huh."

I picked up the baggie with a pair of tweezers, and, with satisfaction, flushed it down the toilet, hoping it wouldn't summon a demon to the sewers or something. Catrick Swayze rubbed my legs as I walked out of the bathroom. "Sam, I'm gonna broach a difficult subject here, FYI, but uh... your friend Abby. Is there any chance that this...?"

"No. I thought of that. But she took prescription pills, not that kind of stuff."

His voice was cautious. "People can take more than one thing."

"Yeah, but she didn't. They said it was prescription pills. And besides, Hex probably wasn't on the street yet."

"Oh. Okay." I could tell he was relieved, and so was I.

I was startled from my thoughts by the chirping of my phone. "What now," Swayze said.

I peered down at the screen. It was a social media alert I'd set up, to keep an eye on what was going on around town. A video had been posted online and was apparently spreading like wildfire. I clicked it apprehensively. Whatever this was, I had no doubt it would spell nothing but trouble, but even so, it exceeded my loftiest expectations.

There were three figures in a darkened room; they all wore ski masks, two guys with AR-15s flanking the one in the center. "The city of Williamsport must pay for its crimes," he intoned, the sketchy audio quality taking away a little of the intended ominousness. "For too long, the North Side has prospered at the expense of the South, leaving it to wallow in violence and poverty. We will not stay silent any longer. We will fight back. We have Zackary Tyler. Taken last night." And if people weren't inclined to believe him, he brought out the proof: reaching out of the shot, he produced Zack himself, a little boy of eight or so, holding him up with one hand like a kitten. The boy was silent, but his eyes were wild with terror. "One million dollars. Or the boy dies." The video ended.

Silence filled the house. In the comments below the video, opinions ranged from enthusiastic support for the kidnappers to demands to put every South Sider to the sword. "Well, this changes the game somewhat," Swayze said after a moment.

"Brilliant observation," I muttered, still fighting down chills.

"Do you know that kid?"

"No, I guess he goes to elementary school. I know his sister, though; well, I know *of* her. Her name is Alexandra. Rich, popular, beautiful. Captain of the cheerleading squad, I think. You'll be shocked to learn she's never spoken to me."

"Really, even with your sparkling personality? That doesn't seem right. Don't the Tylers own about half of Williamsport?"

"Yeah, but it wasn't a very smart ransom demand. He didn't mention how they're supposed to get him the money even if they wanted to. Whatever else happens, this is gonna blow things up even worse than they already are."

"Maybe that's the point."

I knew he was right. I didn't believe for a second this was some merry band of South Side freedom fighters. It seemed a lot more likely this was the Reapers, who the rest of the world believed were an urban legend. "There's gotta be something we can do," I said. "More than nothing, anyway. What if I could track him? King Death, or at least one of his dealers. Through the imprint on the card. Maybe they could even lead me to the kid."

"I doubt the imprint would be strong enough, changing hands as it would have. Even if you could, going in alone and blind would be a good way to commit suicide."

I knew he was right about that, too. Damn it. All that realization did was make me even more inclined to do what I'd already planned on doing. "He outclasses me, doesn't he? King Death?"

Swayze eyed me. "Looks that way. Look on the bright side…"

I stared down at him as his voice trailed off. "What? What's the bright side here?"

His pink tongue darted briefly across his lips. "Uh… I just kinda started talking and hoped for the best. I can't think of a bright side at the moment."

"Oh. Well, I guess I can understand that."

"What now?"

"A walk."

I stuck to side streets to avoid being spotted by Reapers, cops, demons, or anyone else who might be looking, and finally made my way to the east edge of town, still technically in the city limits, but nice and secluded. I hopped a chain-link fence and made my way into the woods, where kids my age usually go to hook up. Unfortunately, that wasn't why I was here.

The woods weren't overly large, but go in deep enough, and the sunlight starts to fade and the noises from the street quiet down. It was as good a place as any for a terrible idea.

I'm going to regret this. "Eressen. Eressen al'Barra. I'm here. Speak to me." I felt power ripple out of me into reality as I cast the most basic of summoning spells. If Eressen was really anticipating me, that should be enough to get the job done.

I waited. I had enough problems without having to add a deal with a Shal'Gasa to the list, but he was right: I needed help and that was all there was to it. The consequences would be tomorrow's problem.

I waited long enough to hope that he wouldn't show, and I could leave with a clear conscience, satisfied I'd done the best I could. Yeah, right.

A gust of wind behind me rattled the leaves. I turned. Eressen stood there, that same placid look on his face. "Mr. Adams. Good morning."

"Good morning."

"I understand things got a bit complicated last night, didn't they?"

"You could say that."

"And now you want my help."

"Let's not get carried away."

"Don't be silly. There's no shame in asking for help; the only shame is being too proud to ask for it when it's needed. My father once said that to me, and I never forgot it."

I resisted the urge to roll my eyes. "He sounds very warm and fuzzy."

"Let's not get carried away."

I growled. "You help me now, in exchange for a favor in the future, correct?"

"Correct."

"And I'm going to get some actual help out of this, right?"

"Certainly."

"How do I know that?"

"As a show of good faith, how about some information, with no obligations either way."

"Okay." I knew I was about to get manipulated.

"I'm aware of the unfortunate events last night. There was nothing you could have done to save those people, you know. I hope you don't blame yourself. You fought bravely."

"Get to the point, if you have one."

"The point is, I had some little winged friends flying about Williamsport, so I had a better vantage point than anyone else did. And as a result, I spotted something significant you couldn't have known about."

"By any chance, was it a kidnapping?"

"It was. Has it become public knowledge then?"

"Yeah, which makes this conversation seem less and less necessary."

"I think you'll still be intrigued by what I have to say. Is the murder public knowledge as well?"

My eyebrows jumped at that. "The murder? No."

"Interesting. When your local law enforcement was engaged elsewhere, one car ran another off the road, near the outskirts of town. Two men shot and killed the young woman driving, then made off with the passenger in the backseat. A little boy. One would almost think the mess at the party was a deliberate diversion."

"Do you have any idea why nobody knows about the murder?"

"None."

"Did your little winged friends think to follow the car?"

"Of course they did." His face colored with the first anger I'd seen on him. "Those *churls* spotted them and opened fire. They *wounded* poor Torvath." He held up a hand. "Fear not, he will recover. But I admit, I was shocked that human criminals spotted them. They knew to be on guard against supernatural threats as well as mortal ones."

"That tracks. I think it was the Reapers. A street gang, led by a guy named King Death. I suspect he's the wizard you were warning me about, out of the goodness of your heart. And I suspect they're the ones who took Zack. Whoever they are, they're in the know, supernaturally speaking."

"I see. Anyhow, the car eluded them after that, so I concentrated my efforts on gathering information. And here I am, ready to be of service."

"That's not much help."

"Well, that's the best I can do at the moment. I'm not a miracle worker. Now, regarding that favor…"

"Yes, yes, I'll do it."

He held out a hand. It was one of those moments in life that feels significant, like you're about to make some important decision. A bad one. I knew I needed help; if the dead cops last night hadn't convinced me of that, the kid's abduction certainly had. And if I was desperate enough to ask Eressen for help, I still intended to use it sparingly, if possible. Backup from the Shal'Gasa is definitely a "break glass in case of emergency" situation.

With an exasperated sigh, I clasped his forearm. "I'll let you know when I need help," I said.

"I'll do the same."

"Terrific."

After Eressen left, I hung around the woods awhile, thinking over what he'd said. Tracking King Death may have been a non-starter, but he wasn't the one I needed to be tracking right now. Zack was. And to do that, there was a whole new dangerous place I needed to go.

I was in for more walking, unfortunately. I made my way out of the woods, downtown, then crossed the Williams River into a completely different world.

The "burned out truck swimming pool" décor common on the other side of the river was replaced by boat dealerships, finely manicured lawns, and houses with bona fide paint. If the people behind me amused themselves with pharmacy robberies and the occasional drive-by, the rich douchebags in front of me may or may not have hunted humans for sport.

I was glad I'd never truly fit in with either camp. Can you imagine? I would have turned out to be a basket case.

Williamsport isn't that big; I knew generally where the Tylers lived, and a few minutes online got me specifics.

I tromped on through the North Side until I reached the out-skirts of town itself. Then I hung a right at an easy-to-miss stone sign reading "Talgarth Woods," and went down another street, up a gradual incline, with forest on either side.

There are North Siders, and then there are *North Siders*. Unfortunately, Alexandra Tyler was one of the latter, and since I didn't have a prayer of talking to the adults in her family, she was the only thing I had that even resembled a lead. I thought about asking Jason for help, have him talk to some of his North Side friends, but I didn't want him involved in this, and I doubt it would have helped anyway.

I don't mind admitting I was nervous as I passed several secluded driveways until I finally got the right one. This neighbor-hood freaked me out. Talgarth Woods, or as it's colloquially known by the high and lowborn alike, The Bluffs, is the height of luxury in our humble city. Most of the local rich and shameless made their homes here, including the town council, and most of the wealthiest business owners. The mayor's mansion was around here someplace. These people had as little tolerance for outsiders as any South Side gang member. At least a South Sider would go to jail if they decided to riddle me with bullets.

Putting such thoughts aside, I adopted the confident gait of someone who was exactly where they were supposed to be and marched up Alexandra's endless cobblestone drive.

It was a pleasant place, with a huge, manicured lawn that put your average golf course to shame, trees forming a U shape around the perimeter, and a gazebo tucked away beyond the house, almost out of sight.

About nine and a half hours of walking later I finally stepped onto the pillared stone porch. The house was enormous, three stories that practically screamed "Do you know who my father is?"

I had spent the entire walk trying to formulate what to say when I got here. I had decided to pose as a member of the school paper, the *Weekly Wildcat*, here to talk to Alexandra about Archibald J. Keller High School's deepest concern for the safe return of her brother. Unfortunately, that was as far as I'd gotten. There wasn't all that much a South Sider could say to keep the door from getting slammed in their face. *Maybe I can tell them I'm applying for a job as the pool boy.*

Before I could talk myself out of it, I rang the bell. Several ominous bongs echoed through the house. I had only been waiting a few seconds when the door flew open. I was fully expecting to see a stuffy British butler named Jeeves. Instead, it was Alexandra herself, auburn hair cascading down her shoulders, her erotically ripped jeans probably costing more than my parents' car.

"Is there something I can do for you?" There was naked impatience in her voice.

I tried to get my brain working again. I'd figured on having to talk my way through the aforementioned Jeeves, but I'd lucked out. Instead of having to run some complicated bluff, I could jump straight to the ravings of a madman. "My name is Sam Adams. You might remember me; we go to school together. And this is an emergency. We can help each other. Please."

She stared at me, blinking, shaking her head a little in bewilderment. I seized the initiative. "It's about your brother," I said, inching forward, hoping she wouldn't slam the door on my face. "I want to help him. I *have* to talk to you about it. Please, Alexandra, I know how this sounds, but this is important."

She stared at me with suspicion and confusion, and, I saw, wary interest. I saw the decision cross her face, that it was unbelievable, ridiculous, but she had to know for sure. She threw the door wide and stepped back. "Fine."

Feeling a naughty little thrill at being the first South Sider to enter this house since... ever, probably, I stepped inside. The place was palatial. An enormous staircase curved upwards in both directions, chandeliers hung from the ceiling, and on one wall was a fireplace so large the architect had to have been being deliberately ironic.

My shoes clicking on the marble floor, she led me to a foyer (I guess; I don't know what a foyer is.) Upon closer inspection, she looked terrible. Okay, she looked like a model, but a model with bloodshot eyes, and a tremor in her hands.

"Is there somewhere we can talk?" I asked.

"Here is fine. What do you want? If you know something, why don't you tell the police?"

I cast a glance around and saw no one, wishing we could have found somewhere with more privacy. I took a deep breath. "This isn't the kind of thing you can tell the police. You don't know how dangerous this is. Alexandra, I want to help your brother if I can. I'm trying to figure out who took him and I want to get him back, but I need your help. Please. It's not just Zack. A lot of lives are at stake here." *Mine in particular.*

Dark suspicion flickered across her face, her eyes welling up. "I don't even know you. Why should I believe anything you have to say?"

I wasn't sure what else I could say to convince her of anything. Maybe if I'd had a couple weeks, I could have come up with some super cunning plan to win her over, but with the time I had, I could only think of one. Glancing around once more to make sure we were alone, I drew in a little power, then reached out, sending it coursing through my fingers, and slowly lifted a vase off a coffee table, from twenty feet away.

It glided silently through the air as I brought it towards me, nice and slow, since it was plainly a thousand-year-old antique. Her eyes became huge, and her mouth opened. She blinked several times. The vase came to rest in my hands, and I held it out to her. She took it without saying a word, staring at it like it was an alien. "Look, you see what I can do. I'm a wizard. I can't make it any clearer than that. That was magic, in case you were wondering. And I can use magic to track your brother and bring him back. I just need something of his. A toy, a piece of clothing, anything. I know this is way beyond a lot to take in, but right now, I need you to somehow find a way to trust me. Please."

She hesitated, staring at the floor, shaking her head like she was trying to make the whole world go away. I knew the feeling. Then her head came up and her eyes were wet with tears but clear and focused. "This is so much more complicated than you realize," she whispered.

Heavy footsteps came down the stairs. A stocky middle-aged man with dark blonde hair came hurrying down the steps, glaring at his phone like it had insulted his mother. He reached the floor and stopped short when he saw us.

He greeted me with a look of aristocratic disdain. "Who's this?"

I held my breath.

"This is Sam," she said. "We're doing a project together at school."

I gave him a grin and a wave.

His eyes flashed. "Damn it, Alex. You're not supposed to have people over right now. I *told* you that."

"I know, but this is really important."

"I don't care. Whatever it is, it can wait."

Her face colored with anger. "Rick, I'm not—"

"Stop being such a whiny bitch and do what you're told for once."

He continued deeper into the house. Alexandra looked down at the floor for a second but regained her composure a heartbeat later.

I searched frantically for something to say. "So… your dad can really pull off a pair of khakis."

"He's my stepdad." She practically spat the words. "My real Dad died a long time ago."

I started to stammer condolences, but she took me by the arm and pulled me toward the door. "You need to leave."

"Look, Alex, I—"

She opened the door and shooed me outside. Just before she closed it, she leaned closer to me and murmured, "Jake's. Six o'clock."

I nodded once.

Slam.

I realized I hadn't had time to tell her to keep this to herself, like I'd wanted to, but that probably wouldn't have done any good one way or the other. Still fearing the appearance of the palace guard, or whoever it was that protected these parts, I beat a hasty retreat to safer territory.

CHAPTER NINE

IN WILLIAMSPORT, THERE'S no such thing as neutral ground, but Jake's is as close as it comes.

Between sleeping in, shady meetings with a Shal'Gasa and a local heiress, and all that damn walking, more time had passed than I'd realized, and my appointment—I wasn't deluded enough to call it a date—with Alexandra was sooner than I'd thought.

I informed the cat of the latest developments, pointedly ignored his opinions of the Shal'Gasa and, as he put it, "femme fatales," and gave him the snack he was loudly demanding.

If Alex brought me something to track him with, this would probably turn into an all-nighter, so I texted my parents, told them I would be staying the night at Jason's place. I thought about looping him in to give me an alibi but decided against it. I didn't want him getting in an awkward position if I got busted. That, I thought, showed a worrying amount of moral character.

After that, ignoring the ache in my feet and calves, I set out again. My stomach rumbled as I walked out the door. Without my noticing, lunchtime had gone the way of the dodo bird.

The sun had sunk deep into Williamsport's horizon as I made my way through the business districts, and beyond, not quite "welcome to the jungle" territory, but where the buildings get a little more run down and the graffiti a little more frequent. The streets weren't overly crowded now, but I kept my eyes open for potential threats, more of the mundane than magical variety this time, until I reached a glowing sign that said "Jake's," perched over a wide metal building once painted red, tucked between a twenty-four-hour laundromat and a free clinic.

Inside, the lights were already on. There were couches and tables here and there, a jukebox in one corner, a pool table, arcade games, things like that. Long ago, some well-intentioned adults from a church or something had imagined it as a place to keep those wacky teens off the streets and out of trouble, but they'd fallen on hard times, and Jake's had plummeted right along with them. Nobody was even sure who owned the place anymore—although it wasn't anyone named Jake—and these days it had a well-earned reputation as a place where you could find any kind of trouble you might be looking for.

Like, I remembered, drugs. I swept a nervous glance around the room, fearing King Death might be lurking nearby, ready to set off a few more magical fireworks.

I didn't see anything like that, but I spotted danger of a different variety: Alex was already here, seated on one of the battered, faded couches, looking like a Disney Princess who had wandered into an episode of *Cops*. Nobody was around her, making me wonder if the first guy to come on to her had gotten punched in the balls.

There were a few of my fellow high schoolers around, albeit not many, all of them plainly uneasy, feeling the tension that had permeated the whole damn city like summer humidity. The dealers who usually lurked around Jake's were nowhere in sight.

I sat across from her. "I'm guessing this is your first visit to Jake's."

"Thank God for that. I'm here to talk about my brother. I'm

not even supposed to be here. You say you know something about what's going on; do you know who has him?"

"Not exactly."

"What does that mean?"

I debated how much to tell her and decided on the direct approach. "I think a wizard has him. A bad one. I can't say for sure yet, but he's the prime suspect. He calls himself King Death. Some kind of drug dealer. And he has others working for him. Other wizards, demons, I don't know, but they call themselves the Reapers. I don't want to scare you but that's what we're dealing with." There, it was out in the open and she was free to run screaming.

She blinked away tears, her voice starting to shake. "Why? It's not just about the ransom, is it?"

"No, I don't think so. I think they wanted to escalate things, get the North and the South to go at each other even harder." A terrifying thought burrowed its way into my brain and refused to leave: that the only thing that would wind up Williamsport more than kidnapping Zack would be murdering him, but I wasn't gonna mention that.

Her gaze was distant, frightened. "I really should be shocked by this. I shouldn't believe anything you're saying to me."

"But you do."

"Yes." I could tell she was groping for the right words. "What you're saying actually makes sense."

I laughed without much humor. "I never expected any of this to actually make sense." I recalled Alex's words back at the house. "You said this is more complicated than I realize. Tell me."

Her voice was flat. "It started a long time ago. Like, as long as this town has existed, it's been going on."

"What has?"

"This…" Her voice lowered. "Supernatural stuff. I've known about it my whole life. A lot of people do. The city government.

The cops. The business owners. The newspaper. Everybody who's in charge of anything, they're in on it. And they cover it up."

"Huh." It was all I could think to say. I sat back on the couch, mind reeling.

"Anybody that doesn't know about it, they pay off. Coroners, clerks, witnesses, anybody they need."

I tried to select from one of the million questions in my head. "Why?"

She scowled. "The official story is they're keeping everybody safe. That they protect us from whatever's out there. That it would be too dangerous if the truth got out. Maybe it's true but I've heard rumors."

"What kind of rumors?"

"That they benefit somehow. Using all this. That that's where the money and power come from. That they're making deals of some kind with... these things."

Damn, damn, damn. This was the absolute last thing I needed. I shook my head, trying to focus. "What are they doing now?"

Her face turned utterly vicious. *"Nothing.* They're doing *nothing."* She massaged her forehead. "Last night, the police chief showed up. Told us they'd found the car empty, the babysitter dead." She shuddered at the memories, then continued. "I thought maybe someone was gonna hold him for ransom, like they said in that video. But the police chief told us he had reason to believe it was 'supernatural in nature.' Told us about what happened at the rave. Some of that was you, wasn't it?"

"Uh... some of it. The part that didn't kill anyone."

I don't think she was convinced but she continued. "As soon as they figured out it was connected to this weird shit they're involved in, they started covering their asses. Talked about how they would 'manage this crisis.'" She shook her head. "I always heard whispers about this stuff. But it was in the abstract. I basically convinced myself it wasn't real. But now…" She gathered herself. "The cops are looking for him, but they haven't found anything so far. My brother is not the priority. They just want to make sure this doesn't rock the boat. They don't do this kind of stuff. They don't rescue people from monsters. Mostly they just make sure anybody who sees anything weird keeps their mouth shut. Nothing like this has happened for as long as anybody can remember."

"And that's why you were able to believe some wizard that walked in off the street. I wasn't sure you'd even come. You knew magic was involved. You knew wizards existed."

"I never expected to meet one, but yeah, I knew wizards existed. When you showed up, I thought I might have found a way to help Zack that didn't involve trusting the people who couldn't protect him in the first place. The people in charge, they were *relieved* when that video came out, because they knew it would escalate things, like you said. They want the North and South to fight. They want them to blame each other to take the attention off the Reapers."

"And by extension their whole conspiracy."

"Exactly."

Head in my hands, I stared blankly at the floor. These people could make a murder disappear without a trace. Risk an eight-year-old boy's life to hide their literal demons. And I was about to add them to the list of people I was pissing off. *Jesus Christ on a donkey.*

"Alexandra, have these people ever killed anyone?" *Like a handsome young wizard?*

She rubbed her eyes with the backs of her hands. "I don't know. I've never heard of them going that far but… I wouldn't put it past them. I wouldn't put anything past those people."

Just walk away, Samuel, I told myself. *Don't say anything, don't do anything, just get up and walk out the door. Tell Eressen it was a dead end. Find another way to get him off your back.*

It was a good idea, and I decided to do it. For some reason, my mouth opened, and I said, "Did you bring me anything to track him?"

She nodded, reaching into a wildly expensive purse and producing a child-size baseball cap, emblazoned with the Williamsport Wildcats logo. "Will this work? I can get something else if you need me to."

I took the cap from her, and closing my eyes, held my other hand over it. I could still feel a faint energy, emanating from the cap. Zack's energy.

"Yeah," I said, "this'll work."

"How?" she said, suspicious again.

I guess I should have clammed up, refused to reveal any trade secrets, but I found I wanted to tell her more. I usually just get to talk magic with my cat. "Auras aren't exactly real," I explained, "not in the way you normally think of them, but every person has a unique… smell, you could say, in a psychic sense."

"Smell?" she said, almost smiling.

"Uh, sure, smell. And if I have something of Zack's, or anyone's, there are spells I can use to track them down."

She stared at me. "Because you're a wizard."

"That's correct."

She shook her head. "Why are you doing this?" she said. "You still haven't told me how you got involved."

Against my will, I thought of Jenna, walking alone across her yard. "I'm involved because I'm a wizard, basically. There's not a whole lot of us around, so when something like this goes down in our neighborhood, we tend to get mixed up in it, whether we like it or not."

"Just bad luck?"

"Pretty much. 'Become a wizard,' they said. 'It'll be great,' they said."

She gave me a brief smile, then grew serious again. "What are you gonna do?"

"After the tracking spell? I don't know. One problem at a time."

She didn't reply, and she looked so lost and gorgeous and forlorn I had the sudden urge to take her into my arms and stroke her hair. This was followed by an image of my getting pepper-sprayed, so I refrained. Instead, I said, "I'm sorry."

"For what?"

"That your life has suddenly turned into my life."

"It's not your fault," she said. "Something like this was always gonna happen."

"It's not your fault, either."

"I know. Trust me, it's not myself that I blame for this."

I stood. "I'd appreciate it if you didn't tell anybody about me, especially your asshat of a stepfather."

She gave me the laugh of someone on the wrong end of borderline insanity. "I won't," she said. Her laughter died away. "Look, I don't care what you have to do, or I have to do, but whatever happens, my little brother is gonna come home safe, no matter what."

A little determination cut through the general terror. "We'll get him back. No matter what."

The little voice in my head didn't even bother to dignify that with a response.

"Sam?"

"Yeah?"

"Thanks. For all of this. I wasn't sure you'd come, either…"

"Neither was I, but…" I waved my hands, trying to think of something heroic to say. "I did."

"Keep me in the loop."

"I will." We exchanged phone numbers, which a few days ago would have seemed like a much happier event, then she went floating out the door.

Well…

Somehow, I couldn't get much past "well." Why couldn't I just pull rabbits out of hats at birthday parties?

I stuffed Zack's hat into my jacket pocket. *Cast the spell to find Zack. That's all you can do right now.*

I paused a moment to check my phone, replying to dad's text that I "certainly" had made it to Jason's okay, then I stepped outside, the day already gone. Streetlights were on, casting the world in a chilly glow. The sign reading "Jake's" flickered on and off. Behind me, I heard music begin thumping from the jukebox.

On impulse, I headed in the direction of Jason's house. I'd hide out in his basement or something, cast the spell there, take some time to figure out my next move. I could have gone home, but that would have involved a lot of bluffing and sneaking around that I didn't have time for.

As I walked, I found myself thinking back to what Alex had said, that something like this was bound to happen. I didn't know if that was true for her, but it was for me.

Wizards are fighters. Pretty much any time in history, whenever Bad Shit was going down, there was a wizard mixed up in it somewhere, on one side or the other. We don't usually move to the suburbs and join the PTA.

Of course, we don't usually live to be much older than I was, either. The stereotype of the wrinkly, white-haired wizard is very, very incorrect.

There wasn't a single person on the sidewalk; no cars passed on the street. It was unusual, even for a slow night. I didn't care for it.

If I hadn't been so distracted, my mind in such a mess, I like to think I would have made a better account of myself when the bag went over my head.

CHAPTER TEN

I CAME AROUND slowly; there was a strange aroma still faint in my nostrils, making the tiny part of my brain that still functioned wonder if I'd been chloroformed or something. Whatever it was, my head was foggy, and it took ages to clear.

My eyes adjusted slowly, finally revealing that I was in a run-down room that might once have been an office, pale light coming from a ceiling fan. My wrists and ankles were tied to a chair and stubbornly refused to budge.

My eyes found two blurry shapes on the other side of the room that coalesced into middle-aged men.

You know what really sucks the terror out of kidnapping? Hearing a portly, balding guy stammering "—my God oh my God what are we supposed to do now?" His gaze fell on me, and he visibly gagged. "Mitch! He's awake!"

Mitch turned to look, his eyes going wide but doing a little better job at keeping a lid on his panic. He held up a placating hand to his buddy. "Stan. Stan. It's fine. Calm down. We're gonna—"

"He's not wearing the hood!"

"What do you mean?"

"You took off his hood! He can see our faces now! We were gonna leave his hood on so he couldn't recognize us!"

Mitch looked abashed. "Um… I was just making sure he was breathing okay."

Stan began massaging his temples, pacing back and forth. "And you just told him my name. And I told him your name. Oh my God, oh my God, this is bad. They're gonna want us to KILL HIM now!"

"Whoa, whoa, Stan, nobody's gonna kill the kid. Nobody ever said—"

Stan was near collapse and his voice was a shriek. "That's how it happens in EVERY GODDAMN MOVIE! When the guy sees the kidnappers' faces, they KILL him!"

Despite his outward calm, I could see Mitch was getting antsy too. "Stan, come on, you don't have to talk like that."

Stan halted his pacing and swept a hand through what was left of his hair. I wondered if he'd had all of it when he'd started out. "I'm sorry, I didn't mean to swear, it's just… I have kids! I have to make a toast at a wedding next week! I can't get involved in a murder."

I fought past the dryness in my throat, a lightbulb coming on. "I know you."

They froze in terror, the room going still.

And I did recognize Stan, although I drew a blank on the other guy. The memories fell haphazardly into place. "Stan Powell. I bought some of your wife's brownies at a bake sale last year. You said they didn't have walnuts, but they did. What if I'd been allergic?"

He gesticulated wildly. "I made a mistake."

"You're on the *school board*, you son of a bitch. You can't kidnap a kid."

"I'm sorry."

Mitch swatted him in the ribs, causing him to yelp. He crossed the room to stand in front of me, giving me what I'm sure was his most intimidating look. "Look, kid. We just want to talk to you about what you know, that's all. What did Alexandra tell you?"

"I don't know any Alexandra."

"Don't lie to me." He waved a fist.

"Okay, okay. But this has to stay between us, all right?"

He watched me suspiciously and I hesitated, drew a breath, and continued. "Allie-Bear and I are in love." Mitch groaned. "We're running away together. Leaving on the midnight train for Kansas City, the Missouri side. We're gonna lie about our ages so we can get married. She's gonna get a job as a manicurist. I'm gonna work for my cousin, selling scrap metal. We may have to live in our car for a while, but at least we'll be together." I gave them a pensive look. "She wants to have kids right away, but I don't know. Do you think I'd be a good father?"

Mitch actually screamed, storming back across the room toward Stan. He pulled Stan closer, lowering his voice, severely underestimating my eavesdropping skills.

There was real fear in his voice. "Stan, we gotta do something. Rick's gonna be here soon and… and if that kid doesn't give us some answers, I'm afraid maybe you're right. I'm afraid Rick might really hurt him."

That killed my amusement stone dead. The only Rick I knew in this town was Alexandra's stepfather, and he was no one I felt the need to converse with.

I closed my eyes, trying to draw power into me. To my surprise, it worked. I had feared they'd found some way to dampen my power, keep me from frying them, but…

It clicked, and I had to fight to keep from laughing. *They don't know I'm a wizard.*

I glanced around the room but couldn't see what I was looking for. "Guys?" They turned, eyes anxious. "What did you do with my jacket?" They stared at me in bewilderment. "That's my favorite jacket. You better not have lost it."

Stan glared. "What do you want with your jacket?"

"I'll talk. I don't want to get killed. There's some stuff in my jacket that'll explain everything. Evidence Alexandra gave me."

They looked at each other.

Stan motioned to the left, toward a dusty old table in one corner. I spotted it then, my denim jacket crumpled in a heap. "It's over there. Had to take it off him to get the cuffs to fit right."

Mitch gave me one last suspicious look. Then he headed across the room, scooping it up.

I braced myself, feeling my body tingle with power. *Surprise, Mitch.*

The door screeched open and all three of us flinched. The magic left me, spells dissipating before I could cast them.

Rick blustered in, closing the door behind them. Stan and Mitch wavered.

He cast a glance at me. "Good. You got him."

"Yeah, yeah, we got him," Mitch said.

Stan pulled himself up to his full height. "Rick, you can't hurt him. He's just a kid."

"Shut up, Stan. Has he told you anything?"

"He said there's something in his jacket," Mitch said. "Information of some kind."

"Let me see."

Stan tossed him the jacket, and he rifled through it, coming up with some lint, an old Taco Bell receipt, and Zack's hat, the knife safe and sound in its hiding place in the lining. I held my breath, frantically pulling in power, fearing he would recognize the hat. Luckily for me, he wasn't a very involved stepfather, and he dropped it to the floor, uncomprehending.

Rick whirled on me. "I'm done playing these games," he

shouted. "Tell me the truth, or you're not gonna live to get your driver's license."

It wasn't the greatest threat, but I knew he was serious. Rick was a very different breed than Stan and Mitch, and it was time to go.

I began directing magic toward my restraints, delicately, hoping I could get them loose before they realized what was happening.

Stall. "The truth, Rick," I said, "is that your stepdaughter is never gonna sleep with you."

His face twisted, and his eyes went dark. Then he reached behind him and somehow, I knew he was reaching for a gun.

"Rick, don't, stop," Stan gabbled.

My blood turned to ice, and as Rick pulled his gun free, I forgot all about my restraints, lashing out blindly with magic, Rick's feet kicking as he was lifted through the air.

The gun went off, blowing a hole in the wall, the sound massive in the confines of the room, and Mitch screamed and dropped to the floor, probably convinced he'd been shot. Rick went surging across the room and into a window. I was hoping he would dramatically crash through it to the street below; that didn't happen, but he slammed into it hard, shattering it into a million pieces and sending him flopping to the floor. The gun detonated again before he lost his grip, and it went skittering into the shadows.

For an instant the pulverizing sound of the gunshots drove all thought from my mind.

Focus, dammit!

I sent another wave of magic toward Stan and Mitch, and they both went skidding back before they could make a move. I directed the magic back down towards my restraints again, shattering them and the chair and sending me crashing to the floor ass-first into the debris.

I hauled myself up and headed for the door. Out of the corner of my eye, I saw Stan make his way unsteadily back to his feet. I briefly considered standing and fighting. I suspected I could quite literally tear these guys apart if I tried. Regular humans don't tend to fare too well against magic. But I'd never used magic to kill anyone before, though I knew it was time to get used to the idea, and besides, three magically dead bodies would cause more problems than they would solve. So instead, I vaulted across the room, grabbed up my jacket and the cap, tore the door open, and threw myself into the dingy, murkily lit hallway beyond.

I ran at full speed, still having no idea where I was, looking frantically for an exit.

I tore to the end of the hall, skidding to a nervous stop. There was a window in front of me, and I realized I was two or three stories off the ground.

I cast about for the stairs, hearing footsteps behind me. I half-turned, and without seeing which of the Three Stooges it was, I sent out a jolt of power, yanking a huge chunk of lights, tile, and other debris out of the ceiling into their path. They were obscured from view for a moment, and my eyes finally lit upon a door.

I flew through it and began pounding frantically down the stairs, around and around.

What the hell was I supposed to do now? Even if I made it out of this dump in one piece, I would have the entire town after my head. *One problem at a time.*

I broke the land-speed record storming down the stairs, bashed through another door and into what was left of a lobby. I paused for a second to catch my breath, then made another dash for freedom. I had only gone a few steps when I froze, fast enough I nearly fell. Three more guys were coming through the glass door at the other end of the room.

They saw me. I whirled back around and dived through the door I'd come through. Behind me, there was a sharp *bang*, and something cracked into the wall next to me, spraying me with tiny pieces of plaster.

Desperate now, instinctively drawing in magic, I at least had the presence of mind to slip onto the next floor up, rather than return all the way to where I'd started.

I was in an identical hallway, this one entirely dark, trying various doors, which were, of course, locked. I finally found one that wasn't, pushing through into another decrepit office. I spotted another window on the wall. *Bingo.*

I turned at a sound, and my mouth dropped open to see Stan charging me, faster than I would ever have imagined he was capable of. Before I could move, he bowled into me, and we both went crashing deeper into the room, landing on the floor with a painful crash.

We wrestled around for a moment, but I wasn't interested in a brawl: with a grunt and a little magic, I sent him flying across the room.

I leaped up and he had made it to one knee when I felt a strange flicker. Stan's fist was clenched, and I traced the source: it was magic. Coming from him. He was trying to cast a spell at me.

I stared, so thunderstruck the fight for my life was momentarily forgotten.

I shook myself back to reality, lashed out with levitation once again. Stan's skill level wasn't all that high, it seemed, and his magic fled as he flew into the air to thump against the ceiling. He hung there, his face contorted with bewildered fright. "Rick was gonna kill me," I grumbled. "Thanks for sticking up for me."

I gave the magic a twist that sent him sailing out the door with a squeak, then far down the hallway, before I released it. It would have sent him to the ground with a thud, but not much worse.

I crossed the room and peered out the window at a dark street I didn't recognize. There was an awning a few feet below. It would be tricky, and in no way resembled a good idea, but I thought I could make it. I began wrestling with the window latch, when I heard shouts behind me, followed by footsteps. I still couldn't get the damn thing open.

Panicking, I dispensed with subtlety, and sent enough magic tearing through the wall to smash not only the window, but an eight-foot-wide section of wall around it and send it shattering out to the street below. Before the debris had even finished landing, I threw myself through the opening after it, haphazardly thudding onto the awning, causing it to screech and rock back and forth precariously. I couldn't keep my feet, rolling toward the edge, managing to hang on for all of two seconds, before I tumbled over.

I landed on the ground with a bone-shaking crash. Laying in a brutalized heap, I found myself looking up toward the sky, wondering where I had gone wrong in life that these things happened to me. I was deep in contemplation when I saw a silhouette at the window with a gun in its hand.

The pain miraculously ceased, and, owing more to coincidence than skill, I hurled myself to my feet and began limping towards some vague notion of safety, taking refuge in a nearby, invitingly dark alley.

I ran, trying to keep the pain at bay, when someone rounded the corner on the far side. It was dark, but I recognized him: Rick. He was winded and his right arm was bloody almost all the way to his shoulder from the glass I'd tossed him into, but he still held his gun. He aimed it at me.

I seized hold of magic and sent a dumpster tumbling end over end towards him, all manner of trash flying, sending his shot far wide, into a brick wall over my head, blowing off a chunk. He and I both fled backwards in opposite directions, and he narrowly managed to flatten himself against a wall, out of the dumpster's path.

I reached for more magic, and it responded, but slower, feebler than before. The fall was catching up to me, and I had thrown around too much magic, too fast, while my power was still shaky from last night.

I tried to spin it into a spell again, but couldn't get control of it fast enough, my thoughts sluggish, the magic trying to squirm away.

Yards away, Rick was back on his feet. He wavered, but he aimed again.

My mind went bizarrely blank.

Then something seized me by the arm, hauling me backwards, unnaturally fast, before I realized what was happening.

Four shots boomed from the other side of the alley, muzzle flashes illuminating scattered trash and weathered brick, the bullets whizzing away into the darkness.

Back on the street, a dark form shoved me through an open car door before I could speak. I caught a flash of long hair that tugged at my memory, just before we roared away, the speed limit a polite suggestion.

CHAPTER ELEVEN

STREETLIGHTS BLURRED PAST, one after another, and it took me a moment to come back to myself. I don't think I'd passed out exactly, but the fall, the magic, and the pants-wetting terror had left me shaken and drained. We were on the outskirts of town by now, taking various side streets with no discernible route, to confuse pursuers, I guess.

I shot a nervous glance toward my rescuer; or, with the way things had been going lately, captor.

It was a girl. Dressed casually in jeans and a long-sleeved shirt under a jacket, long blond hair fell past her shoulders. Bottomless green eyes watched the road with casual interest. Noticing my stare, she flicked her gaze away from the windshield and gave me a smile presumably intended to be nonthreatening. It wasn't.

"Who are you?"

She hesitated, just for a second, as if she wasn't sure she should give me her real name, then said "Elise."

"Sam. Sam Adams."

"I know who you are."

"What do you want?"

"Haven't you figured it out by now? I'm here to help."

"Why don't I find that comforting?"

"You should. I just saved your life."

"Thanks. You still didn't tell me why."

We were outside of town by now, the lights fading away behind us. I wasn't even sure if we had come from the North or the South Side. That concerned me.

"Because," she said, "I know you're a wizard. Don't waste time trying to deny it."

Damn. I thought it over. "Fine. How the hell do you know about me? It's not like I'm listed in the phone book."

"Of course not; those things don't exist anymore. It's not like you were hard to find. Always a good idea to recruit some local talent if you can." Her mouth quirked up into a little smile. "And besides, you haven't exactly been doing a great job of keeping it a secret."

Looking back over the last few days, yeah, I had to admit, the list of people who knew I was a wizard had gotten worryingly long. Something else to file under "tomorrow's problem." "And what could you possibly need me for? Even if I wasn't hard to find, why were you looking in the first place?"

"My associates and I do all kinds of things but the most important one is the least flashy: intelligence. We have ways of hearing what goes on, with the Familiar Clans, the covens, on the other side, with everybody. We've been picking up a lot of chatter about this godsforsaken town and I'm the lucky girl who got to check it out."

"Who is we?"

"Nobody you know."

A thought struck me, and I fished my phone from my pocket. Hall and Oates, inept kidnappers that they were, had forgotten to take it. "Hey," Elise said. "You can't call your parents now."

"I'm not calling my parents." Seeing her eying it, I flinched back. "Don't mess with a man's phone." I fired off a hasty text to Alexandra: "Ricks onto us. Lie low."

I got a reply almost immediately. "I will. Thanks."

One less thing to worry about; I wouldn't have put it past Rick to lock her in a tower or something.

Elise pulled over, into a spacious, barren parking lot in front of the kind of motel that shows up on the news.

She shut off the engine and got out, the grimy red light of the neon sign casting her in a vaguely diabolical glow. I followed. "You still haven't told me a damn thing. Why should I trust you?"

"Do you really have a choice? You nearly got yourself killed already, and you haven't even made your move against King Death."

I felt the hair stand up on the back of my neck and I narrowed my eyes at her, pulling back, hoping I had recovered enough to fight. "What are you? Are you a witch? Are you with King Death?"

Her face twitched with contempt. "No. I have nothing to do with him."

My mind made its way back to when she had first grabbed me. When I first saw her. When I'd been too out of sorts to notice anything. She *moved* different. Something clicked. And she saw it in my face.

Before I could do anything, she flew at me, covering the distance between us before I could blink. Her hand closed around my throat, cutting off my air and she slammed me back against the car, my feet kicking empty air.

Her face had taken on a serpentine cast, her eyes had gone blood red, and her jaw had distended with the fangs of a vampire. "If you're not any use to us," she hissed, "they said I could just kill you."

I flapped around, trying to get free, but I couldn't budge her. I managed to get a grip on the crucifix around my neck, which I wore for pretty much this exact situation, and thrust it as hard as I could against her throat.

She screamed, jerking away, her skin red and sizzling. I collapsed to the ground, trying to get a breath and draw in power at the same time.

Eyes wild, she lunged at me, seizing me again, and as her fangs flashed for my neck I lashed out with magic, blasting her halfway across the parking lot, sending her bouncing and rolling in a spray of gravel.

The effort of casting spells again when I was already depleted blurred my vision and sent me collapsing to the ground, my organs and bones aching with the pain that comes from pushing magic too far.

Thirty or forty yards away, Elise rose unsteadily to her feet, staggering herself. She made her way slowly towards me. I tried to rise but couldn't, in too much pain to feel as much fear as I should have.

She stopped in front of me and held out a hand.

I glared at it suspiciously, but figuring I didn't have much to lose, took it, and she hauled me upward, stronger and quicker than a human could have.

"I think we've both gotten a little too impulsive," she said.

I groaned in agreement.

She dusted herself off. "You're still on this damn hero crusade and you need help," she said. "Bearing in mind you don't actually have a choice, will you let me do that?"

The world was still spinning. "Fine. What's our next move?"

"Track him. You can do that, can't you?"

"Yeah, I can track him."

"So how soon do we get this done?"

I wanted nothing more than to go home and fall into a coma. But no; procrastination is a time-honored teenage tradition, but a kid's life was at stake. "We go now."

"I may not live long enough to pull this off," I reminded her as I followed her to her motel room. "The North Siders still want my head on a spike."

She rolled her eyes. "They're nothing that concerns me."

"That's easy for you to say. You can fly off back to your castle or wherever. I have to live here. They probably have a warrant for my arrest now."

"I doubt that. You have a Guardian at your house, right?"

I nodded, deciding not to ask how she knew.

"I thought so. You're safe as long as you're there, anyway. If I were you, I'd make some arrangements, make sure word of what was going on here would leak out if anything happened to me. And if they bother you again, make sure they know it."

"And what about Eressen al'Barra? If you know about the rest of it, I'm guessing you know about him too."

She snorted. "Contrary to what they think, the Shal'Gasa are not invincible."

"How comforting." I had no intention of stabbing a Shal'Gasa lordling in the back to impress the Bride of Dracula, but she didn't need to know that. Situations like this were exactly the reason I'd broke down and asked for Eressen's help to begin with, and I would have, if it wasn't for Elise's presence. I debated summoning him anyway; maybe I'd get lucky, and they'd kill each other. But even if that succeeded, I'd circle back to my original problem of going it alone, and somehow, I suspected a vampire and a Shal'Gasa fighting over me would end a lot worse for me than it did either of them. It rankled, but, reluctantly, I did nothing.

She unlocked the door and stepped inside, turning on the light to reveal an entirely generic motel room. "You're supposedly the expert here," she said. "What now?"

"Now, just step aside and let me do my thing."

Shrugging, she did.

I pulled Zack's hat from my pocket and directed my magical senses towards it. I got a fix on his energy, cemented it in my mind, concentrated until I was certain I could track it. Then I returned the hat to my pocket, sat down on the floor, and closed my eyes.

I channeled more power into me, feeling it crackle and twist within my soul or whatever you'd call it, like the kindling of a fire deep within me. Then it was time for business.

I cleared my mind as best I could, bringing up the feel of Zack's energy. Then I cast the spell.

In what I'm sure you'll see was becoming a pattern, I hadn't thought this through. Sure, I knew how this spell worked; I had discussed it with Swayze and thought I knew what to expect. I knew it was powerful. But I wasn't expecting *this*.

I felt my mind, or maybe my soul *fly*, thinking for a moment I had been physically torn off the ground.

Images flashed before my mind's eye, so fast I couldn't make them out at first. Houses, streets, stuff I couldn't identify, all whirling faster than any human could ever move, like some hellish Google Earth. I rocked back and forth, scarcely able to feel the floor under me.

The visions went back, forth, up, down, until I lost all sense of time and space. I couldn't have sat there for more than a few minutes, but it felt like all night.

As suddenly as they'd begun, the visions froze, making me lurch.

I saw a big, rambling old bastard of a house, clearly run-down and long deserted. I didn't recognize the place, but it could only be on the South Side.

The image stayed there, crystal clear, for a long moment, allowing me to look at it until I was sure I could recognize it if I ever saw it again. Then, slowly, the image faded away, and I was back in the motel, slumped on my side on the threadbare carpet, panting for breath.

I sat there a long time, gathering myself and trying to replenish the magic I'd used.

Elise finally spoke. "Did it work?"

I gasped down several lungsful of air. "Yeah. It worked."

We stuck to side streets and back alleys, places I would have been afraid to travel this time of night, if it wasn't for the literally blood-thirsty killer in the driver's seat.

I gave her directions now and then, the tracking spell embed-ding the knowledge in my head as if I'd known it all along. We didn't speak much as we drove. I thought about pressing her for details about what she was really doing here, but knew she would only lie to me, so I just let her keep driving us towards what was undoubtedly certain doom. I just hoped the doom was for someone other than myself.

I knew what I was walking into, and I knew how badly the odds were stacked against me. I could be dead in a few minutes. My mind kept returning to my family, Mom, Dad, Ella, Catrick Swayze, at home with no idea what I was about to do. I tried to imagine what they would do if they found out I was dead and found I couldn't.

Hands shaking, I tried to chase those thoughts away every time they appeared.

I found myself thinking back to earlier, when I'd spared those clowns back in that abandoned building. Had I done the right thing? I suspected they weren't done making trouble for me. I had held back. That, I told myself, wasn't something I could afford to do again.

It took us a while, as we wound our way along, taking us deep into the South Side. Somewhere sirens rang, and occasionally some dive bar's neon sign lit Elise's face, making her even more terrifying than usual. We didn't see many people, to my relief. The last thing we needed was for Elise to decide she needed a midnight snack and chew someone's face off.

I would have been content to wander the streets all night, but unfortunately, we arrived. I pointed to the right. "That's it. Right there."

Elise pulled over and parked. "Hey," she said. "You were worried about having to live here. There's a scarf in the glovebox; wrap it around your face. Protect your secret identity, such as it is. Better if the Reapers don't know who's after them."

That made sense. I produced the scarf, wrapped it around the lower half of my face up to my nose, just under my eyes. I examined myself in the rearview mirror. "Do I look like a superhero?"

"You look like a sixteen-year-old wizard with a scarf wrapped around his face. Come on." We clambered out of the car.

The house in front of us was large but dilapidated, with no lights on. It was the most suspicious-looking place I'd ever laid eyes on. There were other houses scattered around, some of them with lights on. I grimaced, fearing they might get caught in the crossfire. There was also the fact that however much South Siders mistrusted the police, particularly lately, the sights and sounds of a magical gang riot would probably be enough to make them break down and call 911.

I returned my gaze to the house, trying to formulate some coherent thought that would let me survive the night. It wasn't working very well.

Elise had no such hesitation. "Okay. Let's get this done."

I scowled at her. "Is there a plan?"

"Yeah, we go in there and murder them, and haul the kid out. I thought that went without saying but I guess not."

"Just like that, no biggie."

"I can handle them."

"Sorry, I'd just kinda like something a little more concrete than 'go in there and murder them.' A wizard who's literally named *King Death*, plus the Reapers, and we don't know how many of them there are or what they're capable of. Plus, this is the South Side, so it goes without saying there's a mountain of guns."

Elise watched the house for a while. "They don't have any guards."

"Guards?"

"Yeah. I thought they'd have some posted."

I glanced around nervously, seeing nothing but parked cars and overflowing garbage cans. I was suddenly convinced every shadowed cranny, of which there were a lot, held some slobbering horror. "Could be we can't see them."

"Could be. Could be a trap."

I sighed. "Probably. What do you think? Some kind of diversion, maybe? Lure some of them outside? Divide and conquer?"

"I don't know. It might work. What do—"

Our brilliant strategizing went out the window when the screaming started. Loud enough to be heard across the street, it went on and on, clearly coming from inside the house, and sounding distinctly like an eight-year-old boy.

I turned to Elise, my whole body tensing up. "I guess it's the direct approach," she said

CHAPTER TWELVE

I DREW IN power, felt it... flicker, somehow. Unfortunately, even magic has its limits. I knew I was burning too much too fast but ignored it.

Elise's face had regained its vampiric aspect. "Let's go," she said flatly, then began... *loping* across the street and across the house's overgrown yard. It was an unsettling sight, to say the least.

I charged after her. I admit, I couldn't help but feel a flicker of excitement, feet pounding as I closed the distance, magic burning in my veins, charging into battle to save the day.

I was close behind Elise, and went bounding onto the porch, towards the door, and my excitement evaporated as I had time to think that hey, I hadn't planned on charging into battle quite *this* fast, maybe we could slow down a little, reconnoiter the situation, and—

Elise crashed through the door. She didn't even bother to kick it down, just threw her body against it and shattered it into a million pieces, dust and debris spraying in all directions. She flew into the darkness and before my brain could connect with my feet, so did I.

It was too dark to get much of a look at the room around us, but I saw a whirl of movement coalescing into a vaguely human shape, bringing a gun to bear.

Elise was much, much faster than he was. Her body blurred across my field of vision and the gun went off, causing me to flinch, the sound reverberating through the room, muzzle flash playing havoc with my night vision, then somehow, the gun was in Elise's hand, there was another ear-splitting bang, a brief, dark spray in the air, and the body flopped heavily to the floor.

The room began to spin violently. *I shouldn't be spinning around like this*, I mused.

I was saved from embarrassing myself by the bullets that began tearing through the walls, breaking glass, ricocheting, sending plaster dust into my face.

I flopped back, trying to find cover and something hot stung my leg.

Something bowled into me, sending me flying across the room, losing my bearings. I finally had enough presence of mind to wrap my shields around me, hoping it would be enough, recalling the way my magic had flickered.

Bullets continued to roar but the impacts didn't seem as close now. We were crouched down in some sort of utility room. The fire slacked, still blowing holes in walls and furniture, but clearly just probing, unsure where we were.

I glared at her. "Again, I ask, is there a plan?"

There was another automatic blast. "Calm down. This isn't exactly my first rodeo." With disturbingly perfect timing, she turned and opened fire, putting four slugs into a guy who had been creeping toward us, AK in hand. He crashed into a stove before bouncing to the floor.

She turned back to me. "I can handle the humans. It's his majesty and whatever he can cook up I'm worried about. That's where you come in." *Lucky me.* "I'll keep it simple so you can understand. I know how to move fast and stay in the shadows. I can probably keep your ass alive too."

"Thanks."

"If we stay here, we're dead. Well, you're dead and I'm even deader. We make our way upstairs, take out whatever we come across. Hopefully between the two of us we can neutralize all the threats and take Zack at our leisure."

"If he's still alive. All these bullets flying around…"

"Yeah, I know. Let's move."

She seized my arm and hauled me to my feet, causing me to yelp with pain as I put weight on my wounded leg. Then we were hurtling forward.

A few bullets tore past us, then we were on a landing, running up the stairs. In no mood to observe traditional gender roles, I let her take the lead.

The firing had stopped, which made me surprisingly nervous. We stepped off the stairs into a darkened hallway. I was having bad luck with darkened hallways lately, I reflected.

My senses painfully alert, I happened to cast a glance down and saw at my feet a huge, dried bloodstain spread across the carpet. I flinched. There didn't seem to be any bodies to go with the blood, which somehow made it more, rather than less, disturbing.

I couldn't see more than a few feet in any direction, shapes indistinct smudges. The whole house was dead silent. I tried not to think how apt that expression was.

I had noticed, before all the violence kicked off, that King Death had yet to make an appearance. For all I knew, he wasn't even here. It was strange, I thought. Either he was waiting to see if his shooters would be enough to stop us, or he was luring us into some kind of trap. With my luck, it would be number two.

It was number two.

The first thing I felt was a surge of magic. It crept up the back of my neck, causing me to clench my fist.

Then I felt the heat.

I spun around.

A long, snaking column of fire made its way out of the darkness of the staircase. It wasn't your stereotypical *Dungeons and Dragons* fireball. Oh no, it just had to go the extra mile of creepy. It was fifteen feet long, and looked like a thick, round cord. It cast wobbling, distorted shadows on the walls. It didn't go blasting in all directions, torching everything in its path. It just glided firmly in our direction, not even making a sound.

And it had a goddamn face.

It wasn't very distinctive, just two eyes and a gaping orange void for a mouth, but when you find yourself face to face with a sentient, flying bonfire, it doesn't take much to send you screaming for the hills.

I would have liked to go screaming for the hills, but I didn't exactly have anywhere to go, so I frantically braced my shields instead, letting out a scream of terror I hoped it would mistake for aggression.

The fire gained speed when it saw us, then flew directly for Elise. I let the magic of my shields twist and writhe, the faintly glowing barrier wrapping around both of us.

The fire slammed into it and let out a growling scream. Recoiling, it attacked again, trying to get to us, then, in frustration, slamming directly into the shields over and over and over.

The flames were nearly white, and the heat was growing painful even through the shields.

"Sam," Elise said, voice sickly sweet, "is there anything you can do about this thing?"

The thing slammed into the shield, shaking it, forcing me back a step, the light burning my eyes. My stomach dropped. "Maybe?"

The fire let out a screech that filled the hall, then spread out into a glowing orange cloud, wrapped around the shield, little flaming tentacles everywhere, all hovering a few inches from our faces like we were in a snow globe from hell. "If you could figure it out, that would be great."

I groaned, tried to concentrate while holding the shield in place. *Please let this work.* Trying to keep the tightest psychic grip on the shield as possible, I did the first thing that came to mind, which wasn't saying much, and hurled a levitation spell.

It scooped up the flames, causing that face to snarl in surprise, and I slammed it upwards, hard as I could, into the ceiling. The flames sizzled through the wood, sending the ribbons of flame cartwheeling out into the night sky. A narrow, jagged hole marked its path, flames chewing at the edges.

I didn't even have time to be relieved, before I spotted two dark silhouettes out the corner of my eye, aiming what distinctly looked like guns, in what distinctly looked like our direction. I shifted my shield around as gunfire scorched the air, bullets sparking against the magical barrier. Without conscious thought, Elise and I were moving, crashing haphazardly through the nearest door.

A man stood in front of us: the glow in his eyes, faint in the dark, marked him as a wizard. King Death? I had no idea.

Panic surged over me.

There was no time for exchanging insults, no long, drawn out moment of dramatic glowering.

We just reacted.

His arms were outstretched, gesturing wildly as he whipped up a spell, drew back his arm to unleash it. Before he could, I fired off my own. A wind roared through the small room, tearing things off the walls, and sending me crashing into a shelf, nearly losing my balance. The wind swirled into a whirlwind, seizing him, fouling his spell. Next to me, two dozen small black knives embedded themselves into the wall with a crunch, and five or six more hit Elise in the torso. She jerked back and forth, her blood spitting to the floor. Apparently conjuring was one of his many talents.

I threw my arm sharply to the left, and the wind tore through the tiny room, so loud it seemed like it would take the whole house down, then it picked him up and hurled him through a window with a musical crash. I thought I heard a thump on the ground below and hoped I had broken his neck.

I stood there gaping, panting, shocked. It had all happened so fast. I glanced at Elise, and she was yanking the knives out of her, scowling at each one, and tossing it on the floor. She saw me staring. "I'm fine." She pulled the last one out while I stood slack-jawed, then reached into her waistband and pulled out the gun she had taken. "Let's go."

I nodded, swallowed. "Right. Let's go."

She glided forward lethally, gun raised, me following less dramatically, into the hallway. A group of shapes appeared in front of us, too fast for me to count, and the automatic gunfire started again.

Elise was hit several times, her body jerking back and forth, her blood hitting me.

Apparently displeased with being shot, her face twisted into a feral shape. She raised her own gun, fired twice, sending another body down.

She lunged forward and with her off hand, lunged out, grabbed a guy's throat as he tried to aim, and *yanked.*

Luckily, I couldn't see much of the results due to the darkness of the hall, although the splats and squelches told most of the story. I saw another guy aiming a rifle at me, sent out a wave of motion that sent him crashing through a door, gun discharging into the ceiling. I noted with grim satisfaction I'd managed to return the favor I'd gotten a couple nights ago.

Elise fired her last few rounds at a target I couldn't see, the shots turning the hallway golden-bright for a moment before the gun clicked empty. Directly in front of her, close enough to kiss, I saw a guy, eyes crazed, aiming a pistol at her face. She pulled him even closer, using his body for a shield from the bullets that came her way. His body twisted spasmodically, then she threw what was left of him to the floor with a wet thump, drew her hand back, reversed her grip on the empty gun and flung it like a tomahawk. I thought I heard a crunch.

She turned to face me, her clothes and hair stained with blood. "Stop standing there," she hissed. "Go check some of the other rooms on this side of the hall. I'll take the other side. If you come up empty, check downstairs." I stared at her in bewilderment. "GO!" she shouted.

She disappeared into the darkness and shaking my head to try and clear the cobwebs away, I followed. I stepped into the next door down. Behind me, I heard the crack of gunfire again.

I glanced around, not seeing much other than the dogs playing poker on one wall. Then I froze.

Heat.

I turned, fear seizing me.

The fire was there. Staring at me.

I threw myself backward until I hit a wall, the thing lunging toward me.

I struck out blindly with magic, sheer force plowing towards it, and it glided to the right, avoiding the blow, contempt plain in its... fiery demeanor.

In the brief seconds that passed before it came back around, I knew that if I stayed here, I was a dead man, and this fire ghost of death was between me and the door.

So, I improvised. Motivated more by terror than strategic thinking, I threw up a shield and tore into the floor, over and over. Power surged and welled within me, twisting and turning and leaping in my blood, my brain. I knew I was pushing myself too hard, but it wasn't like I had a choice.

The floor bucked and trembled beneath me, and it didn't take long for it to disappear beneath my feet.

As the fire began to fill my vision, there was a tremendous roar, and I went hurtling downwards into open air, nails and boards and shredded carpet following me down in a tangle.

I flopped around, boards banging into my head and making me see stars, other stuff pelting my face, the scarf around my face disappearing.

In what was becoming a very bad habit, I crashed to the ground. This time, there was a coffee table waiting for me, which I shattered into a million pieces.

I rolled around in the debris, my vision obscured by dust, blurriness, and terrible pain.

The gaping hole in the ceiling got suddenly brighter.

I hurled myself upwards, staggered a few aching steps in the wrong direction, then began stumbling for my life.

The thing followed me, looping down through the hole, its pace quickening, coming directly at me.

What was I supposed to do, conjure up a garden hose? I doubted if I could outrun it, either.

The look it gave me as it flared toward me was just a blank orange glow, but I still got the feeling it was amused.

I thought back to when I'd first seen it, a couple minutes ago that seemed like hours. When I had been certain, somehow, that it was alive.

And if it was alive, it could become the opposite of alive. It was a rather slim thread to hang my life on.

A thought occurred to me, somewhere in the gray area between a plan and an obituary.

I decided to attack.

Howling, I gathered in all the power I could and unleashed it, hoping vainly to blast the thing into the stratosphere. I didn't, though I did blow out a window on the far wall and smash the plaster around it. The thing reared upward, curling, dodging, then straightening out again.

I got the feeling I'd surprised it, and why not? Who would have expected someone to do something as ridiculous as trying to fight it?

It recovered quickly, flew towards me, and all I could do was throw my shield up. It slammed into me, drove me back several steps, tried another angle, lunged again. I parried, managed to extend my shield to cover all of me, knowing that a whack-a-mole style battle was one I was doomed to lose.

It roared, pummeling against my shield, light blurring my vision. It was hot enough to give me newfound sympathy for a Thanksgiving turkey, and little burns were already beginning to hurt. I was desperate, on the edge of panic, as I tried to think of something, anything, that would hurt it.

I managed to conjure a thick wave of mist that drenched the room, hoping to smother it or at least confuse it, but all it did was hiss and burn away almost instantly.

Clearly unhappy now, the fire attacked, faster, more aggressive, and less controlled than before.

Dispensing with subtlety, it burned directly through an easy chair, and hurtled at me again with another growling scream.

I tightened my grip on the shield, trying to put distance between the two of us.

We danced across the room, still darkened but illuminated here and there by the flames, lunging, slashing, dodging, attacking, retreating. Back, forth, left, right, it was becoming desperate and so was I, as I blocked its attacks with my shields and cast levitation.

My magic flung drawers full of silverware at it, their contents clattering in all directions as they flew across the room. I tossed pots and pans from the sink, picked up the damn refrigerator and flung it into the flames, making them gust out to the sides, but I knew all I was doing was stalling.

More than once, it got close, too close, causing my heart to stop and the heat to become unbearable, but it never touched my skin, always deflected by the shield, though only just, and the flames never quite got to me.

I can't say the same for the room.

As we struggled and fought back and forth across the forty feet or so of living room and kitchen, the movements of the fire became more aggressive, more erratic. As we danced around, it would light up a couch, sear a chunk out of a wall.

I paid the fires beginning to smolder at the edges of my vision little heed. There would be plenty of time to deal with that life and death crisis after I solved this one.

I was beginning to tire again, my exertion and injuries catching up with me. I narrowly dodged another fiery pounce, slower, I was disturbed to realize, than before. If I kept this up much longer, it could simply outlast me and turn me into a human firework. If I was going to do something, it would have to be now. The phrase "do or die" had never been more depressingly appropriate.

I let fly with a burst of wind that made its flames fan out to the sides, pushed it back slowly several feet, buying me just a little breathing room.

With magic not giving me much to work with, I turned to science. What, I had wondered as I scrambled for my life, would kill a fire? Water was the obvious guess, but I sucked at water magic. A lack of oxygen, I thought, proud of myself for remembering something from science class, but if there was some way to suck the oxygen out of this room (other than calling Nana and having her pontificate on her family's life choices, ba-dum-tiss), I didn't know what it was.

Then something clicked. Earth. Earth could smother a fire. One of the more obscure of the four elements, that could be what got the job done. And like I said: there are all kinds of ways to use levitation.

I cast magic out of the house, into the yard. I thought I could feel massive chunks of dirt and rocks tearing themselves free from the ground beyond the house. Then I directed it all towards the windows.

They burst into a million shimmering pieces as massive, misshapen dark clouds hurtled into the room, knocking stuff over, breaking things, whooshing like a windstorm.

An entire mountain's worth of dirt, gravel, rocks, shrubbery, and chunks of sidewalk roared through the windows and plowed straight into the fire, smothering it, making its light dim almost instantly. There was another strangled screech, one last flicker in the air, then nothing. The debris whumped to the floor.

Sweet victory.

Also, my pants were on fire.

I squawked, stopped, dropped, and rolled, flopped and cursed and finally got it out before it did too much damage to the skin underneath. Still smoking, I staggered to my feet. I realized with a sinking feeling that that meant my shields had grown too weak. And my nose had started bleeding again.

The darkness was still illuminated, and for a moment I feared the creature was coming back. But no, as it turned out, it was just the walls and furniture, the flames crackling violently through them. In one place they were already eating into the ceiling.

I guess it would have been too much to hope for my impromptu avalanche to put out the rest of the fire.

There didn't seem to be a bucket handy, so I returned to the mission of finding Zack. There's nothing like a burning building to give you a sense of urgency.

Upstairs, over the roar of the flames, I heard crashes, screams, gunfire, all mingled together in a berserk punk rock symphony of doom.

If I was a kidnapped child, where would I be?

I spotted a door in the kitchen wall. It was old and banged-up, but it had been reinforced with a brand-new padlock.

That's where.

A flicker of magic and a twist of my wrist made quick work of the lock, and I stared for a long moment down the dark, rickety staircase. Nothing with fangs lunged out to eat me, so I stepped through the door.

I'd had enough of this tromping around in the dark bullshit, so I fumbled around, and, for the first time in what felt like years, caught a break. There was a light switch on the wall, and it worked.

I felt the strain as I drew in more magic, had to pause for a second to shake away light-headedness, but ignored it, and stepped down the stairs. Yes, they creaked spookily.

I turned the corner at the bottom and scanned the room, fully expecting to meet the terrors of the underworld. Instead, I saw nothing more dangerous than some exposed insulation.

I started to call out, then stopped, reluctant to give up the element of surprise. Then I spotted the kid. He was in the far corner, curled up in a ball.

I glanced around once more to make sure he wasn't the bait for some trap, and seeing nothing, bounded across the room.

I knelt in front of him. "Zack? Zack? Are you okay?"

He looked up at me, his face bewildered and red from tears. He shrank back. "Stay away."

"Zack, I'm not with these people. I'm here to help you."

He snuffled. "No."

Oh, for God's sake. "Zack, your sister is really worried about you. She sent me here to help you. Because I'm a wizard."

That piqued his interest. "A wizard?"

"Yeah, a wizard. If we get out of here, I can show you some

really cool magic stuff. But you gotta come with me, okay?" *And if you don't, I'll drag you out.*

Upstairs, I could hear the battle still raging, someone screaming for several seconds before abruptly going silent.

Zack looked at me more intently now. "Cool stuff? Like spells?"

"Yup, spells."

"Your shields don't seem to be working."

I saw the knife in his hand, the hand he'd concealed beneath him, half a second before he plunged it deep into my abdomen, pain blasting through me.

I screamed and shrank back, swaying on my feet, head spinning, barely able to keep from falling. Zack leaped to his feet, grinning.

Hot blood poured out of me, spilling from my abdomen down onto my pants. Zack bounded toward me, his eyes now entirely black. The part of my brain that still functioned realized he was possessed.

His voice still sounded perfectly childlike. "I know what you are, *Wizard.*"

I had no interest in his opinion of my kind of people, so as he drew back the knife again, I lunged out with my knee and scored a direct hit to his hip, which made me scream with pain but sent him skidding back across the floor.

Oh, give me a break. If you'd just been stabbed by an eight-year-old demon seed, you'd have kicked him too.

I ran across the basement, in complete panic mode, my only thought to reach the stairs and get the hell out of there.

The adrenaline got me there in record time, but as I began to make my way up, the pain came flooding back, seizing my whole body, and burrowing into my brain. I collapsed. Dimly, I saw a thin trail of blood stretched across the room. But no Zack.

The little bastard is stalking me.

Then the knife flashed again, *under* the stairs, thrusting towards me. I twisted to one side, wincing from the pain it produced, barely avoiding it.

Zack reached up and swung onto the stairs, standing over me.

He gave me an amiable look. "Two thousand years of existence, and I've never killed a wizard before. This is a rare treat. If it makes you feel any better, you're dying for a good cause."

It didn't make me feel any better, so when he stabbed down, I grabbed his tiny forearm and entangled my legs in his, yanking him down on top of me.

He roared, twisting viciously and snarling, trying to bring the knife around. He succeeded in getting a long, shallow cut on my left arm, but thanks to the horrific pain in my abdomen, I hardly felt a thing.

Get that damn knife. I threw him face down on the stairs, got both hands on his wrist, and managed to drag the knife free, letting it clatter between the stairs.

Then I picked him up and threw him under my arm, hauling him up with me, the wound throbbing as I did.

Congratulations, you just won a street fight with a little league player.

I drew more magic into me, hoping to heal the wound, or at least dull the pain, but I could tell it wasn't nearly enough. Maybe if I hadn't burned off so much already, I would have been okay, but as it stood, the wound was too deep and bleeding too fast for magic to give me anything other than a temporary boost.

I hurled myself through the door back upstairs, Zack snarling and thrashing around in my arms, and I could barely keep hold of him.

Off to my right, there was a spectacular crash, as the ceiling in the next room came down in a hail of debris and fire. I didn't stop to see what came falling through.

The flames had spread by now, and the heat was unbearable.

Most of the next room was on fire, and the smoke and flames were licking into the kitchen, forcing me to swerve to avoid them.

I burst through the door, out onto the porch, and staggered down onto the sidewalk, gasping in the cool night air. My socks, I realized, were wet with blood.

Vision blurry, I glanced around while Dark Zack continued to shriek incoherently. Where the hell should I even go? I doubted I could get far like this.

A shape appeared in front of me. A person. Not much older than I was, bloody, swaying on his feet, I recognized the guy I'd seen at the bonfire. And he was aiming a gun at me.

"Son of a bitch..." he mumbled.

"Shoot him," shouted Dark Zack.

There was a click as he pulled the trigger on an empty gun. He swayed back and forth, scowling at it. Then he was airborne, crashing out of my line of sight.

A dark roaring shape flew towards me, startling me and causing me to lose hold of Zack. I got a grip on his shirt and yanked him back before he could escape.

A car had torn in front of me, I realized, and sent my would-be assassin flying. The window was down, and Elise was staring at me with a half-smirk. "This is getting to be a habit. Get in."

Something in the building creaked sharply and roared. She didn't need to tell me twice.

Zack started biting me. I growled down at him, managed to get the car door open, then flung him inside, clambering after him. Somewhere, off in the darkness, I heard sirens begin to whine. Because if there's anything that calms a situation down, it's the fuzz.

I hadn't even had time to get the door closed when the gunfire started again.

CHAPTER THIRTEEN

THE CAR ROCKETED forward, throwing Zack and I into the seats and provoking a new surge of pain from my wounds. We swerved hard to the right, hurling me into the floor, entangled with Zack, who switched to scratching now. "BASTARD! WIZARD FILTH!"

I supposed I should be grateful he couldn't do much in such a tiny body. I shoved him away and got unsteadily back into the seat, holding him off with a straight arm. "Shut up, you little rodent."

"You're *both* children," Elise muttered from the front seat.

Behind us, there was a series of sharp cracks, and the rear window shattered into a million pieces, pelting us with broken glass. My jacket caught most of them, but two or three struck home, adding more cuts to an already impressive collection.

Zack whooped for joy. Then he hurled himself forwards, trying to grab the steering wheel. We swerved, the rear end smacking into a parked car.

I dragged him back and pinned him down. "What the hell are we supposed to do with him?"

Elise tossed a glance behind her, where a dark SUV was ripping after us. "I'm sure you'd never let me hear the end of it if I just wrung his neck."

"Well, maybe we shouldn't make it Plan A."

"Exorcise him."

"What?"

"Exorcise him. I know you banished a demon the other night. It's the same basic premise." That was a house, not a person, I thought weakly, but didn't say anything. It wasn't lost on me how well that had gone.

I don't know what she saw, but it caused her to swerve hard, smashing a stop sign to the ground, throwing me into the air. Behind us, there was a boom and a flash of light.

"Um. Um. Sure. I'll... exorcise him."

I tried to concentrate on the spell. My brain was foggy, too foggy for this.

Zack continued to howl bloody murder. There comes a point when magic is, believe it or not, kinda easy. You just start blasting and hoping for the best. Zack couldn't be a sock puppet for a demon the rest of his life. I had to try.

I drew power into me. It was tough; I was losing strength.

I grabbed Zack by the forehead. How did it work in the movies again? "I command you, demon, to get out. Leave this boy and never return." I thought about dropping a "power of Christ compels you," but doubted that would work for me.

Zack thrashed. "I'm stronger than you, Outlaw."

Ignoring him, I cast more magic. "GET OUT!"

Behind us, there was a long chatter of automatic weapons fire, then the sharp *whump* of another explosion, right next to us.

An invisible force gripped us, slowing the car dramatically, tossing me around yet again. Tires screamed. Elise jerked the wheel violently, trying to escape. The windows on the right side shattered, and one of our tires exploded beneath us like a gunshot.

"Magic," she said. "One of your fellow wizards is in the car, plus a grenade launcher. Can you fire back?"

"Not and still have enough juice to exorcise the kid."

The car bucked as something seized hold of the rear end. Metal crunched, and there was more squealing of tires, then we were dragged grindingly backwards.

"Try!"

Reluctantly, I turned away from Zack and looked back through the shattered rear window. The other car was nearly as banged up as we were, growing closer and closer. We would be on them in a few seconds, and they probably wouldn't wait that long to open fire. I did the first thing that came to mind, seized what magic I could, and sent a ball of fire towards the car.

It wasn't the unnervingly precise thing that had tried to kill me earlier; this was a jagged, haphazard sheet of flame that dipped and swerved before it got to its target.

But it got their attention.

The driver of the car swerved, plowing through a luckily unused bike rack, and the flames raked the passenger side.

Sensing Dark Zack was about to pull another stunt, I lunged back towards him and sent another current of magic into him before he could do anything. "I COMMAND YOU TO LEAVE THIS BODY AND NEVER RETURN!"

Zack continued to thrash, but from the dark magical currents that still emanated from him, I could tell the demon, whoever it was, still had control.

My head was beginning to swim, and I was starting to feel the deep pains in my body that came with too much magic use. The car, still smoldering, flew towards us again.

Then it veered off, abruptly cutting to the left and disappearing down a side street. "Maybe we scared them off," I suggested wearily. Elise didn't respond.

"I think not," Zack declared. A thunderous, inhuman howl came out of nowhere and seemed to vibrate the car.

I heard the thump of enormous footsteps, then the howl mingled with a growl, and it was close, causing me to flinch, and it turned into a roar that drove all thoughts of the spell from my brain.

I tried to get a look outside, saw nothing but a blur of movement at the edge of my vision, there and gone. "Can you see anything? A werewolf? No, the moon's wrong. Maybe some kind of shapeshifter?"

"I don't know, I don't exactly have time for a wildlife survey." There was an icy pause. "That demon you banished the other night... if one could cross over, that means another could."

"Indeed," Zack piped up.

More demons. Wonderful. Ignoring the fact that my magical energy bar was getting dangerously low, I prepared to fight.

Through the shattered windows, I saw fur and claws rear up. I attacked, sending a whirlwind screaming towards it. The car sloughed away from the storm, prompting Elise to growl as she wrestled the wheel.

The winds collided with the beast, whatever it was (I figured it was for the best I couldn't get a good look), and sent it spinning back to crash into a storefront. It roared, the sound juddering through my organs, and I hoped I'd managed to hurt it.

I was disabused of that notion five seconds later, when a gigantic, clawed paw crunched onto the hood of the car, that roar loud enough to make my ears ring.

Elise roared back, fangs bared, the sound spine-tingly fearsome, no matter how small it was next to the demon, then jerked the car hard to the left. I was, yet again, tossed in all directions.

As claws punched through the metal over my head, there was a bone-jarring impact, another growl, this one laced with pain, and with a screeching of metal, a chunk of the car's roof was ripped away and the weight disappeared from the car.

"Please tell me it's dead," I panted.

"I don't think so, but I shook him off on a light pole. We lost him."

Zack growled at that, redoubled his thrashing. Because things were going just a bit too well, I heard the rumble of an engine accelerating, and, of course, the SUV pursuing us came flying around a corner.

"Duck," Elise said.

I threw myself to the floor onto Zack. I'd like to tell you I was shielding him with my body, but I was really just trying to get out of the line of fire, and you wouldn't have believed me anyway.

Elise had gotten her hands on a machine pistol, and it roared over my head, hot shells landing on me, the sound grinding painfully into my ears like a power drill. When the gunfire stopped, I risked a glance behind us. I didn't say anything, but her barrage didn't seem to have affected them much, and they still ripped after us.

A great grinding sound of metal echoing all around us, loud enough to be heard over the roar of the engine.

A burst of sparks filled the darkness, and the grinding changed pitch. There was a brutal crash next to us and Elise swerved. "What the hell is going on?"

"King Death, or whoever's back there. He's throwing street-lights at us."

"Oh."

More sparks flared, accompanied by violent pops, and we swerved violently back and forth as Elise tried to dodge. Huge metal clangs sounded next to us, all around, and I was glad someone with Elise's heightened reflexes was at the wheel. I heard the zap of electrical currents going out of control, saw sparks rain down here and there in tiny showers.

Below me, there was a metallic scream as the rim of the busted tire scraped concrete, throwing up faint sparks, there and gone in the dark.

One of the lights clipped us, sending the car shuddering to one side, but Elise managed to regain control. I saw a long metal pole go cartwheeling, strangely slowly, it seemed, in front of our windshield.

The whine of the sirens came screaming back into my hearing, and two cop cars, sirens erupting with color, came ripping around a corner, directly at us. The lights glared through the windshield, and Elise slammed the wheel to the right, the cop cars barreling past, close enough for us to graze the second one with a thump. I heard rattling pops of gunfire behind us, probably the Reapers trying to strafe the cops.

"Damn it," I growled. I'd forgotten all about the cops. Apparently, we'd made so much noise even the South Side's famously slow 911 response time hadn't been enough. Trying to keep one eye on Zack, I peered through the back window, trying to figure out what was going on from the tornado of light, sound, and motion. "I hope they realize we're the victims here."

"Don't worry," Elise said, a certain murderous cockiness in her tone, "we might not survive the night but nobody in this car is getting arrested."

The cops, I thought, might be safer chasing King Death, and an instant later, I was proved brutally wrong, as one of the cop cars was hurled through the air as if some god had flicked it with a giant finger. It smashed against a building's brick wall, smashing it open, the back half of the car disappearing into the hole. "Damn it," I shouted, thumping my fist against the seat. The supernatural was hurting far too many people who weren't in the game, and I hated it. The other car avoided getting tossed but didn't fare much better: no doubt screaming in terror, they swerved, landing on the sidewalk, and taking out a fence. I heard more gunfire, then the wrecked cars disappeared in the distance as we drove for our lives, the Reapers chasing us.

"We need to get this thing wrapped up before any more cops show up," I said. I knew backup wouldn't be far behind, and more death shortly thereafter.

"Tell that to the Reapers. What the hell are they doing back there?"

"My shadow wyrms will devour you, wizard," Dark Zack declared.

"Quiet, you." I stuck my face out the broken window, into the chilly winds whipping around us. King Death's driver had lost patience with boring old streets and started driving down the sidewalk to spice things up. They were flying, gaining speed, and the reason hit me: they needed more room. They were planning on ramming us.

The fact that that was probably a suicide mission for them didn't comfort me in the slightest.

"Keep going," I shouted at Elise.

"Great idea, I'd never fucking thought of that."

The streets were narrow here; the buildings were packed close together and there wasn't an easy way for us to escape.

They barreled towards us. I only had a few seconds. If I could time it right...

I sent out a bolt of levitation, aiming not at the car's cab but at its tires, its undercarriage. Then I thrust the force violently to the left.

It worked; the car skidded violently, tires screaming, engine roaring in pained protest, and it went bashing haphazardly back across the street, where it overturned with a spectacular, crashing roar.

I wasn't under any illusions I'd killed the son of a bitch. That would have been nice, but wizards are tough to kill. Of course, I should probably be grateful for that.

I leaned back, gasping for air. I didn't have time to rest: Dark Zack had thrust himself into the front seat and was going for the steering wheel again. He got his paws on it before Elise knew what was happening, sending us swerving onto the sidewalks ourselves. I grabbed him by the scruff of his shirt and threw him back to the backseat before she could make good on her threat to wring his neck.

We had bounced back into the place traffic is supposed to be, more or less, when another car came ripping down another street. The only thing they could possibly be doing was pursuing us.

Dark shapes leaned out two of the windows, opening fire with automatic weapons, a long, deafening chatter. Bullets shredded the air around us, hitting the buildings beyond us, shattering glass, throwing up sparks from the asphalt. The fact that they were charging with such wild abandon is probably what kept us from being shot to pieces immediately but that wouldn't last much longer.

At least it was only mere bullets being thrown at us now, a refreshing change from all the dark magic. I reached for magic of my own, prepared to lash out again, a repeat of what I'd done to King Death's car. My head swam, green and blue stars spraying back and forth across my vision.

I couldn't focus enough to get the job done. My magic wasn't gone, not quite, but I didn't think I'd be using it to snipe any more cars tonight. "Uh... Elise?" I slurred. "I'm running out of ammo here." More gunfire rang out.

"Hang on," she said.

"What?"

There was an explosion of sound, glass shattered, metal screamed, and the car shook so hard I couldn't see how it held together.

Lights and colors whirled in front of us, and when I realized what was happening, I felt strangely detached: *Oh. We just crashed into a convenience store. No wonder there was so much noise.*

Without missing a beat, the car followed, chasing us through the jagged opening we had carved in the storefront.

It was apocalyptic. Elise accelerated, smashing through shelf after shelf, sending up a hail of various household products as the shelves dominoed against each other and crashed to the floor. Sparks rained down from the ceiling.

"Um. Elise?"

I meant to inquire about our destination, but she couldn't hear me over the racket, or, given her heightened senses, perhaps she just ignored me. Through all the swirling debris, I could dimly make out a frozen food section and a wall ahead.

I blocked out everything else. I pulled in every flicker of power I could still muster, until my body shook. Then I grabbed Zack one more time, concentrated as hard as I could, and screamed "GET! THE FUCK! OUT!"

Power rushed out of me, making me feel as though my bones were vibrating under the skin. Zack snapped back like he'd been struck and hit the seat unconscious.

I didn't feel pain anymore, from the magic or the stab wound. I just felt a little tired. I was faintly aware of Elise swerving sharply, producing more crashes. Only feet away, the SUV tried to slow but couldn't get it done in time, bashing into a shelf full of ice cream. What was left of our car finally thumped to a stop.

I heard the door open, and Elise disappeared. I heard some shouting, a brief smatter of gunshots, then silence.

The passenger door opened. I was laying on my side on the backseat floor. I didn't remember how I got there.

The last thing I remember was noticing the backseat floor was covered with red.

CHAPTER FOURTEEN

I REGAINED CONSCIOUSNESS slowly and lay there a long time before I opened my eyes.

My everything hurt.

When I finally pried my eyes open a crack, I wasn't in Wizard Heaven, but a small, sparsely decorated room, light shining down on me.

I looked around slowly. I was laying on top of a bed, my brain finally registering that I was in some sort of motel. That sounded familiar somehow.

I saw Elise, sitting in a chair against the wall, reading a book.

She looked up at me, closing her book and setting it carefully on the floor. "You're alive. I wasn't so sure at first. That was just about your last hurrah, my wizard friend."

I groaned quizzically.

"I fed you a little of my blood. Healed you right up."

Marvin Gaye's "Sexual Healing" began playing in my mind.

I ignored the music and managed to get my mouth working, convinced I could still taste vampire blood. "Zack?"

She jerked her head behind her. "I have him locked in the

bathroom. I think he came to a little while ago, but I haven't checked yet."

I reached for magic and closed my eyes in relief when I felt it respond. It was more of a trickle than a flood, but I hadn't burned myself out like I feared. Elise healing my wound probably had something to do with it, which I supposed I should appreciate.

I tried to flop out of bed and nearly collapsed for my trouble.

"Easy, tough guy. That stuff isn't a cure-all. You're still gonna hurt for a few days."

I gingerly made my way across the room, and she rose to join me. "I have to check."

I stopped in front of a mirror on one wall. I looked about as dilapidated as a wizard could look: my clothes were filthy and torn here and there, I had several cuts of varying size and bruises in the double digits, the bottom half of my left pant leg was flapping around, blackened and scorched, and I was covered head to toe in the blood of various parties.

"Maybe you could wash up before you go in there," Elise suggested.

I grunted in agreement and soaked a towel in the faucet, spent several minutes getting the worst of it off my face and arms.

When I finished, I looked nominally less likely to terrify a child.

"Ready?" Elise asked me.

"Yeah."

She stepped to the bathroom door, then disentangled a complicated mechanism involving a chair and some rope that held it shut. I didn't ask why she'd brought all that rope.

She gave me a look that said something to the effect of "try not to get stabbed again, genius," then swung the door open.

Zack was huddled in the bathtub, giving the faucet the thousand-yard stare.

I delicately extended my senses toward him. It was difficult, and my hold was tenuous, but I could tell the dark energy that had reeked from him wasn't there anymore. Yay, me.

I sagged with relief and exhaustion. "He's fine."

She eyed him. "I'm not sure how 'fine' he is. What do we do with him?"

"Take him back to his family, such as it is. We need to talk to him, though. He may have information we need."

"You think he could know something about King Death? What he wants?"

"I know it's a long shot, but he's the closest thing we have to a lead."

Her voice was dubious. "He doesn't look like much of a lead."

"Yeah, well, with the way things have been going, I'll take what I can get."

She shrugged and leaned against the door frame and I stepped deeper into the room. "Zack?"

He looked up, sending a tiny, frightened glance in my direction, as if he was afraid to see what might come through the door. It was a few seconds before he spoke. "Who are you?"

"My name is Sam. I'm a wizard."

"There's no such thing as wizards." His face was still haunted, but he didn't seem afraid of me now. I guess I'm not what you'd call intimidating.

"Sure there is. Watch this." Ignoring the surge of pain it caused, I reached for magic again, twisting and twirling my hand in front of me. When I was done, there was a glowing green dragon dancing in the air, a spray of dark red emanating from his mouth. "Pretty sweet, huh?"

He laughed a little, managing a weak smile, and I got the impression that was a lot closer to his normal personality. "Yeah."

I let the dragon fade, then knelt by the tub. "Zack? Do you remember anything? From when the bad guys had you?"

His face darkened. "You kicked me."

Of course, he remembers that. "Do you remember anything else? Anything they might have said?"

He shook his head vigorously.

"Did they talk about King Death?"

He shrank back against the wall. "I don't want to talk about him." He was clearly on the verge of tears.

I screwed a smile onto my face. "Hey, don't be too scared of him. He can't be that scary if you ask me."

He didn't laugh this time, but his expression softened. I continued. "I mean, how tough can a guy named King Death really be? Think about it: if you're such a badass, you don't need to call yourself 'King Death.' You could just call yourself Steve or something and it wouldn't matter; everybody would know how tough you were. Sounds like he's overcompensating to me." I hoped it was true and knew it wasn't. "Piece of advice: next time somebody scares you, just laugh in their face. It'll freak them out. They'll think you know something they don't, that you have some kind of advantage they can't see and then they'll start rethinking making trouble for you. You can't be scared of something when you're laughing at it. Like this." I let out a wild cackle.

He giggled again. "You're funny."

"Yeah, I'm a hoot and a half, just ask my teachers."

He smiled. "The next time my teacher yells at me, I'm gonna laugh at her like that."

"I fully support that, young man. Did you hear them mention any other names?"

"I don't know."

This was going nowhere, and I had no idea how to draw him out of his shell. I'm a long way from being a child psychologist. I racked my brain, trying to think of something, anything that might help, and a lightbulb came on. One more Hail Mary, then I would get him on his way.

"Only one other question, Zack: did they ever mention a place?"

"A place?"

"Yeah, like a place here around town. Somewhere you might have heard of before?"

He thought that over. "Just that place where we drew the pictures."

"Pictures?"

"Yeah. On the graves or whatever."

"You mean like a cemetery?"

"Yeah."

I sat back in surprise. I hadn't expected that to actually work. He was talking about making rubbings of tombstones, I realized; I'd gone on the same field trip when I was his age. "Zack, when you went on your trip, where did you go?" He looked at me blankly. "Did you leave from school?"

He nodded.

"Did you go down the street with the big sign that says Archibald J. Keller?"

"No. We went down the other street. With the big trees."

Although "the other street with the big trees" wasn't exactly helpful on its face, I knew what he was talking about. Following that street far enough would take you right past a cemetery.

I stood. "Zack, thanks. You helped me a lot. You helped a lot of people."

"I did?"

"Yeah. You're a big hero. I'm gonna call your sister, and she'll come pick you up."

"Ally's coming?"

"Yep. She's gonna be here so fast your head's gonna spin."

Grimacing at the inadvertent *Exorcist* reference, I hurried from the room.

I saw Elise watching me. "Well, that was just about the sweetest thing I've ever seen."

"I'm glad I could warm your little black heart. I'll go call his sister. You can let him out of the bathroom, you know. Just don't use him for a midnight snack while I'm gone."

"Don't worry; he's too skinny to eat."

Elise gave me the necessary directions, then I stepped out into the night air, the cool freshness bringing me around a little, stopping for a moment to look into the distance. There wasn't much to see, just the chilly red light of the neon sign and a dark stand of trees across the road.

Well, I had accomplished... something.

The events of the last few hours didn't even seem real. They seemed like a dream I'd just woke up from. I reached for my phone; I knew I needed to call Alex, make her stop worrying, but my hands wouldn't stop shaking, and it took two or three tries to paw it free. Once I finally did, I had to stop and catch my breath, like I'd just run a marathon. A wave of numbness flooded me, not my body, but my mind. I couldn't make my brain work; I couldn't even remember how to dial her number. My brain seemed filled with an endless void of static. Abby, I thought suddenly, would be proud. She would have been glad I saved a kid.

That brought me around enough to dial Alexandra's number. She answered almost immediately, and I didn't keep her in suspense. "It's Sam. I found him. He's okay."

I think she started crying, but I managed to give her the directions Elise had passed along, and I got the feeling she'd be there.

While we waited, I amused Zack by telling him some of the tamer, more kid-friendly stuff about wizardry. He was still visibly shaken, but occasionally, I'd see his eyes light up, especially when I told him I had a talking cat. He'd wanted to know if he could meet Catrick Swayze, hear some stories. Recalling that Swayze's stories tend to involve graphic violence, strong language, and adult subject matter, I dodged the question.

Then Alex showed up, the door opening so abruptly it caused Elise and I both to leap to our feet, expecting violence. Hopefully no one noticed my exhausted legs went out from under me almost instantly.

"Ally," Zack said.

Her eyes found him, and she flew across the room, dragging him into her arms. "Hey Monkey."

There was cooing and sobbing for a few uncomfortable minutes, then she looked up at me. "I was so afraid... well, you know."

"Yeah."

She glanced at Elise. "You helped get my brother back, didn't you?"

Elise's eyes rolled toward me. "Mostly I just helped keep this fool alive."

"Thank you," Alex said. "I can't thank you enough."

"You're welcome," Elise said, uncharacteristically hesitant, apparently uncomfortable with receiving thanks.

She took Zack's hand and led him to the car. I watched from the door as she got him bundled in back, then trailed after them. She leaned inside. "I'm gonna talk to Sam for a minute, then we'll go home, okay?"

"Okay."

She closed the door and turned back to me. "I don't even know where to start."

I ripped off the band aid. "He's pretty messed up. He was possessed for a little while."

It was a moment before she could speak. *"Possessed?* Like by a demon?"

"Yeah. It's not like you think, the devil or whoever had nothing to do with it. It was just some creature they recruited that lives on the other side."

She shot an anxious glance towards the backseat. "What... I-I don't understand. What happened?"

"If it makes you feel any better, he doesn't seem to remember much of it. They were using him as a trojan horse to kill a certain wizard."

"He tried to *kill* you?"

"Well, I think we can blame the demon for that, and his Reaper friends. I... well, I exorcised him."

Her mouth slack, she looked away, shaking her head. "Oh my God. Can it... you know, come back?"

"I don't think it will. The spells you have to cast to possess someone are line of sight, so he should be okay."

"Line of sight," she muttered at the ground, tears in her eyes. "I guess these are things I talk about now."

"He should talk to somebody, I guess. He needs help and I don't know how to do any of that. I just know magic. Since there's some big cover-up, maybe somebody can find a child therapist on the take or something."

She nodded, still in shock. "You saved my brother's life."

"Yeah, well, eventually."

Some strength returned to her voice. "I guess this is the part where I give you the whole 'if there's anything I can do to repay you' speech. Well, there is something I can do: I'm gonna keep my eyes and ears open. I know what these people do behind closed doors. And they don't expect anything out of me. They have no idea how much I hear. And if they're doing anything that could come back to you, I'm gonna let you know."

"Don't put yourself at risk."

"I'm already at risk. I'm gonna do it whether you want me to or not."

I snorted. "Thanks."

She ran a hand through her hair, looking down at the ground for a moment. "This isn't over for you, is it?"

"No."

"Is there anything—"

"No. Don't get any more mixed up in this than you already are. Things are gonna get out of control and I don't know what's gonna happen."

"I'm pretty sure things are already out of control." She reached out and squeezed my wrist. "Just live through it, okay?"

"That's the plan."

"Thanks for saving my brother."

"You're welcome. Could you give me a lift home?"

"Sure. No problem."

"I'll be ready in just a minute."

Reluctantly, I went back inside. Elise was sitting where she was when I woke up, patiently waiting for me to return.

She gave me a look. I hesitated. "Look, I'm in this whether I like it or not. You can walk away whenever you want. Are you gonna stick around? I'm still not clear on why you're here to begin with."

"Would you be willing to do us a favor, if it came down to it?"

Not really. "Fine."

She nodded. "Fine. I'll be there."

"Thanks. Should we exchange numbers?"

"No, the line wouldn't be secure. Don't worry, if I need you, I'll find you."

"Great." Making deals with creatures of the night was getting to be a bad habit. In no mood for more conversation, I left the room.

CHAPTER FIFTEEN

"WELL, AT LEAST you saved the rug rat," Swayze said as I snatched my talismans off my dresser. I had been regaling him with my many near-death experiences last night.

"True," I said, turning around. "But it's not over. If King Death was the one in that car, I don't believe for a second that crash was enough to kill him."

"I agree."

I felt a thrum of power as I slipped on my healing ring, surprised it was actually working. "He's still out there. And people are going to keep dying."

His whiskers twitched in something approaching sympathy. "Well, that's a wizard's life, pal. People around us get killed."

"I'm not gonna let that happen. I'm gonna do something about it."

"Such as?"

"I haven't quite gotten that far," I admitted.

He heaved a sigh of feline exasperation. "How far *have* you gotten?"

"Well, I have the beginnings of a plan."

"I hope you come up with something soon. Make sure and let

me know, so I can tell you what a bad idea it is. I would tell you to be careful, but I know that's a nonstarter. I don't like the way you're using magic, though: you're going through too much too fast. You're getting too banged up and it's gonna get harder to heal. You don't have enough experience to fight like this. It would be iffy even if you did. You're gonna burn yourself out if you keep this up, and then you're easy pickings."

"I know. I don't see what else I can do. I don't have a lot of choice."

"You gonna keep up appearances and go to school again today?"

"Sort of."

"More bad ideas, huh?"

"Nonsense. I'm just gonna talk to some people, figure out where things stand."

Swayze stood. "And on that note, I should get going. Gonna drop a line to a few connections of mine. Make those arrangements we talked about."

"Great. How are—"

Swayze meowed a word I didn't understand.

There was a ripple of power through the air. My open closet shimmered and vanished. In the rectangular opening I saw faint, warm light, heard discordant voices and music.

I stared at it. "Uh…. what?" I lifted an arm and pointed at it in bewilderment.

"I'll be back in a few." Tail aloft, he strutted towards the opening.

"You turned my closet into a portal."

He stopped and looked back. "I mean, yeah. It's not like it's the first time."

He walked through the opening and disappeared. A second later, there was another shimmer, and my closet was back where it was supposed to be. I glowered at it. *Cats.*

I guess there weren't any credible threats that day, because unfortunately, class was back in session. I kept noticing aches and pains as I walked, particularly from the wound in my abdomen, and knew the magic that kept them from being worse hadn't quite got the job done. Hopefully King Death would be polite enough to wait a week or two to make his move, when my reserves would be nice and replenished. At least there wasn't much damage to my face, which would have raised some awkward questions with my parents, though I'd put on a long-sleeve shirt to hide the ragged cuts on my arms. They'd been rather surprised to see me coming down the stairs that morning, since I was supposed to be hibernating at Jason's house, and I'd "explained" that Jason had driven me home late last night, without waking anyone, since I'd forgotten my backpack here, and of course, I couldn't go to school without my backpack. I managed to convince myself they believed it.

There were cops stationed in the parking lot when I arrived. I looked for Rodriguez but didn't see him. When I got inside, teachers were ranged around the halls, some along the walls, trying to look tough, others walking the halls, heads on a swivel. If trouble broke out, I didn't like their chances. Early this morning there had been a press release saying that Zack had been brought home safe thanks to "the great work of our police department," but that had had pretty much the effect I thought it would, which was none whatsoever. If the North Siders weren't furious before, which they were, now they were convinced some South Side gang members had kidnapped an adorable eight-year-old. A glance at social media on the way over told me that none of those cops had died, at least, although there were three in critical condition. People were abuzz with murky rumors of a high-speed chase. There had also been street fights and busted windows, plus a car lit on fire on the North Side. The same person who torched the bus, I wondered, or a copycat?

It was loud like it always was, as I walked to my locker, but the noise was different somehow, a different pitch, a different vibe. The voices that mingled together were harsh, tense, shaking with barely suppressed fear and tension in need of release. I threw my stuff into my locker, unable to disguise my own.

North Siders and South Siders roamed the halls, eying each other warily, though no one made a move yet. They weren't playing with fire, bringing school back in session, so much as lighting a torch and tossing it into the draperies. I wished they'd invested in a metal detector, too, and maybe some Marines and bomb-sniffing dogs.

I doubted much learning would get done today, from the way students glared at each other and teachers jumped out of their skin at every little noise, but I sat through algebra, because first hour is when the teachers take attendance, and send off the numbers to the Powers That Be. From that moment on, I was officially in school.

When class was over, I took advantage of the noise and crowds to slip out, into a back parking lot. I swiveled my head back and forth, trying to prepare an excuse in case somebody caught me, but I didn't see anybody, and made my way out into town without incident.

It took me longer, but I didn't take the most direct route; I stuck to side streets to avoid onlookers, and awkward questions like 'why aren't you in school?' and 'why are you practicing sorcery?' and finally made my way to the edge of town.

Out here, there were more trees and fields than houses. On the edge of the city limits, I made my way down a narrow, little-used street until I reached a rusted old gate, with a sign over it that read "Woodlawn Cemetery."

The place was small, and there weren't too many gravestones there, probably in the low double digits. It was secluded, set in a shadowy little clearing, and would have been easy to miss from the road. It was a serene enough place, not where you would expect a guy named King Death to hang out, even if it was a cemetery.

Still, I didn't care much for cemeteries these days.

I glanced around, but no one was watching, so I pushed through the gate and made my way inside. All the graves were old, cracked and worn down, most of them overgrown with weeds, a few completely on the ground. *What am I even looking for?*

There wasn't a church, office, or building of any kind nearby. Nowhere I could find some information. That was probably for the best anyway. Better to keep to myself at the moment.

I was still tense, ready to start firing away at the first sign of trouble; I had no way of knowing if King Death or his cronies were around. The longer I was there, however, the less nervous I felt. There wasn't a soul in sight, no sign of magic, no growling of demons. It eventually became clear I was alone, unless you counted the skeletons, and I relaxed.

Unsure what else to do, I wandered around, up and down the rows of tombstones, seeing nothing suspicious, hearing nothing but the occasional chirp of a bird from one of the big trees scattered here and there. The graves revealed nothing, just long-ago dates, and names I didn't recognize. Some were so old and worn the writing wasn't even visible. I didn't have any real plan when I came here; all I'd really planned to do was see if anything stuck out as unusual, and yet, I was still getting nowhere.

I was close to writing this off as the ramblings of a scared kid and an excuse to cut class when I felt it. Just a little flicker of magic; not even a flicker, really. A trace. A residue.

I stopped, peered down at the gravestone next to me. Albert Miller, it read. June 5, 1841-January 29, 1901. Was that significant? I had no idea.

With a little to go on, I increased the pace of my roaming,

feeling it again, more than once. The afterburn of magic; powerful magic; it had to be, to leave a trace even this small.

I still couldn't make out any rhyme or reason to it, so, on impulse, I trotted across the cemetery and clambered to the lower branches of one of the trees.

Surveying the stones laid out in front of me, I began calling up the memories of the ones where I'd felt the magic, marking them out in my mind.

There were five of them. A smile spread across my face as I picked them out.

As I made my way back across the cemetery, I felt my trepidation returning. There hadn't been much to worry about when I wasn't accomplishing anything. Now that I was getting somewhere, it was back to fight-or-flight.

I picked out the nearest of the tombstones to have set off my magical alarm bells. Again, there was nothing out of the ordinary about the marble slab. Hesitantly, I reached out to brush my fingers against it, opened my mind and let my senses stretch over the area.

I shuddered, as something like an electric shock zapped through my mind, causing me to flinch back a pace. It was the same feeling I'd had when I'd confronted Hex before; I was getting depressingly good at recognizing it.

This was where he made it, I realized. This was where he cooked the Hex. Take some good old-fashioned narcotics, bring them here, use the magic as gasoline on the proverbial fire, and pollute it with some bad, bad mojo.

It still didn't answer the question of why. Occam's razor seemed to suggest pure unscrupulousness, that His Deathly Majesty just wanted to make a quick buck and didn't care who he killed in the process. But try as I might, I couldn't quite believe that. Occam's razor doesn't usually apply to wizards.

I considered it from a different angle: pure maliciousness. Some sort of magical serial killer? That, I thought, was a disturbingly plausible new angle.

Some wizards get so deep into magic they don't even think of people *as* people anymore, just mere meat bags as opposed to their majestic power. Some wizards get so deep into magic they lose touch with reality altogether. The idea that some dark wizard might start killing people for sheer sport made more sense the more I thought about it. Of course, I thought, it simply had to be the most horrifying option. Of course, the worst-case scenario was the most likely one. It couldn't just be some run-of-the-mill drug dealer dabbling in things he didn't understand. It had to be a blood mage. A wizard who bypasses "dangerous" and "ruthless" and goes straight to "unstoppable nightmare," drunk on the kind of magic that has no purpose other than sheer bloodthirsty destruction. An enemy far more powerful, more intelligent, and more vicious.

I mulled over my next step and reluctantly returned to my original idea. I had another stop to make. I had made plenty of bad decisions lately, I figured. What was one more?

Williamsport City Hall, located in the historic downtown neighborhood, is a wide, four-story brick building, keeping the riffraff out with an ancient wrought iron fence. Though extensively renovated over the years, particularly after a vicious fire in the 1820s, it's one of the oldest buildings in town. Dad told me once it was also a brothel in the Eighteenth century, which is not something you should point out on a class trip.

It was really just a guess that made me come here; it seemed like a worse idea than usual to be roaming around The Bluffs at the moment and given that Alexandra said the entire city government was involved in the coverup, this seemed as good a place as any to put things into motion.

I had been nervous walking up here, but somehow, seeing this building, with all the secrets and power it represented, my nerves went away. My pace quickened, and I shoved through the double doors, fighting the temptation to make a grand entrance by simply blowing them off their hinges.

I vaguely remembered the layout of the building from that ill-fated class trip, so ignoring the bewildered receptionist, I moved deeper into the building, feet rapping against the tiled floor, then took the stairs to the next floor and examined plaques on doors until I got to the one that said "Mayor Seton."

I threw open the door.

A jowly, middle-aged white guy (are you sensing a theme?) looked up from his desk in confusion. His mouth dropped open.

"Good morning, Mr. Mayor."

He blinked several times. "Shouldn't you be in school?"

"Most likely. You know who I am by now, don't you?"

"Ah... I..."

"You know damn well who I am, and I know about your little cult."

He shook his head, trying to figure out how his day had gotten so screwed up so fast. I knew the feeling.

It was then I noticed Rick, standing in one corner, his arm in a sling, a chair overturned on the floor behind him, as if he'd leaped to his feet. On the other side of the room sat a uniformed guy I took for the police chief, due to his crew cut and blunt faced scowliness. His face was calmer, but he was clearly unsettled as well, and subtly touched the gun at his hip.

Magic instinctively roared to life in my veins, my gaze fixing on him. "I can kill you before you get it out of the holster."

He stared at me intently, hand still on his gun, but made no further moves. He didn't speak. The expression on his face could charitably be called "cautious."

I swung a glare toward Rick. "By the way, did this bastard tell you he tried to kill me last night?"

The mayor's head snapped toward Rick, and I knew he had neglected to mention that part of the story. Seton managed to regain a little composure. "What do you want here? Zack is home safe, we're all still alive, King Death is gone. It's over. Just move on with your life and forget we ever knew each other."

"You don't really think it's that simple, do you? King Death is still out there, and I'm pretty sure he's planning something a lot bigger than just slinging drugs."

The police chief was shaking his head. "No. We've investigated, and we feel certain the man calling himself 'King Death' is dead. Either one of the bodies we pulled out of that burned house, or the ones you killed on the street. The ones we've been able to ID all have a criminal history." He shook his head. "Jesus, you take juvenile delinquency to lofty new heights."

"That's kind of you to say, but he's not dead. It takes more than a car crash or a house fire to kill a blood mage. You don't even know what a blood mage is, do you?"

"We know exactly what a blood mage is," the chief snapped.

"But you've never fought one, have you?" I hoped no one thought to ask me if I had. "You don't know what they're capable of. You don't have anybody that can fight back. Except me."

The chief looked like he was about to keep arguing but the mayor held up a hand. "Hold on. We need to listen to what he has to say."

The mayor's face was corpse pale and I knew what Alexandra had said about Williamsport's Powers That Be was correct. Whatever supernatural know-how they'd once had, they'd gotten dangerously complacent, and despite their bluster, they were scared.

Well, that was mature of them. I decided for once, I'd show a little maturity myself, and told them the truth. I left out most of the gory details, along with several names to protect the innocent and/or guilty, but I gave them a solid summary of what I'd learned so far. They listened intently, Rick fuming silently but even he letting me talk. They tried to maintain that authoritative look of adult superiority, but I could see through it.

Finally, I got to the part about the graves, and you'd have thought I tossed a grenade into their laps.

Rick loudly demanded something I couldn't understand and didn't care about, the police chief leaped to his feet, and the mayor pushed his rolling chair back several feet, arms held up and stammering in denial. Jeez. I hadn't been expecting *that*. I waited a moment for them to settle down, then held up a tentative hand. "So, I guess you know the place?"

There was a moment of guilty, uncertain silence. "We know it," said the mayor.

"Don't," muttered the chief, with the voice of someone who knew it was futile but thought he should say something on principle.

"No," said Seton, voice exhausted. "This is important, and you know it." He turned a queasy gaze to me. "There are things buried in that cemetery."

"What kinds of things?"

"Bodies. Just like any other cemetery, but not quite." The look on his face was so guilty it was downright comedic. "Some of the people buried there... they're not exactly normal people. They're wizards. Like you."

"Go on."

"Blood mages, like you called them. People who used dangerous magic. Summoned demons, killed people. A wizard's body, even when they're dead—"

"Still has power," I said, recalling one of Swayze's lessons. "I know. You can combine the residual power with your own. Do all kinds of nasty stuff."

"The founders of this town knew how dangerous it would be if the bodies fell into the wrong hands. They brought them here, to keep them in one place, out of the hands of people who would use them to do harm."

"But why? A wizard's corpse is usually burned for that exact reason." Almost instantly, I realized the answer. "It wasn't about keeping people safe, was it? They wanted a power source. For themselves."

The mayor nodded gloomily; eyes lost. I could tell he wanted to argue but the words died in this throat. He had spent years hearing the positive, heroic version of that story, but he'd always known it was a lie, deep down, and I'd just confirmed it.

"Whatever they wanted back then, it doesn't matter now," he said. "What matters is that we're in danger. We all are."

"You can't believe anything this kid says," Rick burst out.

The mayor waved a hand in exasperation. "We don't have a choice. We can't take the risk of ignoring him. You know what he is, and so do I."

"Yeah, we know what he is and that's why we can't trust him," said the chief. "Wizards are nothing but trouble, every time."

"The trouble's already here, officer," I said, with more of a sneer than was strictly necessary.

The chief slammed a fist onto the desk. "We could make you disappear right here, kid."

I leaned forward, felt a rather manic smile creep across my face. "Really? Are you sure?"

There was a second's hesitation. No, they weren't sure. "That's actually the other reason I'm here," I said. "I've made a few arrangements. And if you kill me or throw me in jail, or if anything happens to Alexandra—" I singled out Rick for a poisonous look "—if anything happens to *anyone I know*, up to and including my cat, the entire world is gonna know about your setup here. It's in your best interest to make sure I live a long and happy life. You might even say it's necessary for your survival."

The mayor mustered a little courage. "Nobody would believe you. People aren't going to believe a conspiracy theory about demons and magic."

I really savored the next part. "*People* won't. But the 'world' I was talking about wasn't *our* world. It was the spirit world. As of about an hour ago, a friend of mine whispered in all the right ears, and if you make a move on me, they'll all start singing like demonic canaries, and word will spread through every realm there is. See, what you probably don't know about demons is that they have enemies. If you're working with one, you're automatically the enemy of a few more. And a bunch of human chumps are always easy pickings. I'm guessing whatever monstrosities you got your-selves involved with didn't mention that. And I'm guessing they won't be very happy if your little arrangement is public knowledge, either. After that, it's pretty much a crapshoot who eats you first."

There was stunned silence and deciding I could hardly ask for a more dramatic exit, I turned to go. "I don't like King Death any more than you do. Keep me in the loop, and I'll do the same. Something'll be going down soon."

"And why should we believe that?" Rick called after me.

I opened the door. "I don't know, Rick. Quit being such a whiny bitch."

Despite my bluster, I didn't have much intention of keeping them in the loop, and I knew they didn't either. Still, as Eressen pointed out, this was beyond me. If absolutely necessary, I might have to ask for their help and I hoped they'd have the sense to do the same. I wasn't optimistic. At least maybe they'd put the cemetery under surveillance, keep King Death from making more party favors.

As I walked away from city hall, I decided there was one more stop I should make, that I'd forgotten amidst all the violence. I pulled out my phone and placed a very long and very boring call to the Williamsport police station. By the end of it I'd gotten a line on Rodriguez and swung left on Clark Street to meet him for lunch.

Nancy's Diner is one of Williamsport's more pleasant venues.

Located off Main Street, it's on the North Side but lacks the servant-slapping sophistication most venues have on that side of town.

I deposited myself in a booth and ordered a cheeseburger and fries. I only had to wait a few minutes for Rodriguez. The bell clanged and he came in, still in uniform, trying to look like he wasn't up to no good. He didn't seem to have much practice.

He scanned the room, spotted me, and sat down across from me. His dark eyes were serious, but still surprisingly friendly, given the circumstances. "What's the situation?" he said without preamble.

"Just lovely," I said. I hesitated a bit, unsure how much I should say. He seemed like an honest guy, but however nice he might be personally, he was still part of the town's coverup.

Could I trust him? Maybe not, but I found I trusted him slightly more than the jackasses I'd talked to earlier. It could help to have someone dependable on the inside, someone who might be more interested in saving lives than covering his ass, and I got the feeling Rodriguez was that guy.

So, I told him the truth. Again, I left out a number of details, tried to downplay the level of... controversy I'd had with the town's aristocracy, particularly his boss, but by the time I finished, I'd given him an overview of the last few days and a pretty good idea of why we were in Deep Shit.

Aside from a brief pause for a waitress to take his order, he barely said a word. I took several breaks to tear into my food; I felt like I'd barely eaten lately, while he hardly touched his.

When I finished, he stared at me balefully. "So, is that all?" His voice was weak.

I chuckled. "Yeah, that's about it."

He stared through the far wall. "Huh. They didn't cover most of this at the academy."

I attacked my burger again. "Really? I figured you wouldn't be too surprised. I know the cops are in on it, so you don't need to deny that part."

"You're right, to a point. I've only been here a little over a year. When they recruited me, they made it clear early on that this wasn't your average police department." He chuckled without humor. "They made it sound so patriotic and noble, and I ate it up. Oh, sure, protect the streets from those supernatural predators that are just waiting to kill innocent people, be a hero." He shook his head. "I got swept up in it but it's not really like that. The only thing this department cares about is protecting the businesses and the politicians from those dirty poor people on the South Side. I've never seen any of that stuff they talk about, although I know some of the other guys have. It's all pretty hush-hush, even for those that know about it. After a while, I kinda got in denial. Never saw any werewolves or vampires or whatever, so I could almost convince myself they were hazing the rookie or something. Until now."

"So why stick around?"

He shrugged. "I don't know. Thought about transferring to a big city department but I always wanted to be a cop in a smaller town. I've got to know people around here, it's home. And believe it or not, there *are* actual crimes once in a while. Like delinquent teenagers that flee the scene of a crime."

"And King Death."

His face darkened. "Yeah, and him."

"What do you actually know about this guy? I've been chasing him for days and I feel like I'm worse off than when I started."

"We don't know much more. Like you heard, we wrote him off as some urban legend all the dealers told each other. It was always 'my cousin's friend's brother saw him turn himself into a bat' or something like that. Still, they did investigate. The drugs were real enough. It's fairly recent that they've started killing people. They can do freaky stuff. We don't even know what they are."

"They're regular street drugs, hexed with magic, hence the name."

Rodriguez shivered. "I still can't quite make myself believe this is real. I don't want to." He gave me a frown. "But somehow... it's fascinating, you know what I mean? I mean, I thought this stuff was a myth my whole life."

I mustered up a sympathetic smile. "Yeah, I remember that exact feeling."

"You're a..." He lowered his voice. "A wizard. What is this stuff? What can we do about it?"

"To answer your first question, what magic can do to people depends on two things: what you're trying to do with it, and where you get it."

I could see the wheels turning behind his eyes, his cop instincts kicking in despite everything. "And this guy's doing something bad with it."

"Maybe, but I think it's the latter more than the former. I think he's reaching into some *really* sketchy other dimension and taking its power directly or he's made himself a deal with a very, *very* nasty spirit or demon or something. Maybe both, for all I know. And since I'm delivering such terrible news, to answer your second question, I have no idea what to do about it, other than stopping him."

He stared gloomily down at his food. "I'm starting to regret asking."

"Is there anything else you know, anything that might help us?"

"I'm not sure. You know about his calling card already. That hasn't gotten us any closer to tracking him down. Jeez, I really shouldn't be talking about an ongoing investigation with a teenager."

"A *wizard* teenager no less. So, why are you?"

He looked up towards the ceiling. "Because you're right: the people in charge can't handle this, and we need all the help we can get. I'm scared and I don't mind admitting it."

"Neither do I."

"The theory was he was a figurehead of some sort, just a myth a bunch of dealers cooked up to keep us chasing our tails. Now that doesn't seem to be the case. Two things we learned that might be of interest: one, we thought he might be one of the students at your school, or some of his dealers were, anyway. Most of the users are teenagers, so it made sense."

"I don't know. We have our share of drug dealers but I'm not sure any of them are masters of the dark arts. What's the other thing?"

"That there's a connection to the South Side. Not too surprising in itself, but we think it has something to do with the Sixth Street Aces in particular."

"The Sixth Street Aces? You think they're behind this?"

"Actually, just the opposite. Whoever King Death is, we're certain he's not one of them."

"Why?"

"Because they've dropped off the face of the earth. When Hex first showed up, before it lit the town on fire, ground zero was Sixth Street Aces territory. Kind of a trial balloon, we think. And the Sixth Street Aces didn't do a thing. You'd think if another dealer moved in on their territory, they'd try and retaliate. But they didn't. They disappeared. We've hardly seen them on the street in months now."

"You think they're hiding from him."

"Exactly."

"I don't like the sound of somebody that can make the Sixth Street Aces go hide in their basements."

"Neither do I."

"What about the others, the Black Nines or SSK, people like that?"

"They haven't dropped off the face of the earth like the Aces did, but they don't seem to be doing much actual crime lately. They're laying low; some of them probably even joined the Reapers. Especially the smaller gangs, the ones nobody really takes seriously. And there have been six unsolved murders of gang members over the past few months."

"People who crossed the Reapers."

"I suspect so."

I sucked in a breath and let it out. "As depressing and horrifying as all this is, I think it helps. I have a place to start. I'm at square two, instead of square one, anyway. There are things I can do the police can't. Hopefully, I can track him down, stop him there before he does any more damage."

"You talking about killing him?"

I hesitated, then shrugged. "That's the plan."

"I really ought to give you some speech about how I'll arrest you if you do anything like that, but I'm pretty sure procedure is out the window. I want to help."

"If you want to help, keep your eyes open. Don't go after King Death, at least not without every cop in the city backing you up. You'll just get yourself killed. But you need to be ready. I don't know what he's got planned next, but King Death's not done yet. Just make sure everybody's on the lookout."

"I can do that. Anonymous tip, or something, if I need to."

"Great." We exchanged numbers. I stood, then hesitated.

He smiled. "Don't worry, I got the tab."

"Thanks."

"You're a brave guy," he said. "Trying to take this on by yourself. Don't worry. We'll get you some help, sort this out."

I allowed myself to think he might be right. "Thanks."

"Good luck, kid."

"Oh yeah. My name is Sam. Sam Adams."

"John Rodriguez. Good luck, Sam."

"You, too."

I opened the door, the bell above it clanged, and I hit the streets again.

Believe it or not, at a loss for something else to do, I went back to school.

By the time I made my way back and reinfiltrated the place, it was getting late in the day. I wondered if I'd had any homework.

I had been expecting trouble, but there didn't seem to be much other than grumbles and sullen looks. Asking around told me there had been a few scuffles, but nothing major. I wondered if that meant things were blowing over or the calm before the storm, and nearly burst out laughing.

As I made my way into sixth hour as if I'd been there all day, right where a young wizard was supposed to be, my mind churned over what Rodriguez had said.

Come to think of it, I hadn't seen any of the Sixth Street Aces around school so far. I had flirted, very briefly, with the idea of charging after them right away, but no, I wasn't quite ready for that. I needed to think, maybe come up with some kind of good idea for once. It would be better if I had Elise with me, but she couldn't come out in the daytime, and I wasn't willing to wait. Besides, on the way back from Nancy's, I'd gotten a text from Jason. "Need 2 talk," it said, "Important. Where r u?" I needed to touch base with him, see what fresh hell this would be. I surreptitiously pulled my phone free and fired off a text. "I'm here. When u want 2 meet?"

The reply was almost instantaneous, which was worrying. "Soon as school is over. Library."

Sixth hour was nearing its close when my phone vibrated again. I figured it was Jason at first, until I saw everyone else in the class getting similar texts. *Good God, now what?* The teacher shot anxious glances at the noise as the bell rang and we began to make our way out. After leaving the classroom, I found a semi-quiet corner, scrolled through the texts that had gone ping-ponging around the school.

And yeah, this wasn't good. I'd go as far as to call it bad.

Some genius, it wasn't clear who, had got the bright idea to hold something of an impromptu memorial for Reggie, and the event had spread like wildfire. Then some enterprising South Siders had gotten wind of the news and decided they simply had to have the same thing for Nina. It was a recipe for, well, disaster wasn't a strong enough word.

I never thought I'd find myself rooting for the school's authority figures, but Jesus Christ, wasn't there anything they could do about this?

Almost immediately I answered my own question. No. There wasn't a damn thing they could do. There were simply too many of us and too few of them, and the only thing that might momentarily distract them from killing each other was the prospect of a common enemy.

Was this what Jason had been worried about? I didn't know.

At least this crisis didn't seem to involve any magic: I could just hunker down in the library or somewhere until the storm passed. Most probably it wouldn't be as bad as I was expecting anyway.

I laughed aloud, earning me a strange look from a teacher passing by. I laughed so hard I had to lean back against some lockers. I shook my head to keep tears from forming in my eyes and began hustling for the library.

It wouldn't be as bad as I was expecting. Oh sure. Because that had been such a pattern lately. I snorted again, shaking my head at my wacky sense of humor. Once I'd composed myself, I pulled out my phone, texted Ella: "where r u?"

"Hiding in the book closet in the English room," she replied. "Don't tell anybody."

"Definitely will," I shot back. "Stay there. Gonna hide out myself. We'll meet up after school."

It quickly became clear this wasn't going to blow over: people were speaking at a fever pitch, coalescing into groups, ignoring occasional shouts from teachers to knock it off. I picked up the pace. The library, I realized, was too far away and I should have thought of some other hiding place.

Teachers stuck their heads out of doors like nervous prairie dogs. I saw Mr. Perkins leaning out his door, classroom phone pressed tight against his ear, probably calling for backup. Who he thought would show up, I had no idea.

I saw a crowd ahead of me, talking and mingling around a tangled mass of color. My stomach dropped as I recognized it. It was the makeshift memorial Reggie's friends had set up around his locker, now emptied of its contents by administration. Flowers, cards, memorabilia I couldn't make out, a heap of love and loss spilling out into the hall. Nina's locker had looked the same, I remembered. The same way Abby's had looked. The memory came roaring back: it had been massive, cards, flowers, stuffed animals. All things she would have liked, if she hadn't been too dead to enjoy them, stuff nobody would have thought to get her if she hadn't been. I had wanted to put something there, intended to, but nothing I'd thought of had seemed right, and I'd put it off until it was gone. Our relationship in a nutshell. I should have gotten a teddy bear, I thought. She would have liked a teddy bear.

"You okay man?" I looked around, saw Brian standing in front of me, uncharacteristic concern on his face. I realized why he was looking at me that way: my face was wet. I swiped at it. "Uh, yeah, I'm fine, thanks."

I began walking away before he could say any more, picking my way through the crowd. I had just about got clear, when my stomach found another reason to drop: Reggie and Nina's lockers, I realized, were way too close together.

Not a problem when they were alive. Maybe that was even how they'd gotten together, passing by each other every day until one of them decided to flirt. But now, it was bad, bad news, because just a little way down the hall Nina's friends and family from the South Side had congregated around her own locker.

And yes, the two sides had noticed each other.

And yes, yours truly was caught smack in between.

The symbolism around here was getting ridiculous.

Hemmed in, I watched as people went nose to nose, spitting insults, the hall filling with an overlapping tangle of angry voices. I saw Kev Mitchell, a South Sider built like a tree trunk lean forward and sneer something at Rob Masters, a North Sider built like something significantly smaller than a tree trunk. I couldn't make out what he said, but I guess it was what you'd call fighting words: hate swept across Rob's face, then there was an open pocketknife in his hand and he gouged it into Kev's thigh.

Kev screamed, then they all surged forward, straight at each other and me. I let out a squawk, then they collided. Fists flew, bodies bashed together, and I was buffeted back and forth violently, bouncing off people and lockers.

I flailed around, trying to kick and shove people away from me before I got murdered. It wasn't working. I had gotten away with throwing magic during the chaos at the rave, but I didn't want to try that here: too many people in too close a space. Unfortunately, that left fighting my way out.

With nothing else to do, I plunged into the madness.

With all the aggression I could muster, I bashed my way through the press, arms flailing, trying to bob and weave. There were screams, people clawing at each other, going down in heaps. I saw a South Sider slam a North Sider into the lockers, only to be clubbed to the ground from behind. Then I couldn't even tell who was who.

The hallway was a screaming tangle of thrashing bodies. There was no strategy, just sheer blind murderousness. Someone went down directly in front of me, being kicked by his opponent, forcing me to adjust my course. Up and down the hallway people fought, and the damn thing seemed endless. A multitude of endless crashes and bangs filled the air, people slamming against the lockers, and anything that wasn't nailed down flew through the air. I took a couple hard knocks in the head, sending me reeling but I managed to keep on my feet and keep moving. The third time it happened, it inspired me to risk enough magic to put my shields up. A glance around the hallway told me the teachers, it seemed, had wised up and locked their doors. A couple hadn't got the job done: the shop door stood open, Mr. Baker crawling out the damn window, while a few people ran inside and started knocking desks over.

I passed two girls rolling on the floor yanking at each other's hair, someone getting an MMA-style ground and pound (that sounds so dirty), another pair exchanging punches boxing-style. I pushed and shoved and growled and cursed and threw elbows, shoving aside anyone who crossed my path. Every so often a bloody face would wander by.

At last, I shoved a pair of wrestling, grunting figures out of the way, got into open air, sucked down a deep breath and started running. I went down the stairs, clear of fighters, at least, then down to the next hallway, where things were little better.

People were ranged all over the halls now, apparently having spilled out of classrooms. It hadn't turned into a full-scale slugfest yet but pushing and shoving was already breaking out.

The one silver lining in this ridiculous cloud was that people were spaced out here, the hallways being not nearly as packed. I picked up my pace as the cops from outside, a few of the braver teachers stormed into the fray. I wasn't interested in sticking around to see what happened next. I bolted.

Not seeing a lot of directions to run, I turned a corner more or less at random and collided with someone. They didn't even attack me; it was pure bad luck.

With a grunt, I went flying down the hallway, skidding across the tiles and into some lockers, banging my head, shoulder, knee, ribs, and elbow in no particular order.

I groaned, flailing around like a fish. "Sam?"

"Huh?" A door creaked open next to me, and I scrambled towards it.

"Come on, Sam." Someone grabbed me by the shoulder and pulled me in. The door slammed behind us. It was McKinley, panting, as he fumbled with the lock. His sixth hour class was gathered inside, apparently not having stormed out to do battle, watching us with bewildered eyes. A few other students stood around, apparently refugees like me.

I tossed an anxious glance at the door, hoping it stayed good and locked. I could still hear the sounds of fighting outside. "Thanks," I panted.

McKinley's face was slack with fear. "Don't mention it," he said.

We lurked around in McKinley's classroom the rest of the day, leaving the rest of the school to sort out its own problems. More cops finally showed up, administered some tazings, and made off with the few perps they could catch. As might be imagined, school dismissed early, though not by much, by the time the lockdown was over. I could have sworn I heard a collective sigh of relief when Archibald

J. Keller High finally expelled its denizens to go have their battles somewhere else, where it would be someone else's problem.

Unfortunately, I had somehow become that "someone else."

Jason was waiting in the library when I arrived, quiet amidst the hustle and bustle of the school winding down for the day. I spotted him in one of the big reading chairs, leaned forward, face a mask of tension. "Shouldn't you be at football practice?" I said, hoping to start the conversation with something neutral.

He turned to regard me. "No one is going to football practice today," he said, "and do you wanna know why?" His face was uncharacteristically serious again. Almost mature. It was frightening.

"Not really. I'm guessing it has something to do with death and destruction." I sat across from him.

"Yeah, you could say that. That's why I need your help. Because you're reasonable."

"I'm what?"

He almost smiled. "I mean, you don't want this war to happen any more than I do."

"How can I help with that?"

His face tightened. "I don't know. But I can't do it on my own, and you're the only one who'll listen to me. I'm not explaining this the right way." He rubbed his face. "I heard some of my friends talking today. I don't know what they're gonna do exactly, but... they're forming some kind of a posse."

"A *posse?* You mean, like, with horses?"

"Probably not horses. You may not know this, but somebody threw some kind of homemade bomb at the police station today. A couple South Siders got jumped, put in the hospital. And there was a drive-by at Trevor's dad's dealership. Bunch of windows got shot out, and his dad was there, and he got hit."

I recalled the easygoing face of the guy I'd met at the beach. "Oh God. Bad?"

"No. He's gonna be okay. Got hit by shrapnel and he needed some stitches. Trevor went berserk when he found out. I was there. Threw a chair across the room. Started screaming about how he was gonna make the South Side pay, that it was time we stopped letting them 'get away with their bullshit.' And a lot of people agreed with him. Especially after Zack got kidnapped. Even people who didn't want to fight before lost it when that happened. They're going to gather up more people and then they're gonna do it."

"When?"

"Pretty much now."

I rubbed my face. "Damn. Okay. Do you know what they're gonna do?"

"From what I heard, they're gonna drive into the South Side en masse and start throwing rocks through windows, jumping people they pass by, stuff like that."

"Basically, mailbox baseball, but with people."

"Exactly."

"Sounds like they're gonna all meet up somewhere before they go. Do you have any idea where that would be?"

"No, but I can find out." He produced his phone, exchanged a couple texts with Kyle, then looked up. "They're getting together at Trevor's house. Kyle said he was glad I'd changed my mind about going with them."

I stood. "Okay. Let's go."

"What are we gonna do?"

"I don't know. I was hoping we'd think of something on the way over there. I'd tell you not to get involved, but you wouldn't listen."

"Nah. That's why I called you. Because the cops wouldn't do anything, and my parents would have just told me to stay out of it. I knew you wouldn't do that."

"Good thing you have a friend that lacks so much common sense."

He erupted with laughter, his dark mood momentarily vanished, then became serious again. "I'm sorry I got you into this. I wasn't sure if I should, but I just didn't know what else to do."

"Don't worry about it. It'll be exciting. I feel like the sheriff in an old-timey western. Where's Trevor's house, anyway?"

It wasn't far. We scooped up Ella as we left, her having emerged unscathed from the book closet. "There's about to be trouble," I told her as Jason drove.

"What are you talking about?"

"Some North Siders are about to head into the South Side and start attacking people."

"*Attacking* people?"

"Yeah. I don't think they're heading our way but stay in the house, do you hear me? Stay in the house."

"He's right, Small One," Jason said as he pulled up next to our house. "This isn't just obnoxious big brother stuff. You gotta stay safe."

Her eyes roamed back and forth between us. "Okay, okay, fine. I'll stay put."

She climbed out of the car, looked back at us. "How are you even involved in this?" she said. Jason had the sense to roar away before I had to answer.

A few minutes later, we were there, on a wide, tree-lined street on the North Side, a few blocks away from the bridge that led to the soon-to-be battleground. The drive over had been strangely pleasant. Sure, I was anxious, and yet, the impending terrorist attack was almost a relief compared to what I'd been dealing with. Just good old-fashioned North Side/South Side theatrics. It was refreshing, a temporary respite from impending magical doom.

We pulled over on the curb. Ahead of us, I saw teenagers milling around, many of them carrying bats, tire irons, chains, stuff like that. Three pickup trucks parked nearby seemed to be the assault vehicles. We both sat there a moment, studying them.

"They look a little more organized than I'd thought," I said glumly.

"Yeah. Trevor is smart. I get the feeling that he cooled down a little, but instead of calling the whole thing off, he started planning."

"Terrific."

"Last chance to back out," Jason said. "Maybe I could talk to them, make some of them see reason anyway."

"Nah. My family lives on the South Side, remember? I don't want these goons tearing the place up any worse than it already is. People could get killed if this goes sideways."

"I've been thinking about that ever since I heard about it. They go over there, start attacking people, the South Siders realize what's going on. You know they have tons of guns over there; they start shooting, and Trevor... I don't think even getting shot at would be enough to make him back down. The North Siders fight back, cops show up, bystanders get hit."

"A bloodbath."

"Then it really gets bad. Both sides lose people. Stuff like this starts happening all the time, on both sides."

"Full-blown Williamsport apocalypse."

"Yeah. They'll tear each other apart."

All my ideas about how this was a kinder, gentler emergency fled. Suddenly my mouth was dry, and my head was spinning. King Death, I thought, as a cold weight settled at the bottom of my stomach, knew Williamsport was a powder keg waiting for an excuse to go off. Just light all the right fuses and people would be too busy going after each other to go after him. "Well, we won't do anything sitting around here talking. Lousy bastards."

We piled out of the car, walking down the street, towards the gathering. I hoped we looked confident, like a couple of gunslingers walking towards a showdown, to continue with the western metaphor. I didn't feel like it. "What are we actually gonna do?" I whispered.

"I was hoping you might have some ideas. If we can't talk them out of it, it might get physical."

I actually gulped. I didn't know people did that in real life. "Right. Physical. And if that happens my, uh, hobby is gonna give us an edge."

"Right."

It was best for both of us, I figured, that we didn't talk about my magic much. And yet, it had never bothered him, not once. Perhaps that was why I found myself walking into a showdown in a cul-de-sac with him.

By then, people had begun to notice our presence. I saw Kyle step out from the pack. "I'm glad you're here," he said. "Ready to kick some ass?"

He glanced at me, and I expected him to have a fit about a South Sider crashing their exclusive event, but he barely seemed to notice I was there. He didn't even look at Jason in expectation of an answer. Instead, he looked worried, distracted. He hadn't had the determination and enthusiasm that usually accompanies the phrase "ready to kick some ass?" Brian appeared over his shoulder, and he didn't look much better.

"You're having second thoughts," I ventured. "I mean, you guys have a history of douchebaggery, but not a history of violence."

"He's right," Jason said. "You don't have to do this. Come on, just leave with us."

Kyle's gaze hardened. "No. I'm sorry, we can't." I found this new side of Kyle extremely disturbing. "If we don't do something now, they'll never leave us alone."

"Can't you see this'll just make everything worse?" Jason said. "You're gonna get yourselves killed."

"You decided to join us."

It was Trevor. Again. Talking to him twice in the same week was just too often.

"Yeah, I decided to join you," Jason said. "To tell you what a godawful idea this is. Come on, you're gonna get people killed and you know it."

"Yeah. South Siders."

"You're talking about a war."

"The war's already started. Time to start fighting it." His gaze swung to me. "What the hell are you doing here?"

"Magic tricks," I declared.

"He's trying to save people's lives, the same as I am, including yours," Jason said.

He glowered at me. "You just keep showing up, don't you?"

"By any chance, are you related to a guy named Rick?" I said.

"Who?"

"You just have a resemblance to this other North Sider I met."

"Sam, shut up," Jason muttered.

Trevor returned his reptilian gaze to Jason. "You should join us. We're protecting your family too."

"There's a guy over there with a potato gun," Jason said acidly. Chris Greenberg, who I would have pegged as a nerdy AV Club type, shouldered the weapon and shifted uncomfortably, where he stood on a tailgate. "Yeah, I feel real protected."

"You're not gonna stop us, either one of you," he shot a predatory glance at me again. "So, get out of the way while you still can."

"Drop dead," Jason said.

I stepped closer to stand shoulder to shoulder with him, giving Trevor a smirk. "Yeah, I think you'd be a lot safer if you went and found a polo match or something."

Trevor punched me in the face.

I sprawled, rolling over in the street and landing haphazardly on the sidewalk.

From starry eyes, I saw Jason lunge out and land a right in Trevor's face that sent him flying backwards, bouncing off a tailgate and hitting the ground in a heap. A hand thrust in my face, and I was surprised to see Kyle there.

Gratefully, I took his hand, and between the two of us, we got me back on my feet, cheek throbbing.

There were murmurs around us, worried looks. I knew these guys liked Jason; they didn't want to go against him.

As I watched, Trevor lurched up and collided with Jason, sending them both back to the ground. Shouts rose up all around us, more anxious than celebratory. I'd never seen Jason in a fight in my life, and I stared, agog, as the two of them rolled over and over, trading punches.

The fight ended undramatically: Jason was on top, seeming to get the better end of things, but Trevor slammed an elbow into the side of his head that sent him sprawling away.

Trevor stumbled to his feet. Jason didn't. Trevor raised his arms, shouting. "Come on, let's go, let's go." Voices rose in a clamor and people began scrambling around the streets. Some of them did, anyway. Some stood around, uncertain, anxious, casting glances at each other, at Jason, who groaned and stirred and started to rise. Trevor spotted this, stepped in, and drove a foot into his ribs, sending him back down hard.

Before I quite realized what was happening, I'd lunged off the sidewalk onto the street. I threw a lance of levitation at Trevor before I'd stopped moving. I wasn't being very precise. I cracked a window in a car, causing someone to jump and swivel their head to stare at it, wondering what the hell that could have been, but it caught Trevor in a glancing blow that bounced him against a truck.

He whirled, eyes blazing, probably thinking I'd shoved him or something. His mouth twisted to spout some threat, but I got there first to stand over Jason. "Stay the fuck away from him," I snarled, feeling a little spittle leak from my mouth, "or I'm gonna rip your goddamn lungs out of your chest and light you on fire."

Trevor quivered, not from fear, unfortunately, but from unadulterated rage. His eyes had gone completely feral. Then he hissed, reached into his waistband, and pulled out a gun, small, black, aimed at my face. There were shouts of fear, and from the corner of my eye I saw people flinching away. Nobody had banked on getting involved in this.

"Son of a bitch," growled Trevor.

I stared down the barrel of a gun, wanting only to rip him apart, not anywhere near as scared as I ought to be. I was too wound up on testosterone and magic, having faced death too many times lately, to have the proper perspective on this sort of thing.

I knew he was on the edge of pulling the trigger. I didn't know if I could pull off levitation on him without getting my brains blown out. And as Trevor's body tensed, like he was about to fire, in the tiny window I had before things got upsetting, I hit on an idea that might be smarter.

No sooner than the spell had spun to life in my mind, I released it, straight into Trevor.

Looking shocked, he dropped his gun and darted back, then turned and took off running down the street. Around him, several others did the same, one of them diving into a car and peeling away. It seemed the spell had used a little too much juice.

Those still around looked flabbergasted, unsure what to do. "It's over," I called out. "Go home." Slowly, bewilderedly, they began doing so. I turned and began helping Jason to his feet. "Are you all right?"

"I'm fine," he grunted. "What did you do?"

"A fear spell," I said. "It makes you, uh, scared, as you can see."

He studied the rapidly emptying street. Off to one side, Brian nudged Trevor's gun along the ground with his foot until he deposited it in a storm drain. "Are they gonna be okay?"

"Yeah. They'll start to calm down in a few minutes, and a few minutes after that, it'll wear off and they'll wonder what they were so scared about to begin with. A few minutes after that, and the memories will just kinda fade out, like something that happened a long time ago but doesn't seem very important now."

His eyes roamed the deserted street. "Fascinating."

"Totally harmless."

He sighed raggedly. "Well, it's better than the alternative, that's for sure. Come on, we gotta go before the cops show up."

We piled into his car and got the hell out of Dodge.

Jason turned onto my street, heading for my house. "Thanks again," he said. "If you hadn't been there…"

"Forget it."

"That would have been really bad today. People would have died."

"But they didn't."

"I know, but what happens next time, and the time after that? You won't always be around to cast spells at these people. I damn sure didn't get anywhere talking to them."

"That's not necessarily true," I said. "I think Kyle and Brian would have changed their minds when it mattered, and I know for a fact a lot more North Siders weren't there than were."

"True."

"You gonna fight for the North Side if it comes down to it?"

"I don't know. I may not have much of a choice. My friends from the South Side aren't even talking to me, except you."

"Jason, don't get involved, you'll get yourself killed, and we don't need any more of a body count."

"But it's like I said. I may not have much choice."

"I know the feeling."

"What do you mean?"

"Nothing," I said, hoping he would buy it. He didn't.

"Sam, do you know something about this? What's going on?"

I hesitated, but no, it was time for the truth. "There's this drug dealer, King Death, leader of the Reapers."

He nodded. "Yeah. Thought it was a ghost story."

It is. "It's true. He's involved somehow. He's the one who took Zack. He's trying to start a war. I don't know why."

"Well, he's succeeding."

"I know."

He studied me. "And you're gonna try and stop him. Because he's magic-related."

"'Try' being the operative word. And yes, he is. Sorry I didn't tell you about it sooner, but it's been one of those weeks."

Fear crossed his face, but he shook it away as best he could. "Let me help."

"I knew you'd say something like that. If you want to help, the best thing you can do is get everybody talking to each other. You said you have friends on both sides, and I know it's true. People like you because you're honest, they trust you. Maybe you can use that. Try and get some goodwill, talk people out of fighting each other. King Death, he's the real enemy here and the North and South are both playing right into his hands."

He shot a tongue across his lips. "Okay. I'll try."

"Just don't stick your neck out too far."

"Take your own advice, okay? I know you have a reputation for helping people out, but don't let it get you killed."

"I didn't know I had that reputation." Something tugged at the back of my mind, lost in the shuffle of this week's madness. "Jason, is there something happening? I mean, is there something the school has planned, something we're supposed to do?"

"I don't know. Maybe." His face turned sour. "The back-to-school dance?"

I read his mind with growing dread. "Don't tell me they're still having it. After the riot today?"

He nodded. "Yeah. Saw it on their Facebook page. Said they weren't gonna let a few delinquents ruin it for everybody else, or something like that."

I sighed and looked at the ground. "Of course they are." I really shouldn't be surprised Williamsport was more interested in the appearance of normalcy than anything else. "Who the hell would go to a dance *now*," I wondered to no one in particular.

Jason shrugged. "You and I are pretty much the only people at our school who know about the magic stuff. Everybody else just thinks the North and South are at each other's throats, and that's nothing out of the ordinary. Some people are gonna go just to look for trouble."

I groaned. He was right. "Well, they'll find some. You should stay home, at least." I was seized by certainty that King Death would hit the place. I had no proof. No evidence, no magical powers at work letting me see the future. But I was certain.

His voice was mild. "Won't do any good at home. Besides, I already got my suit dry-cleaned. What about you?"

"I don't know. Maybe?"

"Guess I'll see you then."

I wanted to talk him out of it but doubted it would do any good. "Yeah. See ya."

Looking disturbed, he drove away and disappeared around a corner.

Maybe I wouldn't need to talk him out of it. It seemed like a long shot, but I didn't have much to lose by trying. I pulled out my phone and got the mayor on the line. "You have to cancel the back-to-school dance," I said in way of greeting.

I swear, I heard him shake his head. "You don't understand, Sam," he said. "We know exactly what we're doing."

"You can see why I might find that hard to believe."

"Despite what you may think, we're not complete incompetents. We know the Reapers go after crowded, public places like this. And we know you must have shaken him up after last night. He'll be getting desperate. That's what we're counting on."

"Why don't I like the sound of that?"

"We'll have officers stationed at the school, at other high-profile locations around town. And when the Reapers make their move, we'll be waiting."

I struggled to speak. "So, they're BAIT?"

I heard him swallow, apparently unaccustomed to being bellowed at. "Uh, no, of course not—"

I clenched a fist, waved it by my head ridiculously. "Do you have any idea how many people could die even *if* that works? How many will die if it doesn't?"

"I—"

"And you know he causes diversions when he attacks, did you think of that?"

"Sam, you can't screw this up—"

I hung up the phone. *Okay. Pull yourself together.* I took several deep breaths. I needed to stop King Death now. Before he had a chance to pull anything. And I would, I assured myself. Totally. No question.

Help.

CHAPTER SIXTEEN

THERE ARE THINGS teenagers know that cops don't. I'd go as far as to say there's a *lot* of things teenagers know that cops don't.

The one that mattered at the moment concerned the Sixth Street Aces. I had a feeling they hadn't gone quite as deep underground as Rodriguez believed.

To my surprise, it wasn't even four o'clock; the confrontation with Trevor had seemed to last a couple days. But no, there was plenty of time for my next terrible idea.

Ella had texted me earlier, demanding to know "wtf is going on?"

"Nothing," I replied, "I'm fine, it all blew over." With Ella as satisfied as she was likely to get, I turned left on my street and began heading where angels fear to tread.

I passed the street where I turn to go to school, went several more blocks, then jaywalked past an intersection. That's where things get spooky: the pleasant backyards and picket fences disappear, and give way to run-down auto repair shops, shady antique dealers, bars, payday loan places, and my personal favorite, a two-story of indeterminate color billing itself as "Global Finance."

Then you get to Lodge Street. If you get a little taste of the South Side experience before, that's the real jumping off point.

Without hesitating (much) I plunged in.

I try not to spend much time down here, but it was nominally safe during the daytime. Still, I squared my shoulders and quickened my pace, trying to adopt a sufficiently intimidating look, to make sure I didn't look like easy prey.

In truth, it wasn't that scary; just run-down houses and trailers mostly, and I had to wonder how much of its fearsome reputation was true. *Enough to get the job done.*

A few people shuffled by, sometimes looking at me funny, but nobody messed with me as I made my way further south.

When I finally stepped under a narrow, graffiti-soaked overpass, most prominently showing an ace of spades with a 6 in the middle, I knew I was in the right neighborhood. Then I stopped short as I passed another symbol, subtler, easier to miss on the bridge's underside. It wasn't like someone was marking their territory, but like they were being sneaky: with far more precision than you'd expect from a street gang's graffiti artists, a colorful death card was splashed across the dirty grey concrete. Apparently, there was a new sheriff in town. Just when you thought the South Side couldn't get any more dangerous. I walked on, more alert now.

I didn't know the area well, but it didn't take much to track down the place I sought: an abandoned pizza parlor, sitting empty for who knew how many years. A broken-down sign said "Joey's" in what were once cheerful colors. It didn't look like much, but I, like every other South Sider at Archibald J. Keller, knew this was the Sixth Street Aces' favorite vacation spot.

Deciding on caution for once, I studied the place for a moment. Nothing moved, and no sound leaked out. Perhaps Rodriguez and I had both overthought this, and maybe the reason the Sixth Street Aces had gone missing was because the Reapers had simply killed them all. There might be nothing waiting for me in there but a pile of decomposing bodies.

I forced down my fear. A week ago, I wouldn't have even considered this, but the Sixth Street Aces seemed a lot less scary since I'd encountered King Death.

I walked to the door and banged on it.

There was a pause.

Then I heard scuffling feet. Voices.

I continued banging. "Open the door. I'm not a cop, and this is an emergency." More scuffling. "I can hear you in there."

Silence, stretching out for several long seconds.

Then I heard the snap of a lock, and the door opened just a crack, creaking and rattling from disuse. Half a face peered out, its one eye trying to look tough. "What do you want?"

"I want to talk."

"We don't want to talk. Get lost."

"I'm here to do you a favor."

I could tell he was debating closing the door, but some instinct told him not to. "What kind of favor?"

"We have a mutual enemy: King Death."

The guy on the other side of the door apparently misjudged where I was standing, just a little, because the bullet that roared deafeningly and splintered through the door missed me by a few inches.

I squeaked and flung myself painfully to the sidewalk, as more shots echoed. Instinctively, I threw magic at the door, bashing it off its hinges. There were thumps and shouts on the other side. Over my head, a shotgun blast shattered a window. Shit.

I crawled out of the line of fire, then threw myself to my feet and began running. This was not how this was supposed to go. I get that gang members can be on the touchy side, but this was flat-out unreasonable.

Common sense said to just run for my life. But if I was gonna protect the people at the dance, or wherever the Reapers turned up next, I needed the Sixth Street Aces. Common sense wasn't required.

Great. Just great. Growling at myself, I hung a right, taking a long, wide loop around Joey's, shoes eating up pavement. I ran past a tangle of indistinct buildings, keeping it in sight, hoping they couldn't spot me from inside. Just when I thought this week from hell had run out of ways to surprise me, here I was, launching a one-man siege of an abandoned pizzeria.

I crouched in an alley, once I was satisfied I wasn't about to get ventilated and watched the place. Nothing moved. At least they were too scared of King Death, who they probably thought I was, to come out and chase me. I rolled my eyes at that. If they ever encountered King Death, there would be no doubt in their mind which one of us was which. Maybe I could work my way closer; there had to be another entrance. I could sneak in there, maybe magically disarm some of them; if I could keep them from killing me for a few minutes, I could explain myself. That, I figured, probably wasn't the worst plan I'd come up with lately. Seizing on the moment of optimism, I hustled out from cover and began picking my way back toward the building. I kept low, constantly expecting bullets to start flying, but they didn't. I made my way to the back lot behind the building, and yeah, there was a backdoor. The place was two stories. A metal staircase led to a door in the wall of the second.

The back door, I figured, would likely be guarded. The second-floor door... well, it was as good a try as any. Trying to keep my steps light, I eased quickly up the stairs, wishing I knew an invisibility spell. I had reached the landing and was about to try the doorknob when the door below banged open. Apparently the Sixth Street Aces had decided to chase me after all. Three or four of them came boiling out the door, guns in hand. One of them looked up and saw me, all of them beginning to shout.

Whatever happened to their fear of wizards? I guessed they'd decided to conquer it by blasting me to smithereens. Guns were raised. I was so tired of getting shot at.

I didn't really plan what happened next. I just reacted. There was nowhere for me to go, stuck out on the narrow landing like I was. My only thought was escape. I lashed out, hard and fast, with levitation.

I levitated myself.

I won't say I flew; that implies a lot more dignity than what actually happened. Magical force slammed against the metal, hard enough to rattle the whole thing, provoking more shouts from the Sixth Street Aces, then I was propelled upwards, arms flapping, squawking in fear. How, I managed to wonder as wind rushed through my ears and my stomach churned, could they ever find this sight intimidating?

Shots split the air as my torso slammed against the edge of the roof. Ignoring the pain, I threw myself over to flop in a heap before they could find their range. Footsteps clanked up a fire escape. I had got myself good and trapped now.

A gunshot blew a hole in the roof, then another, somebody down below trying to feel out where I was. I was tempted to send a blast of magic down in response, but no, that would kill the people that were supposed to be my allies and might collapse the whole thing and take me with it. Crashing through one floor had been more than enough.

And I doubted I could pull off that flying trick again. I wasn't sure how I'd pulled it off this first time.

There was a big hunk of metal machinery—a heater, an air conditioner, I don't know—a few feet away. I threw myself across the space and hid behind it. I crouched, trying not to breathe, as footsteps clanked upwards and skittered across the rooftop. I readied to fight. If there wasn't gonna be a peaceful end to this, I was prepared.

"Is he up here?"

"No."

"I saw him go up here."

I risked a glance around the corner. There were three of them, guns raised, prowling the roof with the looks of people who desperately wanted to be somewhere else. At least they hadn't conquered all their fear of wizards.

One more try at diplomacy, then it was battle time. They hadn't seen me yet, but the roof wasn't big; it couldn't be long until they did. So, peering over the edge of the metal, I focused on the closest one. Hopefully I wouldn't hurt him, much.

I sent levitation towards him, almost like a lasso. With a brief, startled cry, he flew off his feet and began windmilling towards me. His pistol went off once, then he dropped it. The other guys whirled, too flabbergasted to even lift their guns, which I knew wouldn't last long.

The guy rocketed towards me, faster than I'd intended, and I eased up, hoping to keep him from breaking his neck. His shoes clanged violently into the metal, almost directly in front of me. And he couldn't move. His arms flapped, but he couldn't wriggle out of the spot where I'd pinned him. I jumped up, threw an arm around his neck. "Nobody move."

They moved, waving guns, one of them jumping like a scared rabbit, then trained their guns on me. "Put your guns down," I shouted. "Put them down or he's dead. Do it."

They hesitated, torn, unsure what to do. "Do it," shouted the guy I'd nabbed, "just do it." I couldn't see his face, but he squirmed and wrestled, trying to get free.

They didn't drop their guns, but they lowered them hesitantly, enough that I wasn't in imminent danger of death. "Which one of you is in charge?" I hoped my voice sounded authoritative. The two of them glanced at each other. "I'm not King Death," I said.

"That's why you're still alive. I could have killed you whenever I wanted." I wasn't convinced that was true, but they didn't need to know that. "I'm his enemy. Same as you. And we can help each other. If we don't, we're all dead. So, who the hell do I talk to, to make something happen?" They stared at me with sullen fear.

"Me." The voice issued from over the edge of the roof. A sharp-faced young man with a shaved head and icy blue eyes appeared over the fire escape and clambered to the top. A Tek-9 was held in one hand. "You talk to me. What do you want?"

"Just what I said. Believe it or not, I'm here to do you a favor."

He stared me down and however tough he might have been with human threats, I could see the fear boiling just under the surface of his eyes. He had tamped it down for now, but it wasn't going away. This was far, far beyond anything he'd ever dreamed of, and he had no idea what to do about it. He kept his tone firm and even, though. "How can you possibly help us? Who the hell are you?"

"You've seen what I can do. You know what King Death can do, correct?"

He nodded warily. "I do."

"Magic," I said. No use beating around the bush. "What you saw was magic. King Death can do it. And so can I. I can help you kill him."

His eyes were suspicious, but I could tell he was desperate for a lifeline and couldn't resist the temptation to grab hold of this one, however tenuous it seemed.

Just when I was getting somewhere, somebody shot me.

CHAPTER SEVENTEEN

"YOU SHOT ME, you son of a bitch," I spat at a guy my age someone had called Tommy.

"Damn it," said Michael, Head Sixth Street Ace. "We need to talk to him, and you could have blown his head off."

"You could have blown MY head off," shouted my former hostage from the back of the room.

"And mine," I said, still seething.

"I saw an opening," he said haplessly.

My left arm, where Tommy had shot me, didn't hurt that much, which somehow disturbed me, but it was bleeding all over the place and showed no sign of stopping.

I had blacked out for a time and when I woke up, I'd found myself in the pizzeria.

The place was run down, but they'd made the best of it: someone had gotten an arcade working, there were lights on, sleeping bags. And of course, enough firearms to win the Battle of Stalingrad were scattered around the place, in wild violations of safety procedures. I doubted they'd do much good if King Death decided to knock on the door. At least they had a first aid kit: Michael was dabbing my arm with a cotton ball. I got the feeling first aid wasn't his thing.

Scattered around the former pizzeria were a couple dozen or so teenagers. They didn't look like much. It occurred to me there should be more of them.

They eyed me sullenly. No one spoke. I gave them an insincere smile. "Hello. I'd shake your hands but that would be horribly painful."

There was a pause. "You shake hands with your right hand, though," someone said.

"Oh yeah, that's right. Guess I can shake hands then, if I don't bleed to death."

"There's no way this guy can actually do magic," someone piped up.

"Of course not," I said, "I'm clearly a Jedi."

"Shut up," Michael said. "We gotta deal with this bullet in your arm."

"Yeah, I noticed that." And what, I wondered, the hell was I supposed to do about it? I didn't have time to go to a doctor, and though I could heal the wound, magic wouldn't do anything for the bullet lodged inside me.

Or maybe it would. I tossed a glance at the group. "Hey, you wanted to know if I could really do magic. Let me show you a magic trick."

I smeared away some of the blood over the wound, wincing at the pain it provoked, so I could get a better look. There was a tiny, raw hole weeping blood. Delicately, I extended my index finger over it. Focused. Concentrated. Blocked out everything else. Triple checked to make sure I had everything just so. Then, I let the magic *yank*.

A tiny, bloody dark mass of lead ripped out of my arm to clatter on the linoleum.

I screamed, pain blanking out everything else. I felt more hot blood pour free in the bullet's wake. The pain was so intense my head spun and I rolled out of my chair. Michael reached for me but couldn't get a grip and I slammed down against the floor, laying with my cheek against the cool linoleum, arm screaming. I found myself staring at some little red smears next to my face. Blood, or old pizza sauce, I wondered.

I wanted to scream profanity at the heavens but that would have been too much effort. I just lay there, panting and moaning like a sick dog for a few moments until I felt able to talk again. "Hep muh up," I mumbled, and hands eased me back into my chair. My head spun and my stomach wobbled. "Now," I slurred, "for my next trick." I held a shaking hand over the bloody mess, and let invisible power flow through my hand, into the skin of my arm, vibrating deep within the wound. I groaned. Relief hit me almost instantly and there was a strange tingling sensation as tendons or veins or whatever began knitting themselves back together. I sagged back in the chair as the pain receded. It didn't quite disappear, but it shrank enough for me to think clearly again, becoming a dull, manageable ache. Michael stared at me slack-jawed. "Whoa."

Spotting the tiny piece of metal on the floor a few feet away, I sent a twist of magic that deposited it into my palm. "Think I'll keep this as a souvenir," I said. I wiped off the worst of the blood on my sleeve, then put it in my pocket. Maybe I could make it into a talisman or something. I didn't care for getting shot, but I had to admit, having *been* shot was kinda badass. Gives one a certain street cred.

Mutters rippled through the group as they realized what I'd done, confusion and awe and fear mingled together. Michael reached out a slow hand and brushed against the area where the wound had been. "*Oww.* It's healing, not disappeared."

He snatched his hand back. "Uh, sorry." He gave his head a shake, got his game face back on. "I've seen you around school. What do you want here? I know you're not into this kind of life." He jerked his head, taking in the pizza parlor and crime in general.

I searched for the right words. Were there any? "That's where you're wrong. I am into this kind of life. Just not the life you're talking about. I've been doing magic for over three years now."

"I don't believe in that stuff," Michael said uncertainly.

"You don't have to believe in magic to die from it. Come on, I know you've seen King Death. I know you've seen what he can do. Well, so have I, and unlike you, I have an explanation. He's a wizard. A loathsome son of a bitch of a wizard who's killed a lot of people and who's gonna keep killing until somebody stops him."

"I've seen some of the stuff he can do," Michael said cautiously. "And what you did just now."

"Then I'd say the time for denial is over. You're not losing your mind. I know you're not. I thought I was, but I wasn't either. I know magic's not supposed to be real, but it is whether any of us like it or not."

Michael eyed me. "How do I know you're not working with him? You said you could have killed us when you had a chance, but how am I supposed to believe any of this?"

"I'm not like him. We're not all like that." King Death, I reflected, was giving the wizarding community a terrible reputation. "Look, there's only one reason you should trust me, which is the same reason I should trust you: because we need each other. If either one of us could have taken him out by now, we would have done it, but we can't, so we do. At least tell me what you know about the guy."

He dragged a hand across his face. "A couple months back…" I could see him weighing how much he should tell me, then decide to roll the dice with the truth. Maybe he needed to unload. "We heard about a new dealer, selling some really weird shit. Calling himself that. Thought it was just some loser cooking stuff in his trailer or something. A couple guys went to check it out and didn't come back. We started taking it seriously then. We sent somebody asking around, trying to buy from him, found one of his dealers. We went looking for them and found them. And he found us." He shook his head at the bad memories. "I don't know what happened. RJ got, like, lifted off the ground, smashed into the ceiling. He was my best friend. It broke his neck. There wasn't even anybody else in the room. Then the windows smashed in, tore us up with glass. I'd never seen anything like it. We started shooting, running in all directions. Panicking. A guy standing next to me burst into flames, just like that. To be honest, I don't remember much after that. I just ran like everybody else. It's all a blur. Except for one thing."

"What's that?" I dreaded the answer.

"I saw him." For a moment Michael didn't sound like a gang leader, just another scared kid. I got the feeling that was how I sounded too. "I saw King Death."

"You saw him? Did you get a good look?" I dared to hope that maybe we could get a face, even a name, something concrete to chase down and put an end to this.

"Yes. And no." Michael said. "I saw him. But I didn't get a good look." He swallowed. "He was wearing a mask. I shot him. Point blank. There's no way I could have missed. He just shook it off. Didn't even flinch. I thought I was gonna die. Something picked me up, tossed me into a tree, knocked me out. I guess he thought he killed me. He just waved his hand a little. When I came to, I got the hell out of there. His people were out hunting us down, so I rounded up the ones I could, and we've been holed up here ever since."

I swallowed. "Quite a story."

"Kind of a horror story."

"Tell me about it."

I sketched out the same story I'd told Alexandra and Rodriguez and the mayor, how King Death had spent the last few days trying to murder me in various gruesome ways, all my greatest hits.

Occasionally one of them would pipe up with a horrified question. When I finished, they stared at me in shocked silence. "Damn," Michael finally said.

"Yes."

"What are you gonna do now?"

"Believe it or not, I'm gonna help, if I can."

"How?"

I gestured at my healed wound. "I can do stuff a lot more dramatic than that. The kind of stuff King Death used against you, I can use against him. Does that sound like a guy you'd want on your side?"

"It does. But you're still as outmatched against King Death as we were, aren't you?

I sighed. "I probably am. There's no way around it. He's stronger than me, and he's got the Reapers with him. But I gotta do something. Or try to, at least."

"Even if it gets you killed?"

I thought that over, suddenly, strangely surprised. I had risked my life many times over the past few days, came close to losing it, but somehow, that was a question I'd never actually stopped to ask myself. "Yeah," I said. *Huh.*

"Well, I'm not. Look, I hope you kill that son of a bitch. If it was just my life I had to worry about, I'd help you. I would. But I got people depending on me." He gestured to those around him, watching us with shell-shocked expressions. "Too many of us have died already. And if we go after King Death again, he'll kill us all. I know it and you know it."

I shook my head. "No. Neither of us is strong enough to go after him on our own. But if we work together, if I can find us more help, we can stop him. We can find a way to take the fight to him."

"We can't. You know what happened the last time we went after him. It's not enough. We don't even know who he is, or where he is."

"There has to be a way to figure it out."

"No. It's suicide."

"Damn it, do you want to spend the rest of your lives living here? I mean, what's the long-term plan here?"

"The long-term plan is to stay alive," he snapped.

"I'll help you." It was Tommy, a look of frightened resolve on his round, dark face. "I'm tired of living here. There are mice."

I managed a smile. "It would be nice if you'd shoot at the enemy for a change."

He roared with laughter, like I was his oldest and dearest friend. "So will I," spoke up a tiny, thin-faced girl in a threadbare hoodie, possibly the least intimidating person I'd ever laid eyes on. "He killed my cousin."

There were rumbles of assent, others encouraged by their words. Michael looked around, torn, seeing the tide turning. "This is suicide," he said, more to himself than to anyone else, tossing a glance at me, hoping I would somehow tell him otherwise.

I couldn't. Even if all the breaks somehow went our way, the odds were going to be a long way from being in our favor.

Then a sensation slithered through me. A familiar one. A bad one. I wavered, light-headed. "Oh shit."

"What's the matter?" Michael said.

My voice was weak. "The Reapers. They're coming."

CHAPTER EIGHTEEN

"SON OF A bitch," Michael muttered, visibly clamping down his fear. The room burst into motion, shouting Sixth Street Aces dashing in all directions, colliding with each other, grabbing up guns. Forcing myself into action, I let magic surge into me.

"Put something over that door," Michael shouted. It was still nonexistent, after I'd shattered it a few minutes ago.

"NO!" I roared. "Stay away from it."

"Do something," someone shouted, and I knew it was directed at me, because that's what you shout at a wizard in an emergency. Somebody hustled over to a window, peered out. "I don't see anything," he said, "Nothing's moving. I don't—" He let out a short, sudden little scream as something broke the window and slammed into his face. He thrashed, trying to scream, and failing. Blood gushed onto the walls, then the thrashing, snarling thing hauled him out the open space. It was all over in a few seconds.

Screams of terror filled the room.

"We have to get out of here," I panted to Michael, crouched nearby, gun drawn.

He opened his mouth to reply but was cut off by a sound. It probably sounded bizarre to everyone else in the room, but I knew what it was almost instantly. It was a thrumming, drum-like thumping sound, loud yet soft, weirdly musical. Hellbats. The little bastards liked to nest in their hundreds of thousands in the Caverns of Khorrath, and they could be counted on to show up and make nuisances of themselves when some wizard of dubious character needed two-bit muscle. Michael heard it too, but before he could ask the depressing question "what is it," every window in the room was blown out, prompting shouts of fear, crashing furniture, a few wild shots.

Dark shapes fluttered inside, too fast for me to count, other than "too many."

More gunshots went off, overlapping with each other, absurdly loud in the enclosed space, as the Sixth Street Aces began a general barrage, shattering windows, blowing holes in walls, sending a sign that had once shown the specials crashing to the ground, murdering the poor arcade, seemingly laying waste to everything except the actual enemy. I had to throw up my shields, barely in time to keep four bullets from taking me out. They froze, embedded in the magic, and I made a rather pathetic noise. If we kept this up, the hellbats would be the least of our problems.

One of the hellbats, all leathery wings and fangs, let out a screech and lunged at me, and without thinking, I lashed out with magic as hard as I could, and it spiraled over my head, going for another angle, and I spun on my heel and nailed it. It let out an indignant screech as it slammed brutally against a pizza oven. Bones snapped.

Then it burst into flames. They were a lot bigger than your average bat, perhaps the size of a small dog and when a creature the size of a small dog decides to burst into flames upon its death, you've got a problem.

The sickly green-gold fire flared through the creature's corpse, liquefying it on the inside, and spread across the floor, towards me, coating everything in its path, provoking hisses from everything it touched, and sending me scrambling awkwardly to the top of the counter, like I was hiding from a mouse. *Oh yeah. That's why they're called hellbats.*

"DIE! DIE! DIE!" Their high-pitched, weirdly adorable chant filled my ears. *And they can talk too.*

"We can't stay here," I screamed at Michael.

"What the fuck are those things?" he roared back in terror.

"Hellbats. Exactly what they sound like and they breathe fire."

"DIE! DIE! DIE!" said the hellbats.

There were more shouts, a spray of fire that torched a table. Someone ran by with their arm on fire, having the presence of mind to stop and drop, finally, although they didn't seem to be getting much rolling done. I sent a jab of magic into the ceiling, shattering a sprinkler, and a deluge of water emanating from the ceiling soaked them.

Too fast for anyone to react, a hellbat scooped up one of the Aces in its claws, hauled him off his feet, haphazardly back through one of the shattered windows. I heard him screaming, then stop abruptly. Michael looked ill.

"Come on, we gotta go," I shouted, shaking his arm violently.

"There's a way out," he said. I crushed a hellbat against the ceiling as he spoke, turning it into flaming pulp. He fired his gun into another as it flew through a broken window, blowing its head off and sending the curtains swirling into flame. He jerked his head. "Back there. There's a tunnel."

We began shouting at the others, who had taken cover behind overturned tables while they tried to get off wavering shots.

They didn't have to be told twice, diving from cover and bounding across the room, stampeding past the counter, hellbats swarming after them. A bullet somebody fired back at them whipped past my face with a crack. Michael and I covered their retreat, him firing shot after shot until he ran out of lead. I sent bolts of levitation without a lot of success. When the last Sixth Street Ace had scampered past, I dredged up a pile of magic, spun it into wind, and hurled it into the hellbats' faces.

A massive roar filled the pizzeria, and invisible gusts shook the air, spiraling into the horde, cutting off their chanting, driving them backwards, wings flapping against the current, the fire gusting back into them, producing screams of pain and fear.

The wind kept moving, an invisible, solid, living wall of force, spinning up tables and chairs and a million other unidentifiable objects and whipping the whole mess of furniture, flame, and hellbat into a vortex, tossing up and down and against the walls.

It was spectacular; it also lit the building on fire: flames immediately began racing and chewing along the floor, the walls, the ceiling, faster and hotter than a natural fire could be.

I bounded into the dark of the kitchens after Michael.

I spotted the others, the last of them clambering down into a small hole in the floor, trapdoor open. *Cool, a trapdoor.*

"Come on," I said, "I don't think that'll hold them for long."

"Maybe this will," Michael said. He threw a pair of long tubes into an oven, slammed the door, then pawed at the dial before running.

I plunged into the hole, Michael half a step behind me, slamming the trapdoor shut. I made my way shakily down a grimy ladder, before plopping onto a concrete floor.

Nervous voices sounded around me, and a couple people had had the presence of mind to bring a flashlight. Most of them had drawn guns.

The place was dingy; I wasn't sure what the tunnel's purpose was, or if it even had one anymore, but it clearly hadn't seen any humans in a long time. Even the rats seemed to have abandoned the place.

"Is there a way out of here?" I growled to Michael.

"Yeah." He pointed ahead of us. "Hundred yards or so that way, then almost that much to the right. Leads to a grate onto the street. I check it every day, it's open."

"The Williamsport catacombs," I said. They're something of a legend when you're a kid in Williamsport, the kind of thing adults assure you isn't actually as interesting as you think it is, so you should leave it alone. "Always wanted to check these out."

"I'm glad you could get the chance." A smile slashed across his face, his eyes vaguely unhinged.

"What was that you threw in the oven?" I said as we all began to run.

"Pipe bombs. And this place has gas heat."

"So, we should run."

"Yeah, definitely."

It was dark in the tunnel even with the flashlights, but when you're frantically running for your life, you don't really need lights, you just stampede in the general direction of safety and to hell with anything that might be in the way.

Just when I'd begun to wonder if Michael's fireworks display wasn't going to work, an earth-shattering roar sent vibrations ripping through the walls around us and caused the ceiling to shake and spill plaster worryingly.

I jumped but kept running, convinced a fireball was about to chase us down the tunnel, but nothing worse than plaster dust and smoke followed us.

"Can those things follow?" Michael asked.

"I don't think so. There should be a big heap of burning wreckage over our heads, and they don't have the dedication to sift through it all with their claws."

We ran on, the turnoff Michael had talked about materializing rapidly out of the gloom.

And a man with it, standing there waiting.

My heart leaped into my throat and voices rose up as the Aces noticed his presence. And magic shimmered from him, as he prepared to cast a spell. I picked out his glowing eyes in the gloom.

I didn't give him the chance. I mustered all the levitation I could and flung it at him, sending him spinning into the shadows. "Get out of here," I shouted. I sent another burst hurtling in the direction he'd fallen. They hesitated, which I appreciated. "GO!" I heard more than saw their panicked footsteps pounding away down the tunnel as I braced my shields.

King Death himself? I didn't know, but I was the only one that could hold him off. Only a wizard had even a fraction of a chance of stopping him. They would have been shredded.

A bolt of force slammed into me, muffled a little by my shields but hard enough to lift me off the ground.

I skidded and rolled to a stop on the floor, coming quickly to my feet. He was charging me, leaving the Sixth Streeters alone, at least, and I lanced more levitation. He dodged, disappearing into the shadows, and my spell knocked a chunk from the wall.

From the way he swayed on his feet, I suspected he had taken Hex, rather than being King Death in the flesh, which was bad news, in the sense that I had yet to get my hands on him, but good in the sense that it marginally increased my chances at survival.

He disappeared from sight for a stomach-churning moment, and I sent a beam of fire straight up, casting the tunnels in an orange glow. There he was, the son of a bitch, lurking around at nine o'clock, trying to sneak up on me. I angled the fire down and out, sent it blazing towards him at point blank range. It hit him dead center, bowling him back, fire blooming around him like the Fourth of July.

He staggered, then shook it off. The flames dissipated, and he shook his head, pulling himself to his full height again. They leaked to the floor in burning rivulets, winking out slowly.

I realized what had happened almost immediately, the realization leaving a sour, sinking feeling in my gut. Shields. The motherfucker had figured out how to make shields.

He gave a hard laugh in the shadows. "I was the first one," he drawled. "Took it when it just gave you a little buzz. Took it when it gave you powers. Took the last batch. The strongest one. And I lived." He didn't know what was happening to him, probably hadn't realized it before he took Hex, but he most likely had some latent magical talent he'd never discovered before, so the Hex had affected him a lot differently than it had a garden variety human. Apparently, this would be a little more of a fight than I'd thought.

"I recognize you," I said, something about his face clicking in my brain. "You're the guy I tossed out a window last night. Figured you died."

"I'm tougher to kill than that. That's why he trusts me. The rest of them are gonna drop dead, but I'm gonna live. And King Death and I are gonna tear this town apart."

"Cool," I said, and attacked.

I tried a conjuring of my own, a jagged, ugly piece of metal that scythed towards him, that his shield batted away with ease, but it gave me time to close the gap between us; I knew that turning my back and fleeing was as near to suicide as I could get, but if I could take him down now...

I reached out, tore a section of metal pipe free from the ceiling. It sailed into my hand, and I slashed it down. It collided against his shield, the magic vibrating with a soft hum at the impact. He may have figured out how to make shields, but I doubted he had much experience with them and if I could shatter them, I had a chance. I pounded down over and over, driving him back, and I had no idea how badly it was hurting him, but he managed to send a bolt of force that plowed into my own shield and propelled me back to the middle of the room.

I rose to see the guy coming at me, a long, jagged blade of green fire appearing in his hands, dancing down a jagged pipe he held, having apparently copied my trick and gave it a little extra spin of his own. Fine. I channeled magic down through the pipe, still in my hand, hoping this would work; with the way things had been going, it was even money. Flames sprang along the metal, completely ignoring the way fire was supposed to behave, natural orange, as opposed to that sickly, unearthly green, but fire nevertheless.

Flames licked around my hand but didn't singe me. I found I was happy to have good, honest fire on my side. I swung. The blades of fire collided, flashing in the air, magic vibrating through my entire body.

I slashed again, missing but forcing him back, then he swung the fire at my head, forcing me to duck, the hissing and popping of both fires filling my ears. The flames leapt and lit up the tunnels bizarrely, and his face flickered in and out of focus as the light shined on him one moment, disappeared, did it again.

Even amidst my stomach-churning terror, I was able to think this was just plain cool. I nearly started laughing at the ridiculousness of it all. Sure, being a wizard had been dangerous lately, but where else could you have a flaming sword fight? With my life on the line, I found myself suddenly, weirdly at peace with my life choices. The moment of reverie lasted only an instant before I was blasted back to reality.

In truth, it was more brawl than sword fight. He got past me and slammed blow after blow against my shield, rattling me, magic vibrating painfully through me. I slashed a hard blow against him, relieving the pressure for a moment, before he came after me again.

The magic felt as if it was burning through my blood and about to sweep me out to some primordial sea. I thought the heat would singe my hair; I felt it straining against my shield, and the idea that the same thing was happening to the other guy wasn't much consolation. I couldn't go on like this and I had to do something before he came to the same conclusion.

I sent a bolt of wind directly into him, knocking him down. I took a step forward, intent on ramming the fire into his throat, when he responded in kind, throwing me quite a bit farther than I'd thrown him. My feet kicking, I thumped down on the floor on my stomach. I flipped onto my back, a blaze of green blotting out my view. I barely got my own flame up in time, the impact juddering through me, heat pressing against my shield.

Face contorted, he slammed it down again and again, me managing to deflect a couple blows, but a couple others hit my shield, searing me. Through my haphazard viewpoint, I saw his legs only a few feet away. If magic wouldn't provide the answer, maybe a little playground roughhousing would. I thrust out both legs and entangled them with his.

He let out a short little breath of surprise, staggered, lost his balance, and toppled, the green flame disappearing from my field of vision.

I leaped back up, sent another bolt of levitation into him as he rose, and slammed him backwards against a wall.

I bounded after him, seething with adrenaline now that I had him on the back foot. It was the wrong decision. The bastard had somehow hung onto his fire spell, and he flew out of the dark to club me over the head with it.

Pain exploded through my skull. The vivid green light blotted everything out of my vision as, head spinning and throbbing, I collapsed, taken completely by surprise. My shield kept it from melting my skull off, but not by much.

It slammed down into my ribs. I saw him raise it again, eyes wild, before thumping it onto my leg. Well, this shit couldn't continue. My shields wouldn't hold out forever, and even if they did, he would probably batter or fry me to death anyway.

As he lifted his swinging arm for another try, I caught him up in a whirlwind. Things I couldn't see were torn clattering from the wall and he went airborne, slamming into the ceiling several feet away before bouncing down and skidding across the floor.

I staggered to my feet, intent on finally finishing him. Before I could finish anything, he was coming at me, apparently having more stamina than I had, having jumped right back to his feet after being tossed. He probably hadn't spent his entire back to school week getting mauled, either. A fireball arced out, a big one, twisting and roaring tendrils of flame leaping from the sides, like a tiny version of those close-up pictures of the sun.

It was coming too fast to do much but hope. My hand extended out in front of me, and it stopped, about four feet away.

It burned there for a second, both of us shocked, I think, that I'd pulled that off—then I flung it back as hard as I could. It slammed into him, knocking him off his feet. I could see his shield shatter in a flicker of light.

Mine broke half a second later, and half a second after that, pain lanced through my head, like someone had driven a railroad spike through it and I yelped, collapsing to my knees, head spinning and blue stars dancing across my vision. Some dim part of my brain remembered I had to get up and fight, but I could hardly concentrate on staying upright, let alone fighting.

I felt blood pour out of both my nostrils and onto my lips. I knew what that meant. My magical gas tank was dangerously close to empty. I reached frantically for it, causing fresh pain to ripple and more blood to leak. It wasn't gone; I hadn't burned out completely, but I'd pushed myself too hard, and my power was weak, thready. Damn it. I had felt stronger today, thought I had more left in the tank. I hadn't.

The only way to keep from burning out was to try and conserve magic, now when I needed it more than I ever had.

And he was still alive.

At this point I wasn't even surprised.

I'd hurt him: I could tell from the way he walked, the blood and burn marks on his face, his arms. But he still had his magic. I could tell that much.

He stood over me, mouth slack, pain and fear blanketing his eyes.

He was near collapse himself, but he raised a shaking hand, and I knew it was my death.

I was too weak to cast whatever magic I had left.

I was officially on Plan Z.

I hurled myself upwards, using my left hand to help push off as I thrust my right into my jacket.

It surprised him. I grabbed a fistful of his shirt and drug him down with me as I collapsed again.

From a distance, it might have looked like some nifty move, but actually, I would have collapsed anyway, I just managed to bring him down with me.

My right hand was in the lining of my jacket, and I got my fingers on the hilt of my knife, felt it slip for a heart-stopping half-second, got a better grip, and without much in the way of conscious thought I pulled it free and slammed it deep into his throat.

Hot blood immediately soaked my hand and wrist as he let out a wet gasp of surprise. I jerked it back and forth, and he pulled away from me, causing the knife to rip free, and collapsed almost instantly.

I looked over at him, too beat-up to do anything else. I think he tried to reach for his magic, but it failed him. We lay only a few feet apart and I saw shock glazed across his face. I doubt if there's a wizard alive who expects to be killed via stabbing.

Then he groaned and there was nothing in his eyes at all.

I lay there staring at the ceiling, then found the strength to haul myself up. I didn't want to lay next to a corpse, no matter how tired I was.

I tried to feel my magic, dreading what would happen. I hadn't burned out at least, but it wasn't enough. If I didn't have to fight for my life for a few hours, maybe I could replenish a little, but it was hard to see that happening.

"Sam?" Michael's voice boomed down the tunnel and a flashlight's beam cut the gloom.

"Over here," I called weakly.

The light swelled, revealing his haggard face and a gun held at his side. "Are you okay?"

I jerked my head towards the dead Reaper. "Better than that guy. What about you guys?"

"Yeah, we made it out okay. Thought I should come back and see what happened to you."

"Thanks."

"We better get out of here."

I knew he was right, but I was loath to do it. Now that I had won a tiny victory, I didn't want to leave empty-handed. "Hang on."

This guy, I got the feeling, had been a little more than the average goon. Some kind of lieutenant, maybe, but whatever he was, it was the best I could come up with.

I bent and began rifling through his pockets, looking for his phone. While I was at it, I retrieved my knife, wiping off the blood on his shirt before putting it back in my jacket.

Most of the items in his pockets were perfectly mundane, except for the baggie of Hex I found. A Very Bad Idea niggled at the back of my mind. I thrust the baggie into my own pocket and returned to corpse-searching. It occurred to me that King Death might have gone after the Aces now, after all this time, because he was putting something into motion and didn't want loose ends. Of course, I couldn't actually prove that, since I'd just killed the only person I could question.

I finally came up with his phone and was relieved to see it didn't require a password. I checked the call log and found what I was looking for: numerous calls to someone called KD.

"Smart," Michael said.

Maybe there was someone else I could question after all. Pushing away the twist of fear it caused, I pressed the button, turning on the speaker and holding it a little away from my mouth, hoping that would disguise my voice enough to keep him from figuring out he wasn't talking to who he thought he was.

The phone rang three times. Four. As I began to fidget, there was a crackle that caused me to flinch and my stomach to flip. "Yeah?"

"It's done," I said. I knew I couldn't keep this up for long; for all I knew they had a code word or something. "The Sixth Street Aces are dead, and so is the wizard."

"Good. Who was he?" That voice. It was familiar. I'd heard it… somewhere. It wasn't the ominous growl you might expect; it was downright mild-mannered. I racked my brain.

"Never seen the guy before. What now?"

"Link up with the others. Get ready to head for the school."

I wanted to keep him talking but knew it was too big a risk: I might actually have a little surprise on my side and didn't want to waste it. "Copy that. Be there asap."

I hung up. That voice… I tried to run my brain back over what he'd said, parsing through it like I was trying to translate Egyptian hieroglyphics. I recognized the voice, compared it to everyone I could think of, but came up with nothing.

Think, damn it, concen—

It slammed into me.

I recognized it. When he'd said the word "school." Once I did, it was glaringly obvious; I'd certainly heard it often enough.

Mr. McKinley.

CHAPTER NINETEEN

MY STOMACH ROILED and chills raced along my spine, my entire body, as I began shaking for reasons that had nothing to do with my pain and fatigue. I dropped the phone, dimly heard it clatter to the floor.

McKinley.

It didn't seem possible. But it was. I was certain of it. I ran the voice over and over through my mind but kept coming up with the same result. That was McKinley's voice whether I liked it or not.

I tried to force my mind into gear, figure out what to do. I'd been expecting a stranger. I hadn't expected a man I saw every day, that I'd known and liked for years, that had seemed so normal. Was I supposed to kill him now? If he was King Death, I decided, I didn't have any choice. I had to stop him before he hurt anyone else. But how was it possible? I'd never got any magical vibes from him. But if he hadn't been using any magic around me… yeah, he could have hidden it. It was possible.

"Who was it?" Michael asked. "Did you know him?"

My mouth was dry. "Remember Mr. McKinley, from school?"

"Yeah, I guess."

"It was him. I'd explain while we run, but I have no idea what's going on, so let's just run."

We did, me following him and his flashlight, back through the tunnels. The whys and hows would have to wait. We kept going until we were clambering up a rusty metal ladder, and a moment later I was back above ground, gratefully sucking down fresh air.

We were in a run-down old park, it seemed, ancient playground equipment shadowed in the gathering dark. The remaining Sixth Streeters were scattered around, postures tired and frightened. This didn't seem like a good hiding place.

"What now?" Michael said. Murmurs rippled through the others.

I ran my gaze over them. "You should walk away," I found myself saying. "I'm set up to handle this. You're not."

"I don't think you're set up to handle it either," Michael said. "Even if you are a wizard."

"I won't send you into a meat grinder."

"The meat grinder's already here. We tried running from it and it didn't work. May as well try fighting it. If we're gonna die, I'd rather go down swinging than hiding in some dump waiting for those things to come back."

There were rumbles of agreement. Loud ones. I stared at them. Surely that wasn't a lump in my throat. "Are you sure about this?"

He nodded. "We're sure." I could tell he was. They all were. "What do you need us to do?"

"I need you to go to a dance."

CHAPTER TWENTY

I WAS PLEASANTLY surprised no one tried to kill me on the way back from the park.

I kept up a brisk pace as I hoofed it down the darkening street, torn between the necessities of speed and saving my energy for what was coming. At least the dance wouldn't have started yet.

I had thought about calling someone, anyone in charge of something, demanding they call in the entire Department of Defense to protect the school and take out McKinley, but I knew the response I'd get: "you don't know that was McKinley," "calm down, it's being handled," "we don't trust teenage wizards," etc., etc. I needed something a lot more solid than just a fuzzy, thirty-second phone conversation.

And that gave me an idea. Millions of unanswerable questions continued to buzz through my head, and before they drove me mad, I acted on another impulse, this one more prosaic than some others I'd had lately, but something I dreaded just the same.

I didn't go straight home; instead, I headed for the school, my exhaustion only a faint shadow in the back of my mind. I had to know.

People were milling around, setting up for the dance, so no one took any notice of me as I walked inside, roamed the halls until I got to McKinley's classroom. Once there, I stopped, for the first time in what felt like a very long time. I peered over the desk's contents. In the end, I settled on something deceptively simple: a pen. It would do the trick. I shoved it in my jacket and headed for home.

Well, not quite: I didn't want my neighbors getting wind of what I was about to do, so I ducked onto a more secluded street. Without trying to talk myself out of it, I inflected my words with magic and called out. "Eressen? You there? We need to talk."

Moments passed, then there was a ripple of invisible energy, and he was beside me, calmly matching my pace. "Mr. Adams. It's good to see you again. I've been watching you, you know, keeping abreast of things as best I could from Shal'Gasa'Nor. You took my drop of information and turned it into quite a flood. You should have alerted me sooner, though. I could have been useful at that brawl last night."

Had it really only been last night? "I didn't want to bother you. How is it you got mixed up in this, anyway? What's your angle?" I knew I wouldn't get a straight answer.

He affected a look of nonchalance. "Oh, well. Things have been a bit complicated amongst the Shal'Gasa lately, a bit of a family situation, you understand. Mistakes were made, and I can own my own part in it, though what transpired can hardly be called my fault." I found myself smiling. Perhaps Eressen was out on as much of a limb as I was. "Anyway, well... success here might help me get back in certain good graces."

"You still haven't told me what you actually want."

"Well, that part's a bit complicated. Wouldn't want to overwhelm you, our partnership being so new and all. Don't worry, I have everything completely in hand. But that's not why you called for me."

"No. We're going to take the fight to the enemy. I have a way to do it."

"Excellent. How?"

"I may have a way to track him." I didn't mention that I hoped it wasn't true. "If we can track him back to his lair, we'll take him out before he tries anything." I gave him the rundown on what had happened since last I'd seen him. "If tracking him fails, we fight him at the dance."

He nodded. "A sound plan. A little shaky, but that's what makes these things exciting."

"Don't get too excited. There's part of it you're not gonna like."

"Which is?"

"A vampire. She's going to be helping us, because we're going to need all the help we can get."

His eyebrows lifted. "Where in all the realms did you find a vampire?"

"I didn't. She found me."

"And you trust her?"

"No."

"Well, that's good." He sighed. "Very well. You're right; I don't care for it, but I suppose the terms of our deal never said you couldn't bring in other allies. How do we find this daughter of the night?"

"Most of the time she finds me, but I know she's holed up in a motel outside of town."

"Ah, well, shouldn't be too hard, especially if she tends to 'find you,' as you said."

"Thank you," I grumbled.

"I'm sorry?"

"Thank you," I said. "It's not just my life you're saving here. There are a lot of others at stake."

"Not at all, Mr. Adams, not at all." He clapped me on the shoulder. "Fear not, I will follow you into the jaws of the Beasts themselves, if need be, ready to gain glorious victory or glorious death, sword in hand." He tapped the blade at his side.

I eyed it. Swords are cool. "Impressive."

"Ah, thank you," he said, clearly enjoying showing it off. "It's served me well all my life." He pulled half the blade from its scabbard. The blade twinkled with grey-black fire. It looked like any other piece of steel, yet, somehow, I knew it wasn't, the certainty lodging itself abruptly in my mind. I shivered. That was not a normal sword.

"Shal'Gasa steel," Eressen said proudly. "Nothing like it in all the realms. Ensorcelled with all kinds of wonderful wickedness." He slipped it back in the scabbard. "Mr. Adams?"

"You can call me Sam."

"Sam, does that vehicle strike you as odd?" I started to turn but he gripped my arm softly. "Easy now, easy."

I glanced back more subtly and spotted the vehicle he was talking about. A dark SUV prowled slowly down the street a little behind us. I got the feeling they were trying not to look suspicious. "Yeah, I'd say it's a little odd."

"I see. I wasn't certain, being unfamiliar with your traffic customs. Any idea who they might be?"

"Take your pick."

I guess my glancing hadn't been subtle enough. The car gunned its engine, came racing alongside us. A hand jutted out the open window. "Gun," I yelped, just before they opened fire, the shots echoing down the empty street.

Things happened fast. I sent a haphazard thrust of magic at the car, not nearly as accurate or powerful as it should have been, but I managed to throw it off course. Then Eressen was airborne, sailing farther and faster than a human could, light from the streetlamps glowing and shimmering up and down the blade of that sword, now held aloft in his hand. The image was frozen in my vision for half a second, then he shifted his grip and came down on the roof of the car, sword thrust in front of him, punching through its roof. The car continued to roll, Eressen nimbly pulling his sword free and dancing down the car's length and onto the pavement, while the car finally rumbled to a stop in some bushes. Its engine continued to hum.

Eressen appeared next to me, where I had crouched in a vain attempt to dive for cover. He gave me a smile. "That was invigorating. Keeps the reflexes sharp, those sudden attempts on one's life." Gasping down air, I glared at him. That was not how I felt about the situation. "Shall we ascertain his identity?"

"Yeah." We walked to the car, both of us cautious, but no more shots came out of it; Eressen had clearly handled whoever it was. I opened the door, peered inside. The dead man lay sprawled back in the driver's seat, empty eyes staring at the broken windshield, his chest stained dark red. A pistol lay on the floor at his feet.

"Do you know him?" Eressen asked.

"No. I... Wait a minute." I peered at the corpse's face, felt wheels turn in my brain. It was the guy that shot at me last night; the first of many, back at that abandoned office. There was a buzzing sound. The vibrating of a cell phone. It happened again and I traced the sound to the dead guy's pocket. As it vibrated a third time, I pulled it free. The name on the screen was less than surprising. Rick, it said.

As it vibrated again, I answered it. Rick's voice crackled in my ear. "Is it done?"

A dark smile crept across my face. "Not quite, Rick. Your friend missed again." I hung up the phone, wiped off my prints with the hem of my shirt, and tossed it into the dead man's lap.

Eressen gave an approving chuckle. "Off to a good start, my friend."

"At what?"

"At making enemies. A man can scarcely call himself such without a few of them."

"I'm glad you approve."

"Quite a show." I jumped and whirled, ready to attack. Elise sat in a car with the window rolled down, engine idling. Oh good. We'd found her.

"You picked a fine time to show up."

"You seemed to have it under control."

"This must be the vampire," Eressen said, not bothering to disguise his contempt.

"This must be the Shal'Gasa," she said.

I could already see this had been a wonderful idea.

CHAPTER TWENTY-ONE

LEAVING ELISE AND Eressen in her car—I couldn't imagine what they would talk about—I dashed across the yard, mumbled a warning to Big Al to be ready for trouble. I heard him say something that sounded fierce and determined but was in too much of a rush to make out the words. I pounded across the front yard and into the house.

I heard my parents' voices but didn't see them and didn't stop as I wound my way up the stairs, finally reaching my bedroom, slamming the door and collapsing. I knew I had to get moving, but couldn't for several long moments, just slumping against the door, gratefully choking down gulps of air. All this was really starting to catch up with me.

"You could have hit my tail, you know." Catrick Swayze was curled up on my pillow, watching me.

"You were nowhere near the door; you weren't in any danger."

"How did it go?"

"Bad," I said. "I doubt they'll come here but it's about to get ugly. You may want to sharpen those claws."

"They're always sharp."

I changed hurriedly into fresh clothes, ignoring how Swayze

yowled and covered his eyes with a paw. I haltingly filled him in as I did so, then fumbled with my phone. Jason answered on the second ring. "Sam. Are you okay?" He seemed to have a sense of how things had been going lately.

"I'm fine," I lied. "Are you going to the dance?"

"Yeah. You?"

"I don't know. I guess you wouldn't listen if I told you to stay home."

"Probably not."

"Fine. If you're gonna go, expect trouble. I mean it. Worse than the beach. A lot of people are gonna get hurt if we don't do something."

"What do we do?"

"Just tell people to be careful and get ready. This might turn into a fight, and I don't mean with the South Side. With King Death, and his people. I don't think you're gonna get any help from the people who are actually in charge, so we're gonna have to do it ourselves. And if anything looks fishy, even for a second, pull the fire alarm or something. Get everybody out of there. Maybe we can throw them off their game a little that way."

"Jesus," he sighed. "Okay. I can do that. I'll be ready."

"By the way, did you get anywhere with your North Side buddies?"

"I don't know. Maybe. Only one way to find out."

"Yeah, I know all about that. You might have more help than you think. I talked to the Sixth Street Aces. They don't like King Death any more than we do, and they're heading over to help."

There was a long pause. "Huh."

"I know the feeling."

"I just hope they know what they're shooting at."

"They seem like very dependable people. Hey, thanks. I'm sorry I dragged you into this."

"You didn't drag me. Be careful."

"You, too. Thanks again. You're a good friend."

"So are you."

Hoping he was right, I hung up. Then I fired off a text to Rodriguez, outlining my suspicions as succinctly as possible. He texted back right away, telling me he'd do the best he could on his end. Even in a text, I could sense his pessimism.

That done, I pulled the pen from my jacket pocket and ran a hand over it, got a sense of its energy. It seemed like suspicious energy, but maybe that was my imagination talking. I kicked clothes and junk out of the way until I had a clear spot on the floor, then sat and cast the same spell I'd used to find Zack, telling myself that my magic would have to last long enough to pull it off, whether it liked it or not.

My mind dived and swooped around the Williamsport streets again, this way and that, until I lost my sense of direction. Then the images stopped, the vision slowly focusing. It wasn't as helpful this time. A hallway, doors on either side. An apartment building, most likely. Probably in the North Side, judging from the lack of stray crack pipes, flickering ceiling lights, and holes in the plaster. The door in front of me read 9F. I focused, trying to get the magic to do an x-ray on the door, but it didn't work, and I quickly gave up. I didn't have time to learn any new magic tricks.

"Find anything?" Swayze said, pouncing down from the bed to stand beside me.

"Yeah, apartment 9F. That was the best I could do, but I can get us there."

"You really think it's McKinley?"

"I don't want to, but I do."

"What are you gonna do?"

"I'm gonna head over there," I said. "Stop him before he can hurt anybody else." I was surprised at the firmness in my tone.

"Just like that?"

"Just like that."

He licked his lips. "This ain't smart."

"I know."

"You're gonna face off with a guy who outclasses you? A guy you know?"

"That seems to be what we're dealing with, yes."

He eyed me. "Good luck."

"Thanks. Look… if I don't come back from this… I—" He scratched me, swiping his paw across my hand. I shrieked. "What the hell was that for?"

"You know I hate big emotional scenes like this. Good luck at the bloodbath. Try not to die. Of all the wizards I've worked with, you're undoubtedly one of them."

"Thanks. The depth of your concern is touching as always."

"Open the door, would you? I'm hungry."

I did, reaching down as I did so to give him his usual goodbye head scratch. If he noticed that it lasted a little longer than usual, he didn't mention it, though when he flounced from the room, he leaned over to give my shin a rub.

One more time, I went over it all in my head, and in truth there wasn't much. I had my talismans, my knife. Whatever magic was still in the tank. Good intentions, allies of questionable character, and a righteous cause. Yahoo.

I headed downstairs and ran smack into Mom. I flinched, as one does when one is guiltily sneaking away to assassinate an evil wizard.

"Are you going to the dance?" she said.

"Yep."

"I don't think that's a good idea. It's not safe out there lately. You should have come straight home. I heard about that fight at school. And Ella told me some North Siders wanted to attack the South?"

"Oh yeah, that. Look, that thing was totally overblown. They got scared and chickened out."

"What happens next time when they don't?"

I debated what to say. Having to sneak out would make things far too complicated and cost me time I didn't have. "There are gonna be cops at the dance," I said, "but believe it or not, the people there have kind of committed not to fight each other."

"What do you mean?"

"Jason. He's trying to broker a truce. You know both sides like him. The idea is to keep North and South Siders from fighting each other, let everybody have someplace where they can coexist for a night." Every word of that was technically the truth.

"That's a good idea, but I still don't think you should go."

"I just want to help Jason, that's all. I encouraged him to do it. I want to make sure he can pull it off."

"Sam, this is the exact opposite of not getting involved. I don't like it."

"Neither do I, but the North Side and the South Side have to start patching things up sometime. I wanna do my part."

"That's very noble of you."

"Thanks. I've never been noble before. And I'm telling you, I know it's hard to believe, but I really don't think the North Siders and South Siders will fight each other tonight."

"I hope so. If they do, don't get mixed up in it, okay? Be careful."

"You don't have to tell me twice."

"I really do. Be careful."

"I will. Does this mean I can go?"

She blew out a breath. "Yeah, I guess. Don't stay long." She gestured at me. "Is that what you're wearing?"

"Huh?"

"Isn't it semi-formal?"

"Could be."

"Aren't you supposed to wear your suit?"

I put on my suit.

If I died... well, they wouldn't have to change me into it for the casket, I supposed.

Freshly styled, I made my way back downstairs. I could hear Mom and Dad rattling around in the kitchen, talking. I hesitated, swallowed, got my voice working. "I'm going to the dance. It shouldn't be too late. I'll see you later." They called their goodbyes.

"Sam." I froze. Ella had always been a sneaky walker.

I turned and gave her a weak smile. "Hey, Sister Act."

She frowned. "Gonna head out?"

"Yep, that's the plan. Dance the night away."

"Sam, what's going on with you?"

"What do you mean?" I knew I didn't sound very convincing.

"You know what I mean. You've been acting strange for days."

"I'm sorry. I've just been really busy."

"Damn it, Sam. I want to know that you're okay."

Guilt began to creep through me. I'd never wanted my problems to affect her. But they were. I gripped her shoulders. "El. Really, everything's okay. I'm gonna be fine, I promise."

"'Gonna' be? As in, not currently fine?"

Oops. "Yes. I'm gonna be fine. After tonight, I'll stop being so hard to find. Things will go back to normal, okay? Even better maybe." I found that very hard to believe but didn't tell her that. Instead, to her surprise, I gave her a quick hug.

She looked at me, confusion and worry written on her face. "Are you sure?"

"Yeah, of course I'm sure."

I thought about saying "I love you" but that would have made her more suspicious, so I just walked out the door into the dark blue night.

"How much farther?" Elise said.

I sighed. "Slightly less far than the last time you asked me. Turn right here."

"It wouldn't kill you to exercise a little patience," observed Eressen from the back seat.

"It might kill you," she muttered.

"Oh, I shudder in terror."

"Will you two have your sexual tension somewhere else?" I growled.

That brought me a moment's blessed silence in the car. Then I knew, as much as I knew any other piece of information, that we were close. "Here," I said. "Stop the car."

She pulled over and we piled out. A nearby sign read "Crown-view Apartments." There would be people in here, lots of them, and I doubted collateral damage would be Eressen and Elise's number one concern. "Remember," I said, "the rest of these people are innocent. We can't let them get hurt." I feared we might not be able to stop it; when wizards fight, stuff gets broke.

"Then what is the plan?" Elise said.

How, I wondered, had I become the leader of this expedition? "He might have a guardian," I said. "To keep anything supernatural out."

"Which includes all of us," she said, "so we may as well not worry about it."

"That's the spirit. You and I will go through the building, right through the front door like we're doing nothing wrong. Eressen, you climb the fire escape and come in through the window. You think you can find the right one?"

"I'm certain I can."

"Good. He doesn't know about you, so you might be our ace in the hole. Once we're in there, we kill King Death, whoever he is." I still held out a delusional sliver of hope it might be someone other than McKinley.

There weren't any questions, so we parted ways, Eressen disappearing into the shadows and Elise and I simply walking up the sidewalk. "What about the authorities?" Elise said. "Did you get them off our backs?"

"I don't know about that, but they know they're screwed if they come after me. If they do, then boom, there are magical bounties on their heads."

"Good. We won't have to worry about the cops screwing things up."

"Yeah, but I doubt we'll get much help from them either."

"We can handle it. How's your magic?"

"There's enough left to kill King Death."

She didn't answer, but I got the feeling she was skeptical.

We went inside without incident, took the elevator to the ninth floor. You'd have thought it would have been more dramatic, but it wasn't. We stepped off the elevator, into a nondescript hallway. I cast a nervous glance at the doors around us. Hopefully no one decided to stick their heads out once the commotion started. I didn't think there was a way to be subtle about wasting King Death.

"There it is," Elise said, voice low. "9F."

I extended my hand over the knob cautiously. "I don't feel anything."

"That doesn't make me feel any better. Oh well. Let's go."

"What about Eressen? He might not be in position."

"We don't have time to wait."

I gave the knob a magical shove. It creaked and snapped, and I kicked the door open. Elise darted inside, me after her.

As it happened, Eressen was already there, standing by the couch, sword lolling at his hip. When my eyes found him, he shrugged. "The place was empty. Didn't see any need to lurk around on the fire escape. I have to say, this isn't quite what I was expecting when you said we were raiding his lair."

He was right. It was just a messy one-bedroom apartment. I glanced around the room, desperate to find something. I spotted something framed on the wall. Not a picture, something more official-looking. I stepped closer and peered at it. A college diploma. For Eric McKinley. "Goddamn it."

"Bad news," said Elise lightly.

"Yeah. It's McKinley." My last shreds of hope floated away.

"I believe I have more bad news," Eressen said from the hallway. He jabbed his blade at the half-open closet door.

Elise and I approached, and I risked a peek inside. It was a shrine of some kind; at least, that's the best word I could think of, though if it was devoted to any particular god or demon, I couldn't guess who it was. Oh God, what if McKinley's patrons, if he had them, decided to show up and help him out? Actually, that wasn't a major concern. If that happened, I'd be dead before I even knew what hit me, so there was no reason to worry about it. What a relief.

The closet was about what you'd expect: sagging shelves were covered with bones, feathers, goblets, candles, a dagger, jars and vials, holding strangely colored mixtures I decided not to examine too closely. Old books were stacked here and there, and something smelled strange. I made sure not to breathe too deep. *Damn. Even your closet is a cliché.* But I knew it wasn't just some goth affectation. Cliché or not, this only added to my unease, which I wouldn't have thought possible. This wasn't the work of someone ruthless; this was the work of someone unhinged, someone so deep into bad magic there was no coming back from it, someone who might well have lost their grip on reality altogether.

There was nothing to be gained here, I decided. I wasn't about to go rummaging through this stuff.

I felt something, like a faint minor key, somewhere in my soul. I knew it was trouble the second I felt it. *That'll be the trap.*

"Back, back, back." They reacted instantly, the three of us scrambling away.

Before anything could happen, I threw up my shields and headed for the door. It was the right move. I don't know how King Death had rigged it up, not to give off any vibes until the sucker had walked right into the noose, but whatever it was, it was alive now, and had designs on the three of us.

We were halfway across the living room when I heard the roar.

Against my better judgment, I turned around. A wall of surging green fire roared down the hall towards us, vaporizing everything in its path, every door and wall and appliance.

It would devour us, and probably a good chunk of the ninth floor too. I barely had time to expand my shields, covering my friends, expanding them further, to cover as much of the room as I could.

Before I could breathe, it slammed into us. The shield shook and quivered, the roar drowning out all other sounds, and I redoubled my efforts, pumping as much magic as I could into the shields even as I felt them being chipped away. It consumed the room, the entire apartment disappearing in a green blaze; here and there, the fire licked past, where the magic didn't quite cover.

I clung ferociously to the shields, impact driving me back. Endless seconds passed. Then the pressure on my shields vanished, the shields themselves a second later. I stood there, doubled over and panting. The fire alarms had begun to blare.

Half the apartment was a vaporized wreck, like someone had seared it with a giant blowtorch. There was nothing left but debris and ash. Most of the walls were gone, making the place seem oddly large. The rest was untouched, except for a few scorches here and there. Smoke fogged the place, smelling faintly wrong, somehow. That was not normal smoke.

Eressen and Elise picked themselves off the floor. "Well done, Sam," Eressen said.

Elise stared at me. "Sam." She pointed at my face.

I touched it and my fingers came away bloody. I became aware blood had gushed from both nostrils, all the way down to my neck. Red tears had leaked from both my eyes too.

There was a wrenching sensation, deep within my soul, and pain poured from it, stealing the breath from my lungs, and causing me to double over, nearly collapsing.

My head spun and my limbs weighed a ton, though at least the pain receded quickly. "You burned out," Elise said.

"I don't think so; I wouldn't be conscious if that happened. But the magic's too weak. I can't reach it. Damn it, I'm sorry." I couldn't win a fight with King Kitten in this condition, let alone King Death.

"What now?" said Eressen.

"Plan's the same," I groaned. Outside, fire alarms were howling. "Get to the school. King Death McKinley will probably be there already. We have to stop him."

He nodded briskly. "Very well. I know the location of your school. I'll go there at once, offer some resistance if the attack has begun and get prepared if not." With a flick of his wrist a portal appeared again. I guess it was night in Shal'Gasa'Nor because the hole seemed entirely black. More strange noises leaked out. He gave us an apologetic look. "I'd invite you two along, but... well, it wouldn't be quite safe. Wouldn't do the cause much good for you two to be devoured before you even arrived at the battle."

Elise nodded. "Fine, we'll catch up."

"Don't be late." He turned with a flourish, the portal vanishing behind him.

"Wanna go to a dance?" I said.

"Aww, I'd love to," Elise said. "I was afraid no one would ask me."

"Nobody likes a sarcastic vampire." We started running.

Well, Elise ran, and I staggered. Crowds of people, their voices a frightened buzz, were making their way to the halls, to the lobby, and outside, driven by the alarms. We lost ourselves among them, until we were able to peel away in the parking lot. After I finally collapsed, on the way back to the car, she growled in exasperation and hauled me along, wrapping my arm around her shoulders and letting me lean against her. When we made it back, she stuffed me inside, dived in, and the engine roared.

She must have been lurking around town for a while, because she didn't have any problem following the hasty directions I gave her. It wasn't far, especially when you drove the way she did.

For all the good it would do, I had the presence of mind to call 911. "911, what's your emergency?"

"King Death and the Reapers are about to attack Archibald J. Keller High School," I said. "I repeat, King Death and the Reapers are about to attack Archibald J. Keller. I don't know who the hell's in charge or what you people are doing, but you need to dispatch all units." Deciding that any more conversation would probably be unproductive, I hung up. Hopefully the phrase "dispatch all units" would sound official enough to get something done.

I spent most of the rest of the drive with my head leaned against the window, watching the streetlights blur by, and willing my power to come back. It didn't.

"You're not in any shape to fight." Elise's voice surprised me.

"I know. I don't have any choice."

"What are you gonna do, stab King Death like you did that other guy?"

"If I have to."

Despite my strong words, I knew I was done for. Our already

dismal chances had plummeted into the basement. What could I do, hide behind Elise and make cutting remarks? Unless…

Unless…

I remembered the baggie lurking in my pocket.

Oh, shit.

I think that was the little voice of reason in my head, much abused lately and finally pushed past the breaking point.

This was a long shot. The longest shot I'd taken in a week of them.

But a long shot was the only one I had.

I guess that shouldn't have been much of a surprise.

Silently, guiltily, I reached into my jacket pocket and pulled out the baggie. I hadn't planned this, I swear; it had just been a half-baked impulse that made me take this stuff along.

I stared at it for a second, thinking, weighing. "Don't tell me that's what I think it is." Elise's voice cut through the fog in my mind.

I winced. "I don't know what else to do. I'm at the bottom of the barrel. I can't cast any magic like this."

"Haven't you noticed that everyone who takes it dies? You'll be even more useless than usual if you're dead."

"No. I'm a magic user, remember? It'll affect me a lot differently than it will the average person." *I hope.*

"Yeah, it'll probably be worse. You'll melt your face off like *Raiders of the Lost Ark* or cause an earthquake or something."

I swallowed.

She had raised very valid points that deserved serious consideration, and while she'd been doing that, I'd gulped down two of the pills. I gave her a sour smile as they dragged themselves down my throat to my gut. "Never was very good at taking pills. Guess it kept me away from drugs until now, huh?" I laughed madly. My stomach tossed from the abuse I'd given it, but nothing happened.

I didn't feel any different yet, just as beat-up and weak as I had a moment ago. I wondered how long it would take to kick in.

Elise shook her head in exasperation and glared through the windshield. "I think we have one thing going for us," she said. "King Death thinks you're dead. And when he finds out you're not, he's gonna be pissed. I think he hates your guts because you've survived everything he's thrown at you, and he wants to know if he's really stronger than you. Because deep down he's afraid he's not. And we're gonna use that."

"Cool. I've always wanted to be bait."

We flew past a stop sign in what might optimistically be called a "rolling stop," then we were there, slowing down precipitously, sending me lurching.

"We're not all immortal, you know," I grumbled.

She set the car down in the parking lot, somehow herding it into an open space, and we climbed out. Nothing seemed amiss. I'd half-expected the place to be on fire and allowed myself to think we weren't too late to do something. "See anything?" I asked.

"No. Nothing."

"Maybe we'll have time to hit the dance floor before everything gets violent."

We headed down the sidewalk for the entrance. Here and there other students mingled, migrating towards the door. Elise surveyed the scene with unveiled contempt. "This is high school, huh? I'm glad I was born before this was a thing."

"You'd like it. Lots of kids you could bite." I jerked my head to one side. "There's something out of the ordinary."

Rodriguez was stationed by the entrance, another cop nearby, who gave us a suspicious frown. "Sam," he said, coming closer. "Good to see you."

"Good to see you, too. How's it going?"

"All quiet so far." He glanced at Elise and his face visibly quivered. He pulled himself together. "This must be the vampire who's helping you wreck the city."

She gave him a smirk and stuck out a hand. He shook it, and from his moon eyes, I got the feeling it was his first time shaking hands with a vampire. "Elise."

"Rodriguez."

"What's going on here?" I asked him. "Did you make anything happen?"

Rodriguez rubbed his face. "Not enough. I'm sorry. I told them I got an anonymous tip, about McKinley and the attack on the school. They put out a BOLO on McKinley, but that's the extent of the good news. They let me be the one to cover the school, but they said it wasn't enough to change the plan."

"What about the 911 call I just made?"

He wore the expression of someone being sent to the firing squad. "They radioed it to us, but we're not gonna get any help. Not fast enough. About five minutes before you got here, there was a Hex attack on two different banks, simultaneously. Multiple people starting fires."

My heart sank. "And every cop in the city went charging in to protect the money."

"I'm afraid so, yeah."

"So, we're on our own, as usual," I said. "Well, McKinley sure knows how things work in Williamsport."

"How many of you are there now?" Elise said.

"Four."

"Four," I said incredulously. That was even worse than I'd been expecting.

"Yeah. The two of us and two more on the other side of the school. They had a lot of ground to cover, said if trouble started to call for backup and the cars on patrol would head this way."

"Well, the trouble's here and apparently the backup's a non-starter. We have to get everybody out."

"I agree," he said, "but we have to be careful about it. Don't want to cause a panic, or tip him off. Go inside, get the lay of the land."

"Copy that."

Elise and I breezed through the doors into the main hallway, now dim. There was a table set up outside the gym door, Ms. Collins, English teacher, sitting wearily behind it. Beyond her, music thumped. "Three dollars for couples," she said, plainly eager to get back to the *Cosmo* that sat at the table's corner. She made only a desultory protest when we hustled by.

We stepped through the doors into a gym transformed, with people milling around, a pop song playing from the speakers. Sparkling, multicolored lights twirled across the floor. It was all very teen comedy, completely incongruous with the danger we were in.

Of course, the veneer faded once you looked closer. The dancing had an uneasy quality, a few people scattered around the gym floor, their swaying vaguely anxious. Scattered on both sides of the gym, some sitting, others standing anxiously, a few pacing, like they were ready to leap into action, were clumps of my fellow students.

I looked around for Jason, finally spotted him, dancing several yards away. He was not what you'd call naturally rhythmic, but I got the feeling he was trying to force the dance into some normalcy. It clearly wasn't working. I approached him, Elise stalking behind me. That seemed to be her natural walk. "Jason."

He turned. "Hey Sam. You... look like you came straight here from whatever it was you were doing."

I looked down. Yeah, the eldritch explosion at McKinley's apartment had gotten my suit rather rumpled. "Well, I did."

He frowned, then glanced at Elise, looking a little flustered.

Down boy. He stuck out his hand. "Hi, I'm Jason Clay, Sam's friend. How do you two know each other?"

My stomach flopped. I didn't care for these two sides of my life colliding, especially when I wouldn't put it past Elise to eat him. She took his hand. "I'm Elise. Sam and I are getting married—"

"She's been helping me fight King Death," I said abruptly. "Don't ask me why, because she won't say." I decided not to mention the vampire part.

He gave her a disturbed look. "Nice to meet you."

"Sam?" I turned towards the familiar voice to see Alexandra, curiosity and confusion sketched on her face.

"Alex. Hi. I'm surprised you came."

"I'm surprised to see you, too."

"You shouldn't be here," I said, unease beginning to rise within me. "This is about to be the most dangerous place in Williamsport."

She shrugged. "You're here."

"Yeah, but I'm... you know."

"I know. Jason tried to talk me out of it too. I just... I wanted to see this through."

There wasn't much point in arguing about it now, I supposed. "I understand, unfortunately. How's your brother?"

Her face turned sad. "He's home, at least. Sometimes he's fine. Sometimes he just wanders around, or cries. He has nightmares. I'm trying to help him feel better."

I noticed she didn't mention her mom or Rick. "I'm sorry. Has Jason said anything to you?"

She gave me an incredulous smile. "About your big North/South alliance idea? Yeah, he told me."

"You don't think it'll work?"

Her lips curled. "I mean, the Sixth Street Aces are here, patrolling the halls or something." She jerked her head towards a small group of them over by one wall. Michael caught my eye and gave me a nod. "I'm sure we're in good hands."

"Has anything happened?"

"Just one thing," Jason said. "A few minutes ago, I heard there was an explosion or something; a couple people saw it on social media."

"It's true," I said. "I think it's a diversion."

"Oh God," Alex said. "It's happening here, isn't it?"

"Yes."

Fear crossed her face, and resolve. "What are we supposed to do?"

"We need to get out of here, that's what."

"We'll tip off King Death if we do that. We might lose our chance to take him down."

I was surprised at this new side of her, but then, maybe it wasn't new, I thought, recalling her determination back at Jake's. "I won't take that risk. Too many people have died already."

"But if we don't take the chance now, more people will die later. We finally have a chance to stop that son of a bitch, and we can't let it get away."

"Oh yeah, that's another thing. Regarding the son of a bitch in question. I know who he is."

"Who?" Jason said.

"We know him. It's Mr. McKinley. He's King Death."

They stared incredulously. "He's King Death," said Alex.

"Yeah. I know it for sure. I went for him at his apartment, but he made it out before I got there."

"The man wears sweater vests for God's sake."

"I guess they're sweater vests of doom."

"You gotta be kidding me," Jason said.

"Nope, I never joke about unspeakable evil."

Alex snorted, and I saw amusement under the fear. "Yeah, that sounds so unlike you."

"Oh yeah, he's cold as ice in an emergency situation," Elise muttered, and then the phrase "cold as ice" became terrifyingly appropriate. McKinley was there. Standing on the opposite side of the gym. I guess it was his night to chaperone.

He saw me. There was no mistaking it. His gaze locked onto mine from across the room, laser focused. His eyes were utterly barking mad.

I didn't think he'd known I was a wizard; if he had, I figured he would have come after me like I'd gone after him. But he saw me with Alexandra. If he didn't know Elise, the Reapers must have told him about the blonde vampire who'd helped slaughter them. And he knew. I knew he knew. I wondered if he was as flabbergasted as I had been to find out his enemy's identity.

The sounds of the gym faded away. Fear and anger, but mostly fear, flared white-hot through my veins. I instinctively reached out for magic, felt my stomach drop as I remembered it wasn't there.

The three of them saw where I was staring, their bodies tensing and their gazes locking as well. I thought Elise might just bound across the room and tear his throat out on the spot, witnesses be damned. For that matter, I thought Alex might do the same thing.

McKinley vanished. Whether it was magical or not, I didn't know, but he was there, then he was gone.

This, as they say, was it.

CHAPTER TWENTY-TWO

I BOUNDED ACROSS the gym. "Michael. Michael." I caught his attention, the Sixth Streeters clustered around him stirring. "It's happening, right now."

"Damn it. Okay." He turned to those around him. They suddenly seemed pitifully few. "You heard him. Get ready." They milled uneasily, Tommy patting his jacket, where the gun that had shot me undoubtedly waited. He gave me a meaningful nod, which I returned. Alex and Elise had followed me. "Quite an army you got here," Elise observed. Alex just eyed them suspiciously.

I bounded back the way I had come, waving a hand. "Jason. Is there any help?"

"I think so. I'll try." He trotted over to another sullen clump of teenagers. North Siders. I saw the incredulity on their faces, and the suspicious glances towards the South Siders, me in particular, as Jason spoke low but emphatically. The question of "what the hell do we do?" kept banging through my mind but there were no answers on offer.

We were penned up in here like a bunch of sheep to the literal slaughter, and I returned to my first impulse: we had to escape. But that presented its own problems. A giant stampede for the doors would cause chaos, turning us into sitting ducks to be picked off when we scattered in all directions. That could be exactly what the Reapers wanted, for that matter, and it would be impossible to protect everybody. I wouldn't be fighting alone this time but that only made me more anxious. Looking around, at the frightened faces, I promised myself that if anyone here died tonight, it would be me.

No, I corrected myself. It would be King Death.

I'd spent most of the last few days feeling doomed, buffeted all over town by forces beyond my control that I could barely survive against. But I had survived, hadn't I?

I was tired of this. Tired of people dying, tired of getting my ass kicked, tired of being too weak and blind to do anything about it. I wanted to fight back. We may have been bait, but this bait would have teeth.

I focused, tried to call up magic. It didn't work. I'd been hoping for a surge of power to come rushing into me, but that hadn't happened. So far, the Hex hadn't even given me a buzz. What if, I feared, I had it backwards: maybe because I was a magic user it would take a lot more than just a couple pills to affect me. What if magic gave me a tolerance to it, rather than being a match in a can of gasoline? I couldn't worry about that now.

A small crowd of the local jocks had gathered around Jason, and the Sixth Street Aces ambled over as well. The looks exchanged were vicious and I feared a hair trigger was about to get pulled, maybe literally. I spoke up before that could happen. "Easy now, everybody. We have a common enemy here."

Most of Jason's crew looked at me with undisguised disdain. Trevor, unsurprisingly, wasn't among them, but still, Jason had rounded up more than I'd expected. I kept talking before things could get away from me. "Jason told you what's going on, didn't he?"

There were uneasy rumbles. "Yeah," one guy spoke up, "that

we're under attack from the Reapers." There was barely suppressed laughter in his voice.

"It's true. King Death is real, and he's trying to play the North and South against each other. I don't know why, but he wants a war that burns the whole city to the ground."

"Do you actually expect us to believe any of this?" demanded someone else.

"You should," spoke up Brian, pushing his way up from the back, Kyle a pace behind him.

"He's right," Kyle said. "You need to listen to this guy."

"And if you won't listen to him, listen to me," Jason said.

"And me," Alex spoke up. "It wasn't a bunch of random South Siders that kidnapped my brother. It was King Death."

They looked at me, still incredulous, uneasy, but listening. That was a start. "We don't have time to fight each other anymore," I said. "If you don't care about each other, that's fine, but I'm guessing none of you want your own side getting destroyed, your friends and family getting killed. Which they will. I guarantee it. It's already happened, and you know it. Is it really that hard to believe? Do you think everything that's happening is a coincidence? Do you think the Sixth Street Aces would come here if it wasn't important? There's about to be a fight, right now, right here and it needs not to be with each other. Do you understand?" If I'd been hoping for a roar of approval, I'd have been sorely disappointed, but there were a few reluctant mutters that sounded agreeable. "We have to keep anyone from getting killed. I don't know how, but that's the most important thing. That's what I want all of you to do."

"And what do you do?" said Jason.

I swallowed. "I fight."

"You fight?"

"Yeah. I go on the offensive with Elise."

Kyle gave her a look of horny skepticism. "Are you some kind of assassin or something?"

"Yes."

While Kyle mulled that over, Jason said, "Sam, that's suicide, you'll get yourself killed."

"Uh... Jas, you know there are ways I can defend myself."

His face was pale. "Will it give you that much of an edge?"

No. "Maybe. I have to try. I'm the only one that stands a chance of taking him down, and you know it."

"And what about her?" Kyle said, jerking his head towards Elise, still with a rather thirsty look on his face.

Apparently, she was a fan of radical honesty. "I'm a vampire," she said. Kyle blinked. "What about you?" Elise said, nudging me. "Are you back in the game?"

I tried to concentrate. It was hard. I felt... something strange. Like a squirrel scampering around in the back of my mind.

"What is she talking about?" Jason said. Then he glared into my face. "Wait... are you high?"

"Oh yeah," Elise said, venom dripping from her tone. "That."

Now that he mentioned it, I was feeling a little... discombobulated. My head was light, and despite our dire circumstances, I felt strangely happy. What a nice night this was. What a nice universe we lived in. It was so vast, with so many things to discover. So many truths, just waiting to be known, out there, amongst the stars.

"What the hell did you take?"

Oh. Right. Jason's demand brought me back to earth. Awareness slammed onto his face. "Jesus Christ, did you take Hex? How? Why?"

I giggled. He was so funny.

"Sam, pay attention." Something jerked me upright and I found myself staring into Elise's eyes. Her hands clutched my arms. "Do you feel anything?"

"Your eyes are so pretty. They're green, like Ireland."

She swatted me away in exasperation. "Do you feel any magic?"

That was important, I remembered. I stretched out with my awareness. "No. No, I don't think so. I'm sorry." The world seemed to be buzzing, but even in my altered state, I knew it wasn't the same thing at all. "Where the hell is Eressen?" I said, coming back to myself enough to remember him. "He was supposed to be here." I glanced around, half-expecting him to make some dramatic entrance.

"I don't know, and I'm not going to sit around waiting for him, or for you to start levitating things. Let's go."

"She's right," I said, my giddiness fading. "We have to get everybody out of here. Quickly and quietly. With a little luck, maybe we can do it without any bloodshed."

A popping sound came from outside, muffled, but distinct: gunshots, two or three of them.

Shouts rose up around the room. Everyone knew what it was. Jason held up his hands. "Stay calm," he bellowed. "Everybody stay calm. We'll be fine if we stick together, just listen."

There were a couple more shots, closer, then the door burst open, a terrified Ms. Collins boiling through being urged along by Rodriguez. He was shouting into his radio, and I distinctly heard the phrase "officer down." Ms. Collins was incoherently demanding to know what was happening, which seemed to be going around.

"They're here," Rodriguez called to me. "Something got hold of Wright and just tossed him. There's no way he could have survived."

My blood ran cold. The other gym doors boomed as the other two cops bashed through them, guns drawn. "Did you see anything out back?" I called to them.

They scowled at me in confusion. "Answer him," Rodriguez practically shouted.

"No," one of them said. "We just came to back up Rodriguez."

"Then maybe they're not out back. They surely can't have the numbers to surround the place. Maybe they figured they'd come in the front, take us by surprise." They would likely have succeeded, too, if it wasn't for the motley crew of misfits I'd rounded up.

King Death/Mr. McKinley's plan was becoming depressingly clear: in the morning, when the smoke cleared, there would be dozens of dead high schoolers from both sides of town, lying in the rubble, and any survivors would have no idea what the hell had happened. I didn't know how the city of Williamsport would react, but it would be extreme. "International headlines" extreme.

"What's the best way out?" I asked no one in particular. "I—"

Something hit me, and I felt like I'd been knocked into next month. For a moment, I thought someone had cast a spell on me. I tried to cry out in shock but couldn't even tell if I got any sound out. Was I on the ground or was I floating?

The sights and sounds around me screamed into me, devouring my organs, lighting my mind on fire, flooding every vein in my body. I swore I could even feel it in the tips of my hair. Magic smoldered at the edges of my fingertips. It was like waking from a dream. The world had only seemed alive before. Now it was part of me. I was the world, and it was me, and all its power roared through me, waiting, hungry, eager. No, not just the world. The entire universe, out into infinity. I was connected to something so vast, so powerful, unfathomably far away, beyond human comprehension. Something alive. It was glorious. Indescribable. Beyond indescribable. There was something out there, all the way at the end of that long, long chain of power, winding its way through our reality and all the others. But that didn't matter now.

I looked at my friends. They stared back at me in bewilderment. There was a gasp or two, and it took me a second to realize why: I couldn't see it, but my eyes had begun to glow with magic. The wild grin probably had something to do with it, too. Elise was the first to speak. "Guess it worked, huh?"

I felt more lucid now than I had before I'd taken the Hex. "Yeah. It worked. In the immortal words of Bill Paxton, let's rock."

As Elise rolled her eyes, I felt it. A wave of magic, powerful, strong enough to make me flinch in shock despite the Hex. That wasn't the kind of magic that came from a spell, even a powerful one. It was the kind that came from a lot of spells at once. "They're here." I tossed a glance at Elise, who nodded in response. Her face shifted, becoming fangy. I heard a squawk I recognized as Kyle, and we headed for the doors. Before I reached them, something caught my arm gently, and I turned to see Alex staring at me. "Be careful, okay?" she said. "Promise me."

I gave her the most confident smile I could muster under the circumstances. "I promise."

She let go, reluctantly, and walked back towards the others.

Elise was opening her mouth to say something I'm sure she found hilarious. Before she could, I bared my own fangs at her and growled and she lifted her eyebrows in surprise. I stuck my head out the gym door, where Ms. Collins' table sat abandoned.

There were crashes and whoops, and I didn't need magic to spot the source. The Reapers, a big pack of them; all the ones left alive, most likely. They were pounding through the front doors and down the hallway, toward the gym.

I put my magical high to the test, threw up a shield, and was relieved to see it worked. The power surged and leaped within me again, and I wanted to cackle with glee, start casting spells in all directions just for the sheer joy of it, and it took an effort of will not to. I could see why Hex affected people the way it did.

One of the Reapers let out a feral shout, then dirty orange light flared in the shadows, a basketball-sized fireball jetting down the corridor, throwing bizarre shadows across the walls, a long, sputtering trail behind it like some evil comet.

I yelped, then slammed a bolt of pure levitation straight at it. Magic collided in midair, and there was a thump, a flash of light that sent me rocking back. The fireball went searing backwards, nearly as hard as it had flown towards me, and slammed into the chest of the guy who'd cast it.

No, *through* it. The fire blazed a hole into his chest cavity, then, almost immediately, out his back, before flying on down the hall several more feet to light a bulletin board on fire. His blackened, smoldering chest smoked, and I caught a glimpse of a scorched ribcage before, eyes glazed, he crumpled to the floor.

All his buddies opened up at once, too fast for me to see what was going on. I clutched tight to my shields trying not to whimper as magic pummeled me, light flashing in my eyes, impact buffeting me, laying waste to the hallway beyond, glass breaking, furniture flying, pieces of the ceiling coming down. Every one of them was tripping balls on Hex, I realized, like magical suicide bombers.

I cast a lance of levitation, picking up the closest one and hurling him through the glass doors at an awkward angle that looked bad for his health, and as he hit the ground, I picked up a vending machine, sent it careening through the air. It smashed directly into the Reaper in the lead, sending both him and the machine hurtling down the hallway and out of sight, the Reaper's arms and legs flapping in all directions. It looked downright silly, if dark comedy is your thing. I ducked back inside and saw one thing, at least, was going well: Jason and his buddies were herding everyone else for the rear doors, guarded by the cops and the Aces, all of whom had guns drawn. Hopefully the Reapers would throw enough of a scare into them to make them momentarily forget they were natural enemies. "The bus terminal," I shouted after them in a burst of inspiration. "It's not far, get there." I had to hope they understood me. I looked for Alex but didn't see her in the press. I did spot Ms. Collins, being hustled firmly along by Kyle.

The magical hurricane increased outside, and I knew I couldn't stay here. Elise and I danced back, deeper into the gym, and I levitated the big metal doors shut.

It was all of two and a half seconds before the Reapers bashed them open. The first of them came bursting inside, like barbarians storming some medieval castle. All I could think to do was buy enough time for the others to get away.

The Hex was still howling within me, and I stopped fighting it. Trusting Elise to get out of the way, I let magic whip around, a vortex of levitation that spun faster and faster, sucking up tables and chairs, causing me to flinch, as one or two of them got too close for comfort. When there was an enormous, spinning tornado of plastic and metal in the center of the gym, I flung it directly into the bastards. The ensuing noise, a cocktail of falling debris and screams, was tremendous. The mess took out the first ones through, made the rest fall back, fear cutting through even the influence of the Hex. The Reapers had shown up expecting easy pickings, but that was a mistake I was long past making.

I risked a glance back, and the others, though I could still hear their panicked shouts and stomping footsteps, seemed to be well on their way down the hall towards the exit. "We can't let them pursue," I roared at Elise.

"You don't have to shout. My hearing is better than yours."

"Sorry," I shouted.

A fireball slammed into my shields, taking me completely unawares and sending me spinning and sliding across the hardwood until I whumped into the stage.

I heard the Reapers come bursting back inside, having screwed up the courage to fight.

I felt a buzz of magic and heard a whoosh. Eressen flew into my vision, someone else right behind him. Another Shal'Gasa. The new guy went after him, sword in hand. Eressen parried three or four attacks, then did something fancy with his footwork, closed in, and rammed his blade through his opponent's chest, tearing it free, and as he went to his knees, Eressen's hand shot out again, his blade darting in and out of his enemy's throat.

He was dead before he hit the ground. I goggled. Eressen spotted me. "Sam, forgive me, I was unavoidably—"

A Reaper cast a fireball at him, which he dodged with ease, then, contrary to all logic, threw himself at the mob.

He closed with the fireball's caster, sword still in hand, to slice open his belly. The guy already had fireballs spinning in both hands, and as he gushed blood, they had nowhere to go, ending up in his clothes. He blossomed into a human torch, tried to run, and made it a few steps before he tripped and fell, sending puddles of fire spreading out around him. I'd lost sight of Elise but heard a growl nearby that sounded distinctly like her. I guessed I should really get back in this fight.

Just as I resolved to do that, one of them appeared in front of me, another damn levitator, and hurled me straight up, the floor disappearing from beneath my feet. I didn't quite hit the ceiling, but I went on the ride of my life, screaming haplessly as I careened upwards, shapes below me getting smaller, then went flailing back down, the gym floor looming terrifyingly large in my vision. Before I slammed home, I thought to send a blast of levitation down into the floor, crunching a hole into the hardwood, hoping the gravity or the centrifugal force or whatever you call it would lessen the impact.

I'm not sure if it was that or the strength of my shields, but I didn't break my neck, though that didn't keep me from brutally aggravating the bullet wounds, and let's not forget, the stab wound, as well as skinning my knees. I saw stars upon impact but narrowly managed to stay conscious.

As I thumped brutally back to the floor, I extended a hand, and fired off bursts of levitation, short ones, over and over, into my attacker's chest. If he'd been shielded like I was, it would have knocked him on his ass, but he would have lived through it. But he didn't know about shields, and the blows ripped into him like bullets, blowing red holes in his chest, sending him jerking backwards and into the tangle of debris by the door.

I wanted to scream but I didn't, instead scrambling off the floor and looking for another enemy to kill. I saw a Reaper about to cast a spell at Eressen, whose back was turned, and before he could I picked him up and sent him cartwheeling into the gym wall with a wet, crunchy thump.

Eressen bashed the hilt of his sword into a Reaper's face, then drew back and ran him through. He turned to give me a bluff smile. "My thanks, Sam. I— Duck!"

I did. He sidestepped, and a chunk of fire and debris went roaring past me to splatter and clank against the far wall.

Eressen leaped forward, in front of a dark silhouette, cut off his hand as he tried to cast again, then opened his throat on the backswing. As the dying man gurgled, Eressen kicked him to the floor.

I finally caught sight of Elise; in what you might call the last place I'd looked: the ceiling.

Perched over the death and wreckage as easily as if she'd been enjoying some fresh air on a balcony, she crouched on one of the light fixtures hanging over us. There were two of them after her, both levitators firing shot after shot. They were brutal, pummeling hits, some of them blasting chunks out of the walls, better-aimed ones shattering light fixtures. This didn't seem to bother her; she just hopped from one to another, and when she ran out of space, she threw herself even farther, easily landing in a crouch on the bleachers, before appearing back on the ground. One of them threw a spell, and it was close, but she threw herself flat to the floor, letting it knock a hole in the bleachers, then she was back up and both guys were dropping dead.

It was obvious instantly. One guy hit the floor bonelessly, dead before he hit the ground and the other scrabbled frantically at his throat, all thoughts of magic forgotten, gurgling softly as he sunk to his knees, then his stomach. He kept flopping but Elise was already turning away.

Not guns this time. Knives.

I'd hoped we'd massacred them sufficiently by now, but we weren't that lucky. Something surged into me, flooding my vision with light, throwing me through the air. My shield hummed and vibrated, shaking my bones.

As I landed in a heap, I caught a glimpse of what had hit me: a bolt of electricity, scorching the bleachers now. No fair.

I spotted its caster, looking vaguely like Emperor Palpatine, waving his arms as the electricity spun around him. The power surge caused more lights to blow out, sparks raining down from the ceiling here and there. He seemed to be having trouble controlling it, but he had the presence of mind to turn his gaze at me. I tried to reach for magic, but my brain was scrambled, and my response time was slow. Then there was a shot, and instantaneously, his head exploded.

More shots echoed through the gym, then Rodriguez appeared in my view, firing away. I scrambled to my feet.

Another cop was with him, blasting shot after shot at the Reapers. Bullets tore into two or three more of them, sending them twisting and jerking to the floor as they tried to hurl magic, a stray spell producing a crash whose source I didn't see. A moment later, the firing died away, and I heard the clicking sounds of reloading.

I sent a wobbling glance around the gym. It was a mess: blood and wreckage and bodies sprawled in all directions. Rodriguez's partner was down with a piece of metal sticking in his leg, dark blood staining the gym floor, and I wanted to heal him but knew I didn't have time. We hadn't entirely defeated the Reapers; I could hear a few of them moving around in the hallway, but the barrage had tipped the scales in our favor and driven them back for the moment.

I sagged, leaning forward, and resting my hands on my knees. The Hex still seethed in my veins, but exhaustion sank into me anyway. This wasn't over; it had barely even started. And if I was gonna save the day, I needed to do it before the Hex wore off. Before everybody here ended up dead.

"They're too exposed out there," I growled raggedly. "We can't stay here."

"We can't exactly let the Reapers come roaming through here, either," Elise said.

"You and her, go after them," Rodriguez said abruptly. He cast a glance at Eressen. "Uh... he and I will hold them off."

"Eressen al'Barra," Eressen said helpfully.

I hesitated, torn, knowing he was right but reluctant to leave them behind. "I don't like it."

Elise didn't have any such hesitation. "Let's go," she said, and without another word went through the backdoors, down the hall, after everyone else.

I hesitated a beat longer, growled, awkwardly raised a hand in what was supposed to be a manly battle salute, then ran after her. I was doing far too much running lately. Behind me, the gunfire started again.

As we left the gym behind, I cast a paranoid glance over my shoulder, and was damn glad I did.

Two Reapers, having detached from their buddies, perhaps to attack the gym from the rear, came around the corner, and settled for chasing after us.

I grunted a warning to Elise, threw up a shield as a machine gun fire barrage of daggerlike shards of ice came hurling towards us. They shattered with bizarre quiet against my shield, but they would have ripped unprotected flesh to shreds.

Running as I did, I sent a bolt of levitation at the caster that took him off his feet and bashed him into the far wall, eight feet off the ground. Dead or wounded, he was done making trouble for tonight.

Then the other guy ripped a door off its hinges with a demonic scream and sent it barreling towards us. I did *not* like being on the other side of levitation. Elise flung herself through another door, smashing it to pieces. I didn't stop to look back, just dove inside after Elise.

I crashed into a desk and went skidding across the floor. I saw the Reaper's silhouette in the door, and as he stepped through, Elise pounced, her fangs tearing deep into his throat before he knew what hit him. She growled, squelching and popping filling the air, shaking her head back and forth, looking like a dog chewing on a pair of shoes. With one last jerk of her head, she let his corpse fall to the floor. Even in the dark, I could tell she licked her lips.

I made my shaky way to my feet, only half-paying attention to my surroundings, when something clicked. I recognized the room.

I stopped dead in my tracks. *Not now*, I thought. But no: now.

As vividly as the day it happened, I found myself in class, in this room, a year ago.

I hadn't seen much of Abby that summer, for one reason or another, and I'd found myself missing her, looking forward to the day when I'd see her again. That was strange, I had thought. We'd been friends since kindergarten, but I'd never felt that. But that summer, I felt it more keenly every day, at first a little. Then a lot.

This class had been the first time I'd seen her in a month or more. I had looked across the room, where she sat next to another girl. Shawna, my brain dredged up.

Shawna must have said something funny, because Abby was laughing uncontrollably, her eyes glittering, her head thrown back, oblivious to everything else. I had stared, not caring if I was being weird, unable to look away, completely enraptured. It was the most beautiful sight I'd ever laid eyes on.

That was when I knew I'd love her until the day I died.

Luckily, I didn't have any classes in here this year. Being in here every day would probably have turned me into a gibbering loon.

But maybe I'd never left this room at all.

"Sam?" I jumped, found myself back in the murky darkness, that day a painfully fading memory again. Elise's touch on my arm had been surprisingly gentle, and the concern on her face seemed almost genuine. "Where did you go? What's the matter with you?"

"Nothing. We have to move."

And we did, leaving all the ghosts behind.

"It's not far," I panted to Elise. *If they made it.*

As the exits loomed closer, gunfire crackled, somewhere outside. Close. My heart lurched and I redoubled my speed, slamming through the door.

There was more gunfire, and I caught sight of muzzle flashes. The Sixth Street Aces, and the other cop, putting up some kind of a fight.

A vicious roar split the night, chilling me to the bone. It was the demon we'd failed to kill last night, revealed in all its glory now: ten feet tall, a bulletlike head swiveling around massive shoulders, doglike ears, reptilian green eyes, grey-black fur, and talons on each massive hand that I couldn't count but clearly exceeded the standard five. Behind him, I saw a jagged hole in the school's brick wall, which he'd apparently crashed through.

It lumbered towards the knot of shooters, who fell back, but didn't completely lose their cool. They fired a barrage of shots, some seeming to hit the creature, others going wild and setting off sparks in the night. It closed the distance, lashing out with a paw, taking out the closest one.

His body, ragdoll limp, flopped through the air in one direction as a long ribbon of his blood fountained in the other. I screamed in futile rage and sent a vicious blade of fire streaking towards it.

I took it completely by surprise. It was nice to be the one doing that for a change.

It slammed into the creature, hurling it backwards in a spectacular orange rain. It growled again, in what I hoped was pain, but whatever it was, the thing leaped back up quickly, its fur smoking.

The good news was it turned its attention from the others. The bad news was it began hurtling towards us.

"I'm not sure what exactly a vampire's supposed to do about this thing," Elise muttered tightly as it bore down on us.

There was something a wizard could do, though. I didn't retreat, and when it was almost on top of me, I cast a spell of levitation that picked him up bodily, and tossed him a hundred yards, through the first-floor windows and deep into the classroom beyond. Hopefully I'd broken his neck.

I waved an arm, jumped up and down, hoping the Sixth Street Aces and cops wouldn't decide to shoot me. "Hey. Over here." I jogged over to see Tommy and a few others, all of them swiveling guns around and plainly about to faint. "Tommy. What's going on?"

His gaze went to the broken windows. "It hit us right before you showed up. Oh God, Lucas…"

"I know. Did anybody else get hurt?"

"I don't think so."

"Where's Rodriguez and Ellis?" shouted the cop, his gun trained towards the hole in the school's wall.

"They're inside, holding off what's left of the Reapers, buying us time. Where's everybody else?"

He jerked his head behind him. "Back there. At the bus terminal. Your friend the Sixth Street Ace is trying to get one hotwired."

"Good."

"Sam." Jason's voice boomed over the parking lot, and we hustled towards him. "Thank God." He gave Elise a nod. "I was afraid you didn't make it. Are you okay?"

"Fine, never better. You guys?"

"We're okay so far, I think. We gotta get out of here."

"That's the plan. We'll take care of things around here, while you get in the nearest thing with wheels and make tracks."

"I can't just leave you here."

"You don't have a choice. You'll die if you stay here. This isn't over yet."

"Then come with us."

"I can't. He'll pursue you if I go, and I don't know if I can keep any of you safe then."

His face contorted. "Fine," he muttered flatly. "But once everybody's safe, I'm coming right back here."

I didn't try to talk him out of it. By the time he got back, it would be over, one way or another.

Seven or eight gunshots went off back in the direction of the school, and I saw Rodriguez, the wounded Ellis propped up with one arm and both of them waving guns, come backing out the doors. A few steps behind, a Reaper surged after them, arms flinging into the air, and he flopped face down on the gravel.

Jason scrambled towards them, grabbed Ellis under his other arm, and he and Rodriguez began hauling him along towards us.

"If I survive the night," I told Ellis, "I'll come find you, see if I can heal that leg."

"Thanks," he said, voice thready. "I—"

"Sam, look out," Jason shouted. Another Reaper flung himself through the door, and without hesitation, levitated a long chunk of chain-link fence and sent it rocketing towards us.

I flung up a hand, caught the twisting metal in midair, sent it clattering away into the darkness. A split second later, I sent a whirlwind of fire swirling up around the Reaper, drenching him from ankles to face. His scream was loud, but brief, and he collapsed next to his buddy to smolder on the ground.

"Oh shit," muttered Jason, clutching at his throat like he was trying to keep vomit from bursting out of it. I really wished he hadn't seen that.

"Where's Eressen?" I said. "Did he make it?"

"I don't know," said Rodriguez. "A group of them was trying to flank us; he went after them, and we got separated."

"Damn it."

An engine roared, and I saw the last knot of my classmates climbing aboard the bus. "If we're going after King Death we have to move now," Elise said.

"She's right," I said. "Saddle up."

If anybody was gonna make any emotional farewells, they didn't get a chance. That roar sounded again, ripping out of the hole I'd left in the school. "GO," I yelled. We pounded the remaining distance, the Sixth Street Aces clambering inside, Jason right behind, helping the wounded cop. "Good luck," I heard him call as he disappeared inside. Here and there windows opened, gun barrels poking out.

Rodriguez and the cop whose name I hadn't got stood at the bus's entrance, covering the retreat of the last few stragglers. Rodriguez glanced at me. "And don't you get any ideas about selfless heroism," I told him. "If things go sideways on the bus, they'll need every gun they can get."

Rodriguez gave me a forced smile. "Don't worry. As soon as we get out of here, I'll get us help, come back here with every cop in the city. All you have to do is hold out long enough for us to get back here."

I forced a smile of my own. "I can do that. Thanks." Whatever Rodriguez thought, I knew help wouldn't be on the way. The local constabulary might risk their lives to save their own men, or the students at the dance, but a teenage wizard and a wayward vampire? It wasn't going to happen.

There was a rattling crash that sounded distinctly like a demon hauling itself out of a heap of rubble.

I finally spotted Alex. She had been supporting a kid named Jose against her shoulder, him having apparently got hurt in the confusion. She handed him off to Rodriguez and the other guy, who helped him the rest of the way aboard, all of them disappearing into the darkness of the bus. There was another roar that vibrated my shoes. I took a step towards her. She saw me, turning around as she climbed onto the steps.

There was another roar, noticeably closer. It seemed like I should say something, but I wasn't quite sure what, and time, as usual, was running out.

I gave her a smile I didn't know if she saw, then turned towards the sound, and a second later, the bus roared past, spraying Elise and I with gravel, barreling for the street.

The demon lumbered out of the blackness, and I saw his shadowed head turn in the shadows, his gaze swiveling toward the bus. I let out a feral growl that, in my own head, at least, sounded as loud as his own.

He began lumbering after the bus. Its taillights were distant now, but I knew he wouldn't have much trouble catching up. It gave me an idea. *Here's a bus, motherfucker.*

"Duck," I told Elise. Without waiting, I threw an arm around her shoulders and flung us both painfully onto the gravel. As I did so, I sent magic behind us, a lot of it, lifting two more buses screaming from the ground. I heard, rather than saw, them burst through the ceiling of the terminal, never designed to stop *that*.

Wind whistled for a heart stopping second as they sailed over our heads. Once I'd felt them pass, I dared to look up, got a haphazard glimpse of them flying through the air, smashing directly into the demon.

He disappeared, completely buried under a mountain of pulverized metal and exploding glass. Debris was flung upwards from the impact, a tire bouncing madly across the ground into the shadows. I didn't want to gamble on even that much killing him. My stomach still in the gravel, I threw out a hand, aimed a spell towards the wreckage, aiming for the undersides of the buses.

Fire. Jets of fire sprayed all over the shattered hulks. I kept going, not sure how much it would take, the fire spreading precipitously. It didn't take much.

The two gas tanks went off almost simultaneously, a hot fist striking me in the face, the impact ringing my ears and reverberating through my guts. Gorgeous blooms of fire erupted out and up, briefly scorching away the darkness in an eruption of violent light. It dissipated quickly, leaving behind a blazing, unrecognizable heap of metal.

I chuckled with weary triumph as we made our way unsteadily to our feet.

"Sweet," said Elise. "I—" She let out a tiny noise and flew through the air, backwards, hard and fast. She flew across the parking lot, across the street, where she bounced hard off a tree, twisted to the left and disappeared in the darkness.

Shit. I ducked into a crouch, for all the good that would do. I looked but didn't see her. I wanted to go searching but knew I didn't have the time.

I let anger fill me, and power, and turning back I saw him: King Death stood in the open double doors of the school. Watching.

Waiting. A bone-white mask hid his face. He hadn't been blindly throwing magic; he'd wanted to level the playing field. Just me and him.

That was fine with me.

"Sam," he said. My heightened senses made his voice loud even across the distance.

I didn't stop to think how unwise this was: fists clenching, magic dancing within me, its music humming through my body, I began walking towards him, fast, gaze aimed straight at him, nothing in my mind but his death.

"You can take that mask off," I said. "I know who you are, Mr. McKinley. Don't you have papers to grade or something?"

He pulled his mask off and tossed it to the ground, revealing the same familiar face. A cold fist wrapped around my guts and squeezed, and my heart sank. It would have been nice to have been wrong, somehow. "Sam," he said. His voice was no different than it was in the classroom, but his eyes were. Even in the darkness, I could see their distant, wild gleam. "I—"

Perfect. I'd had the feeling he'd want to hear himself talk; any guy named "King Death" must like the sound of his own voice. And that was just what I'd wanted him to do, because it meant he'd let his guard down, even if only a fraction.

I attacked.

I didn't even know what I was trying to do, but by gods, it was going to be something.

It was.

Fire mingled with wind, a blazing whirlwind that roared out of me and through me, burning through the night, screaming as it slammed into King Death. There was a massive flare as the magic collided with his shields, blotting him and everything around him from my view, bowling him back into the shadows of the doors, the blowback sending me staggering back a few steps.

Calm. Calm. Think. Don't let up.

Then all I could do was focus on my shields, as a storm of fire drenched me, heat making sweat and pain blossom all over me. It roared, storming down from every direction, and I screamed in terror, seizing the magic of my shield and holding to it tighter than I ever had.

The fire slammed against me, the shields barely holding together, straining and fraying from the effort, the molten glow blotting out my vision, heat that should have melted me an inescapable pain. Tears of blood slipped from my eyes down my cheeks and I knew the Hex wouldn't keep me from burning out forever.

It wasn't an ordinary jet of fire—that seemed to be a theme with King Death. It was a hurricane, a tsunami, a wall of orange-red, mingled with traces of that demonic green to form a sickly hue, and it swirled and rushed like the ocean as it tried to gnaw through my shield to get to me. I didn't know how long it lasted, just growled until my throat hurt, keeping my shields in place. I felt more blood leak, from my nose this time. And then it was gone, the night going still again. I panted, not quite believing I was alive. I stumbled to my feet. I hadn't even realized I'd fallen.

"I see you sampled a little of my product," said King Death, still with the blasé voice he used in the classroom. "I can see why you would."

And he just keeps talking. I supposed I'd spent my life mouthing off, so there was no reason to stop now. "Isn't there some kind of rule about killing your students?" I sneered at him. "Doesn't that go against board policy or something?"

To my surprise, I saw a flicker of something resembling regret on his face. Almost, anyway, somewhere deep beneath the lunacy. Then it was gone. "I'm not killing them. I'm saving them."

"Oh, for God's sake."

"I don't have a choice." His voice was disturbingly firm, and I realized he actually believed this shit. "I—"

I wasn't interested in his ranting, so I opened fire. Literally.

Two whips of fire, twenty feet long, snaked through the night air, pummeling towards him, him throwing up his hands frantically to block them as they scoured against the red brick walls.

This was amazing. I'd never wielded power like this, and exhilaration sang through me, mingling with the magic itself. Was this how it felt for King Death?

That thought stopped me cold as the whips hammered at his shields.

I'm not too sure what he did next; debris and force slammed into my shields, throwing me back with a thunderous concussion, light blinding me for a heartbeat.

Should I make a run for it? Hoof it into the school or the grounds, make him follow me, try and get him off-balance? King Death answered the question for me: he conjured a horde of spinning, razor-sharp little half-circles of black metal, all of them hurtling towards my face.

I flung my arm desperately, sending a gust of wind that swept them away into the night, a couple of strays scoring my shields, one of them hard enough to draw a little blood. If I tried to run, I'd just get those or something worse in the back. Apparently, the only option, if you'll pardon the expression, was a full-frontal assault.

Before I could stop to think that logic through, I charged.

I let out a roar and a wave of magic that made me feel as if my body was about to fly apart. Jets of fire scorched holes in the walls and levitation blasted him away, off his feet, and he disappeared into the deeper shadows of the school.

I followed him inside, the darkness throwing off my vision for a second.

I looked around frantically, saw nothing but the rubble we'd caused. *There might not be a school standing when we're done.* That brought a little smile to my lips.

Then McKinley was there, appearing from a dark recess, throwing magic, and I tried to react, but he was quicker, sending me flying backwards even as I cast my own spell, smashing me into a trophy case.

What the movies can't communicate about crashing through glass is that it HURTS. Shooting stars flew across my vision and I screamed in pain, as the pointy relics of Williamsport's athletic triumphs dug into my back, my ass, my ribs, my shields doing nothing to prevent me from being poked and prodded by those hateful things.

I was comforted by the fact that McKinley still came out on the worse end: he windmilled over my head and past me, off the floor and into the ceiling, through it, crashing through the tiles and, making a pained squeaking sound you wouldn't expect out of a guy named King Death, bounced and crashed and rolled down the hall, between the tiles and the next floor, until he finally came bursting out again to crash haplessly to the ground.

I hauled myself out of the jagged mess and pursued, the pains in my body making me wish I hadn't. *Finish him.* It wasn't a triumphant war cry, it was the full-scale terror of finally having the bastard where I wanted him, with one slim little chance to stop him before the moment was lost.

I cast a twist of magic that tore chunks of brick from the wall with a grinding snap, let them swirl in the air in front of my fist until they were a nasty little mass of pain, then slammed it down at his head.

The chunks shattered, little bits of them flying in all directions, and he shouted in pain. Without pausing, I tore a long section of jagged rebar from the hole I'd made in the wall and let it land in my hand, sending magic, raw supernatural power, through it until it tingled.

As King Death made his way up, I envisioned myself in Game Seven of the Wizarding World Series, and aimed the metal, glowing blue-green with sorcery, at his head. He dodged back, and I got his chest instead, raised it again and lashed out with the backswing. It collided with his ribs, made him give a satisfying grunt of pain, and roll away. I started after him; rebar raised. As I was about to bring her down, something hit my chest and sent me flying backwards, heart stopping as I lost my grip on the rebar and heard it clatter away. Blood oozed out of the half-healed, still ragged wound in my abdomen. I really should have remembered to put a bandage on that. Magic can make you forget little things like that.

I bounced off the wall, realized he had thrown levitation at me, slashing it like a dagger, and my shield had barely stopped it.

Through blurry vision, I saw him advance, arm extended like he was about to finish me off. I threw a haphazard fireball towards him as I scrambled back, but it went wide and collided with the wall, breaking up into little tails of fire that faded away before they hit the ground.

Little black barbed chunks of metal, almost too dark and too fast for me to see, slammed into my shield, stopping centimeters in front of me as I struggled to keep a grip on it. Sensing his advantage, he kept throwing them, advancing on me as I scrambled back.

Frantic, on the ragged edge of panic, I threw my old friend levitation at him. The good thing about levitation is that it's tough to defend against; your shields might stop some magical nastiness from perforating you, but they can't exactly stop you from being tossed through the air, which he was.

"Tossed" wasn't really the word: I picked him up and slammed his ass against the lockers, trying to smash him like a bug, then flung him hard in the opposite direction, bouncing him off the opposite side. He skidded to the floor and as I moved towards him, my movements slow, too slow, he shambled up, and charged me.

I'd hoped all that thumping would have slowed him down some. Fire blazed from his hands as he ran, and my own roared out to meet it, the brilliant orange bars colliding in midair, swirling and spraying, as I charged him in turn.

We hit hard, bounced and crashed and rolled, through a swinging door to slide across tiles. Something slammed against the side of my head, making me see stars. The wall of a stall, I realized blearily. We'd ended up in a restroom. Of all the places to die. I would have burst out laughing if the very idea didn't make my head hurt even worse.

I threw myself vaguely skyward, was immediately blown off my feet, backwards, through one flimsy wooden wall, another, another, before finally crashing to the floor, my left foot in a toilet.

He sent another smash at me, his form dim just inside the door, but I managed to dodge painfully away, throwing myself out the stall door and to the floor. His spell shattered the mirror into a thousand pieces. I ripped the sink out of the wall with a crunch, flung it back.

He roared as the whole porcelain mess, along with some plaster and metal piping, smashed into him, driving him out of the room, debris erupting. I swayed to my feet. Sound military strategy would indicate I needed to press my momentary advantage, but the pain and exhaustion that sucked me down had other ideas. At least he was wearing down as well. As I followed him back out into the hall, I could tell his movements were pained and sluggish as he crawled back up.

He looked awful: blood streaked his face and clothing and part of his scalp seemed burned away. I felt a bloodthirsty stab of pride I'd managed to inflict all that.

"Sam," he panted. "You don't understand anything."

"I guess I had a bad teacher." I tore a chunk of the ceiling free, lobbed it at his face. He got his shields up, shattering it in a storm of plaster and dust, but it knocked him back into the shadows.

Two streaks of fire, long and thin, barreled towards me from the direction he'd fallen, burning into me, knocking me back smoking, but my shields kept the flames off me.

They lit up the hall briefly, then died away. The sprinklers had begun to chitter, coating the halls with water and making the tiles slick.

I saw light flicker around his dark silhouette, suspected he was about to try the same trick again. I grabbed up another trophy case and thrust it at him, its surface grinding across the floor, its contents rattling.

If it smashed him to a pulp, so much the better, but my main objective had been to keep that fire off me. I was losing faith in my shields, and I wanted to preserve them as long as I could.

The fire leaped onto the box, crackling into the wood instantly, and he scrambled back, before he got smushed, crashing through another set of double doors. The gym, I recalled, my sense of geography as hazy as everything else.

I forced myself to charge the door, then ducked back, kicked the doors open with one foot. Another fireball hissed through the opening, but I was already running to the opposite set of doors and throwing myself through.

The place was on fire, I noted with dismay. Then I spotted McKinley making his way backwards, watching the doors, ready to attack, but I'd taken him by surprise and as he turned, I picked him up again and tossed him onto the stage. Rodriguez and Eressen and Ellis were nowhere in sight. I hoped that was a good sign.

I bounded after him, stumbling through the wreckage and bodies, tromping up the short steps onto the stage, sending a spiral of fire into the curtains and then tossed them in his direction with a ripping sound, hoping to wrap him up. It succeeded, but only for a moment; the charred remains sloughed off him, then I was off my feet, slamming against the stage's backdrop.

"I'm making things better, Sam," he said. "An idealistic teenager and a wizard, of all people, should understand that."

This time, I thought it might be smart to keep him talking. My voice came out as a rasp. It felt like an eternity since I'd used it. "You can see why that would be a little hard to believe."

"The North Side is evil," he snarled. "You have no idea what they're capable of, Sam, NO GODDAMN IDEA. I have to stop them."

"You're killing South Siders, too, genius."

"I KNOW," he roared. "I hate them too. More. It all has to burn. Everything. That's the only way to stop it."

"Stop what?"

"The Black Moon."

This wasn't going the way I'd expected. "What the hell are you talking about?"

"North Side, South Side. When they're all gone, all that's left will be me. I'm gonna rule the wreckage. And I'll be the one strong enough to stop it." He bared his teeth. "This is so much bigger than you or I can fathom." His voice was breathless and his eyes regained their unstable gleam. "There are things out there waiting. They're gonna sweep everything away. Everywhere. This pathetic little city is just the beginning." He smiled. "You could join me."

"Fuck you," I said, and cut loose.

Wind and fire mingled together in a miniature tornado, devouring him, provoking a shout of fear and pain, lifting him off his feet, throwing him back into the gym, into the fire and debris.

I had hoped to toss him into the fires and fry him, and got close, but his shields apparently held out long enough for him to send the flames gusting away from him.

I leaped off the stage, bounded after him, bashing my way through the rubble. I tore the basketball goal off its bracket and sent it flying into him, tossing him across the room, into the bleachers.

He held out a feeble hand, and that slashing levitation hit my chest again. The fabric of my shirt tore, and blood welled. It sent me reeling, then McKinley was back on his feet, charging me, and I lashed out to rip the boards out from under his feet, sending him flailing comically into the air.

"I gotta hand it to you," he wheezed as he made it to his hands and knees. "I never expected you to fight like this. Never dreamed... that crazy ninja wizard that scared my guys so bad was one of my students. But now it kinda feels like destiny or something."

I picked up some debris without even looking to see what it was and flung it. He managed to send it crashing away, and if his deflection was pretty weak, my attack had been the same.

He spun up a whirlwind, but he was too weak to be precise, and it swept up both of us, sending us rolling and bouncing painfully through the mess and out the already-shattered doors to roll onto the tiles of the hallway.

I must have blacked out for a second, because it seemed I blinked, and he was standing over me. "It's better this way," he rasped, a giggle bursting from his bleeding mouth. "It wouldn't have worked if you'd taken my offer. We always would have ended up like this." I tossed him back, cracking spiderwebs into another trophy case. He didn't seem to notice. "You would have figured it out eventually."

I picked up some of the trophies from the mess and thrust them into his gut. How much his shields stopped, I couldn't tell, but I saw blood. I guess he saw I was more interested in killing him than taking the bait. "You would have figured out what happened to Abby," he said.

Every blood cell in my body turned to ice. The world around me faded away like someone turning off the sound on a TV.

"It was too easy," he said, clambering to his feet. "Distance magic was never my thing, but it worked on her. Looked like an overdose. That's where I got the idea for Hex."

I was frozen, completely paralyzed. I tried to speak and couldn't. I didn't even know what I would say. "Why?" I managed to pant, unable to make my voice rise above a whisper.

"That's complicated," he said. "Don't blame me, it wasn't my idea. Look out behind you." I half-turned and a dark, hulking mass was next to me, roaring, and something tore into my leg and then I was unwillingly hauling ass down the hallway. The thing growled and snuffled, hard to make out in the darkness, though I was pretty sure I recognized it: the demon I thought had had the decency to get blown up a few minutes ago.

I tried to concentrate, to attack, but it was impossible, my head and back bouncing up and down on the floor, claws digging into my lower leg, producing even more blood. That was just a dim murmur, however, next to the chaos that pounded through my mind. *You would have figured out what happened to Abby.* My mind couldn't progress any further than when I heard those words, even if it meant saving my life. Classroom doors bounced by one by one, my vision shaking, as we made our way into an undamaged part of the school. Fear was beginning to creep in, and it was almost a relief because it gave me something else to focus on. If I didn't do something fast, I was going to be this thing's dinner. My consciousness wobbled and flickered, and I knew I was on the verge of passing out, injuries and magic and shock all conspiring against me. *You would have figured out what happened to Abby.*

Suddenly the undamaged hallway became very much damaged. A window burst inward, the rain of falling glass sparkling in the glow from the streetlights.

A cape-wearing form sailed through the space, planting itself on the ground in front of the beast. There was a sword gleaming silver-blue in its upraised hand. Eressen of the House al'Barra, sworn to the Crimson Throne. "Good evening, Sam," he said.

The pressure on my leg vanished, although the pain stuck

around. I thumped to the floor. The demon roared distantly. "Good evening," I slurred into the tiles.

"That turned out rather perfectly, didn't it? I've always wanted to crash through a window. I'll keep our friend here occupied, and you finish your duel. What do you say?"

That sounded like a terrible idea, but I staggered to my feet. "Thanks," I said grudgingly, then trotted, fast as a wounded wizard could trot, back the way I had come, as both of them snarled battle cries behind me. It was easy to find my way, due to the helpful trail of blood. I didn't have to go far before I spotted King Death. He seemed to be in the spot where I'd left him, waiting for me. "I had a feeling you'd be back," he said.

Abby's face filled my head, the image I saw over and over, the last time I'd seen her, when she'd given me a smile and walked away, but rather than send me reeling like it usually did, it filled me with indescribable power and rage. All my hurts forgotten, I flooded myself with magic.

The idea that the phrase "taking you down with me" couldn't have been more appropriate was a tiny echo in the back of my mind, and I paid it no attention. Recalling Michael's hellbat strategy, I flung long jets of fire, not at King Death, but at the walls, aiming for the pipes I knew were there. My aim wasn't very precise, but it didn't need to be.

The effect was almost instantaneous. There was a school-shaking roar, walls torn to shreds amid a maelstrom of orange and red, filling my entire vision until there was nothing else in the world. I was blown off my feet again, propelled into the air, crashing, again, through a rickety wooden door. Debris pummeled me, and I tried to cry out, but it turned into a harsh gurgle, as rancid smoke scoured my lungs. A chunk of brick slammed into the side of my head, and I felt blood pour from my scalp, onto my face, ears, neck. I was dimly aware that my shields were about to announce last call. I should have taken a hundred mortal wounds already, but the shields and magic in my body had managed to scrape up enough power to keep me alive.

I passed out for the umpteenth time that week. That really can't be good for a person's brain health. When my awareness kicked into gear again, I realized I was in the shattered ruins of a classroom.

He lurched through the door after me, barely on his feet. I tried to bring up an image of Abby's face again, but it wavered and flitted away. There was too much blood and death and destruction to be able to think of her. My magic, at least, was still there, although it was getting dangerously low. I was running out of—

Something slammed into me, bowled me over the desk, spraying paperwork and breaking a computer. I knocked over the chair to land on the floor. McKinley lurched towards me, not saying anything now. He punched out with an invisible fist again, knocked me into the whiteboards, making my head snap to the side and my vision to lurch precipitously.

I tried to roll away, got a glancing blow in the leg.

I couldn't last much longer. I was going to die here, away from my family, Abby unavenged. Abby. Why? That was a question McKinley was never going to answer.

Maybe it wasn't anything to fear, I thought. Maybe wherever wizards go when they die, I might find Abby there waiting for me. She'd be so happy to see me. Maybe I'd have an eternity to say the stuff I'd never said when we were alive.

There had been so many times I'd feared for her. I wasn't under any illusions about the kind of darkness that existed. And I had been afraid it would swallow her up someday, that all the things I loved about her would cause her to be crushed by it, the darkness I knew was so much greater than even the most fearful or cynical of people ever realize.

I had thought her kindness, her warmth, would make her dangerously vulnerable. Weak, even.

Now, in this hellscape, I thought perhaps those things had made her strong.

It was so, so tempting to just let go. And it wasn't any strength of mine that made me refuse. It was all hers.

I knew what she'd say. I knew what she'd want me to do. Those words would have to wait. If it really was an eternity, I guessed we had time.

I let power fill me again. It was waning fast, but there was enough left to fight a little longer.

Or to land one really, really hard hit.

McKinley stood over me, swaying slightly, blood bubbling out of his open mouth. The left side of his face was a ruin, and half his shirt was torn off, his pale chest stained with blood and filth. The telltale tears of blood that come from hitting magic too hard stained his face, and he held his body at an odd angle, like it hurt to walk normally. He held out a shaking hand to finish me.

I closed my eyes, filling myself with more power than I ever had before, until I could actually see the bones in my hand glow, until I was certain my blood actually boiled. I'd never done this spell before; it was far too dangerous.

The idea suddenly seemed hilarious.

Body sagging with relieved finality, I cast the spell.

Thunder, loud as thunder could ever be, filled the confined space, shattering my mind. A jagged blade of lightning, bright beyond comprehension, ripped through the ceiling and devoured McKinley, crackled along my skin, made my hair stand on end.

The impact blew me off my feet and across the room, feeling as if I was floating rather than falling, time slowing. *Is this what it's like to die?*

During that long, stretched-out moment, I saw the flesh scoured away from McKinley's bones by the blast, knew even a wizard as powerful as him couldn't survive that, and wanted to weep with relief, because it was over.

Finally.

I tried to call up that image of Abby, her head thrown back in pure joy, but it was so hard to concentrate.

The light swallowed me.

CHAPTER TWENTY-THREE

I DREAMED.

It was raining, as is appropriate for scenes of bittersweet romance. "Sam?" Abby's voice stole my attention from messing with my door's lock and I spun around like I'd been shot. Her backpack was held over her head, and with two or three big steps, she bounded onto the porch. "Ugh. Hi. I need to borrow your porch for a few minutes if that's okay. Or even if it's not."

"You don't have to wait out here; you can come inside if you want."

"Thanks, but it's fine. My Mom's gonna be here in a couple minutes to pick me up."

I shrugged, trying not to stare. Flecks of rain shone in her hair. "Do you have a crush on somebody?" she said abruptly.

I nearly fell off the porch. "No."

She gave me a smug look. "That was a rhetorical question, because I know you do. I've seen how you mope around, staring at nothing, with, like, this vacant look on your face. Those are the tell-tale signs. Come on, who is it?"

"That's just my normal face," I protested. "It's nobody, really." How had she noticed my vacant looks?

"All this denial just makes me believe you even less. Come on, you can tell me. I'll tell you who mine is if you tell me yours, I swear."

I swallowed. I was about to stammer more ridiculous denials. The words jammed in my throat. She was staring at me, her dark eyes warm, always with a hint of laughter dancing behind them. I still couldn't speak. I could only stare at her, befuddled and over-whelmed and bizarrely happy, like I always was in her presence.

She stared at me, her amusement slowly slipping away, replaced by understanding. I saw the instant when the truth slipped into her mind. But the warmth was still there. Why, I wondered, had I ever been afraid to tell her, of all people, the truth?

Abby's voice was soft. "Sam," she said.

That's when I knew it was a dream because it hadn't happened that way in real life. The dream slowed, became sluggish, as if we were moving through molasses, and her face went fuzzy. In real life, I had cracked some joke and assured her I wasn't interested in anybody, and she had groaned, rolled her eyes and muttered something about the exasperating nature of men, before bounding across the yard, into her mom's car. I'd waved goodbye wondering if I'd done the right thing. Four days later she was dead.

My mind moved through a long, black, empty void.

Then I was back in my body, with all the pain that came with it.

My senses felt as if they were scrambled. It was a long time before I could even pry my eyes open. Once I did, it took me a moment to recognize the faded plaster of my bedroom ceiling.

And there was something warm and furry on top of my head. Again.

I didn't push it away this time. I could barely lift a finger. My mouth was Sahara dry and tasted like chemicals. I could barely even manage a groan.

Whiskers appeared in my blurry vision. "You're awake. Good."

I managed to croak out a word. "Happened?"

"Well, it's about ten a.m. on Saturday. You were out for some-where in the neighborhood of thirty-six hours."

"Parents?"

"They know you're sick, but that's about it. They stick their heads in once in a while, but they let you sleep. There was some dried blood on your face that would have raised some questions, but don't worry, I licked it off."

"Thanks."

"Jason and Elise brought you in."

"Elise?"

"Yeah. Vampires are tough to kill."

I was almost happy she survived. "Wasn't sure she made it."

"She's the one that found you in the wreckage, from what I understand. Apparently, Jason dived out of a moving bus or some-thing to that effect and came charging back to the school. Between the two of them, they sorted it out: Jason texted your Dad from your phone, said you were gonna go have a late-night snack at his house and not to wait up. They waited until your parents were asleep, then they borrowed your key and snuck you in through the backdoor."

I licked my lips, tried to work up a little saliva. "While I was unconscious?"

"Yeah. I told Big Al it was okay. Oh, that reminds me: I had to invite Elise into your house. Somebody had to pick up your ankles and I don't have thumbs. Hope you don't mind because it's not like you can do anything about it."

"Oh well. Throw it on the pile."

"Then, Jason came back that morning, told them you'd come down with the flu and he'd brought you back without waking any-body up. Said the nausea made you fall down a flight of stairs."

I tried to laugh. "That's the worst excuse I ever heard."

"Well, he figured it was more believable than the truth. I thought the poor kid was gonna have a stroke. I get the feeling he's not used to lying to adults. You should have seen his face when I said hello. Oh yeah, I told him you'd shoot him a text when you woke up."

"Am I, like, dying?"

"No. Your shields stopped the worst of it and the magic helped heal the rest. Still, you messed yourself up pretty bad." He was right about that; I didn't seem to have one specific injury, rather, it was more of a general pain radiating through everything. "The reason you're so weak and sick is because you burned yourself out. Happens to every wizard once in a while. You were a mess that first night. Does weird stuff to you, getting your magic ripped out. You coughed up blood for a while, which was gross but didn't last very long. Had a fever. Then you were delirious. Mostly just nonsense." From the look on his face, I knew Abby's name had come up in my delirium. His whiskers twitched. "There was something else too; something weird even by your lofty standards. Towards the end, you started talking about wings."

"Wings?"

"Yeah. 'It has wings,' or something like that. Said it several times. Any idea what that was about?"

I shuddered as a sudden image flashed into my mind, so brief, so indistinct I could almost think it wasn't real. Almost. I put a hand on my head and nearly passed out from the effort. "I don't know," I said slowly. "There's something in my mind. It's hard to describe. It's like... a memory? Not one of mine. But somehow, I know that's what it is. I know it's not a dream. And I can see... something. Something huge. Really, really huge. Like, 'huge isn't even the right word for it' huge. And I can see wings."

Swayze's feline eyes were huge. "Huh," he said.

"Any ideas what it is?"

"No. That's what's really scary about magic, kid. What we know about it is only a fraction of what there actually is."

"Terrific."

"The good news is, magic's like lifting weights: the more you do it, the stronger you get. When you can do magic again, you'll be better than you were before."

I became aware I was still in my much-abused suit from last night, the night before, whenever it was, bloody and filthy, although someone had had the presence of mind to remove my shoes.

I laid there over an hour, my body still a wreck but my head slowly clearing. Despite my pain and weakness, I had the urge to get out of bed, clean myself up and try to get a little human again. Ignoring Catrick Swayze's protests, I tried to get up and promptly collapsed to the floor.

The people of Williamsport were informed things were back to normal.

Williamsport had gone even wilder than I realized, with multiple fires and shootings caused by the Reapers attacking the banks. Two cops were dead, the one I knew about at the school, another in the fighting across town. The news vaguely alluded to the "shooters killed in the incident," without going into much detail about the Reapers. By my count, we'd dispatched more than twenty of them at the dance and hopefully that was all of them. Rodriguez, I was pleased to hear, came through with nothing worse than some stitches, and got a commendation for bravery.

There was a big candlelight vigil for all the people who died over the past week, in what was attributed to a "surge in gang violence," which I guess was technically true, even if it was a gang that included hellbats. Luckily, I was still too weak to attend. I was told it was very moving; there was singing and everything, and not a single fight broke out. I wasn't under any illusions that anything had changed around here, but at least we'd held off the war for now.

McKinley was hailed as a hero who died protecting his students, with no one mentioning the freak lightning strike that killed him.

Speaking of gangs, I didn't hear from Michael, but I did hear through the high school grapevine that the Sixth Street Aces were back in business.

Alexandra sent me a massive bouquet of flowers, along with a card reading "I'm glad you're okay. My brother is doing better. Thank you again, Sam." I put it in my wallet.

Despite my blackmail scheme, I had still feared retaliation from the Great North Side Conspiracy. That is, until I got an awkward, rambling phone call from the mayor where he lauded me as a hero who had saved the city. Somehow, I found that more disturbing than the alternative.

Archibald J. Keller, to the disappointment of every teenager in town, reopened sooner than expected. An army of contractors worked at a furious pace, thanks to generous donations from several prominent North Siders, including Rick, and, though parts of the school would be a disaster area for weeks, there were enough undamaged classrooms to squeeze us in. There was also talk of raising money with a bake sale, which prompted me to laugh so hard I almost fainted and earned me a bizarre look from Mom. Her and Dad seemed to buy my own version of the official story. I had taken pains to tell them we'd skipped out on the dance before the fireworks started, but I saw concern mingled with skepticism every time the subject was brought up.

Ella finally got ungrounded. You'd have thought she would have leaped at the chance to roam free, especially since school was closed, but she mostly kept bumming around the house. One afternoon, while our parents were at work, and I felt strong enough for holding conversations and standing upright, I sought her out. I found her in her room again, sitting at the foot of her bed. "Hey."

She turned from her phone, tossed it on the pillow. "Hey."

There was an awkward pause, neither of us knowing exactly what to say, but unable to escape the feeling it should be something. If I had ever been good with feelings, I wasn't anymore, but I took a shot. "We should talk. I've been wanting to."

Her face was unreadable. "Yeah, I know. Me too."

"Are you okay? Everybody seems like they're worried about me, but you were there at the beach. You saw that fire. I've been meaning to say something, I just…" *Got a little busy fighting for my life.*

"I'm okay," she said, "really. Like I said, I didn't see those bodies like you and Jason did, and I'm glad. It's just… I don't know." She shrugged. "I've always heard, like, how out of control this town can get, I just never…" She sniffed and wiped at her eyes. "I can't believe people wanted to kill me because I live on the wrong side of a river. I was scared, that's all."

"I know. I'm sorry." I stepped closer and slipped an arm around her shoulders. She leaned against me, wiping her eyes again.

She pulled back. "I was scared for *you*, too. I know you got mixed up in everything that was going on somehow, even if you won't say so."

"I was," I admitted. "I'll tell you everything someday, just maybe not now."

"That's not the only reason I was worried."

My skin turned cold but I pushed past it. "Abby."

"Yeah. Abby. I know how much you're hurting. I can see it. Everybody can. Everybody but you." I tried to speak but my mind was blank. I could only nod. I still wasn't up for talking about her much. Maybe I would be someday. But not now. "Abby was my friend too," Ella said. "There were lots of people who cared about her. And you, too. I'm just saying you don't have to hurt alone."

I tried to smile. "You're too smart to be twelve." I sighed and rubbed at my face. "And you should go out and do something fun."

"What do you mean?"

"You don't have to admit it, but I know you're nervous about going out, with everything going on. 'Going back to normal' isn't really an option in Williamsport, but the war's over. The Reapers are wiped out. You don't have to hide out in here."

Her eyes flicked toward her window. "Yeah. I guess. Ava wants me to come over again."

"You should go. You'll be glad you did."

"You're trying to get me out of the house again."

"Yep."

She snorted. "Fine. Okay. I'll go to Ava's." She stood. "See you when I get back." She stopped at the door. "Hey Sam?"

"Yeah?"

A look crossed her face I couldn't quite identify. I'd always been able to read her before, but this eluded me. Then she gave her head a brief shake and it vanished. "Nothing. It can wait." She disappeared into the hallway.

It was a week before I was strong enough to return to school; Swayze estimated it would be more than twice that before I could do magic again. I couldn't even remember what it was like to be a teenager rather than a teenage wizard.

After all the death and terror I'd faced down, I didn't know what to do with myself now that it was over. The last couple days before I returned to school, I went with Swayze for short walks down the street in the evenings, trying to get my strength up, finding I had a new appreciation for peace and quiet.

Swayze and I were on one such walk, him trotting, me slouching, in companionable silence, when we came to the big friendly elm tree at the end of my street, which marked the limit of my endurance. I stopped for a moment to catch my breath. Then I saw the open void, under the tree. "Lovely battle, wasn't it?" Eressen stepped out, unruffled as ever.

"Eressen. You made it."

"Was there ever any doubt? We have fiercer creatures than that in our foothills. Still, it was a fine skirmish."

Swayze let out a low growl. "I take it that's him."

"Yeah, that's him."

Eressen looked down at Swayze and gave him a broad smile. "What an adorable creature. Hello there, little fellow."

Swayze hissed.

Unease filled me. "If this is about that favor, I'm in no shape to do anything for anybody right now. My magic is shot and will be for quite a while."

He waved a hand. "Nonsense. It's all quite delicate, and this isn't the right time. Rest yourself, and don't give it another thought."

I had the feeling I'd give it another thought. "This favor... It's not just some vague IOU for the future, is it?"

"Ah, well, I'd rather keep that to myself for the moment. The fewer that know, the safer we all are; wouldn't do to have the information falling into the wrong hands. Although you're correct: I do have something in particular in mind."

"How are things back home? You get everything straightened out?"

He sighed. "Well, one always has problems one must tackle, but yes, the current situation is thankfully in hand. And I'm afraid I must be going; I just thought I'd spare a word for an old comrade-in-arms. Only proper after going through a battle together. Good evening."

"Good evening."

He turned to go, then stopped, returned his gaze to me. "You know, Sam, I get the feeling you like all this excitement. Sure, you hem and haw, and grouse about the danger, but deep down, you have the heart of a warrior."

"I find that very hard to believe."

"Well, I don't. And from one adventurer to another, and in

recognition of the service you've done me, I think I can afford to give you a little hint about our task ahead." He dropped his voice in conspiratorial glee, then said, "It's a heist."

With a swirl of his cape, he disappeared into the void, leaving me staring mutely at the tree.

The day before I was set to go back to school, we returned from our walk and flopped down on the porch swing to rest a moment before dinner. I was close to my full strength by now, but still tired easily. And, I was somewhat surprised to discover, I wanted to enjoy the sunset for a little while, like an old guy or something.

We sat there, watching cars go by and the sun sink, me stroking his head, him purring. "Things are gonna get complicated now," I said.

"What do you mean?"

"People know about me now. In town, in the other realms. Even the mayor knows I'm a wizard, for Christ's sake."

"Well, it might have helped if you hadn't announced you were a wizard to everyone you met."

I glared at him. "That was a strategic move, based on fluid circumstances, as I've explained."

"Uh-huh."

"Anyway, I get the feeling Williamsport's problems are a lot bigger than just King Death."

"If his big evil plan was to crown himself king of Williamsport, he sure wasn't setting his sights very high."

"No. But there's something we're not seeing. More to it than that." Against my will, I recalled what McKinley had said, about the Black Moon. Swayze hadn't known what that was either.

"Yeah. There always is with wizards." There was an uncomfortable pause. "You killed the man who killed Abby, at least, even if that wasn't what you set out to do."

"Did I?" He stared at me expectantly. "What McKinley said,

it wasn't just some random act of violence. I don't think he acted on his own. He may have cast the spell, but I think someone else put him up to it."

"Could be he was lying, just to mess with you. Who the hell would send a blood mage to kill a random fifteen-year-old girl?"

"I don't know. But I'm sure he was telling the truth."

"How can you be sure?"

I didn't want to say it because that would make it real. "Because we didn't study."

"What do you mean?"

"Abby died early on a Wednesday morning. Four or five a.m., something like that. I found out when I woke up that day." My whole body tensed as I fought those memories down. "The last time I saw her was a Monday afternoon. We were supposed to study the next day, on Tuesday. But we didn't. Between the last time I saw her and the day she died, I'm missing a day."

Swayze sat in silence for a long moment. "Well," he said finally. "That's a worrying development."

"Tell me about it."

He shook his head, stretched, and stood. "Well, there's nothing we can do about it tonight. And I know you're not gonna do *anything* dangerous without your powers, so we may as well have some dinner."

"You go ahead. I'll be right behind you."

As he disappeared through his cat door, I turned my gaze back to the street, watching the streetlights come on. The blood, the chaos, wasn't over yet. It was just taking a little break. I found the idea marginally less terrifying than it used to be, and that gave me an uneasy feeling in itself. As much as I wanted to go on some bloody crusade of vengeance against the people who'd killed Abby, if they even existed, the thought of actually doing it overwhelmed me. If I investigated Abby's death, if someone really had murdered her, I would have to face a lot of things I'd intended to spend the rest of my life running away from. But I didn't have a choice, did I? Had I ever?

What all this meant, I was too terrified to contemplate. More terrified than when I'd been risking my life.

It was then I saw Elise, standing on the sidewalk, half-obscured by the twilight shadows.

I started, then remembered Big Al, watching silently. I relaxed.

"I wasn't sure you'd come back," I said.

"Had to look in on my date," she said, that strange smile on her face. Whatever was going on behind those green eyes, I couldn't read it. "I have to go. I have things to do elsewhere. Our paths will cross again soon."

"I'm sure they will."

"Something is coming, Sam."

"How clichély vague."

"Something is coming, and we have no idea what it is. Not Armageddon, not Ragnarök, nothing that's ever been prophesied."

I felt a chill. "Maybe that can be our second date."

"I guess I'll see you then." She turned to go.

"Wait a minute," I said. She turned back, studying me. "These people you work for. Who are they? What do they want with me?"

"Well," she said, smile returning, "they're not exactly people."

And then she was gone.

I drew in a long breath. The evening suddenly seemed a lot darker. I needed to be heading in.

Then I felt something else, a sense of unease in the back of my mind. Magical? No, my magic was busted. It was just some weird human feeling. Something was about to happen, something that couldn't be avoided any longer.

I didn't relish the idea but ignoring it wouldn't make it go away.

Reluctantly, I hauled myself to my feet and went back in the house.

My parents were waiting in the kitchen, looking at me expectantly.

"Hey, family. What's going on?" It was more of a formality at this point.

There was a moment of hesitation. Dad spoke up first. "We need to talk," he said.

That old chestnut was never a good sign. I was tempted to run back out the door. "Okay," I said. "So, I kinda got involved."

END OF BOOK ONE

Sam Adams will return

ACKNOWLEDGMENTS

I'd like to thank my parents, for their invaluable support and encouragement; Sarah Chorn, for her skills as an editor and her indispensable, much-appreciated advice; Luke Tarzian, for turning my confused mutterings into actual artwork; r/Fantasy, for rekindling my love of the fantasy genre; and all of you out there who followed Sam Adams on his misadventures.

ABOUT THE AUTHOR

Daniel Meyer tried his hand at a few careers, but fearing they were too realistic and achievable, he became a fantasy writer instead. Now he spends his days writing about magic and explosions. He is a lover of Eighties rock, an occasional kilt-wearer, and a supporter of raccoons. He lives in Missouri, where, as ever, he's working on his next novel.

www.danielmeyerauthor.com

Twitter: @dmeyerauthor